One ❦
French
Summer

Also by Lucy Coleman

One Perfect French Summer

LUCY COLEMAN

embla
books

First published in Great Britain in 2024 by

embla
books

Bonnier Books UK Limited
4th Floor, Victoria House, Bloomsbury Square, London, WC1B 4DA
Owned by Bonnier Books
Sveavägen 56, Stockholm, Sweden

A CIP catalogue record for this book is available from the British Library.

ISBN: 9781471416958

This book is typeset using Atomik ePublisher.

Embla Books is an imprint of Bonnier Books UK.
www.bonnierbooks.co.uk

Dedicated to my husband, Lawrence, and fond memories of the New Year's Eve we arrived in France to find that it was snowing and our last-minute hotel booking had fallen through. Cold and hungry, we stumbled across a cosy little place to stay with a restaurant next door. It was the best New Year's Eve ever and made me fall in love with him – and France – all over again!

'What Luke helped me realise, is that we learn from each other. Striving to be the best version of me is all I need to focus on. And wisdom is the result of life experiences, because age is . . . just a number.'

Freya Henderson

Freya

June

Sevenoaks, Kent

1

The Price of Success

'Yes!' I punch the air as I place the phone back down on my desk.

When I glance around me, I'm conscious that the whole team has stopped what they're doing. 'Sorry . . . youthful exuberance,' I laugh. 'I've just landed the contract for that barn conversion at Edenbridge.' Not a bad way to kick off a delightfully sunny Monday morning in June, taking on a million-pound-plus property.

Naturally, constantly striving to up our game and knowing that at least two of our competitors were asked to value the prestigious property too, there's a chorus of whoops.

'Well done, Freya,' my best friend and business partner, Beth Masters, calls across the office. 'The photos are going to make an awesome display in the centre of our window.'

She's right, but now the pressure is on. I'm fully booked through until next Tuesday morning and while our photographer is good, he's going to need my direction on this one. It must be literally picture perfect, because the Fosters happened to drop into the conversation that one of their neighbours is thinking of downsizing too and will shortly be looking for an agent.

Our office manager, Ethan Edwards, saunters up to my desk, indicating towards the chair opposite me. 'I know you're busy, Freya, but can I have a quick word?'

Ethan has only been with us for eight months but he's more than proven himself. Everything runs smoothly now after a period that Beth and I refer back to as the *twilight zone*. The previous incumbent came with a glowing CV and while she was great with the clients, her IT skills fell far short of what was promised. She not only managed to delete a whole load of files, which we managed to recover from our backups, but after a routine system upgrade none of us were recognised as users. We lost an entire day's work online when we had to call in a troubleshooter to sort it all out.

'Always. What's up?'

'Nothing's wrong,' he assures me, hastily. But, as he lowers himself down onto the seat, I can tell that his thoughts are churning. 'I've been speaking to this couple on and off for a couple of weeks now. They're moving into the area and are getting desperate to find a property. I've sent them details of everything new that we've taken on within their price range but they're looking for something *special*. I think the barn could be it.' He raises his eyebrows, his eyes shining with optimism.

I know what's coming next. 'We don't let people view until the property details are online, Ethan. Besides—' I pass the file over to him ready to be actioned '—until you've emailed Mr and Mrs Foster the contract and they've returned it duly signed, the barn isn't officially on our books.'

'I know, I know,' he states, putting up his hands to reassure me he understands our strict protocol. 'But when the Fosters rang to book the appointment and they were telling me a little bit about their property, I had that eureka moment.' He flashes me a pointed look.

I nod my head, because I know that feeling well. 'Right client, right time, right place?'

'I think that might just be the case with this one. If I get the contract printed off and drop it in to them on my way home from work this evening . . .' He's keen, I'll give him that. And that's exactly what this business is all about.

'The couple you're talking to are proceed-able and vetted, I assume?'

'Yes. The cash is in the bank and they're growing more and more dispirited by the day because he's about to start a new job.'

A quick sale would suit the Fosters down to the ground. They're downsizing now that the last of their three sons is at university. They have a smart new camper van parked up in the paddock next to the barn; it's sitting there waiting for them to start a six-month tour around Europe in a week's time. It will be Mrs Foster's sister who will be giving us access to the property.

'Look, Ethan, the reason we don't jump the gun with viewings is to protect both ourselves, and our clients. Until the marketing campaign begins, we have no idea what level of interest we're going to get. A good response could see them getting multiple offers above the initial selling price we agree to list it at.'

His smile fades. 'I understand that, Freya. If you don't mind, though, I'll get the paperwork sorted this afternoon and, as I said, I'll pop it in to them on my way home. Just to help speed things along.' Now that's commitment.

'OK, that's fine with me. If they ask you to wait while they sign it, then I'll broach the subject of your prospective purchasers with them when I call to book the session with the photographer. How's that?'

Ethan's smile returns. 'Ace,' he replies, as he hurries back to his desk to start work.

Only Ethan could talk me into that. I guess I'm a sucker for a cheeky smile when it's backed up by a genuine desire to get a result.

I head out to the staff kitchen to grab a coffee and seconds later Beth enters. 'Did Ethan just sweet talk you into bending the rules?' she muses.

'Hmm . . . maybe a little, but we'll see how it turns out. Actually, I valued the barn at a tad over what I think it will achieve because it has quite a bit of land and the location couldn't be better. It'll make a perfect home for a discerning purchaser, and it should attract a premium.'

She shakes her head at me, laughing. 'What is it with you and younger men?'

Beth has hit the nail on the head but it's a sore point right now. 'Do you fancy going for something to eat after work?'

'That sounds good to me. Shall I book our usual table?'

Are we creatures of habit, or what? 'Perfect. Right.' I glance at my watch. 'I'm off to do a viewing in half an hour and I've a few calls to make first. It's going to be another busy day and all I can say is *bring it on*!'

I wait for Beth to join me at our favourite restaurant, Fresh and Wild. They do the most amazing fish dishes, and you won't find the word *fried* anywhere on the menu. Everything is either steamed or baked *en papillote* – the old traditional French style of cooking items in an envelope of greaseproof paper.

I start thinking about how the business has grown. I don't often reflect on what we've achieved, as there's always another milestone seemingly within reach and that's where our focus lies.

Hearth and Home Estate Agency was started by Beth's father back in the early nineties. Following his death almost six years ago, his estate passed to Beth and her brother, Harry. As a civil engineer, Harry had no interest in the business and it left them with a dilemma. Beth had been working alongside her father since she was twenty-five years old and if their mother were still alive they knew even she would have expected them to step up. However, Beth couldn't manage to run things on her own and Harry felt he was letting his sister down.

When Beth asked if I was interested in buying Harry out of his share, I was a sales negotiator at an estate agency across town. While I had some savings in the bank, it was nowhere near the sort of figure a 50 per cent stake was worth. In the end, we struck up an arrangement and by the end of our fourth year of running the business together, my debt to Harry was fully paid up.

'Hey . . . you were deep in thought there!'

Beth sinks down gratefully into the chair opposite.

'Yes. I was thinking about how far we've come.'

'It's been quite a journey, hasn't it? Is this carafe of house wine to share?'

'Yes, and as the saying goes, sharing is caring,' I reply, reaching out to pour the wine.

We chink glasses and she eyes me, suspiciously.

'There's something you're not telling me. You know it'll come out some time or other, so why not get it off your chest?'

It's hard not to look guilty. 'I haven't been to the gym for six days.'

Her face falls. 'What? You were doing so well. The doctor said you need to go at least three times a week, four if possible. It's not like you to quit on anything, Freya, and this is about your health, so that makes no sense whatsoever.'

I can feel my shoulders beginning to slump. 'I know. I had a nice routine going, too. And I haven't had a takeaway in well over a month. I'm following his recommendations to the letter.'

'No,' she states, firmly. 'He told you that exercise is important to help combat the symptoms.'

I sigh. 'I know and it did help, but I . . . um . . . need to find another gym.'

'Freya, that's a lame excuse. Admit it, you've had a scare and it's a wake-up call.'

Working long hours, having your evening meal delivered to the door and then after only four hours' sleep, lying in bed clock-watching until dawn breaks, does not constitute a healthy lifestyle. I get it, though, I was overloading my system.

Too much time spent on electronic devices, a poor diet and not enough exercise . . . no wonder my heart would suddenly start racing and I'd break out into a cold sweat. Having it spelt out to you that you're putting your body into a constant flight or fight mode, which is why I couldn't sleep, isn't what you want to hear. I was looking for a quick fix solution. Drink less caffeine maybe or eat more veggies. But like everything else in life, nothing is ever simple.

'I don't feel comfortable there,' I explain, hoping she'll think it's all the he-men lifting weights putting me off.

'Oh no . . . it's that guy . . . What's his name?'

'Luke.' I can't help smiling to myself as I think of him. That long, dark curly hair, usually neatly tied back at the nape of his neck because he's always on the go. It suits him, though.

'Ah . . . your cool surfer dude.'

'He isn't *my* anything,' I reply, pointedly.

'Doesn't he live in Cornwall?'

'Yes, he's staying locally with friends of his.'

'Hmm. He's been here quite a while; that's very accommodating of them.'

'OK, I admit we've been spending a bit of time together, but it's starting to get a little awkward now.'

Beth's expression freezes. 'Oh no! You said it was just the odd drink you've been having together. He hasn't stayed over at your place – has he? You said he was way too young and frivolous for you to take him seriously. And he doesn't have a job, I mean, you two are like opposite ends of the scale.'

'Did I use the word *frivolous*?' I question, trying my best to remember the conversation. That was a tad condescending of me. Beth said I had a sparkle in my eye that morning and she'd started quizzing me.

Luke is good company but now I know him a little better . . . a lot better, actually. 'I didn't want to make a big deal out of it; he's spontaneous and fun to be around,' I reflect.

'Just like you then,' she snorts, and I start laughing as she sips her drink.

'Unlike me, but it's good to have a little fun for a change. Except that—' I draw to a halt, as Beth is now staring at me, and I know I can't leave it there. 'He's been teaching me how to meditate, he says it's a good way of slowing everything down.'

'Really?' I can see she's keen to know more. 'So, he's both energetic and an advocate for peace and tranquillity. Isn't that the epitome of a balanced life? He could be a good influence on you, Freya.'

I roll my eyes at her. 'Luke is interesting and flirtatious because he's young and hasn't really found his thing in life yet. He says he's keeping his options open for now, but he's hopeful that one day he'll find himself in the right place at the right time.'

'Hmm . . . now that sounds a little naive to me. Reading between the lines, you've had a little fling – which you've been ominously quiet about – but you're regretting it already.'

Is that the problem? I wonder. What scares me is how quickly Luke has become the highlight of my day and that's not a good thing. I love my life just as it is. Work inspires me, I'm free to do what I want – when I want. My cottage in Eynsford, six miles from Sevenoaks and a thirteen-minute train ride away from the office, might be bijou, but it's the home of my dreams.

Besides, my life is perfect without a man in it because, in my experience, it's a complication I don't need right now. Beth and I intend to make Hearth and Home the number one estate agency in town, as second place simply won't do.

'It's been great, but he's a traveller and now he wants to whisk me away for the summer. A mate has let him down and he thinks it'll be cathartic for me to step outside of my comfort zone.'

Beth's eyes widen. 'He does? Where? Some exotic island?' She's jesting with me.

'No. As far as I can tell, it's a working road trip through France in a van.'

She sits back in her seat, looking relieved. 'He doesn't

know you then, Freya. In a van? You like your creature comforts way too much to be tempted by that. If it's a working holiday, he obviously has an itinerary.'

I nod my head. 'I assume so, but I didn't ask any questions because I didn't want him to think I was taking his offer seriously. It's a trip he first undertook when he was just eighteen years old, apparently. Luke and his friend have done it every year since, but this year the guy can't make it.'

'Hmm . . . it sounds interesting. What exactly does the trip involve?'

'He mentioned something about helping at an old manor house in northern France to prepare for a week-long gourmet extravaganza and picking fruit and vegetables, I think. We were in a rather noisy bar at the time and I certainly wasn't going to quiz him. He raises the topic every time we meet and I change the subject the first opportunity I get.'

'And he sleeps in a van?' Beth starts giggling. 'Unless it's a luxury caravan with a toilet and a shower, and there's somewhere to plug in a hairdryer, he doesn't have a chance of enticing you to join him.'

I look at her, straight-faced. 'I'm not thinking of going. It's a two-month trip!' I exclaim.

'On the other hand, maybe in your case it's just what the doctor ordered. A couple of months away from work to de-stress, enjoy nature and all that wonderful fresh air. Getting hands-on doing a multitude of tasks is free exercise and, no doubt, you'll be eating a lot healthier. Pub meals and takeaways won't be an option.'

'Ha! You couldn't cope without me,' I chuckle.

'I could, if it puts you back on track, Freya. I've been doing some online research, and I don't want you burning yourself out. Ethan is keen to get some experience as a sales negotiator, and if we hired some temporary help to run the office side of things, he could take on a part of your role. To be honest, if we don't offer him a chance to step up before too long, we could lose him.'

Suddenly, she's taking this seriously. 'But how would that work?'

Beth sits quietly for a moment as her mind ticks over. 'He could split his time. As office manager and trainee sales negotiator, he'd keep an eye on a new administrator, but in between I'd start training him up.'

'Are you ladies ready to order?' the waitress checks.

'I think we are,' Beth confirms, as she glances at me. 'We'll have our usual, please.'

The waitress gives a little smile. 'No problem.'

'That's us to a T, isn't it? The usual,' I mumble.

'But it needn't be, Freya. You're overdue a relaxing holiday. I pop off to the Canary Islands every summer to spend two weeks at my aunt's luxury villa. You take a few days off in summer, usually to spend time in your beautiful garden and that's it. All I'm saying is that if you really do enjoy his company, think about it. What an experience it would be, and you'd come back refreshed.'

Goodness. That's not the way I thought this conversation would go. I'm just about to enrol at a gym that's a car ride away from the office, simply to avoid Luke. He's getting desperate because I won't answer his calls anymore. I told him straight; I'm happy with my life exactly the way it is, and he needs to go off and have a wonderful summer in France – without me.

2

Persistence is Irresistible

I love Sundays. It's my only day off, even though the office is open from ten o'clock until four in the afternoon. We have a little team of part-time staff who help with the viewings at the weekend, as it's often busy. But it's the time of year when if I turn my back on the garden for more than a week, the weeds start to become really noticeable, and the grass starts looking shaggy. I'm as OCD about the garden as I am my beautiful, Grade II listed cottage by the river.

After a productive morning, it's wonderful to sit and relax with a cup of tea to survey my handiwork. There's something about nature that is calming and after a frenetic week at work, I can already feel the tension in my shoulders beginning to ease. I spent way too much time hunched over my laptop, even though in the evenings I'm now fighting the urge to check out what the other agents have taken on. That's the trouble with being competitive.

What doesn't help is that Hearth and Home do realistic valuations, even when it's clear the seller is disappointed. Other agents will match the price expectations of the client and are content to let a home sit on the market for a while to prove a point. Then, when it doesn't sell, the negotiator suggests a price drop. Sometimes it works, and the client listens to their advice, but sometimes it doesn't, and the customer goes elsewhere. It's not immoral, but some clients who walk away after that scenario aren't happy. Obviously, people like to share their opinions when they feel that they've been let down by a professional and that's why we don't play games.

'Freya?' a voice calls out.

Inwardly, I groan, as I jump up out of my seat and make my way around to the tall scrollwork gate at the side of the cottage. A smiling face peers back at me from between the ivy that I can't bring myself to cut away, but which prevents me from using the side entrance.

'Luke. What are you doing here?' I sigh.

That wicked little smile of his continues to grow.

'You won't answer my calls or my texts, what was I supposed to do? I have a little surprise. Have you eaten, yet?'

'No. And I'm not hungry.'

He holds up a carrier bag as he pulls a long face. 'Sorry . . . I thought you might appreciate a little company; and I knew you'd be working on the garden. I went to quite a lot of trouble to—'

'OK! I'll go back inside to let you in.'

I'm such a sucker. He did look apologetic, but also a tad wistful. When it comes to perseverance, he is the main man.

As I swing open the door, my heart leaps in my chest. Sometimes there's this air of vulnerability about him, despite the fact that on the surface he appears to be the sort of guy who sails through life with ease. I guess I was like that when I was his age, but life has taught me to rein myself in. When it comes to one's emotions, it's not a good idea to say the first thing that pops into your head. Experience tempers everything and that, I've come to discover, is a good thing.

'You look great,' he blurts out.

That's exactly what I mean! I step back, to allow him to come inside. 'You'd better take that little lot into the kitchen.'

'You said you weren't hungry.' He turns his head to glance at me, knowingly, over his shoulder.

I turn away while I shut the door, thinking this is a huge

mistake. 'That was in the hope that you'd go away,' I call out as he disappears from view.

If he believes that, he'll believe anything because it wasn't at all convincing. It's really good to see him.

'It's been a while, Freya,' he comments, as I lean back against the countertop and watch as he begins to unpack a carrier bag full of goodies. 'Here,' he says, pulling out a bottle of red wine. 'Take this and two glasses out to the garden, and I'll join you shortly.'

This is my cottage; he's been here less than two minutes and he's taking over the place again as if it's his second home.

'A quick lunch and then you must leave, because I have plans,' I state, firmly.

He looks at me askance. 'What plans?'

That throws me. 'I have a date with a good book.'

He begins laughing, softly, as our eyes meet. 'I think I can beat that. Now . . . go! Don't spoil my surprise.'

What am I going to do about Luke? I ponder, as I sip a rather nice glass of red wine. When I glance at the label, Le Manoir du Bois sounds so inviting. The black outline of a grand house, with a long curving drive leading up to it, sets me daydreaming until a voice breaks my reverie.

'*Voilà*!' I jump up to move the wine bottle and the glasses, so Luke can lower the tray carefully down onto the glass tabletop. 'Impressive, *non*?'

I'm sunk, as I look up into those charismatic eyes of his and see an air of expectancy.

'It's . . . wonderful. A real French experience by the look of it.'

Luke has literally raided a delicatessen and purchased anything that was sporting one of those cute little French flags.

He passes me a paper plate and a napkin, and I glance up at him, puzzled. 'Happy anniversary?'

'Oh . . . they're left over from a little do I hosted for the friends I'm staying with. They've been married for two years.'

'Ah, I see.'

'Right. We have *rillettes Saint-Jacques*.' He points to a small Mason jar.

'That's scallops, isn't it?'

'Yes, with crème fraîche. And *saucisson sec*, a rather nice salami. Then my personal favourite, lobster mousse with cognac.' He looks pleased with himself. 'Then onto the cheeses. A soft Camembert and a creamy blue Saint Agur and Port Salut with the infamous orange rind. Oh . . . and a *pain de campagne*, fresh sourdough country bread and a classic *fougasse*.'

The *fougasse* dough is shaped to resemble an ear of wheat, and this one also has green olives in it.

'It all looks amazing. What's that?' I ask, pointing to a film-covered dish.

'That a classic French dessert: mini *babas au rhum*. While I didn't bring any vanilla ice cream with me, it's lush with a cup of coffee served on the side.'

'There's a good quality ice cream unopened in my freezer,' I confirm.

'I hoped as much,' he says with a cheeky grin. We've often lain together in bed sharing a carton, which is why I buy the smaller round tubs. You can't stick it back in the freezer once it starts to melt and Luke doesn't like to hurry anything.

'Luke, I know what you're trying to do, and it won't work.' I start digging in and he joins me.

'Don't you fancy a little French adventure with me? It's for two months. That's not a lot to ask,' he states, as if I'm being unreasonable. 'Just July and August. I'm about to disappear for a few weeks and we'll be able to catch up on the drive to Picardy.'

'You're going away?'

'I have some work to do, so I'm heading back to Cornwall.'

'Work?' I query. I assume he's joking, as you can only stay with friends for so long.

'You seem to think I spend my life living from day to day, but that isn't strictly true. This job is important, so I need to focus. When I return, the van will be all loaded up and I hope you'll change your mind and come with me, Freya.'

'*The van.*' I give a gentle sigh. 'It's not really my thing, Luke. I don't do tents, either.'

He makes a dismissive sound. 'It's just a means of transport, Freya. If we do, and I say *if* we do, end up spending a night in it, then I'll make sure we stop somewhere with excellent facilities. In between travelling, we're going to stay at some truly amazing places.'

'You mean, you are,' I correct him.

He frowns. 'Are you enjoying that wine, because Le Manoir du Bois is the first stop on the trip. Admittedly, they only grow the grapes and they're processed and bottled elsewhere, but it's an incredible place. I guarantee that you'd fall in love with it.'

My plate now has a fine selection of mouth-watering titbits and I sit back to watch Luke in earnest. 'But you said that it's a working holiday. So, what will *you* be doing there to earn your keep?'

'Helping them to get everything ready for an influx of guests for their annual gourmet food festival. I did tell you a little bit about it, but you never take me seriously.' He looks a little dejected and I can sort of understand why.

'I just . . . Our lives are so different, Luke. I can't just drop everything and take two months off.'

'Why not? You work long hours week in, week out; everyone deserves a break. I'm not giving up that easily, because I think it would do you good. I've seen people burn themselves out and it's a long road to recovery. Anyway, this little array in front of you is merely a taster to get you hooked.'

I spread a little lobster mousse on a chunk of crusty bread and there's a definite whiff of cognac in the air. As I pop it into my mouth, I'm unable to comment, other than to let out a satisfied 'Mmm . . .'

The way to my heart is through my stomach and, unfortunately, Luke has already sussed that out after a few midnight raids on my fridge. He hasn't been in my life for very long, but he doesn't miss a thing and, like it or not, I find that rather endearing.

The next day, around mid-morning, I call Mum and her cheery voice echoes down the phone line. 'Where are you, Freya? There's a distinctly hollow sound, like footsteps.'

'I'm on my way to a viewing but I'm a little early. I decided to have a walk around the area in case any new "for sale" signs have gone up today.'

'Oh, Freya, only you would think of that, my darling daughter. Your dad would have been so proud of what you and Beth have achieved.'

Hard work does pay off and, boy, have we worked hard. That's why I'm calling Mum to tell her my news. 'I'm going to take a couple of months off to do a little tour of France. Beth is fine with it and we've approached Ethan to help cover part of my job. Do you think I'm being a bit rash, though?'

There's a stunned silence and when Mum starts talking, I can tell she doesn't quite know what to say. 'A . . . um . . . tour of France? That's a bit out of the blue, isn't it?'

'I'm teaming up with someone else. They'll be doing the driving.'

'Oh, right, I see. That makes more sense then, as you hate driving on the other side of the road in a right-hand drive. Dad gave up on trying to convince you that the more you do it, the easier it becomes.'

That thought makes me smile. 'Ah . . . I remember that wonderful New Year's Eve,' I reply, wistfully.

'Everyone was wishing us "*Bonne année*",' Mum chimes in. 'If I said it once that night, I said it fifty times over and just thinking about it makes me smile.'

'It was fun, wasn't it?'

A last-minute search online saw the three of us bundling suitcases into the car and heading for what was supposed to be a New Year's Eve we'd always remember. And it was certainly that, all right.

'I'll never forget the look on your dad's face when you informed him that the ping on his phone was a message saying our reservation hadn't gone through. Even though we'd received a confirmation email before we left home.'

'Yes, but Dad wasn't one to make a fuss, was he?'

It's funny how things turn out. We were on our way to Mont-Saint-Michel at the time. It had started snowing quite heavily and with our posh evening frocks and Dad's dinner suit in garment bags laid out carefully in the boot of the car, we decided to head for the first hotel we could find.

It was eight o'clock before we found somewhere with two available rooms, and we were feeling a tad sorry for ourselves. And hungry. They weren't offering room service as it was, after all, New Year's Eve. With our limited French and their smattering of English, the woman behind the reception desk managed to talk the restaurant next door, called L'Escargot, to make up an extra table just for us.

It turned out to be a truly wonderful evening. Everyone there gave us a warm welcome, and considering they were mostly large family parties, the kissing on each cheek seemed to go on forever. It was magical, and the last time the three of us were together. The memory of that trip is dear to our hearts because what seemed like a disaster turned into a night of pure joy with lots and lots of raucous laughter, and manic dancing between courses.

'It's wonderful to look back on that, Freya, isn't it? Even though each of the eight courses came with a different wine, it was just a taster, and every mouthful of food was a sheer delight. We were the only non-French-speaking people there, but they made us feel so welcome. And now you're going back to make another memory. It's about time.'

That was nearly ten years ago now. 'This will be a little different. It's actually a . . . um . . . working holiday.'

'It is?' Mum sounds surprised. 'Is this some sort of estate agent exchange programme?'

I burst out laughing. 'No, nothing like that. I'll be turning my hand to lots of different things.'

'Like?'

'Working at a manor house, and picking fruit and vegetables, for starters.'

Mum draws in a sharp breath. 'Really?'

'I'm going with a friend. His name is Luke Stevenson. He lives in Cornwall but has friends here in Sevenoaks. We sort of bumped into each other at the gym. Luke has spent every July and August for the last . . . I don't know . . . six or seven years, I think, doing this and I thought it might be fun.'

'Well, Freya, it's about time you took a break. I mean, a *real* break. It doesn't matter what you do, as you're not one to lie on a sun bed. They do say that a change is as good as a rest. In my opinion, if anyone needs to step outside of their daily routine for a while, it's you, my darling.'

Now that's a real surprise. I thought Mum would be questioning me about Luke, not jumping on the same bandwagon as Beth about how I need to get away for a while.

'So, you think it's a good idea, too?'

'I'm assuming that means Beth has been actively encouraging you?' Mum is no one's fool.

'Yes. But I wondered whether I was just being a bit rash . . . or trying to recapture my youth. You know, having hit my mid-thirties and all that.'

She giggles. 'Ah, you're still a spring chicken, as your grandma would say. Get out on the road and have a good time. You'll come back the better for it.'

I groan. 'That's exactly what Beth said. And now Ethan's aware of it, he can't wait to take over my desk. But Luke is away working, and we don't head off until the first of July.'

'That's perfect then. I know you; you'll want to brief Ethan on every little thing. Learning to let go isn't easy, Freya, but there comes a time when it's for our own good. This is that time for you. And when you're on your travels, I want you to send me lots of photos, so I can be a part of your trip, too.'

Oh, Mum. 'Of course I will. And is everything good with you?'

She makes a disparaging sound. 'There aren't enough hours in the day, Freya. I don't know how your dad coped with all the committees he was on. Allowing the local Residents Association to talk me into being his replacement is bad enough and it was a big mistake. I don't have his patience and even after all this time I'm still the one hurrying the committee along. Honestly, some people just seem to enjoy the sound of their own voices, anything to avoid making a decision. Your dad would laugh, as instead of taking his place and being a placater, I'm the one calling people out. But things are getting done a little quicker these days, just not quickly enough for me in some instances.'

Mum won't put up with any nonsense, whereas my dad was a gentle giant of a man. He was a peacemaker but Mum always said people took advantage of him and maybe, in hindsight, they did. But he made a lot of good things happen for our local community and he'll always be remembered for that.

There's a bleep and it's an incoming call from the office; after a quick goodbye I'm surprised to hear Ethan's voice.

'Please don't say my viewing has been cancelled,' I groan.

'No. Nothing like that. I have an offer for you to put forward to the Fosters . . . you know, the barn conversion at Edenbridge.'

'An offer, from someone who hasn't even stepped over the threshold?' Being keen is fine, but we're professionals and most vendors would reject an offer like this. I know he was disappointed when he learnt that the couple he originally thought would snap it up had found something else, but it happens.

'This couple called into the office just after you left this morning. I showed them the brochure and the photos you took when you did the valuation. It's perfect for them, Freya. They went straight out to do a drive-by, in fact they parked up and had a general walk around the area. Half an hour later, they rang offering the full asking price with a six-week exchange and completion date.'

It's unusual, but now the contract has been signed we're honour-bound to put forward all offers we receive. 'As soon as my viewing is over, I'll pop in to see the Fosters and explain the situation. They didn't think there would be any viewings until after they'd left for their holiday, so this will come as quite a surprise. They're packing, so they'll want a bit of notice. Text me the clients' availability and I'll arrange something.'

It seems Ethan might just have made his first sale and starting with a property priced at well over a million pounds is impressive. It's all about gut instincts, trying to distinguish serious buyers from those who are serial viewers. Some people are looking for the impossible: a bigger property than their budget will buy or wanting a bargain at the seller's expense. But full asking price off the bat is quite something. And talk about timing! Any guilt I'm feeling about my trip is beginning to fade fast. I think Ethan will enjoy stepping up and with Beth keeping a close eye on him, he'll do well.

That night as I lie in bed, part of me is nervous about what I'm getting myself into. Luke is hard to resist and he's growing on me in a way I haven't experienced before. He's kind and thoughtful, which is lovely, but I don't know what he's expecting from me. I've told him several times not to read anything deep into this little jaunt of ours. But is he really listening to me? I wonder.

Tomorrow he's leaving Sevenoaks and after a meal together at the local pub earlier this evening, I struggled to remain upbeat. I felt sad. I don't know what his life is like back in

Cornwall. I know he doesn't have a partner, or even an ex he's close to. My own love interests have come and gone. So far, no one has really left a long-lasting impression on me.

Naturally, Mum worries about the fact that I don't have a significant other in my life. It wasn't that long ago she actually mentioned the biological clock. At the time I'd laughed and reassured her that if I hear that tick-tock sound, I won't just grab the first available man I see. But she was serious. After having a series of boyfriends in my twenties, I simply got tired of dating. And it's true to say that since I became a partner in the estate agency, my life has been focused on securing my financial future.

Yes, there has been the odd occasion when I've gone for a drink with someone. Usually after a party where a friend, and not just Beth, made the introduction. However, Mum says she doesn't want me looking back on my life with any regrets. It didn't help when Beth said that a part of my problem is that I always pick the same type of man.

'It's like you have this mental tick list. If they don't measure up to it, then you write them off.' She was joking around at the time but maybe she has a point.

'What if I'm one of those people who just aren't able to commit to someone long term?' It was a bit of a scary admission and I was a tad concerned when Beth didn't immediately dismiss it.

'You just haven't met the one, yet. When you do, believe me, everything simply falls into place. There is no such thing as Mr Perfect, Freya,' she'd replied. 'A professional man with no baggage, a good work ethic and a heart of gold would probably turn out to be unbearable to live with.'

'So, what's the point of looking?'

The expression on her face had been one of sheer exasperation. 'You can't judge someone before you get to know them properly. It's about making an effort and taking a risk. It also means listening to what your heart is telling you, before your head takes over. No one is perfect and that includes you and me, too. Thankfully, it doesn't make any of us unlovable, does it? As a couple you grow together and, from personal experience, you end up changing in ways you couldn't have imagined.'

Beth got engaged to David five years ago and they finally got married in June last year. They honeymooned in her aunt's beautiful villa in Tenerife, knowing that each year they can return, and it will always hold special memories for them. I thought that was rather romantic, and it did make me start to wonder whether I'd ever find a special someone of my own.

And now here I am, about to spend the best part of the summer with a man nine years my junior. My instincts tell me that Luke is a genuine guy and when we're together we have an awful lot of fun. But if he's looking for a long-term commitment, given our different lifestyles and the age gap, it's a recipe for disaster. Somewhere out there is the woman of his dreams, he just doesn't know it yet.

I draw in a deep breath, straighten my back and clear my mind, as Luke has taught me. It's time to go within and stop worrying about what might happen way down the road. I'm in *the now* and I'm . . . happy. He is, too.

I'm beginning to get excited at the thought of stepping outside of my comfort zone for a while. I mean . . . what harm can it do to let my hair down before I give some real thought to what I want out of the rest of my life. And with Luke around, there'll never be a dull moment.

July

The journey to Danizy, Saint-Quentin begins . . .

Freya

3

The Departure

When Luke raps the door knocker, my bags are already packed. I'm under strict instructions to travel light, but we're talking about two months away from home. He suggested I choose items that don't need ironing if at all possible and said that if it will roll up without creasing, then it passes the test. Beth and I spent a long time, both online and searching in stores, for my new summer wardrobe. Items I could dress up, or down, with a few simple touches. And shorts and T-shirts for the stint on a farm.

When I swing open the door, he's standing there, his face alive with a smile that reaches from ear to ear. 'Are you ready?'

'I am. Is this light enough?' I ask, proudly, as I indicate to my new cargo hauler sitting on the floor behind me. It's a backpack, and wheeled luggage, all in one and it's super lightweight. Next to it is my all-purpose travel bag. In there is something for every occasion, hopefully, including everything for a full make-up job and my trusty hairdryer.

'Pretty impressive,' Luke replies, eagerly stepping forward to plant a kiss on my lips.

As I stare up into his eyes, I can see the excitement bubbling up inside of him and I'm feeling it too. 'We're really doing this,' I sigh, slightly breathlessly. 'I can't believe it. Where are you parked?'

'A bit further down the road. I didn't want to pull into your drive and risk churning up the gravel. Come and meet Reba. I'll grab the big bag; you take the other one.'

He lifts my luggage with ease, considering how much I managed to cram in there. But it's actually a huge relief to know that I don't have to worry about anything getting creased. It's a tip I could have done with years ago, as on the occasions I have gone abroad I've always taken a travel iron with me.

We step through the double gates, and as we pass my neighbour's car, I immediately spot Luke's van. 'Wow! What a beauty!' I exclaim.

'She certainly is. I gather from your reaction it's not quite what you were expecting.' Luke glances at me, teasingly.

'If you'd mentioned that it was a VW, I'd have had an entirely different image in my head.'

He chuckles to himself. 'Oh, so you thought I'd turn up in a rusty old ex-works van that I'd tarted up?'

I give him a droll look. 'No.' Although, I have to admit that he's not far off the mark. 'Did I hear you right . . . R-i-b-a?'

'Nearly. R-e-b-a. She's just come back after a total refit. With a brand-new engine, we'll get eighty miles an hour out of her no trouble at all.'

As he unlocks the double doors and slides them back, I'm in awe.

'It's immaculate, Luke, and I love the colour of the upholstery!' White leather inset with a lime green has a distinctly summery, and contemporary, feel. Considering he's a surfer, I was sort of expecting something rough and ready, with a few . . . OK, a lot of stickers on the rear window. The sort you see in shops that were the forerunners of memes, like *surf's up* and *surfing ninja*, or maybe well-known beaches he's visited. But this is way too grand for that. The paintwork gleams. You're talking serious money here.

'We're the first to take her out on the road after two months in the garage.'

Ah, so he's borrowed it. Luke's friend must really trust him or owe him a huge favour.

'All I can say is, lucky us,' I reply.

In a way it reminds me of my cottage. What Reba lacks in size, she makes up for with a sense of uniqueness. Everything about it smells new and the upgrade must have cost a small fortune.

Luke leans forward to turn the key and I put out my hand to stop him for a moment.

'I'm just filling in for a friend. No strings attached. Just a summer of fun and new experiences, right?'

He raises his hand and we high five. 'Agreed. Unless, of course, during the trip you end up falling in love with me. Now wouldn't that be something?'

I start laughing. 'There's a reason that I'm still single, Luke. I'm not prepared to settle and I've yet to meet a man who ticks all the boxes.'

With that, he gives me a cheeky grin. 'Don't judge a book by its cover. Do you know that old saying "still waters run deep"? Well, I might end up surprising you!'

I roll my eyes at him. 'And you think you can do that in just two months?'

'Maybe,' he replies, playfully.

As our eyes meet there's an undeniable buzz between us but with age comes wisdom. I'm used to men going all out to impress me. With Luke it's more a case of what you see is what you get. And yes, that is rather appealing . . . if you're looking for a puppy, that is, but not necessarily for a lifelong partner.

He fires Reba up, and seconds later, we're on our way. 'Day one,' he remarks, with a lift in his voice. 'I guess I'd better start turning on the charm.'

With Le Shuttle behind us, Luke effortlessly joins the busy network of roads leading away from Calais, and Coquelles Terminal. I'm not really surprised that there's no satnav in the vehicle, given his carefree attitude to life. However, I find myself glancing at his side profile, thinking he's a guy full of surprises.

'What?' he asks, nervously. 'I can feel you staring at me. You can relax, your life is in good hands. I know every inch of this journey and I'm a competent driver.'

That makes me smile to myself. 'Oh, I'm not doubting your abilities, just marvelling at the fact you don't need a map.'

'Not for the French summer tour, I don't; and if I head off somewhere I haven't explored before, I like to wander at will and discover new places.'

That sort of sums Luke up, really. I'm a meticulous planner and having entrusted the next two months of my life to him, I am beginning to get a little anxious.

'The first place we're staying at, you said it's very grand. They know you, but what will they be expecting of me?'

'Don't worry. What they need is helpers who are prepared to be flexible. Don't start worrying about it, Freya. This is supposed to be fun.'

'Yes, but I'm going into this blind, Luke. It's a bit daunting, if I'm being honest.'

'Max and Erin Daniels are a lovely couple. Max was in the banking industry. When he hit fifty, they sold everything and bought Le Manoir du Bois outright. It's a large property, so the upkeep alone is enormous, but he and his wife have succeeded in making a success of it.'

'So, the guy who usually travels with you . . . what does he do?'

Luke turns his head to check the passenger-side wing mirror, as he pulls off onto a slip road. 'Mostly hands-on in the kitchen but Erin is quick to pick up on an individual's strengths and weaknesses, and she'll soon suss you out.'

Well, unless she wants someone to market her property, I do hope she understands that whatever task I'm assigned it will be a case of doing my best. Luke is just so calm all the time and I envy him that.

'Right, that's the worst bit over. The roads will be much quieter from here on. It's about a two-hour drive if we're lucky, depending on traffic. Now, stop worrying, Freya. Sit back and enjoy the scenery. We'll find somewhere quiet to park up and have lunch. I've come prepared, you know.'

My eyes widen, faking surprise. 'You have?'

He chuckles softly to himself. 'Oh, you have no idea how long I've been planning this trip.'

Now I'm confused. 'But it's been the same for the last what . . . seven years, hasn't it?'

Luke takes one hand off the steering wheel and reaches out to grasp my hand, lying on the armrest between us. 'This year I've reinvented myself, just like Reba, and we're on a mission.'

'Hmm . . . I hope it's not a mission to convince me this is how I should spend every summer, because that's not happening. I can only hope I have the stamina for this,' I remark, only half joking. But my fear is that Luke hasn't listened to a single word of warning I've given him. It's simply a summer break and this is definitely a one-off event for me.

Hopefully, next year his friend will be accompanying him, and this will be a delightful memory I'll look back on with fondness. After all, a handsome young guy, a dream of a VW that no one could possibly turn their noses up at, and even the air smells different.

'We're just coming up to a tiny village. Most places close on a Monday but there's a wonderful boulangerie on the left and they also own a *tabac* next door, which sells amazing coffee. They open for a few hours and we can pop in for a drink and to use their facilities. I know the perfect spot for our picnic and it's only about a ten-minute drive from here.'

It sounds heavenly to me. I'm famished.

Standing at a small counter running along one wall of the tiny *tabac*, intermittently sipping an espresso and a tall glass of water, is surreal. Usually, I'd be popping into The Coffee

Shack, a short walk away from the office, for a takeaway coffee. The old man next to me, who speaks no English but clearly wants to chat, is a real test of my basic school-level French and I'm glad when Luke comes to my rescue.

We end up laughing as I make faltering attempts to join in, even using my hands at times as if that somehow makes things clearer, although it doesn't. Arnaud tells us that he comes here every day because the walk from his cottage is good for his legs. He wiggles his walking stick in the air and gives us a toothy grin. I can't understand everything he's saying as he talks very fast indeed, but enough to catch that he's lived in the village all his life and has never been further afield than Paris.

In true Brit style, we both shake his hand as we bid him goodbye, and I'll never forget those happy, twinkling eyes. As we step outside, I turn to look at Luke.

'I think that little interlude made his day,' he says, smiling away to himself.

'It's lovely to have the time to stop and chat, isn't it? I wonder how often English people pull up here. I'm surprised it's even classed as a village, it's more of a hamlet.'

'I suspect that very few would venture into the *tabac*, although I'm sure people stop at the boulangerie to grab a quick snack for the road. Most people coming from Calais would drive further on, looking for a café.'

As we stroll back to the van, which is parked in a lay-by on the opposite side of the road, Luke catches my hand. The baguette, wrapped around the middle with a small piece of greaseproof paper, is tucked beneath his other arm as if it comes naturally to him.

'Did you know that the French have precise guidelines in place to govern the production of baguettes?'

'You mean the actual recipe?' I query.

'Yes, but it covers both the dough, and the size and shape of it. Essentially, it's made up of wheat flour, water, yeast and salt – nothing more, nothing less. And the length, width, height and weight – approximately 250 grams – are all regulated. Now that's what I call having a real sense of pride in what you produce. In the UK only the real artisan bakers – who insist on making everything by hand – understand what we've lost over the years. It's kind of sad that the vast majority of people are content to go to the supermarket and buy whatever's on the shelves. The mass-produced stuff is filling but not satisfying in the same way.'

I totally agree and this lunch wouldn't be anywhere near as enjoyable with the rubbery version from my local store, even though they have little French flags hanging from the shelf. A French person would be insulted.

'A genuinely handmade product from start to finish is a labour of love. Even so, I had no idea it was a source of national pride to ensure the standard is maintained. The humble isn't quite so humble after all,' I reflect as I slip into the passenger seat. Behind me, Luke stows the bread away in one of the cabinets before joining me in the front.

The traffic is surprisingly light for the most part. Even in the short drive to our next stop, our journey has that distinct holiday feel to it. A seemingly never-ending series of roundabouts are connected by a good network of roads bounded by fields and trees. Everything looks green and fertile.

It isn't long before we're driving alongside a small stream and when we enter a section of the road with a splendid avenue of trees, Luke slows down. A few cars are parked up next to a wide grass verge and he draws to a halt.

'Here we are. It's picnic time.'

'Can I give you a hand?'

'Sure.' Luke eases himself out of the seat and I wait as he slides back the double doors.

'If you hop in and pass me the items, I'll load up the cool bag.'

He opens a latched hatch that backs onto the passenger's seat and pulls out a bag. 'The fridge is that first door beneath the sink.'

It doesn't take long to gather everything together and it seems that Luke has thought of everything we need to make up a delightful lunch. From bottles of water to a selection of French cheeses, and even a tinned chicken liver and raisin pâté, that have, ironically, made their way back home.

'Can you grab the picnic rug, Freya? If you feel beneath the bench seat, there's a lever. Just slide it to the right and the front panel will pop open.'

I stoop to slide myself onto the floor of the van, sitting cross-legged as I investigate. 'Ah . . . right. Got it. So, this seat pulls out and turns into a bed?'

'Yep. The whole thing slides forward to butt up to the edge of the sink unit. The back of the bench seat folds down and another, third section behind that raises up to make a good-size double.'

'Only the rear window is tinted. How do you manage at night?' I ask, as I gaze around.

Luke starts smirking. 'Thinking ahead, I like that. See those tiny black oblong shapes on some of the windows? They're magnetic catches. Instead of curtains, we have solid plastic privacy panels. The one for the windscreen rolls up, but affixes in the same way. Don't worry, unless there's a change in plan, we'll be sleeping in a real bed every single night, I promise you.'

'But you don't usually?'

He shrugs his shoulders, dismissively. 'No, but it's a sacrifice worth making.'

I turn to look at Luke and I'm overwhelmed by a sense of peace and happiness as we set off on a short walk. This really is living in the moment and what could be more delightful than strolling down a grassy bank to sit beside a babbling brook? Nothing comes to mind.

'If you spread out the mat, I'll unpack lunch.' He grins.

After that day he turned up at the cottage with a picnic in a carrier bag, it doesn't really come as a surprise that he's so organised. But it's still nice that he's trying so hard to make even the small things enjoyable.

Birds are playing among the tall trees that line the road. They're squabbling and every now and again they fly off in tandem to perch somewhere else. I chuckle to myself as I slip off my shoes and sit in anticipation, my stomach rumbling. It makes no sense as to why the birds follow each other around when they have such a vast playground, but I guess it's a game they always play. A bit like people, really. We're all creatures of habit and never seem to tire of doing the same things over and over again.

Luke places a summery green melamine plate and a bottle of water in front of me.

'What time are we expected?' I enquire.

I watch as he uses wet wipes to clean his hands and then passes them to me. 'I said mid-afternoon, but there's no rush. We won't start work until tomorrow. Tonight, we'll be welcomed like guests.'

'You mean, you'll be welcomed back with opened arms, and I'll be under scrutiny,' I half joke.

'No. It won't be like that, honestly. I wouldn't take you anywhere you wouldn't feel instantly at ease.' Luke narrows his eyes as he stares back at me and suddenly, he's very serious indeed.

'That was just my silly sense of humour kicking in. This looks like a real feast.' When he said he'd been planning the trip, I wasn't expecting such attention to detail. There's even a tin opener, the sort of thing it's so easy to forget. As we tuck in, my smile is enough to reassure him.

Ripping off chunky pieces of crusty, brown baguette adds to the ambience of this picturesque setting. There's a hint of a breeze blowing through the trees and even though the sun is high in the sky, it's very pleasant sitting here eating.

'The pâté is amazing. Good choice.'

'It doesn't really need butter, but there's some here if you want it,' he replies, sounding content.

'Thanks.' The food is so good that all I want to do is focus on eating and taking in my surroundings. But whenever my eyes stray back to Luke, he seems to be watching me.

As my appetite starts to slow, curiosity gets the better of me. 'Is this always your first stop?'

'No. We normally sail by, but it's a place that has always stuck in my mind as somewhere that would be lovely to sit and while away a little time. But maybe not with my usual companion.'

'Aww . . . that's so thoughtful of you.' And touching.

'One summer, and I intend to make it special.'

We sit in companionable silence for a while, before packing up and getting back on the road. I'd be lying if I didn't admit that there's a little knot in the bottom of my stomach. Is it a warning sign? I wonder. In some ways Luke is very *together* considering he's only twenty-five years old. In others he's what I regard as rather cavalier.

He takes on casual jobs to allow him to enjoy a lifestyle and freedom most of us can only dream about. But there will come a point when he has to put down roots. Then what will he do? Goodness, I'm sitting here worrying about Luke's future and suddenly I wonder where the fun me has gone.

4

Bon Appetit!

'Erin, Max – it's good to be back! Let me introduce you to Freya, Freya Henderson.'

After the couple both greet Luke with a kiss on each cheek, I'm expecting a handshake but am surprised when I, too, am greeted in the traditional way.

'Welcome, Freya! We're so very grateful you were able to step in and help. Everyone around here is stretched thinly at this time of the year anyway, and our little festival has grown beyond our wildest dreams,' Erin explains.

'We were panicking a little.' Max jumps into the conversation, smiling broadly. 'But Luke told us not to worry as he had the perfect person in mind.'

The eye contact between Erin and Max is a little worrying. I have no idea what Luke has told them about me, or the nature of our relationship.

'Well, I'm delighted to be here. I'm prepared to roll up my sleeves and have a go at anything. As long as someone shows me what to do, especially if it's in the kitchen. I'm usually quick to pick things up but my French is very basic, I'm sad to say.' I think it's best to be upfront.

'Oh.' Erin's hand flies up in the air, dismissively. 'You'll be just fine, Freya. Everyone works as a team, and we support each other. Now, I'm just preparing afternoon tea, so I'll ask Chloé to show you to your room. We'll reserve a table for the two of you out on the terrace, so that will just give you time to bring in your luggage.'

'That's most kind of you, Erin,' I reply, not expecting such a warm and friendly welcome.

As we head back to the van to collect our things, Luke turns to smile at me. 'Do you feel more at ease now we're finally here?'

I give him a fixed stare. 'You didn't say anything about it being set in its own parkland. Or mention the magnificent, chestnut-tree-lined horseshoe drive through a forest, before it arcs in front of a grand manor house. This is grandeur on a huge scale, Luke. How much land do they have?'

He grins back at me. 'A mere nine hectares, which I think is around twenty-two acres. They grow vines in a number of large fields way over there.' He points to a place somewhere behind the main buildings. 'But a local vineyard has taken over the bulk of the work. In return, each year they bottle up a good supply with the manor's logo, which keeps Max and Erin happy. To be honest, they're just an ordinary couple running a business, Freya. There's never enough help on hand, and you can see how delighted they are to bolster their team by two. That's why I couldn't let them down.'

We're parked in an area just a short walk away but hidden by the trees. As we make our way back to Le Manoir, I'm glad my all-in-one travel bag has robust wheels. The gravel paths are well compacted though; the extensive lawned areas look way too velvety to risk doing any damage.

'Luke!'

A young woman hurries towards us, waving both hands in the air.

'Chloé! *Comment vas-tu?*' Luke puts down his heavy backpack and rushes to meet her. He kisses her three times on alternate cheeks, and they hug like old friends.

I can't keep up with the torrent of words that pass between them, but the body language is telling. At one point she looks tearful, placing both hands over her heart and the look on Luke's face is one of intense sadness. He seems to be reassuring her that he's fine, for some reason. As I get closer, he turns away from her, indicating for me to join them.

'Chloé, this is Freya. She doesn't speak much French.'

'Ah! Bonjour, Freya. It is good to meet you.' Her accent is charming.

Rather awkwardly I let go of my suitcase and put out my hand, which she duly shakes.

'Welcome to Le Manoir du Bois,' she continues. 'Your room is ready. Please to follow me.'

I fall in behind them, as the path isn't wide enough for us all to walk side by side. They obviously know each other well and I'm curious. She's probably around the same age as Luke, but he could be a year, or two, younger. Chloé is wearing a black skirt and a white blouse with a pintuck front. She manages to wear her uniform with style, but then she is tall and willowy.

'The journey was good for you?' she enquires.

Luke responds and there's a lot of back-and-forth chatter, half in French and half in English when Chloé remembers I can't keep up.

Instead of listening, I turn my attention to the facade of the building. The large windows at ground and first floor level, are all flanked either side by white shutters that are pinned back. The entrance is through a sizeable conservatory set up with a number of white bistro tables and chairs. There are overhead fans and semi-opaque blinds covering the ceiling. I am surprised that instead of a stout internal door, it has a pair of glass French doors that open inwards. I suppose security isn't really an issue when the conservatory is locked up for the night. But what it does create, despite the scale of everything, is the feeling that you're walking into a family home, not a grand country hotel.

The main staircase is, as I would expect, very elegant. It curves around a stairwell, and as I peer upwards, I can see two distinct landings. To one side of the entrance hall there's an upright piano against the wall and a writing desk alongside it. Both have been well used and it adds to the overall ambience.

As we start the climb, a young man appears from seemingly nowhere and insists on taking my cargo bag. Luke is already breaking out into a sweat, so I'm more than grateful to hand it over.

'*Merci.*'

'You are welcome. I'm Oskar.'

'Freya,' I reply, and he nods his head at me, smiling.

'Oskar, this is Luke. Oskar joined us at Christmas,' Chloé explains.

'Luke. I have heard a lot about you. It's good that you are here again.' His German accent is quite pronounced, but even so his English is perfect.

I ask him where he's from and when he realises I can speak better German than I can French, he's delighted to tell me a little about the small town in which he was born.

The wooden stairs creak a little as we cross a wide landing and ascend another curving flight of stairs. The top floor is cooler; windows at both ends of the long landing are open to get a breeze through. Up here in the angled roof, the rooms have dormer windows and Chloé swings open the second door on our left.

Inside there are two double dormer windows and the room is flooded with natural light. The sloping roof to one side is higher than one might expect and to describe this as an attic room wouldn't be doing it justice.

'How lovely!' I exclaim, turning on my heels to take it all in.

A king-size bed is set against the far wall, and I should imagine that even lying down, it's possible to look out over the charming vista of the parkland.

'Do you have any other bags to bring in?' Oskar asks.

'No. This is it. Thank you.' I indicate to the small holdall slung over my shoulder and the handbag swinging from my arm.

'Tell Max I'll be down shortly to help serve afternoon tea on the terrace,' Chloé confirms, and he gives her a nod of his head. 'Luke, Erin asked me to check if this room is suitable for you?'

There's a little awkward eye contact between them.

'Oh . . . yes . . . it's perfect, thank you.'

He seems a little distracted.

'Spare towels and bedding are in the linen cupboard.' She gives Luke a wide smile. 'But then you know where that is. I'm so glad you made it, Luke . . . and Freya.'

There's a hint of sadness to her tone, which is perplexing; as the door closes behind her, I turn to look at Luke.

'What was that about?'

'Oh, the room. Erin usually puts me . . . me and my friend . . . in the one next door; it has two single beds.'

That wasn't quite what I meant, but he's already pulling open one of the drawers and beginning to unpack his things.

I wander over to swing open the double, triple-paned windows. Closing my eyes, I take a few deep breaths in – everything has that warm, heady scent of summer. Suddenly, Luke's arms are around me and I tilt my head back to gaze at him.

'Is the bed big enough?' he teases me.

'And some. This is amazing, Luke. It's hardly a chore to work for your supper when you're staying in accommodation like this, is it?'

'Good people, good food and an eighteenth-century manor built on the remnants of a twelfth-century castle isn't too shabby a start, is it? Anyway, as much as I'd love to throw you on that bed, if we don't appear on the terrace without delay, Erin will probably come looking for us.'

He grabs my hand and spins me around to face him. As our lips touch, I feel strangely carefree. Yesterday's worries have vanished into thin air and Sevenoaks feels like it's a million miles away.

* * *

While the parkland setting feels decadent, my surprise when Luke leads me around the side of the property out onto a terrace almost takes my breath away. There's a profusion of colour, mostly vibrant red and pink geraniums, which line a low stone wall. It's obvious that there's a sheer drop on the other side, as I'm looking at the leafy tops of a clump of sizeable trees literally within reaching distance.

Beneath our feet is a mix of old stone cobbles that are clearly original and a swathe of gravel that mirrors the paths to the front. Greeting us are two life-size, weathered metal stags. Their coats are almost a pure rust colour; they stand with their heads erect as if greeting their visitors.

'My gosh, aren't they magnificent?'

'You wait until you see the view,' Luke insists. 'The best is yet to come. Keep walking.'

We weave in and out of the elegant white tables and chairs that half-fill the terrace, nodding in acknowledgement to people already seated, and make our way to a wide space devoid of trees. Even before I can engage my brain, out pops the word 'Enchanting!'

The drop isn't as sheer as I thought, but it slopes gently away in front of us.

'That's the Oise Valley,' Luke explains. 'The river Oise eventually joins the Seine, so it's also a link in the canal system and waterways of northern France.'

Framed by the vibrant geraniums, whose heads pop up a few inches above the waist-height wall, the river appears to be forked. The first expanse of water is wide, then there's a long strip of grass, trees and bushes forming an island, beyond which is another expanse of water. On the far bank, the flat landscape is mainly forest as far as the eye can see.

'It's a wonderful view, *non*?' Chloé approaches and we turn to acknowledge her.

'Yes, mesmerising. I could stand here all day,' I reply, happily.

'Not me,' Luke joins in. 'I'm starving.'

'Then let me show you to your table. You might as well sit and enjoy the view.' Chloé leads us over to the far corner, where there is a little shade, but we can gaze to our right, down over the full length of the valley. 'We have a full range of teas and coffees.' She indicates to the small, printed menu on the table as we take our seats.

How lovely. 'Early Grey for me, please.'

Luke nods his head in agreement and Chloé hurries away.

'Erin does a slightly French twist on the good old English afternoon tea. They serve dinner from eight o'clock and don't stop until around ten, so this is very popular with the guests.'

Oskar arrives with two white, three-tiered cake stands and Luke's eyes instantly light up as we make room for them on the table. Behind him, Chloé carries a tea tray. She double-checks we have everything we need, before rattling off in French the marvellous selection in front of us. From the tiny sandwiches, which are a lot daintier than the ones I've had back in the UK, to a lavish display of cakes, it's mouth-watering. There's everything from delicate mille-feuilles, to raspberry tarts and shell-shaped madeleines; the strawberry mousse on a sabayon base looks delicious, as do the green macarons. I'm in foodie heaven!

After a leisurely walk around the extensive parkland to the front of the property, we head back to the room and, as it's so hot, we lie down on the bed. We end up drifting off and waking up over an hour later. A shower for two is enlivening; Luke has this way of making everything fun and his passion is spontaneous. He always grabs the moment and he's so difficult to resist. But the price he ends up paying is that I'm still sitting down in front of the vanity unit applying my makeup, when he's ready and eager to go downstairs.

'Don't wait for me. You'll find someone to chat with. A

woman doesn't like to be hurried and I should give Mum a call to let her know we've arrived safely.'

He stoops to kiss my neck, sending goosebumps down my spine. 'I love that cologne,' I half-whisper, as he pulls away.

'Cologne, is it? It just came in a bottle, and I spray it on for special occasions,' he laughs. 'I think my mother gave it to me.'

It's the first time he's ever mentioned his family, but I wave him off as it will do him good to have some time to catch up without me constantly by his side.

'See you in about half an hour?' I tilt my head at him. He rolls his eyes. 'It's not just makeup, I want to put my hair up, too.'

'Fine. I'm sure I'll find something to pass the time.' He laughs to himself as he closes the door behind him.

I dial Mum and put it on speakerphone.

'At last! I'm assuming you're there and everything's fine.' Mum's voice fills the room, making me smile to myself.

'Sorry . . . I really am. I meant to text you the moment we arrived, but it's been quite an experience already.'

'I can tell that from your voice. Come on then . . . what's it like? Have they put you to work already?'

'No, far from it,' I exclaim. 'We have a fabulous room, with two huge windows that open up to look out over parkland as far as the eye can see. From what I've seen already, most of the pieces of furniture are classic, French antiques. It's all very grand and yet you sort of feel you're in someone's actual home. In here, we have a king-size bed with white voile drapes. And two gilded chairs with fabric to match the headboard wall. It's pale blue and white. Actually—' I peer at the pattern a little closer '—it's a hunting scene.'

'Hmm . . . you kept that little development between the two of you very quiet!' Now I'm grinning to myself, as it's a tiny detail I purposely skipped over. 'Anyway,' she continues, 'how are you coping with the language?' Mum is such a worrier.

'I think I might be able to get by. The owners are British, and I've met two other people. One is French and the other German, although they both speak some English. Everyone is very welcoming and the atmosphere here is incredible. We even had afternoon tea out on the terrace. I'll send you some photos in a bit.'

'Are you dining there this evening?'

'Yes. The staff all eat together early, which I think is lovely. Guests are served from eight o'clock onwards and tonight we're guests, so I can take my time getting ready. Besides, I don't want Luke to feel he has to be constantly by my side.'

Mum gives a soft 'Mmm.'

'What?'

'I know you said this thing with Luke isn't anything serious . . . but I wish I'd had a chance to meet him before you left.'

'Oh, Mum! I'm all grown up. He's sweet, young and fun to be around. Besides, I'm going to meet a lot of people on this trip, as tomorrow I'll just be one of the staff. Goodness knows what I'll be doing, but this place is so vast that the list of tasks to be done must feel endless at times. I don't think I'll be on kitchen duty, but who knows?'

Mum starts laughing. 'Well, I can vouch for the fact that you can wash up, but I'm sure they have commercial dishwashers. You said something about a gourmet food festival, though.'

'Mum! I'll admit that cooking isn't my strong point, but I can slice vegetables and make salads. Or maybe have a go at waitressing. How hard can that be?'

Now we're both laughing, and if I'm not careful my mascara will end up sliding down my cheeks in this heat.

'Whatever task you're given, you'll do your utmost best, Freya. Enjoy it, my darling, it'll do you good not to be the ultimate professional in the room for a change.'

I gasp. 'I can't believe you just said that!'

'What I meant,' she labours, 'is that it's important to

wander outside of your comfort zone once in a while. You're much too serious sometimes. Just relax and have fun.'

'Ah . . . fun. Well, with Luke around, it will be nothing but that.'

Mum makes a disapproving sound. 'Hmph.'

'Now what have I said?'

'Do you ever listen to yourself, Freya? There's nothing wrong with being carefree. Or trying something and finding out that it isn't your thing. You live and learn, that's the whole point of life. But if you never stray beyond what you know—'

'As Dad used to say, you stop growing and life gets stale.'

'Good. Then enjoy yourself and . . . don't be too hard on Luke. You were his age once.'

Argh . . . from the little I've told her about him, even Mum thinks I'm too old for him. 'I have no desire to turn back the clock, believe me. Knowledge is power and while I admit that I probably will benefit from a change of scenery, by the time we head back at the end of August at least I'll be fighting fit.' If I can resist those wonderful little French pastries and cakes, of course.

Luke

5

I Think I'm in Trouble

As I saunter down the stairs my mind is in overdrive. Watching Freya get ready was agonising. How am I going to get her to take me seriously, instead of seeing me as a mere distraction?

'Luke. Just the man I need!' Max calls out to me as my foot touches the bottom step of the staircase. He looks frazzled.

'What's up?'

'This darn PC. If it goes any slower, I swear I'll . . .' He pauses, draws in a huge breath and plasters on a smile. 'Could you possibly take a look?'

'It's no problem at all. How long has it been like this?'

He shakes his head, sadly. 'Weeks. Every day it gets a little slower. The trouble is, I'm loath to buy a new one because setting it up and transferring all the files across is time-consuming. I'm better off in the kitchen where I belong.'

I did warn Max last year that he needs to find a good IT guy to call in when he gets stuck. I've done a bit of remote work for him on their website, but the real problem is that the minute something goes wrong he has no idea what he's doing.

'Let's try to find out what the problem is and see if it's fixable.'

The look of relief on his face is worrying. If I can't fix it quickly, it might mean buying some new kit. The money isn't the problem, it's teaching an old dog new tricks, as they say.

In the kitchen, Max is a genius. On a PC if one little thing changes, he panics.

'Ah, here you are!' Erin walks into the office, closely followed by Freya. When I catch sight of her, my heart begins to race. She looks stunning in a long, silky floral-print dress and her blonde hair up in a twist, instead of the usual, very neat ponytail. 'Problems?'

Max immediately turns to look at me questioningly.

'Well, I've managed to get rid of the dreaded black screen but it's still painfully slow. There is a whole batch of software updates that are outstanding which doesn't help. I'll set those going but it will probably take a couple of hours for them to load.' It's hard to sound positive, when every time you press a key you have no idea how long you're going to have to wait for the PC to respond. It's way past its prime and I can totally understand his frustration.

'Will I be able to get the handouts and menus Max has put together printed out in time for the start of the festival on Wednesday? I told you we need to replace it, Max.' Erin looks like she might be about to have a meltdown, as she stands there wringing her hands together.

Max looks decidedly guilty. 'I know, m'dear, but what do I know about computer specs? And I've been busy—'

Before Erin has time to reply, I interject, 'Look guys, it's not the end of the world. I'll jump online later and cost out some new kit for you. With a bit of luck, we might be able to get it delivered tomorrow by courier, if not Wednesday morning, and I'll get it all up and running in no time at all.'

'I have my laptop with me,' Freya joins in. 'Are your files backed up somewhere?'

'Yes,' Erin replies. 'Everything is stored in the cloud.' She glances up at the heavens, as if to say *wherever that is*.

'Perfect. First thing in the morning I can download whatever you need and connect up to your printer to get that sorted,' Freya offers.

Erin breaks out into a huge smile and Max simply looks relieved. 'Oh,' she sighs, 'what an angel you are!'

I glance at Freya, and she gives me a cheeky grin. I'm the computer bod who's going to install a new system and get it up and running, and Freya's the angel? I can't help grinning to myself.

'Max, you'd best get back to the kitchen,' Erin remarks, glancing at her watch. 'And, Luke, you don't keep a lady waiting, eh, Freya?'

Now I'm being chastised, but Erin is right. 'I'm done here anyway; I'll pop back later to check how it's doing, and I'll catch up with you after the dinner service, Max. It shouldn't take us long to thrash out what sort of kit you need and get it ordered.'

'Thanks for coming to our rescue yet again, Luke.' Max isn't a techie by any means, and he could really do with some support. 'Every year you manage to sort out our problems, but I know an upgrade is overdue. I can't have Erin getting stressed.'

With that, Erin bursts out laughing.

'I'm stressed about everything!' she exclaims. 'So why not the computer, too? Welcome to the madness that is the run-up to the start of La Fête de la Gastronomie, Freya. Tomorrow things will get even crazier.'

Sitting opposite me in Le Manoir's formal dining room, surrounded by countless antiques and original, cut-glass chandeliers, Freya looks completely at home. She has an air of natural beauty and elegance that is captivating. When I'm not with her, I'm thinking of her and even I don't feel comfortable about that. I know she wouldn't be, because we're just . . . friends with benefits, I think is the polite term.

As one of a recent batch of new waiters places a plate in front of her, she smiles at him, and he sees what I see. It's hard not to sigh, but I promised Freya a summer she'll never forget. I raise my wine glass as he places the starter of *salade gourmande au saumon* in front of me.

As I watch him walk away, I consider what would be an appropriate toast for the first night of our adventure together.

'Let me!' Freya insists, beaming from ear to ear. 'Here's to ten days of fixing computers, calming troubled waters and rolling up our sleeves to work off all the wonderful food we're going to be eating.'

When I gaze back at her, her eyes sparkle and, as we chink glasses, the candles on the table reflect shards of light off the crystal chandelier overhead.

'You're not put off?' I ask, keeping my voice low.

'What, by problems? No, of course not. Anything I can do to help is fine with me. This salmon looks amazing.'

'Most of the salad and veggies are grown on site. You wait until you taste the main course; Max's beef in red wine is unforgettable. The cheeses to follow are all local and the biscuits freshly baked.'

Freya looks happy, as she takes a sip of the house wine, savouring it. 'Well, I'm not sure after that little lot I'll have room for the *sabayon aux fruits frais et sa glâce maison*.'

'Oh, something tells me you will.'

She bats her eyelashes at me, lowering them as she places her glass down on the table to pick up the knife and fork. 'So, I find some things in life hard to resist,' she admits, placing the first sliver of salmon in her mouth and rolling her eyes. 'Oh . . . I'm going to have to walk this lot off afterwards.'

'Ah . . . I'm . . . um . . . going to have to slope off to spend a bit of time with Max as soon as he's free. I'll get it sorted as quickly as I can, though. No more than an hour tops, so you could while away the time sitting under one of the magnificent trees with a coffee, maybe.' Ugh. Best laid plans and all that. I was hoping after this rather romantic dinner that we'd take an equally romantic stroll around the grounds. Abandoning her for a while wasn't on the agenda.

'Hey, it's fine. I understand and don't worry, I'm perfectly capable of keeping myself occupied.'

But that's the whole point – I don't want Freya to spend time alone when we could be together. I want her to see that I'm reliable; that there is a serious side to me and one day I will put down roots somewhere. Right now, I'm working through a few issues, but crossing paths with Freya out of the blue has blown any chance I have of focusing on anything else right out of the water.

'That's a serious look on your face, Luke. You can share anything with me, you know.'

Her remark catches me off guard, and I immediately turn my frown into a smile. 'I . . . um . . . was just thinking of the best option to meet Max's needs. I think I might steer him away from a hard drive to an SSD; its processing capabilities are much faster.' Oh no, I've done it again. Whenever she gets serious, I change the subject.

Instead of sitting back and sharing my turbulent thoughts, I sit forward and pour her a little more wine.

'This is lovely, Luke. I know it isn't quite the same with me tagging along. I can't even begin to imagine what two single guys on a working holiday get up to, but I'm sure it's not romantic dinners together.' Her eyes sparkle as she looks at me.

'Actually, it's a nice change,' I quip, raising my voice a little as the dining room is almost full.

Never in my wildest dreams did I ever think I'd get Freya to agree to come away with me. What would I have done? So many people would have felt let down and yet I don't think I could have dug deep enough to do this trip alone. Too many memories . . . too many regrets.

With Freya by my side this is like a fresh start, putting to bed ghosts of the past and hoping I can finally move on with my life once summer is over. In my heart, I'd give anything for it to be with her, but I'm realistic enough to know that I only have a slim chance of that happening. I'm not exactly some suave man of the world, who has the wherewithal to sweep her off her feet and take all her worries away. And I'm never going to be Mr Nine-to-Five, am I?

'OK, Max. This is what I'm recommending and it's quite an upgrade, but when you check out the price—' I indicate for him to turn the page '—you'll see that you're getting a lot for your money.'

Max slips his glasses down off his head as he reads the specification sheet and then looks at the bottom line. 'Hmm . . . the price works for me. How soon can you get this organised? And, more importantly, how long will it take me to get my head around using the new kit?'

The latter is a tough question to answer. Max regards what he does online as a necessary evil, but he begrudges every minute he doesn't spend in the kitchen. However, Erin has her hands full organising the staff rota, keeping on top of housekeeping and liaising with the head groundsman. 'I've been talking to Oskar and he's very IT literate. Obviously, staff move on, but if it's likely he's going to be here for a while, what if I go through everything with you both once it's all set up? That way, it won't all fall on your shoulders if you get a problem.'

Max puts the printout down on the desk and rubs his hand along his chin as he considers my proposal. 'He's a bright young man and he's certainly keen to learn.'

'You don't have to make a decision now. I'll text my mate, he said Wednesday is probably the earliest he can get it delivered but he'll ask them to send it via Paris Express Courier. He has a contact who has this model in stock. The monitor is twice the size of the one you have now.'

It's clear that Max skipped over that part of the spec and his eyes widen. 'No more peering at the screen to check if a comma is a full stop then,' he laughs. 'I'll have a word with Erin about Oskar. That could be a smart move. I know he's ambitious and he isn't going to be satisfied just being a waiter.'

All I can do is offer what I perceive to be sensible suggestions. Erin and Max are the management team and between them they run everything around here. But a year on, what I'm noticing is a level of stress and maybe even a little dissension between them that hasn't been apparent before. Perhaps it's time to add another layer to their management structure to ease both of their workloads.

Unfortunately, by the time I get back to the room, Freya is fast asleep. Max was in the mood to talk, and we ended up sitting on the terrace with a nightcap. He isn't a big drinker, but he downed two double brandies in the time it took me to drink a cappuccino.

Usually, the hotel is closed during the month of December so that Erin and Max can fly back to the UK to spend time with family. Erin wants to change that and would like to host a special Christmas and New Year event going forward. He isn't happy about it, but fortunately, he wasn't looking for input from me. Max simply needed someone to listen to him. That was just as well, because I did feel a little out of my depth. When does a work problem become a relationship problem, if two people run a business together?

When we parted company, he clapped me on the back, saying that he owed me a huge favour for coming to his rescue on the computer front. Now I'm lying here wondering if it felt like the final straw to him today. I certainly hope not. In my head I need to believe that having someone special by your side means you can overcome anything. Otherwise, what's the point?

I turn to look at Freya, wondering what she did with the remainder of her evening. Her laptop is on the coffee table next to one of the quaint old French chairs and I reckon she spent it checking in with Beth, to see how Ethan's doing. I hope I can wean her off that habit – the need to be needed. I've seen what that can do to someone, and it didn't take long after we first met for me to recognise the signs in her.

Everything in moderation, as my mother would often say. On the other hand, my father was all about achieving. If you pleased one of them, you disappointed the other.

As for me, every step I take on this year's trip is a challenge but, in a weird way, a triumph. My plans were on hold until that fateful day I bumped into Freya at the gym. One thing led to another and even though she wouldn't admit it, every time she walked through the door her eyes scanned around the room. As soon as she spotted me, her face would instantly light up.

It was fun flirting with her, but I knew from the start she was a woman of substance. What I need to figure out is how to prove to her that even though I'm a bit of a mess right now, the lessons I've learnt are changing me in ways I couldn't have envisaged. And age is just a number. Freya gets hung up on that but she's wrong. My life has been like a roller coaster and for what I lack in years, in terms of life experiences I feel I'm already a fully paid-up member.

Freya

6

It's Time to Roll Up My Sleeves

After a quick breakfast with the staff at six thirty this morning, it was good to feel that Luke and I are really a part of the team.

But with up-and-coming chefs from all over France arriving with their support staff to set up in the grounds of the park surrounding Le Manoir du Bois, my first job is rather mundane. I yearn to be outside, getting hands on, but after Luke downloaded a folder from the cloud onto my laptop, there are menus and handouts to be printed.

Luke has been assigned to help the kitchen staff this morning, as the visiting chefs will be lunching here. They'll be too busy setting up their tents, ready for the influx of visitors who will begin arriving tomorrow. Some are staying locally, and others have arrived on site in camper vans. The head groundsman, with whom I had an interesting conversation at breakfast, is in charge of the site arrangements. He said that this year is even bigger and better than last year.

I guess that's why the pressure is on, and the strain is already starting to show. Watching Erin and Max working is like watching two people on separate timelines. Whenever their paths cross, it's brief and they are completely focused on the job in hand. It's understandable, of course, but to live here in this wonderful setting and be stressed tells me something isn't quite right.

'Can I give you a hand?' Oskar pokes his head around the half-opened office door.

'If you can help me suss out who gets what, it will save me bothering Erin,' I reply, soberly.

'No problem, Freya. I came in early in case I could be of assistance.'

I give him a warm smile; he's so very polite. 'This whole pile of A4 sheets needs to be put through the guillotine. Erin decided we should print out the restaurant menus for the entire week, first.'

He raises his eyebrows. 'Ah, she fears the system will go down and it will take a while to get the new one up and running again. I understand that, but Luke will get it sorted quickly.'

I glance at him. 'You sound very confident about that.'

Oskar grabs a pile of the sheets neatly stacked on the desk and starts cutting. 'My father is in IT, and I can tell a pro when I see one. Luke knows what he's doing.'

I smile at him. 'But your interests go in a different direction.'

'You can't escape new technology these days, no matter what you do. However, it is not where my main interest lies.'

'Which is where, exactly?'

He gives a little laugh. 'A humble waiter can aspire to be a maître d'hôtel one day.'

'Ah . . . I see.' I can tell from the way he's taking his time to ensure every cut he makes is perfectly aligned, that he pays attention to detail. 'And why not?'

Oskar turns to look at me. 'And what do you do, when you're not . . .' he grins at me, revealing his perfect teeth '. . . coming to someone's rescue?'

'I sell houses.'

'Really?' For some reason he sounds impressed. 'Is it something you enjoy doing?'

I nod my head. 'Yes, I do. When a buyer steps over the threshold of a property and you see them instantly connect with it, it's rather special. To watch them visualising the house as their new home as you walk them around it is really satisfying. Like any job, it has its ups and downs, but on the whole, I love what I do.'

He stops what he's doing, a look of curiosity suddenly reflected on his face. 'Luke said he does this every year, but you . . . don't?'

'No. I'm just stepping in for the person Luke usually travels with; he couldn't make it this year. Luke didn't want to let Erin and Max down.'

'Ah! Now I understand. That's what friends are for!'

I like Oskar. If he asks a question, it's because he's genuinely interested in the answer. It doesn't take long for us to complete the task, and when Erin appears in the doorway, her smile grows exponentially.

'You're not done already . . . are you? And what are you doing here, Oskar?' She sounds a little breathless and her cheeks are flushed. It's obvious she's been rushed off her feet.

Oskar glances at me, not sure how to reply.

'With two pairs of hands we've literally flown through the printing. Everything is in neat little stacks, Erin, so you can relax.'

She seems surprised. 'That's so kind of you both. And thank you for coming in early, Oskar. That's very thoughtful of you.'

Now he seems a little embarrassed. 'Um . . . what can I do next, Erin?' he queries.

'Me, too,' I join in.

She tilts her head back, closing her eyes as if she's consulting a list that's imprinted on her memory. 'Another hour or so and it will be time to begin setting up the terrace for the grand welcoming buffet for the festival teams. Our regular guests will be taking lunch in the conservatory today, so it's going to be a bit of a juggling act. Max is obviously under pressure in the kitchen, and he'd be delighted to have two extra pairs of hands.'

Oskar and I answer in unison, 'No problem,' which makes us both laugh out loud.

Great minds think alike, but when we walk through the swing doors into the kitchen, it's a daunting scene. Aside from Max and Luke, there are three other people, and they are all beavering away. Luke gives me a wink for the briefest of seconds, as we walk past him. He's slicing raw potatoes and a dozen greased dishes are lined up ready and waiting.

It's the first time I've set foot in here. It's a large kitchen with stainless steel benches in the middle and the walls are lined with fridges, freezers and, at the far end, a series of ovens. And there's the biggest gas hob you could ever imagine, with an enormous hot plate next to it.

It's stuffy, despite the air conditioning and two huge extractor fans over the main cooking area. Max immediately looks up.

'Erin said you needed some help?' Oskar enquires.

'We do, thanks, guys. Aprons and hats are over there.' Max points to a cupboard in the corner. 'Once you've washed your hands, there are one hundred and twenty small tartlets that need filling. That should keep you busy for a little while.' With that he breaks out into a smile. 'Marie will show you what to do.'

After a quick introduction to Marie, the pastry chef, she gathers together the ingredients we need; she explains that there are twenty-four event tents getting set up in the grounds. Each one has its own team and we're catering for around a hundred people in total.

She demonstrates how to fill and decorate the classic *tartes aux fraises*. She makes it look easy, piping the velvety crème pâtissière into the two-bite sized, buttery pastry shells. Then she takes one of the small, washed strawberries and slices it so that it splays out, laying it carefully on the top. Finally, she takes a brush from a pot of apricot glaze standing in a bowl of hot water and coats the fruit, until it glistens.

Left to get on with it, Oskar and I fill the piping bags and it requires pure concentration to recreate the masterpiece that Marie produced with ease.

'Don't worry,' Oskar whispers, leaning into me. 'By the time we've done this lot we will have mastered it.'

This is my induction to assisting in the kitchen of a grand French *manoir* and I'm glad that I'm working alongside another novice. No one who knows me will believe it when I tell them about this. And Marie said we have three other desserts to assemble in only two hours. Eek!

Lunch at Le Manoir du Bois is never rushed and today is no exception. Once the hot and cold buffet is set up on the terrace, two of the temporary kitchen staff greet the fête attendees. When I wander out to see if there's anything I can do, there's a real buzz going on. Marie appears carrying a platter and she makes her way over to me.

'Luke is looking for you, Freya. Erin has reserved a table for you both in the conservatory with the guests.'

'Oh, right. Thank you.' I hesitate for a second. It doesn't seem right sloping off, but things seem to be ticking over well.

'Go on . . . he's waiting,' she encourages me with a smile.

I walk around the side of the property to enter via the front and am surprised to almost collide with a courier in a smart uniform trundling a trolley stacked with boxes, all labelled '*Distribution exprès*'.

'*Bonjour!*' He follows it with a torrent of French words, only a few of which I catch.

It looks like it's computer equipment, so I indicate for him to follow me, leading him back around to the side entrance and the storeroom. With his few words of broken English and my basic French, I check the boxes as requested and sign the sheet on his clipboard. '*Merci*, madame.'

How could a simple thank you sound so flirtatious? I find myself wondering. It's that French accent that makes everything sound so enchanting, no matter how mundane. I smile to myself as I watch him walk away, just as Luke turns the corner.

'There you are!' He gives the delivery man a nod and strides towards me. 'Is that the kit I ordered?'

'Yes.'

'Perfect! It was a huge favour to call in but my contact did me proud. I guess I know what my next job is going to be once we've had lunch. Come on, I'm starving after prepping all that food and you must be, too.' He cocks an eyebrow at me.

'What?' I ask as we walk briskly back towards the conservatory.

'I was watching you and Oskar. You make a great team.' With that he starts laughing. 'The look of panic on both your faces when Marie left you to it, made me feel bad. Talk about being thrown in at the deep end. But you did it.'

We hurry over to the only empty table in the far corner. As we take our seats, I do have a look of satisfaction on my face.

Chloé appears and gives me an acknowledging smile. 'What would you like to drink?'

'Something cold and fruity, if possible,' I reply.

'Make that for two, thanks, Chloé,' Luke confirms.

As soon as she's out of earshot, I lean in. 'It feels wrong that we're having a leisurely lunch and everyone else is working,' I remark.

Luke gives a dismissive shake of his head. 'The staff will eat together afterwards. Usually they eat before, but no one can relax until everyone else has been served. This is their busiest day because of the welcome buffet. The hotel is full, obviously, but all of the gourmet tents run cooking demonstrations and even the produce stands have tasting sessions. There will be a lot of visitors coming and going after today, but only some of them will stop for lunch. Afternoon tea on the terrace is very popular, but it gets quieter late afternoon as everything shuts down at five o'clock.'

Chloé returns with a jug and two tumblers. I can smell

the fresh fruit from here as she pours our drinks. A few paces behind her, one of the waitresses places our entrée in front of us.

'*Céléri rémoulade. Bon appétit!*'

A simple celeriac salad sits on a bed of leaves in the middle of a stoneware plate, and it looks so inviting. The slight crunch to the matchstick-sized vegetable bathed in creamy mayonnaise, with a squeeze of lemon, is seasoned to perfection with a hint of Dijon mustard.

'Hmm . . .' Luke savours his first forkful. 'Now this was worth waiting for. I reckon I could make this.'

'You looked at home in the kitchen,' I reply.

'I'm learning all the time and I do enjoy it.'

'Oh . . . of course, your friend was the kitchen hand, wasn't he?'

I glance across at Luke and he looks a little uncomfortable as he nods his head. 'As I have no training at all in that department, I'm slow, but I've always loved food and that helps.' His deadpan expression changes into an enigmatic smile. 'Do you know what you're doing this afternoon?'

'No. I can't wait, though. It's fun to just muck in and try something new. Assembling what was it . . .' I do the calculation in my head '. . . four-hundred-and-eighty bite-sized desserts, well, half of them, was a challenge, but Oskar and I got there in the end. I don't think it will turn either of us into wannabe chefs, but it did inspire me a little. Who knows, when I get back to my normal life, I might find myself actually cooking in my kitchen, rather than plating up takeaways.'

Luke lets out an exaggerated gasp. 'If that's the case, I hope you intend to invite me to join you.'

I gaze at him for a moment. 'You haven't mentioned your plans once the summer is over.' Argh! The minute I finish talking I instantly regret asking. If he wanted me to know, he'd have told me.

'That's because I haven't decided yet. I don't want to

outstay my welcome with my friends, although I've been helping out with a little project they're both involved with. However, it's almost done, and I don't think they'll need any more input from me.'

Why do I feel that Luke's answers never give the full picture? Why not say what the project is, just on a conversational level? It makes me want to quiz him, but if I do, he might take it the wrong way and think I'm . . . What? Interested because I'll miss him when he moves on?

I lapse into silence as our plates are cleared. Luke refills my glass and I sit back to enjoy the ambience of the conservatory. There are probably at least three, or four, different nationalities eating and, because of the size of the conservatory, there's a hollow ring to the conversation going on in the background.

Oskar and Chloé appear with the main course.

'Duck confit,' Oskar says, putting the plate down with a flourish and giving me a smile.

'And gratin dauphinois.' Chloé places the dish between us and gives Luke a thumbs up before she heads off.

'Oh, this is one of the dishes you were preparing this morning.'

He grins at me, and the awkward moment has passed. 'Yes, and I managed to slice a mountain of potatoes without shredding my fingertips on the mandolin, which is no mean feat.'

I hold up my plate and receive a generous serving-spoon full.

'Mmm . . . I can smell the garlic from here. Did you make the sauce?'

'Of course.'

I'm not sure if he's joking, so I put him to the test. 'What's in it?'

A little self-satisfied smirk creeps over his face and my heart flutters. He's so different to any guy I've ever known and that constantly throws me.

'Let's see . . . milk, cream, some crème fraîche, garlic, nutmeg, a little butter . . . well, Max's recipe calls for quite a lot, actually. Then coarsely grated Gruyère cheese. He did the seasoning with the sea salt and black pepper himself, but I think I have that sussed now, too. I'll definitely be making this at Christmas.'

Do I bite my tongue, or ask the question?

'And where will you be spending Christmas. In France?'

'No.' He pops a forkful of potatoes into his mouth and nods his head approvingly as he surveys his plate. 'I'll most likely be with my parents, down in Cornwall.'

As much as I'm enjoying the beautifully crispy duck and the velvety smooth potatoes, that's so typical of Luke. Does he have any siblings? I wonder. Is it a tradition? There are times when I find him infuriating and others when something inside of me simply melts. We're spending two months together and, even as friends, it's nice to share.

'How about you?'

I can't resist and throughout the rest of the meal, which includes a wonderful blueberry galette – an open-faced pie with a thick, crispy crust around the edge sprinkled with brown sugar and oozing fruit – I give him the lowdown on my family Christmas at my mum's house. Aunts, uncles and family gossip, the lot! The only person I don't mention is Mum's next-door neighbour, George. He's very *friendly*, and a bit of a handyman. Being on her own, I will admit that he has come to her rescue a couple of times. But last Christmas, she casually mentioned that she almost invited him to join us for dinner and I gave a little laugh. I told her that the last thing she wanted was for an act of kindness to be misinterpreted. Besides, she knows very little about him, as he's been there for less than a year. I'm keeping a watchful eye as a lonely widow is an easy target.

'Goodness; that sounds chaotic. Organised chaos, of course, knowing you.' He sounds a tad apologetic now.

'Oh, it's nothing to do with me. I'm always put on

plate-clearing and loading-up-the-dishwasher duty. Usually with my cousins' kids.'

He starts laughing and I can see that he loves it when I share things like that. Why won't Luke share things about his life with me?

7

Fun, Laughter and New Experiences

I end up spending the afternoon in the company of two Dutch guys, Willem and Johan. It's their job to get the industrial-sized generators set up. There's a stone outhouse with fridges and freezers for use by the festival chefs, but various cables need to be run to some of the individual ovens, refrigerated cabinets and lights.

The pitches are laid out on a section of rolling, flat lawn a good walk from the main buildings. The marquees back onto a large square of grass, where the generators are essentially hidden from view.

My job is relatively simple, thank goodness. I unroll cables to each of the stalls while Willem and Johan make the connections. It's hot work, but it's appreciated, and various chefs and retailers ply us with cold drinks.

At one point towards the end of the afternoon, the three of us sit down in a clearing, glad to take a break. The park is a little over twenty-two acres, so even a virtual field of tents – well, rather graceful marquees with high peak frames that are very upmarket indeed – is cloaked by trees. None of this is visible from Le Manoir.

'Do you come here every year?' I ask, out of curiosity.

'It's my third time,' Willem informs me, 'and Johan's first. We both do contract work for the company that supplies generators for various events.'

'Oh, so the chefs and exhibitors rent both the tents and the general facilities?'

'Yes,' Willem confirms.

'It's not a travelling festival?' I assumed it moved around the country.

'No, only a few of the tents are selling local food products and wines, etcetera. But as for the chefs, they travel here from all over to take part. It's become quite a thing for foodies, apparently. Me, I'm happy with a burger, aren't you, Johan?'

'Yep, and keep them coming.' He laughs.

My new companions are also roadies for a couple of rock bands. The other aspect of their work takes them all over the world. It turns out that both of them are divorced, although Willem has recently married again for the third time. It's no wonder their wives don't last the course, given how much time they must spend away from home. I guess it's like everything else in life. We make our choices, and we have to live with the consequences. If nothing changes, then it's like going around in one big circle, and while absence probably does make the heart grow fonder, long spells away from each other can't do a relationship any favours.

'Hi Beth, how are you doing?'

'Good, thanks. You've been on my mind all day. Well, come on, don't keep me in suspense. What has Luke gotten you into, or is it a ruse to have some quality time alone together?'

I start giggling. 'Our paths haven't crossed much today, well . . . aside from our leisurely, almost two-hour lunch,' I declare.

'Hmm. And this is supposed to be a working holiday?' She sounds suspicious.

'Oh, it is!' I tell her about my experiences so far and I can sense her amusement.

'Seriously? The two Dutch guys sound interesting but kitchen duty is so not you.'

'I found it rather inspiring, actually. As for Johan and

Willem, they were telling me a bit about what goes on behind the scenes at some of the rock gigs. Honestly, you wouldn't believe what obsessed fans get up to just to catch a glimpse of their idols up close. Anyway, that's enough about me. What's going on there?'

'The new lady, Nancy, is settling in well. She's a toned-down version of Ethan, very efficient and a bit of a stickler for detail.'

'Am I sensing a little note of disapproval in your tone?'

Beth tuts. 'Day two and she's already returning some of my paperwork with a couple of blank boxes highlighted. I mean, using a highlighter pen; it's like being back at school.'

'Oh, that's so funny.' I laugh. 'It's just what we need. If you're missing bits out, that tells me you're rushing. Is Ethan taking up more of your time than you thought?'

'No. Not at all. He's doing viewings and popping back into the office in between to check on Nancy. Mind you, having shown her the system, she's already off and running. And, to her credit, if she doesn't know something, she asks.'

'There's a but coming, I know it.'

'I don't know whether it's just her dry sense of humour, or her tone, but I'm not joking when I say it's like having a schoolteacher in the room. At least she treats everyone in the same way, so I'm not the only one being quizzed on why I've circumvented some of the office rules. As for other news, we had two completions go through today and Mrs Bennett popped in with a huge basket of fruit for the staff as a thank you. Oh, and I took on another two new properties, which is why I've been a bit pressed for time.'

'Ah, how thoughtful of the Bennetts and well done you.' This conversation is beginning to make me feel homesick. Goodness, I don't really miss my lovely cottage, I miss work. How sad is that? 'I'm glad things are going well.'

'Now, tell me all about where you're staying. What's your room like?'

It's hard not to make it sound slightly romantic given the setting, so I go on to tell her a little about Erin and Max.

'It sounds like they're old friends of his,' she replies with a chuckle. 'Not that the words "old" and "Luke" belong together in the same sentence! They aren't related in any way, are they?'

Now she has me wondering. 'No. I'm sure it would have come up if they were. They do seem to hold him in high regard, but then it is his seventh summer here.'

'I guess anyone who can tackle IT problems, and take on a role as commis chef, is going to be highly prized.' I don't know if that comment is tongue in cheek, but it's true.

'Anyway, I must go. It's time to shower and change for dinner.'

'Don't rub it in. Still, at least it's David's turn to cook this evening. I'm in the lounge with my feet up sipping a well-earned glass of wine.'

'You picked a good one, there, Beth. He's such a sweetheart. So, are you missing me already?'

She chuckles. 'Between Nancy breathing down my neck if I don't cross every T, and Ethan out to prove he can conquer the estate agency world, I guess I am a little. I liked the old normal. But I want you to come back nicely tanned and feeling that your batteries have been recharged.

'There's more to life than just work, Freya. At the end of the day, I have David to unwind with. Everyone needs someone, my dear friend. It's time to drop your guard and I have a sneaking feeling that's why Luke has come into your life. A summer fling is just what you need to make you think about the longer-term future. Enjoy every second of your well-deserved break and, as you've probably sussed, I am a tad jealous. Lucky you!'

After a wonderful dinner in the restaurant, Luke suggests we have coffee out on the terrace. It's twilight already, as we're eating a little later than anticipated. I smirk to myself as I think about how easily lovemaking dispels physical tiredness. And the cool shower we enjoyed together afterwards was enlivening.

In between enjoying tonight's wonderful menu, Luke told me all about his afternoon setting up the new kit. Oskar gave him a hand at one point, and he was pleasantly surprised at his level of knowledge. Max desperately needs someone on site to jump in when he's left scratching his head over something.

It was only then that it occurred to me that Luke is Max's troubleshooter not just when he's here, but all year round. I tried to draw him on that, and he simply said that most things can be fixed remotely.

As I gaze at him now, sipping his coffee, he senses I'm thinking about him and probably have a question brewing, so he beats me to it.

'That's enough about me. How was your afternoon?'

Timing, I reflect, is everything. It's like he's psychic sometimes.

'I spent it unreeling countless drums of cable.'

Luke looks surprised. 'You did?'

'Yep. No skill involved, but it was quite a workout for my upper arm muscles as the drums are very heavy to lift. And my calf muscles are aching a little after all the trudging back and forth. I hasten to add that I wasn't allowed to plug anything in. Willem and Johan did all that, but it was different, and we had a laugh.'

Luke narrows his eyes. 'Oh, you had a laugh, did you? I know Willem, although I can't remember a Johan. Willem can be a bit of a charmer, with his tales about all the famous bands he meets.'

I can't help grinning. 'I know. It was fascinating, though.'

'There's a reason why he's been married several times,' Luke points out.

Is he a little jealous that I spent the afternoon with two burly, fun guys?

'Yes, he said it costs him a fortune in maintenance as he also has children with two of them. His current wife is much younger.'

Luke's eyes widen. 'You must have spent quite a while chatting. I had no idea he has kids.'

It's sort of fun seeing Luke looking a little uncomfortable but I'm not trying to be mean. Anyway, the guys drove off in their lorry late afternoon to do another installation somewhere near Périgord and they won't be back until the festival is drawing to a close.

'I also managed to speak to Beth.'

Luke rolls his eyes at me. He looks so adorable sitting there in the white linen shirt I watched him ironing in the room, as I lay naked in bed beneath the cool, crisp cotton sheet, wishing he'd come back to bed.

'Honestly, what don't you understand about detoxing? A break from work means switching off completely.' Luke's tone is contrite.

I hold up both hands, as if fending him off. 'OK . . . point taken but if I didn't have some contact I'd only be worrying about what's happening. Everything is fine, sort of.'

I tell him about Nancy, and Beth feeling like she's being scolded.

He looks at me a little cagily. 'How's Ethan doing?'

'Good, by the sound of it. He's wasted as just an office manager. Ethan has that ability to suss out exactly what a buyer is looking for. It's all too easy to waste a lot of time showing people properties that don't even come close to their tick list, if you don't ask the right questions at the start. He has the knack, all right.'

Luke does a bit of a body shift in his chair. 'And you don't . . . um . . . see that as a . . . dare I suggest it, a bit of a threat?'

I'm a little shocked at his observation. 'No. The way things are going we'll need to take on another sales negotiator sometime soon, anyway. I'm one of the bosses, Luke, and if I see someone who's good, I want them on our team.'

Now he's embarrassed. 'I didn't mean anything by that.

It's just . . . I'd hate to think you were regretting letting me talk you into this trip.'

As the candlelight flickers over his face, he looks sombre.

'Luke, it's an eye-opener. I can't remember the last time I felt so chilled out. The only slight anxiety I have is if I'm asked to do any waitressing. I'm not sure I can balance two plates on my forearm like Chloé and Oskar do.'

Luke gives a dismissive laugh. 'Don't worry. Erin is much too savvy to inflict that on you. She told me that experienced waiting staff make it look easy, but it takes a lot of practice. They are like ghosts in the dining room, saying little and clearing plates without the diners really noticing them.'

Gosh! That's so true. Tonight, when Chloé served us *le plat fromage*, Luke and I were holding hands across the table. One moment she was there, the next she was gone. I couldn't let go because Luke had just said, 'I've never met anyone quite like you before, Freya. I feel I can be myself and just enjoy each moment as it comes.'

His words made me feel a little sad. I remember a time when I worried what other people thought of me and it's only in hindsight I realise that was because I hadn't found that true sense of self. Luke will get there, eventually.

Lying here with Luke's arms wrapped around me, and a soft breeze coming in through the open window, is bliss. It's been a lovely day and I feel very grateful. It's as if I've been existing in a little bubble and discovering that the world is a much bigger place sounds obvious, but until you're reminded of that, it's not.

I thought I'd feel awkward, tackling things I couldn't even have imagined myself doing but I'm looking forward to tomorrow and the new challenges I'm sure it will bring. But it's the time I'm spending with Luke which is touching my heart. He's like this big question mark in my head. On the surface he breezes through life, seemingly without a care. He doesn't have a permanent job; he seems to move between friends for accommodation and he doesn't have a master plan. But the more I see of him, the more of a puzzle he's becoming.

'Are you asleep?' I whisper, so softly it's as if my words instantly disappear.

'No,' he replies, rolling into me. 'Obviously, you're wide awake by the sound of it.'

'It's perfect here at Le Manoir du Bois, but what's next?'

Luke's face is in shadow but as our eyes meet, his smile shines brightly.

'This break is about living in the moment. What if the world were to end now? It wouldn't matter what tomorrow was supposed to bring, would it?'

I can't help tutting. 'Seriously, Luke? That's such a lame answer. You said you had an itinerary.'

He pulls me even closer until I can feel his breath on my cheek.

'I do, so relax.'

'Yes, but . . .'

'No. I said relax.'

I roll over onto my back, staring up at the ceiling. A few minutes pass in silence until I can't stop myself. 'Just tell me where we're heading next.'

He lets out a tired groan. 'We're going to a campsite about an hour's drive from here.'

Argh. Another half-answered question. 'To do what, exactly?'

'To be on hand to welcome English guests and um . . . stand in for the owners while they shoot off for a few days. There, are you happy now?'

'It's a short stop, then?'

'Hmm . . . maybe.'

'What does "a few" mean?'

'Freya! Stop with this obsession that everything has to be precisely timetabled. It's a working holiday in exchange for bed and board. It might be a week, maybe two. We'll find out when we get there.'

And with that, I watch as Luke closes his eyes. 'I'm tired.' He stops to yawn. 'Uhh.'

Without warning, I start yawning too.

'Sweet dreams, Freya,' Luke mutters, drowsily.

The last thought in my head, as my eyelids droop, is that if the world were to end tonight while we're sleeping then I can't complain. The man lying next to me only has my best interests at heart and I'm in a beautiful place.

Suddenly, in my mind, I'm walking around the park and noticing little details as if I'm seeing it for the first time. Then my whole body jumps; I'm falling, and as I open my eyes, I realise I've been asleep. But for how long?

Luke is lying on his side, and I snuggle into his back, feeling safe and secure. I have nothing at all to worry about. Is this what it feels like to have a man in your life you can really trust, someone who won't let you down? But trusting someone implicitly requires a huge leap of faith. I've never met anyone who has made me feel I can take that leap and it's scary.

I'm used to being in total control of my life; men come and go, like fleeting distractions. Beth is lucky, because David is a keeper, and she knew that from the day they first met. But from my experience, men who are ready to commit are few and far between. Even when they profess that's exactly what they're looking for. I've heard it several times before, only to find a little down the line that isn't the case.

I once thought that I might have found a *potential* Mr Right, but there was this niggling little doubt at the back of mind. It just wouldn't go away. Then, out of the blue, he mentioned that he'd never marry a woman his mother didn't approve of. To say that put me off is an understatement. When he took me to meet his parents, the rose-coloured spectacles came off. In hindsight, it was obvious that I didn't make an effort that day to play by his rules. Either they liked me, or they didn't. Even though I wanted the search to be over, if he truly loved me he wouldn't be seeking approval from anyone else. Needless to say, I wasn't heartbroken when we split up. But what if I never find *the one*?

I won't settle for someone who isn't prepared to go all in; but with Luke it's complicated. He's kind and thoughtful, caring too. On the other hand, there are times he's like a closed book. Why that is, I have no idea. To me, it signals that until he can organise his own life, he's not ready for a full-on relationship with anyone and that's a real shame because he's special. Very special indeed.

8

The Atmosphere is Electric

Wednesday starts off with a dusky blue sky, which means it's going to be a hot one. The festival is due to open at eleven o'clock and with the Le Manoir's kitchen back to normal today, it's just a full restaurant and terrace to service as usual, for the kitchen and waiting staff.

I'm rather surprised when Erin seeks us out just as Luke and I are finishing breakfast.

'Good morning. I hope you both slept well. Max said you're going to have a session with him in the office first thing, Luke, to bring him up to speed using the new system. He's quite excited about it. That old computer was becoming the bane of his life. A bit like me sometimes,' she jokes. 'I was just wondering whether Freya would do me a favour this morning?'

I instantly look at her, nodding my head. 'Yes, of course. I'm done here, so I'm all yours.' I stand, easing back my chair. Luke gives me a parting smile. 'See you later!' I'm half tempted to stoop and plant a kiss on his cheek. However, I'm conscious of the other people around us and, dare I say, what Erin might think. It's not like I'm Luke's girlfriend as that isn't the way he introduces me. And rightly so.

As I follow Erin across the terrace and around the side of Le Manoir, I can tell from her pace that the pressure is on.

'Problems?' I ask.

'Oh,' she sighs, sounding weary. It's not a good sign as it's only eight thirty in the morning.

Before we retired to bed last night, both Max and Erin seemed content that after a hectic day yesterday, everything was all set, ready to go. Le Manoir hosts the event, but now it's over to the participants to do their thing for the next eight days. Max and Erin can finally relax, as long as the generators keep working.

'We're one short on housekeeping today,' she explains. 'And we have four new arrivals due in at noon. I was rather hoping you could lend a hand, but something else has come up and I'll be filling in. Come, let's sit on the bench over here and I'll explain; this is personal and rather sensitive.'

Erin's usual bubbly persona is a little subdued as we make our way across the grass to sit down. Seeing Le Manoir from this angle, with hardly a soul around, it's hard to believe that within the grounds there are dozens of people busy preparing for an onslaught of visitors. After Luke's session in the office, he's on parking duty today; he'll be one of two people at the entrance, directing cars into a gravelled area on the far side of the site.

'A lady named Iris Beauchêne is going to join us, shortly. She's English but has lived in France for many years. She just had a little *episode* and Chloé is sitting with her while she has a cup of tea. She's a great friend of mine and Max's. Her husband, Timothée . . .' Erin sighs, biting her bottom lip. 'Well, almost three months ago he had a massive, and fatal, heart attack. They run a vineyard near Soissons, it's less than an hour's drive from here. She's one of the producers taking part in the festival. The thing is . . . grief is an awful thing, Freya. She has good days, and bad ones. Iris is a strong lady, and she was determined that Le Château de la Fontaine would have a presence here, as usual. It's what Tim would expect of her but it's easier said than done. This morning she arrived, and as they were setting up, she literally went to pieces.' Erin pauses for breath, and I can see that she, too, is tearful.

'Poor lady. Whatever I can do to help, I'll be only too glad.'

Erin turns to look at me with a watery smile. 'She has two young men from the vineyard to dispense wine and canapés, but she's feeling fragile today. Having another woman around might help. Especially if she has to dash off suddenly . . . or is in need of a bit of moral support. I'm not much good to her right now. I, too, am missing Tim today. He was one of those larger-than-life personalities. Always up for a party and a real joker. I feel badly that I'm in danger of starting her off if I break down.'

Goodness, what a dilemma. 'As long as there are two people there who know what they're doing, I'll focus on supporting Iris.'

A look of relief flashes over Erin's face. 'It's not an easy task, I know that, Freya. But, in truth, there isn't anyone else I would feel comfortable asking. You're a kind person and I can see why Luke chose you as his travelling companion.' She's being cautious, which I appreciate, and I'm about to reply, when she looks up. 'Oh, here they are. If you're sure you don't mind, let's hurry over and I can introduce you.'

'I'm sure and it's not a problem.'

'You're such a dear. No wonder Luke is smitten with you. I knew one day he'd turn up with a woman on his arm; I'm just glad it's someone who can see what lies beneath that cheeky grin of his. Still waters run deep, but it's easy to miss that.'

There's no time to ask what she means, as the well-dressed woman in front of us looks across rather nervously as we approach.

'Iris, this is Freya, Luke's girlfr—I mean, friend. She's at a loose end today, because Luke is tied up with Max. I thought she might enjoy giving you a hand and learning a little about the art of winemaking?'

Iris hesitates for the briefest of moments, before giving me a warm smile.

'It's nice to meet you, Freya, and it would be my pleasure.

91

Thank you so much for the tea, Erin. We'll talk later, my dear. Do you know anything at all about wine, Freya?'

Iris and I leave Erin to return inside, and we talk as we walk. Sometimes a simple distraction can still the mind and I'll do my best to keep a close eye on Iris as the day unfolds. She's a brave woman indeed, as others in her situation would no doubt have made an excuse not to take part this year. But I understand she's doing it for her late husband, and as painful as it is, somehow life has to go on.

'As a wine drinker I like to think I'm a little discerning, Iris. I don't just pick the first bottle off the shelf.' I give her a modest grin, and she smiles back at me. That's not always true, but I want Erin's excuse to ring true. 'But I learn quickly, and if someone asks a question to which I don't know the answer, I'll ask the expert.'

She gives me a knowing smile. She's grateful to her friend for understanding that while Iris is imparting a little knowledge to me her mind will be occupied. But above all, she can see that my intentions are well meant.

'It's really about being a people person,' she explains. 'The wine and the canapés will do the rest.' She smiles to herself. 'Nature appreciates when something is nurtured with love and the proof is in that first taste. In the words of the late Robert Mondavi, who put the wines of the Napa Valley in California on the map, "Making good wine is a skill; making fine wine is an art." Having met him once many years ago, Tim perfected that art at our vineyard here in France. Our son, Frédéric, now looks after the vines and his father taught him well. He's disappointed not to be putting in an appearance this year but he's busy replacing some fencing. When animals get in they can do a lot of damage, but there's always something pressing to attend to. If it's not wildlife it's equipment breakdowns.'

It's clear to me that Iris is going to have to dig deep to get through today. Hopefully, once day one is over it'll reassure her that she has the strength, and composure, to overcome yet another challenge, in a life that will never be quite the same again. My heart constricts in my chest, because I can see the pain etched on her face but she's a proud lady and it's like a switch has been flicked on. She raises the corners of her mouth, and this is the face she will show the world.

Over dinner, Luke quizzes me about my day as we didn't get a chance to have lunch together.

'Erin said you were helping out at one of the exhibitor's tents. I was going to walk over to see how you were doing, but there were so many cars it was non-stop. Erin ended up bringing over a picnic lunch in a basket as, with only two of us, it wasn't easy to take a break.

'Tomorrow we're going to put up some signage as a few cars took a wrong turn and ended up driving around the horseshoe track and back out onto the road. Last year they had three people, but Erin couldn't get any extra help until Friday. Anyway, tell me all about your day. Are you now an expert on *la dégustation de vin*?'

'Hardly, but I do understand a lot more about what's involved in a wine-tasting session. Considering it's the general public and not professionals, the French really know their wines. Well, what they like and don't like.'

We dip our soup spoons into a small bowl of classic French bouillabaisse, and I think it's my favourite entrée so far. I love seafood and I don't know what to choose first: a mussel, one of the small clams, a colourful shrimp, or a small chunk of haddock.

'Foodie heaven?' Luke smiles at me as the look on my face obviously says more than words.

'Absolutely! This is divine.' I stop to take a sip of wine but instead of putting the glass straight to my lips, I swirl it around, sniff the contents appreciatively, and then take a sip. Then I burst out laughing. 'See! I know all about colour, clarity and consistency now and this Chardonnay is perfect.'

'I'm glad you've had a good day. My session with Max

was productive. He and Erin have offered Oskar a permanent full-time role. He's delighted, as the high season doesn't allow him to earn enough to supplement his lower earnings during the winter months. In future, he'll be splitting his duties between the office and the restaurant. Max is relieved as it will free up quite a bit of his time. The restaurant is popular all year round and it's a lot of pressure.'

'When I was working alongside Oskar in the kitchen, he mentioned he was engaged. He said that he was keen to advance his career and realised that it would probably mean moving away at some point. That's an amazing result all round, Luke.'

He does look rather pleased with himself tonight.

'By comparison with a productive start, the rest of it was spent dashing around directing the flow of traffic. A sedate day spent dispensing wine and nibbles sounds so much more appealing.'

I glance at him, soberly. 'It wasn't quite as simple as that, although it did end up being an experience I wouldn't have missed for the world.' I continue eating, conscious that he's watching me.

'You didn't get any hassle, did you?'

'No.' I break off a piece of rustic bread to mop up the last of the delicious bouillabaisse, not caring whether anyone is looking, or if it's not acceptable. 'That hit the spot. And, no, my presence was really appreciated, actually.'

'But you're not quite as bubbly as normal this evening.'

Our eyes meet and I can see he's concerned, so I tell him about Iris having lost her husband. 'Iris said she was fine until she saw Erin and they both broke down. It's the first festival since his passing.'

'Oh, Freya, I'm sorry to hear that. What a difficult day it must have been for everyone involved.'

I let out a long, slow sigh. 'It was at first, but as it went on everyone livened up. The customers were so appreciative of the prize-winning Château de la Fontaine pink champagne, although the white and red wines sold well, too. Iris's son was back at the vineyard, but she brought two of their staff with her. It was a struggle to cope at times even with another, unexpected, pair of hands.

'More importantly, looking out for me gave Iris something to distract her. She enjoyed teaching me a little about the wines and we had quite a few English visitors whose French wasn't much better than mine. The helpers she brought with her were both French, although one also spoke Italian. They were relieved when we came to their rescue. I think most of the customers drove off with a least one case of wine in the boot of their cars. There were also some restaurant owners, eager to find a new supplier and Iris took their details, saying her son would be in touch.'

'Then you did well to cope with that.' He reaches out to place his hand over mine and we don't pull away when Chloé arrives to take our plates. She smiles briefly but disappears as quickly as she came.

Luke changes the subject, and the rest of the meal passes quite pleasantly. But the restaurant is noisy tonight, one particularly large table has several people with loud voices, and he can see that I'm flagging.

'Oskar!' Luke stops him as he's passing. 'Is it possible for us to have dessert and coffee out on the terrace?'

'Of course! Get yourself settled and I'll bring the wine bottle and your glasses out to you.'

'Thank you, but I think we're done and looking forward to . . . two double espressos?' He looks in my direction and I nod my head.

In truth, I think I really need something sweet, and to counteract it, something bitter. Luke walks around the table to help me out of my seat. He can tell I'm not my usual self.

As we make our way between the tables everyone is smiling, and the atmosphere is enchanting. It's a night for romance, for family gatherings and celebrations, it seems. But I don't particularly feel like celebrating.

There are only a handful of people sitting at tables out on the terrace. There's a slight chill to the breeze tonight and I do an involuntary shiver.

'You need something around your shoulders,' Luke says.

'I have a shawl but it's in the bedroom.'

He pulls out one of the cast iron chairs for me. 'Then I'll go and fetch it.'

'That's kind of you. Top drawer, right-hand side. It's soft and fluffy, a pale taupe colour.'

He looks at me as if he has no idea what colour taupe might be but it's the only shawl in there. 'You sit and take in the view as the sun sets.'

When he returns, Oskar is just unloading a tray onto the table.

'Max thought you might like a dessert taster plate to share. Enjoy!' With that he lights the candle in the centre of the table and slips quietly into the shadows.

Moments later, Luke lays the shawl around my shoulders and my goosebumps start to disappear.

'Today left you a little . . . sad,' he reflects.

There aren't many people I've only known for a relatively short space of time with whom I'd open up, but maybe that's why our paths crossed. Luke needs to see that there's no shame in feeling vulnerable.

'I was twenty-four when I got the phone call that my dad had passed away. At the time, it was almost impossible to take it in. He hadn't been ill and there were no warning signs. A blood vessel in his brain suddenly ruptured and just like that he was gone.'

I pause, taking a sip of coffee to fortify me.

'I like to think that letting Iris talk about Tim helped, but it did drag up some very painful memories for me. My mum went to pieces at the time, because the bottom had fallen out of her – no, our – world. It took her months to get to the point that she didn't dread opening her eyes every single morning, only to . . . re-remember he wasn't there.' The words are hard to get out.

I pick up the tiny coffee cup once more and take another sip, this time pausing to savour it. The robust, velvety richness of the thick dark coffee is like a pick-me-up.

Luke is staring at me, his face expressionless. 'I'm sorry, Freya. Listening to Iris was a kind thing to do, but it must have taken a lot of courage under the circumstances. If Erin had known, she wouldn't have asked you to step in.'

I'm back in control; it's time to take a deep breath and put this into perspective. 'People say well-meaning things, platitudes really, because what can you say to someone who has lost the love of their life? In a way, I was the right person in the right place, at the right time. Iris was so grateful, it was humbling.'

Luke carries his rather weighty chair over so he's sitting directly alongside me. He reaches out for my hand, and we sit contentedly, for a while.

'That view is unreal, isn't it?' he eventually whispers, leaning in so that I can feel his breath on my cheek. 'Nights like tonight are few and far between, Freya.'

I understand exactly what he's saying. Our loved ones don't want us clinging onto the past; life is for living.

'I guess it's time to sample these desserts,' I reply, determined to shake off my sorrowful thoughts.

Max has literally given us every dessert on the menu. Even though the portions are small, there is no way we're going to be able to demolish this lot, but we give it our best try.

When I can't manage another mouthful, I stare out at the wonderful pink hue in the sky. In my head I hear myself saying, 'I love and miss you, Dad.' I like to think he can hear me and relax, knowing that as I sit here, I'm feeling a sense of peacefulness and contentment wash over me. The stresses and strains of life have drained away; the surprise is that this trip seems to have morphed into an emotional journey for me.

Ironically, tonight, there's no one I could imagine sharing such a poignant moment with other than Luke. And that comes as quite a shock.

Luke and I skipped breakfast this morning. We woke up later than planned, when the alarm he set didn't go off. It was a mad dash to shower and dress. We part ways after a quick kiss, and I watch him walk away. Suddenly, I'm running after him, my feet travelling over the springy turf with ease. He's surprised when I reached out to grab his arm.

'There was something . . .' I pant, slightly breathless from emotion, more so than my little sprint. 'I wanted to thank you for listening and being so thoughtful last night. It meant a lot to me, Luke.'

He turns on his heels and wraps his arms around my waist, staring down into my eyes. 'I'm always here for you, Freya. No matter what happens between us, or where the future takes us. Remember that.'

'OK, I will. Promise. Anyway, I didn't mean to hold you up. Signs don't make themselves!'

He gives me a boyish grin. 'Hopefully, we'll catch up at lunch, having missed breakfast. But something tells me it's going to be another frenetic day.'

This time he lingers over our parting kiss, and a little thrill courses through me. He's a beautiful man, both inside and out. It sounds strange, but there's a quality about him . . . a sensitivity that I often see reflected in his eyes.

When I was in my early-twenties, I thought I was invincible, that nothing could stop me. After losing my dad, each new experience seemed to add a layer of hesitancy and even self-doubt at times. It crept up on me unawares, and it wasn't until I turned thirty that I really found my stride. Then, when I managed to repay Beth's brother in full for his share of the agency, it suddenly hit me what an achievement that was. And using what funds I had left to secure my beautiful dream cottage, I realised that while boyfriends came and went, being self-reliant is empowering.

And now Beth and I dream of expanding the agency and opening a second office. However, what if one day I wake up and feel it's not enough . . . self-doubt, I reflect, can come at you out of nowhere just like that, no matter how content you are with your life.

I stopped dating because I grew tired of searching for my soulmate and constantly being disappointed. Will I live to regret that? I wonder. Maybe it's time to start looking again for that perfect match before my career totally takes over my life. However, I want someone who knows exactly who they are and what they want out of life. That might sound rather cold-hearted but my personal growing pains are behind me, and I need someone who is at the same stage.

Luke isn't there yet. I could be wrong and perhaps living life one day at a time is the answer to finding true happiness; focus on fixing today and worry about tomorrow when it's here. That thought is enough to put a smile on my face, as I go in search of Erin. The trouble with life is that it can blindside you when you least expect it; without a plan you could end up going backwards and losing everything you have. And I'm talking about having a job and a roof over your head, not possessions that are simply nice to have.

'Morning.' I pop my head around the side of the office door and see that Max and Erin are poring over some paperwork. 'If you're busy I can come back later.'

'No. It's fine. We're done here.' Erin stands, placing her hand on Max's shoulder and giving it an affectionate squeeze.

It's noticeable how much more relaxed they are with each other now that the festival is in full swing, and the new PC is up and running.

'We've just had a delivery of new bedding arrive,' Erin explains after we bid Max goodbye. 'The boxes are all stacked in the storeroom, but we can't move them upstairs until the linen cupboard has been sorted. Sophie has volunteered to take on the task but it's too much for one person. Or, if you fancy being outside in the fresh air today, the gardeners are always grateful for a little help.'

'I don't mind giving Sophie a hand. I should imagine it's a bit of a daunting task for one.'

Erin grimaces. 'It is rather. Let's go and find her. And I just wanted to say thank you for what you did yesterday, Freya. Iris rang me last night and asked me to pass on a message. She said if you get a moment, pop into the tent as she has a little gift for you.'

'Oh, that's not necessary,' I reply, rather taken aback. 'It was my pleasure. I learnt a bit about champagne and the wines of Picardy, and I even impressed Luke with my wine-tasting skills at dinner,' I giggle.

Erin laughs. 'That would have gone straight over his head. You know what he's like. He finds pleasure in the simplest of things. Just because something is expensive, or marked "finest", doesn't influence him at all.'

'I've never looked at it that way before, but you're right. He does have a real appreciation for gourmet food, although he's just as happy with a simple picnic.' I'm thinking out loud, rather than making a comment.

'That's his brother's influence. Watching the two of them working side by side in the kitchen, well . . . what a sight to see. Two ends of the spectrum. The IT genius and a young man born to be a chef—' Suddenly, Erin stops full flow, as if she's said too much. 'Oh . . . it's probably best not to mention his brother for fear of . . . upsetting him. I didn't mean to babble on like that.' She increases her pace as we begin to ascend the second flight of stairs.

'Luke does seem to know his way around a computer,' I reply light-heartedly, not wishing to make her feel awkward. I also don't want Erin to feel that I'm quizzing her by asking questions, although I'd love her to continue.

I can't help wondering whether Luke and his brother fell out and that's why this year's trip hung in the balance. The fact that he hasn't mentioned him to me isn't surprising if it's a sensitive topic. Sensitive enough for Erin and Max to avoid raising the subject, too. Maybe at some point Luke will open up to me, although it's none of my business, so why should he?

'When you use the skills that come naturally to you, it can look like success comes easily. However, in some cases the pressure proves too much. What do you do back home, Freya?'

That's so typical of Luke. Erin and Max were obviously expecting him to bring along another helper, but he didn't think to mention I have no related experience at all.

'Together with my best friend, I run an estate agency in Sevenoaks, Kent.'

'It's a beautiful part of England.' We've reached the landing, and she stops for a moment for me to join her. 'That's why your people skills are so intuitive and it's obvious you understand the pressures of running a business. It's all about flexibility, isn't it? Ah, Sophie!'

And with that our conversation is over, as Erin leaves me in Sophie's hands. However, something tells me that Erin wasn't about to add to what she'd said. The look on her face told me it was probably a slip of the tongue, and she was cross with herself. Did Luke have some sort of breakdown in the past? I wonder. I assumed it was a personal choice to avoid carving out his career path going forward. Maybe the reality is that he's not sure he could cope after what he's been through. That thought is chilling. But if it's something he's not ready to discuss, it would be wrong of me to try to draw him on the subject. I don't want to traumatise him; that would spoil everything.

I heave a heavy sigh. Bad things happen to good people, and it changes them. Sometimes for the better, sometimes for the worse. And Luke is right, age is just a number; it's the life experiences we go through that give us wisdom. But he said his *friend* let him down. Falling out with a friend, is very different to falling out with a sibling. If other family members get drawn into it, that could cause a huge rift. It's rather sad to think that he's been through some sort of family drama when his life was just taking off. And it's affected him enough that he doesn't want to talk about it.

I tune back in, as Sophie is explaining in her halting English what she's trying to do. There are piles of bedding lined up against the beautiful wrought-iron spindles that line the landing.

'Some is fine,' she explains. 'Some not so good. We look and decide, yes?'

If that means each and every item, this could take a while.

Luke

9

It's Time to Move On

It's Friday the twelfth of July, and our last breakfast at Le Manoir du Bois. Yesterday was a long one, as the exhibitors set off home and a small team of us started the big clear-up. This morning, Max and Erin insist we have breakfast together. Instead of joining the other guests either in the conservatory, or on the terrace, Chloé leads us out through the French doors to the front and across to the large half-brick, half-glass building referred to as the orangery. In truth, it used to look like an oversized greenhouse that had been left untouched for a long time, despite the magnificent glass roof with its inset lantern protrusion.

I clasp Freya's hand and she rewards me with one of her warm, sunny smiles. We're both feeling a little sad to be leaving. When we woke up this morning, she admitted that she could have cheerfully spent the entire duration of our trip here. I guess she's not one for constantly moving around. Ironically, being flexible in what she does isn't a problem at all. To her credit, she's tackled just about everything except waitressing. But having a firm plan is her comfort zone, even when she's not at work, and that's a bad habit.

The moment Chloé opens the door, and we step inside, Max and Erin come hurrying over to greet us French style. Goodness, we're all feeling emotional this morning. They've known me long enough to accept that I'm a very private person and always will be. However, just the fact that I turned up with Freya, speaks volumes. Give them their due, they've been very circumspect, their quiet acceptance no doubt hiding a multitude of questions left unasked. And that's why I'll always drop whatever I'm doing to help them.

'Wow. Breakfast in style,' I remark as I look around. 'This is quite something. The jungle is gone, and it truly is an orangery again.'

Considering how drastically everything has been cut back and given that what we're seeing is really only one season's new growth, it's a profusion of colour set against a backdrop of greenery. The solid brick walls are covered with old wisteria vines, several climbing roses, and something that I can only describe as having bunches of hanging flowers much like those on a geranium. It's like walking into an indoor garden. I suppose that's what an orangery is, even though I can't spot any citrus fruits.

'It's all down to Erin's vision,' Max replies sounding a tad disconcerted. 'It kept us busy during the quieter months over the winter, although where we're heading with it is still to be determined.'

It's clear he's not fully on board with the overall proposal. Only one table is laid up, but it's been done beautifully, as if we're breakfasting in a deluxe hotel in Paris.

'This is amazing, guys!' Freya declares, turning on her heels to gaze around, enthralled. 'And the beautiful pattern of tiny strawberries and curling green tendrils on the chinaware is so unusual. Together with the ambience, there's a real sense of elegance to this vast space. It reminds me of having afternoon tea at Harrods, but even better!'

'There you go, Max. I told you this would make a perfect setting for intimate wedding parties. Right, let's take our seats.' Delighted by our combined reaction, Erin extends her hand, touching Freya's arm and giving it a little squeeze. 'Saying goodbye is never easy and it's been a wonderful visit this year. I wanted our last meal together to be special.'

Max and I walk on ahead. I pull out a chair for Erin and he does the same for Freya. 'Well, you've succeeded and we're both touched,' I reply.

As Max and I settle ourselves down, he glances first at me and then at Freya. 'It's been a productive one, too. With the upgraded computer equipment and Oskar's new role, it's going to have a huge impact, isn't it, Erin? And your input, Freya, has been gratefully appreciated. There's no doubt we dodged a crisis, or three, having you here to fill in wherever needed.'

'I can second that; a few times I thought I was in danger of having a bit of a meltdown,' Erin states, her cheeks colouring up. 'But no matter what the task was, you rose to the challenge. Anyway, I'm sure everyone is hungry and . . . ah, here comes the coffee.'

Marie, our chef this morning, opens the door for Chloé as she carries a loaded tray across to the table. While Chloé adds another jug of juice to a buffet of fruit, cheeses and various charcuterie, a variety of cereals and a large platter of French pastries and croissants, Marie walks over to our table.

'Can I take your orders for hot food, or should I come back a little later?' Marie asks.

Max looks at each of us in turn and no one hesitates because everyone has a favourite breakfast dish. As they're both about to leave, Erin gives them a warm smile. 'Thank you, ladies.'

No one is taken for granted here and that's what I love about this place.

Ever the attentive host, Max pours the coffee while the rest of us raid the buffet. Freya and I fill our bowls with beautifully plump strawberries, a good dollop of crème fraîche and I grab a croissant.

Erin turns to look at us, letting out a wistful sigh. 'If only the two of you could stay all summer.'

'They've better things to do,' Max reprimands her. 'They've

both worked like troupers and your itinerary isn't all work, is it, Luke?'

A little smile plays around Freya's lips as she stares at me with interest. This fixation she has on an itinerary is never far from her mind. Before I have a chance to reply, my mouth full of crispy, flaky pastry, she responds.

'Luke mentioned while we were getting ready that we're taking a detour before starting the next leg of our journey.'

'I did,' I confirm. 'Freya is still learning to go with the flow.' She gives me what I can only describe as a disapproving glance, before she resumes eating. Strawberries are her favourite fruit, and these are plump, sweet and delicious. 'Iris has invited us to lunch at the vineyard.'

Freya's eyes widen. 'You didn't tell me that!'

'She thought it would be a nice surprise, but as you don't really seem to like surprises, I'm sure she won't mind me sharing it with you now.'

'Oh, Freya, you'll be totally enchanted by Le Château de la Fontaine. It's a truly special place. We love spending time there, don't we, Max?'

'We do, we just don't get to visit often enough.' The look between them tells me it's still a source of contention between them. Max thinks they should be easing back a little, but Erin doesn't agree.

Freya, rather politely, changes the subject. 'This is one breakfast that I'll remember forever. An orangery is such a delightful setting; it's very romantic.'

I can see that it was probably the first thing that popped into her head and the moment she spoke, she realised it might be a mistake, given that Max isn't in agreement with Erin's plan to hold weddings here.

Erin frowns. 'Well, I'd like to hire it out for parties – birthdays, anniversaries, maybe even corporate events. Max is on board with that, but he thinks using it as a wedding venue will be too much work.'

Max sits back in his chair, empties his coffee cup and

pours himself another before replying. 'We'd be stretching ourselves even thinner, especially during peak season.'

The ensuing silence is a little awkward.

'The solution is within our grasp, Max. We need a proper sous-chef, for a start. Someone who can step in for you and literally take over. Having Marie step up, and planning ahead when you take time off, is getting by but it's not a permanent answer. It's madn—' Erin's face pales as she gives me a look of desperation.

When I'm not forthcoming, Max has no option other than to answer his wife. 'It has to be the right person, Erin, you know that.'

Now my conscience is weighing heavily upon me. That's short-sighted, and I know them both well enough to understand that Erin only has his best interests at heart. 'Then maybe it's time to start looking in earnest, Max.'

Our eyes lock and he can see that I'm in total agreement with his wife.

The door to the orangery opens and the hot food arrives. Pancakes ladled with summer fruits, two lots of French toast – *pain perdu* – liberally dusted with icing sugar and summer berries, and one traditional sourdough croque-monsieur. As the serious eating begins, the mood shifts. One can't eat in France and have discord around the table.

It's a fitting last breakfast among good friends. There's a little laughter as Max presses Freya to share some of her highlights of the visit. Her cheeks glow as she reminisces and my heart swells in my chest to see her this happy and relaxed.

The fact that Freya clearly feels a real connection to this place means so much to me. As an eighteen-year-old tagging along in the company of a talented sous-chef, I wasn't that confident when faced with a task I hadn't tackled before. Then Max set me to work on the computer and I was in my element.

I'm ashamed to say that during my first few days here I slept in later than I should have and didn't really appreciate the allowances everyone was making for me. I soon realised that each individual's efforts count when you have a property and grounds this size, and a relatively small team by comparison. It was the start of quite a steep learning curve, and that summer was a bit of a turning point for me. I ended up feeling I was a part of something and every year since that bond has grown. In between visits, Max reached out whenever he had an IT problem he couldn't solve, and I was more than happy to fix it.

However, that closeness makes the parting even harder, and this year is the toughest of them all.

'It's good to get Reba out on the road again.' I wind down the window, and take a deep breath, as we pass field after field, some peppered with clumps of wildflowers in between the crops. It's a nice pop of colour.

'Is Iris's vineyard much of a detour?'

Freya's trying not to sound concerned while worrying that we're going to end up arriving late at our second official stop on the tour.

'Hey, this is a working *holiday* as I've reminded you before. We get to our destination when we get there, it's as simple as that.'

'Yes, but . . . aren't people expecting us?' Freya's tone is enough to tell me that she thinks I'm being cavalier.

'They are, but a little delay of a day, or two, isn't a problem. Don't worry. I've been in touch, as I have a feeling Iris might invite us to stay overnight. As long as we get there some time tomorrow, everything will be fine. I never leave anyone in the lurch. It's not my style.'

'What exactly did Iris say when she spoke to you?'

'She mentioned that it's her son's birthday. They're throwing a bit of a party this evening. All of her neighbours are invited, and I think she's hoping it will help to lift everyone's spirits. She said, "The more, the merrier, and we have plenty of spare rooms if you don't have to rush off."'

'And you said what, exactly?'

'Nothing. It's not my decision to make. There are two of us on this trip, we're a couple.'

Something catches in Freya's throat, and she gives a nervous cough. 'I see.'

'Well, we are while we're travelling. Aren't we? Or would you have preferred separate rooms?'

I don't have to look at her to know that she's smiling. 'Of course not. But the word "couple" has a certain connotation.'

'Of?'

'A relationship with a future. In fact, Erin started to introduce me to Iris as your girlfriend and then apologised, changing it to just friend.'

'You are. My girl *space* friend.'

Freya starts laughing. 'There is no way you said that to Erin; not in that way.'

'I didn't say anything at all. I simply said I was bringing someone with me. Does it matter?' I query.

I was expecting a glib reply, but she stops to think for a few moments. 'Not when it comes to other people, but I think it does when we're talking about you and me. There isn't really an *us*, is there?'

'But there could be, couldn't there?'

'Oh.' She tuts, sighing. 'What do I really know about you, Luke? Not a lot as it turns out. I have no idea whether, when you drop me back home, I'll stand there waving you goodbye for the very last time. Besides, I'm Ms Nine-to-Five, six days a week. There's no way to merge two lifestyles that are poles apart and we both know that.'

I can't dispute a single word as I've thought the same thing myself, but that doesn't mean I'm giving up. Freya laid out the ground rules at the very start but she's changing by the day, and so am I. Surely she's aware of that?

'OK,' I challenge her, 'ask me a question.' We're on a dual carriageway and the driving is pleasant. We're not in a hurry and I understand her being curious.

111

'Where do you live in Cornwall?'

'Newquay.' Knowing Freya, she's expecting more than that. 'I have a house that overlooks the Gannel Estuary.'

'I thought you said you lived with your parents?' she questions, seemingly surprised by my answer.

'No. I said I'll probably spend Christmas Day with them, but I like my own space.'

'So . . . that's your base?'

'Yep. It's the place I go back to when I get fed up with being somewhere else.'

Out of the corner of my eye I can see that she's now studying my side profile, having lost interest in the scenery.

'But you regard it as home?'

Now that's a tough question to answer. 'I don't like being tied to one place, but everyone has to have somewhere they can lay their head, as it's bad manners to outstay a welcome.'

Now she's laughing softly to herself. 'It's not a beach hut, is it?'

'No! Like everyone else I have lots of . . . things, and I have to store them somewhere.'

'What sort of things? Oh, let me guess . . . computer equipment, surfboards, clothes—'

She's enjoying being a detective but she's asking all the wrong questions. None of that matters to me but I'll play the game. 'Yes, yes and yes.'

'Right, now I get it. I'm glad you have somewhere you can go back to . . . in between your jaunts away.' Her tone has changed. I guess when roots are important to someone, they find it hard to understand a person to whom bricks, and mortar, are simply just that.

'When we get back,' I labour my words, 'the first weekend you have free, I'll take you down there.'

All I hear is a sudden intake of breath and I can feel her eyes on me again.

'Really?'

'Just to prove that it's not a beach hut, although I'd dearly love one. I mean . . . sleeping on a roll-out bed and waking up, dashing out because the surf's up. Now that would be my idea of heaven!'

Freya

10

A Warm Welcome

We can't fail to spot the sign for Le Château de la Fontaine, but having made a right turn, the tree-lined lane leading down to it seems to go on forever. There are a few potholes to negotiate, and Luke is naturally being very careful driving Reba. When the lane finally opens out there's a huge car parking area and beyond that a vista that takes us both by surprise.

'Wow! Now that's what I call a château,' I declare.

When I glance across at Luke, he looks equally impressed. The pale, honey-coloured stonework of the building with the dark-grey slate roof, combined with the size of it, makes a grand statement. It might not have turrets, but the roof reminds me a little of photos I've seen of the Palace of Versailles. The roof itself is set at quite a steep angle but a row of dormer windows adds to the charm. As we walk towards the building, what commands the eye is the seemingly never-ending vista: field after field of neat rows of vines going off in all directions.

Luke clasps my hand in his. 'The grapes for that bottle of wonderful pink champagne Iris gave you, that we shared on the terrace at Le Manoir du Bois, were grown here. I hope we get a tour. After all, we are in the Champagne region.'

'Even though, as you pointed out, I don't usually like surprises, I do love this one! When I thanked Iris for the champagne, and the little souvenir, I had no idea she'd invite us here.'

Luke pulls me close, planting a kiss firmly on my lips as I stare into his eyes. 'I knew you wouldn't want to turn down her generous offer. And, I will admit, I was excited about the prospect of getting a tour of the vineyard and seeing how they turn the grapes into wine.'

'Freya, Luke! *Bonjour!*' It's Alain, one of the guys who accompanied Iris to the festival.

We hurry across the vast space to meet him halfway and shake hands. 'Iris is on a phone call. Come, I will take you inside. She will not keep you long.' Alain's English is very good. When he was chatting to Luke at Le Manoir, he told him that he spent three summers touring the UK with an ex-girlfriend. He's probably around Luke's age and they got on very well, so he's delighted to see us.

The stone steps leading up to a large terrace are very grand indeed. Each of the stone pillars on either side has a carved statue of a lion in repose. There's something so romantic about aged stone with its weathering and the various lichens that it attracts. All around us are borders with a multitude of shrubs and a backdrop of tall trees: oak, beech, chestnut and pine to name a few. But it's the variety of rich colours and spotting some of my favourite plants, like climbing roses and regal irises, that remind me a little of an English country garden. Someone here pays attention to detail and it's a wonderful contrast to the vast swathes of leafy greenery.

We stop to appreciate our surroundings and then walk to the edge of the terrace to gaze down over a beautifully manicured lawn, on the edge of which is a magnificent fountain. Seconds later, Iris appears, smiling from ear to ear.

'My dears! I'm so glad you could make it.' She greets us in the French style and is clearly overjoyed to see us. 'Frédéric has taken the minibus to collect some dear friends who are going to help set up the terrace ready for this evening, but he won't be long. When he returns, I know he'll be eager to give you a tour of the vineyard and the bottling plant.'

Luke's eyes light up.

'If it's not an inconvenience, we'd love that,' I reply, happily.

'Oh, for him it's a pleasure. He has some big ideas for the future and is always grateful for a listening ear. In the meantime, how would you like a little walk around what I call my little piece of home, Freya?'

Luke's enthusiasm fades a little, even though he's trying to plaster on a polite smile.

'Perhaps Alain would be kind enough to show Luke some of the outbuildings. They're not all in use, as some are badly in need of repair, but it makes for an interesting walk around.'

Alain nods his head, and the two men take their leave.

'It so pretty what you've done to the terrace, and you have your namesake flowers.'

'Another week, maybe two, and the flag irises will turn, their flowering season over. I will miss them when they're cut down. I'm particularly proud of the dahlias; I do spend a lot of time out here tending and watering them, but Frédéric's wife, Sabine, also gives me a hand. They're expecting their first baby in November. Frédéric, of course, has a small team that takes care of the vines and we have two gardeners who maintain the trees and the boundaries. Nature is bountiful.' She gives a tinkling little laugh. 'But it means it's a constant struggle to keep things in check.'

Iris leads me across the terrace and down a mirror-image flight of stone steps the other side, into what could be described as a secret garden. The entrance is via a perfectly formed doorway cut into a tall, ten-foot hedge. She opens the wooden gate, inviting me to step through.

'Oh, a cottage garden! How delightful. Back home I have a little cottage on the edge of a river, and I spend every spare minute I have in my garden. It's the perfect way to relax after a hectic day at work.'

'Luke told me that co-owning an estate agency means you work long hours.'

'Yes, but I love what I do. It's the best feeling in the world when people step over the threshold of a property and instantly feel a connection. It's like it was destined to be.'

'Ah, that's exactly what I felt shortly after I was married, and Tim brought me here. He thought I'd be horrified at the amount of work that needed doing, but I felt that pull and even though I was a little overwhelmed by it, I could imagine us living here. He was grateful, and relieved that I felt the same way.'

Her words are touching. 'That's fate, isn't it?'

'Yes, Freya, I believe it was. And he indulged me when it came to the cultivated gardens here, because although his focus was always solely on the vines, he knew that there were times when I got a little homesick. It was a long weekend in Paris with some friends, who ended up changing the whole course of my life forever.'

'Gosh, that must have been exciting, but daunting, too.'

'It was,' she admits. 'Never in a million years did I ever imagine myself living in France, let alone a vineyard as grand as this one. Of course, it was well over a year until he confessed that shortening his Christian name was partly why his parents didn't um . . . *take* to me.' She smiles to herself, as if transported back in time. 'Timothée is such a mouthful and, besides, he found his nickname endearing.'

'Did your relationship with your in-laws improve over time?'

'Not until Frédéric was born, three years later. They had the heir to their heir, and when it came to naming him, I did the right thing. So, he took Tim's father's Christian name, and his middle name is in honour of my father. Frédéric Samuel Beauchêne. Life has been a little complicated at times, but we got through it.'

Her smile is whimsical, and I sense it's not an easy topic of conversation, so it's time to change the subject.

'We really enjoyed that wonderful bottle of champagne, Iris. It was totally unexpected and a lovely gesture. I was also touched by the little gilded plaque in the small wooden box; it looks antique.'

'You were very kind to me that day, Freya. Sometimes my strength leaves me and, in those moments, the last thing I want is pity. You seemed to instinctively know that.'

She falls silent, but as I cast around for a suitable response, Iris begins talking again.

'It's one of three little amulets that we found when we had one of the old fireplaces opened back up, many years ago. This house belonged to Tim's grandfather but had been empty for some years when we took it over. Only the grounds had been maintained, when his father took over the running of the vineyard. They have a country house not far from here, with too many memories to leave it behind. Tim and I made it our life's work to restore this place and I like to think we did a good job.

'The words on the little plaque – *porte bonheur* – means "bearing happiness". The image of a four-leaf clover was a traditional emblem of good luck in France, and they probably date back to the early nineteen hundreds. I don't know what made me think of them, as they hadn't seen the light of day for well over twenty years. The fact that the thought popped into my head, I took as a sign. I knew the champagne wouldn't last long—' she gives a little chuckle '—and I wanted you to have a little keepsake to express my gratitude.'

I don't know quite what to say. 'Oh, Iris. I'll treasure it forever; it's a memory of one summer I'll never forget.'

'One, hopefully, of many more wonderful summers in France.'

I hesitate for a moment. 'I fear it might be a one-off.'

'Surely not? Luke said to me it was like coming home.'

'He used the word *home*?'

'He did. Although he loves his house in Cornwall. He

told me that to wake up each morning and look out over the water is a blessing.'

Iris has no idea how jealous I am that Luke has opened up to her and shared things he hasn't shared with me.

She seems to sense my disappointment. 'Time is a great healer when people are battling with life's trials, Freya. Be patient. Give him time. I don't know Luke that well, but Max and Erin speak so highly of him. There was doubt as to whether, or not, he would turn up this year. I don't know why, but when he did, they were overjoyed to see that he wasn't alone. It put their minds at rest.

'Now, I think it's time to pop into the kitchen. We have a chef and two helpers busy preparing a light lunch for when Frédéric gets back. Then, it'll be manic this afternoon setting everything up for tonight's party. I hope you like dancing and loud music.'

'It sounds wonderful!'

'Then let me show you to your room.'

I guess we're staying overnight; it would be rude to refuse. And maybe an evening of celebratory laughter and dancing is exactly what I need to stop my mind trying to unravel the puzzle that is Luke.

There are moments I wonder who exactly he is; in his laid-back, understated way strangers quickly become friends. He seems content to flit in and out of their lives and that seems to be enough for him. Now I'm beginning to wonder whether he doesn't want to get too close to anyone; possibly, because someone hurt him in the past. Then I realise I'm overthinking it and, being totally honest with myself, it's none of my business.

People come and go in our lives and not everyone we meet leaves a lasting impression; but some do, and Luke is one such person.

'Freya! I've been eagerly awaiting a call. I know you've been on the road again and I hope you're settling down for the second leg of the journey.' Mum sounds relieved to hear my voice.

'We aren't going straight there, as we're staying overnight with Iris. It's her son's birthday. There's a big party this evening, and this afternoon we're getting a tour of the vineyard.'

'Oh, how lovely! Now that's the joy of a road trip. You can make a little detour whenever you want. And how is the dear lady doing?'

'Happy to be back with her family and making an effort to shake off her sadness.'

I really hadn't meant to tell Mum about the time I spent with Iris but a few days later when I rang her, I suddenly found myself dissolving into tears. Obviously, Mum was concerned to know why I was upset. And, of course, then we started talking about Dad, that made her emotional too. But it ended up in us both sharing some things we'd never voiced before. In doing so, it was yet another step towards letting go of misplaced guilt that's so easy to cling on to.

In Mum's case it was for not dealing with it better. She was emotionally overwrought, which was only natural because she was grieving and in shock. For me it was that awful feeling of helplessness. Mum was inconsolable; at the time, I wished there were something more that I could do, other than make her cups of tea and sit on the sofa beside her as we shed tears together. In hindsight, the tears were a good thing, as left alone I would probably have bottled up my feelings and put on a brave face.

'Well, it's early days for the poor woman. But what better way to keep her spirits up than a birthday party with family and friends? I've no doubt that it's what her husband would have wanted.'

I let out a positive sigh. 'It's a blessing to be able to help someone in a moment of great sadness, isn't it?'

'It is, my darling. No good deed goes unrewarded and what a lovely gesture to invite you and Luke into her home to share in a special celebration. And how is Luke?'

'He's . . .' I give a little laugh. 'He's impatiently waiting for our tour of the vineyard.'

'Well, send him my best regards. This trip is doing you the world of good, Freya. I can't wait to hear what surprises he has planned for you next. Have you heard from Beth?'

Unseen by Mum, I grimace to myself. 'I haven't spoken to her for about a week. I . . . well, I know she's busy and she said she wouldn't keep bothering me, but it's been a hectic time.'

'Oh. If she hasn't got in touch, then it means everything is going well. You don't want her to think you're constantly checking up, do you?'

'No, I guess not.' But I do feel guilty, and I will call her when we get to our next destination.

'And how is life back in Sevenoaks?'

'After the hot spell we had, two days of continuous rain means I haven't stepped outside the door. I swear the grass has grown at least an inch, but the garden in general is looking so much fresher for it. Tomorrow I'm meeting up with my ladies for a relaxing lunch at our favourite restaurant. Oh . . . that's the doorbell, I'd better go. I have a delivery due. Take care, Freya, and enjoy the party this evening.'

'I will. Love you, Mum!'

Frédéric is what my mum would call a man's man. He's very polite, his English is as good as his French, but when we begin our tour of the bottling plant, his conversation is aimed mainly at Luke.

A lot of the information is quite technical, and Luke is naturally curious, asking question after question. Some I find interesting, others not so much.

However, I am interested to hear the answer to what he asks next. 'What makes a sparkling wine sparkle?'

'Excess carbon dioxide,' Frédéric replies. 'There are two basic techniques, one artificial and one involving a second sugar fermentation, which is the method we use.'

Now it's my turn. 'Having sampled your wonderful rosé champagne, does the process involve using both white and red grapes?'

'Interestingly, no. We use Pinot Noir and Pinot Meunier, which are both red grapes. There are only seven varieties of grape allowed by the Champagne AOC, which stands for the *appellation d'origine contrôlée*. Most champagne is white, because when you crush red grapes you get white juice, although there are a few exceptions. By letting the juice sit with the grape skins for a little bit, it soaks out some of the colour. *Et voilà!*'

Frédéric seems delighted by our interest and mine is growing by the minute.

'Iris said that the vineyard was started by your great-grandfather. You're the third generation; that's quite something.'

'Yes, although the pressure is immense. This plant is old and in today's terms, inefficient.'

Luke frowns. 'But it does the job?'

Frédéric extends his hand, tilting it back and forth indicating that things don't always run smoothly. 'We get a lot of breakdowns, which is to be expected given its age, but it's getting harder to find replacement parts. My biggest complaint is that we could be helping out our neighbours, smaller producers, if we could afford an upgrade. Faster, more efficient machinery would give us additional capacity. But that would require investment on a scale I simply cannot raise.'

And that's where the pressure comes in.

'Right,' he continues. 'It's time to walk among the vines. It's only then you can fully appreciate the bounty and the glory of nature. We may even turn you into *vine* lovers, although it will also make you so much more appreciative when you taste your next glass of wine.'

Frédéric is obviously very in tune with the land, the vines and the potential of this place. I can't help feeling that somehow, he'll find a way to bring his plans to fruition, over time. And with their first baby due in just a few months, it's a blessing after the loss of his father. Both for them as a couple and for Iris.

11

New Friends

After a wonderful lunch on the terrace surrounded by a dozen of the family's closest friends and neighbours, while it's hard to remember all of their names, both Luke and I are made to feel like we belong here.

Luke helps three of the guys to set up the equipment for what will be a mixture of both live and recorded music. Another group erect a large, open-sided marquee on the lawn in front of the Le Château de la Fontaine.

Frédéric, Sabine and I have been charged with sorting out the bunting.

'*Alors!*' She laughs, as we begin opening a stack of boxes Frédéric carried over from one of the many stone outbuildings. 'Why do we not pack them away tidily?' Her voice has a wonderful lilt to it.

'We'll soon untangle these,' I reassure her.

She turns to look at me, smiling. 'Shall we simply tip it out and see what we can rescue?'

'I'll leave you ladies to sort this lot and start carrying over the chairs. Let me know when you're ready for me to put them up.' Frédéric stoops to plant a kiss on his wife's cheek and as their eyes meet the look that passes between them makes my heart melt.

'Go,' she says, shooing him off. 'You do not have patience for this.'

As I empty a box out onto the large rectangular table, Sabine pulls up a chair and immediately begins looking for the end of the bunting.

'Is almost impossible,' she states. Her efforts seem to be making the tangle even worse.

We end up starting somewhere in the middle and it takes a lot of twisting, turning and teasing to unravel one half. The little cotton flags are in an array of muted colours, probably faded by the sun over the years, but it's going to add a lot of cheer to the marquee.

'This is a special birthday for my Frédéric,' she informs me. 'He is . . . uh, thirty? I kid him he has his first grey hair already. He'll get more when the baby comes.'

I give a little laugh as she grins back at me.

'It's an exciting time and good to have two celebrations so close together.'

'Yes.' A frown appears on her forehead, dulling the sparkle in her eyes. 'It has not been an easy time here. Not for my mother-in-law, or for Frédéric. Tonight is good. This is a place made for gathering people together.'

'It must be hard work running the vineyard,' I reflect.

'It is different now that Frédéric has sole responsibility and a future to guarantee.'

Her smile hasn't returned.

'Of course, but I'm sure his plans will do just that.'

'We hope. I hope, anyway. The renovation work on *le château* was . . . what do you say . . . a money pit?'

'Ah, yes. I can understand that.'

'Having a grand passion comes at a cost and the lack of investment in the vineyard itself is something Frédéric must now deal with.' Suddenly her expression changes. 'There, we did it!'

The bunting laid out on the table in front of us winds back and forth at least a dozen times. Putting this up isn't going to be easy and we have four more boxes to detangle.

Sabine helps me to lift off the bunting and we place it on the flagstones before tackling the next lot.

'You met Iris at *la fête*?'

'Yes. I helped dispense the wine and the canapés.'

'She would not let me go with her that first day, even though I could see she was feeling fragile. She said you were an angel.'

I give a little shrug. 'I was there to help, as they were really busy, and I was glad to lend a hand. I learnt a bit about the wines and the champagne and met some lovely people.'

'It got her through the day, Freya,' Sabine replies, letting out a gentle sigh. 'And Luke . . . he is your boyfriend?'

I take a moment to consider my response and she laughs. 'Or not?'

'It's complicated.'

'Ah, I see. But he is taken with you. I can see it in his eyes.'

I can feel the heat rising in my cheeks as she scrutinises my face, looking for clues. 'There's quite an age difference between us. My life is very settled. This is just a summer experience we're sharing.'

'I see. Well, I hope it will be full of wonderful memories that you'll both remember forever.'

What a lovely thing to say. 'Being invited to join in with your celebrations today is a real highlight, Sabine. It's the first time I've had the pleasure of walking around a vineyard and it's wonderful knowing that it's passing from generation to generation. Standing among the rows of vines, we both felt an overwhelming sense of being at one with nature and Luke literally said that as I was thinking it.'

'My Frédéric, he says there's a soul connection with plants, but not everyone can feel it.'

'I've always loved gardening, so maybe that's why I felt it, too.'

Her mouth twitches. 'I was born and brought up in Paris; busy streets, big buildings and the noise of the people and the buzz, it was what I was used to. When I met Frédéric, I had no idea this was his life, but we fell in love. And now, here I am, and I wouldn't want to be anywhere else.'

Love, it seems, can change everything in an instant. But does that guarantee life-long happiness? I wonder. When one person has to give up more than the other to make it work as a couple, the danger is that if either one isn't happy, resentment will set in.

'Ah!' Frédéric is back. 'Well done. Now I will need to go and get some stepladders.'

For all the pressure he has on his shoulders, the look on Frédéric's face tells me he's a very happy man indeed. I think he knows exactly what Sabine has given up for him and he'll cherish her all the more because of it.

'Oh . . .' Iris walks past, leaning in for a moment as Luke and I dance on the spot. 'You two make such a stunning couple. Don't stop. It's good to see you enjoying yourselves!'

She moves on through the crowd and Luke smiles down at me. 'Well, with a beautiful woman in my arms I guess that means I cleaned up a bit better than usual tonight. I didn't want to let you down.'

That makes me chuckle. 'You look handsome and you're a much better dancer than I am.'

The music is brilliant. The French DJ has played a whole host of artists I've never heard of before. Tracks by Alonzo, Zak and Louane. It's just a pity that I can't understand most of the lyrics.

When the next track strikes up, I catch the name – La Zarra – but not the title. It's a melody I can imagine playing over and over again in my head.

'I like this song.' I turn to look at Luke.

'Yeah, it's good. "Tu T'en Iras". It's a bit sad though.'

'Is it?'

'It means "You'll Go Away". It's about a woman who awaits the inevitability of her man leaving her, after being hurt before.'

'Oh, that is sad.'

'You won't do that to me, will you?' he jests. Luke's grip tightens slightly, as we circle around the temporary wooden dance floor.

I laugh off his comment. 'I'm all yours until the end of August. If I leave you now, I'd be stranded, wouldn't I?'

But his eyes don't stray from mine.

'I mean, cut me out of your life after we return to the UK.'

'I like to think that we'll always be friends, Luke. Why wouldn't we be?'

'Exactly. Would you do this again, next year?' My feet falter as we get out of synch and Luke leads me off the dance floor. 'Well?' he presses.

As we walk towards the bar area to get a drink, I consider my answer.

'Maybe. It's been thoroughly enjoyable so far and surprisingly re-energising.'

'You've definitely switched off from work.' He sounds triumphant.

'That's true. A change, as they say, is as good as a rest. And it is. I'd never turn my back on you, Luke, but I think in the song the words are probably referring to a relationship that wasn't destined to last. You said you'd never been through that experience.' And I remember being very surprised to hear that.

'No, I haven't. I've never been in one place long enough, I guess.'

'Not even in Cornwall?'

We each pick up a glass of white wine from one of the trays, acknowledging the bartender with a tilt of our glasses. Then we make our way over to the fountain.

It's quieter away from the speakers, and as the light fades, it's nice to stand in the shadows cast by the ground-level floodlights.

'It's my sanctuary. It's where I go to think, create and escape the world. That's why I don't invite people back to the house when I'm there.'

'But you've invited me for a weekend stay on our return.' Has he forgotten already?

'That's different. You're not *people*.'

'You know what I mean.'

Our eyes meet and I can see I'm not the only one beginning to feel uncomfortable about the way this conversation is going.

'You understand me. It's easy being around you, Freya.' He raises his glass, and we chink, just as the DJ turns off the music and summons everyone to the terrace.

That inner voice of mine starts a dialogue all of its own. *That's the problem, Luke, I don't really understand you even though we're spending a lot of time together. It's what you're not telling me that matters. Of that I'm very sure.*

The distraction comes right on cue. There's a lot of laughter as we wait for the thirty candles on the enormous cake in the centre of the table to be lit, but eventually there's a chorus of 'Joyeux Anniversaire'.

We all raise our glasses to toast Frédéric and there's a cacophony of good wishes winging their way through the air. Then Iris indicates for him to say something. Having turned up empty-handed, I wish we'd stopped off somewhere to buy a small gift. But what do you buy someone who, at the start of the day, was little more than a total stranger?

Frédéric's speech is quite short, but he talks fast, and I catch very little of it. With in excess of fifty people here in total, the air of gaiety and support is wonderful to witness. I glance at Luke, and he leans in closer.

'He just thanked everyone for coming, for helping to get things set up and said we should all enjoy ourselves. And at the end he said it was a day to count his blessings. He thanked Iris and Sabine, but also his grandfather and his father. And then he said we're in for a treat. And judging by the group of people taking centre place on the terrace, it's a string quartet.'

'How wonderful, but aww . . . what a touching speech.'

'I bet it brought tears to Iris's eyes, but she's surrounded by people, both French and English, who knew her husband well. That must be a comfort. Frédéric's passion for the vineyard was nurtured by his father and he must really miss him.' The tinge of sadness in Luke's voice surprises me.

I wonder whether there's an underlying sense of something a little deeper than empathy going on here. 'Are you close to your father?'

Luke instantly shakes his head. 'We're civil to each other because of my mum, but he gave up on me when I quit university after the first year.'

'Oh, I'm sorry. I didn't mean to pry.'

'It is what it is. I don't hide the fact that we don't get on. That's why I have a place of my own. I visit my parents regularly whenever I'm in Cornwall, but an hour at a time is enough. At least at Christmas, there's a house full of people and that makes a huge difference. Anyway, let's wander over and grab a seat. There's something about Puccini's "Nessun Dorma" that deserves one's full attention, don't you agree?'

He's right and by the time they play the final chord, I have tears in my eyes. It's been a fabulous day and a truly magical evening. I love classical music, but when you hear it in the grounds of a vineyard, in the shadow of a grand château, with a magnificent fountain in the background, it's surreal. It's as if we're among friends; everyone is smiling and life feels good, really good.

The following morning, it's time for another round of goodbyes. It doesn't get any easier, as a whole group of people wave us off after breakfast. And it's with a promise that we'll be back before too long. In my purse I have Iris's email address and phone number, which she pressed into my hand as we kissed goodbye.

We set off in silence. I imagine we're both feeling the same way, wishing our stay could be longer because the house party isn't over and will continue throughout the day. However, it's with great regret we had to leave suddenly, when Luke received a text which seemed to set him on edge. It only took us about ten minutes to get all packed up and take our leave.

'Where are we heading?' I ask, wondering how long we'll be on the road.

'It's a campsite a couple of miles outside of Limoges. It's quite a drive, but we need to get there as quickly as possible as there's been a change of plan.'

'What's that in terms of miles?'

'It's just under five hundred kilometres, so about three hundred miles.'

'It's ten o'clock now. If we hit traffic or any sort of hold-up, even a tractor, it's got to be a good six-hour drive surely,' I point out.

'We'll do it in five,' he says, adamantly. 'Half of it is via toll roads and if it's OK with you, we'll only stop for comfort breaks. I'm sure I can beat that. I know the route, so it's not a problem. Just sit back and enjoy the scenery.'

He's determined, but I can tell that Luke's not quite as confident as he's making out. Will it really matter if we're a little late, though? I guess I'll find out when we get there.

As the hours tick by, he pretty much sticks to the maximum speed limits, so he's strangely quiet as it commands total concentration. He's obviously on edge and, quite frankly, I'm not sure what to think. It's as if he can't handle pressure and he withdraws into a little world of his own.

We stop briefly at a small roadside café to use their facilities, buy two filled baguettes to go, and although they didn't do takeaway coffee, they kindly filled the two thermal mugs Luke ran back and grabbed from the van. All the while his brow was furrowed. Whereas yesterday was fun and relaxing, today, even driving through picturesque leafy lanes on some of the back roads as we headed into and exited hamlets and small villages, he's been constantly watching the speedometer.

* * *

'Luke!' We haven't even pulled to a halt, when a woman, who is probably in her early fifties, waves in the direction of the van. He winds down the window and raises his arm.

Behind her, a man exits the office building just inside the entrance to Camping au Coeur de la Forêt, carrying a suitcase in one hand and a bag in the other.

I hear him say, 'There, Daphne. I told you he'd make it!'

Luke yanks on the handbrake, opens the door and leaps out. I give them a few moments before I saunter over to join them, but the couple are already heading towards their car. They're obviously in a hurry, but as we stand watching the car drive past, the woman turns to give me an apologetic smile.

Luke lets out a huge sigh of relief. 'The timing was perfect. Thanks for being so understanding, Freya. That was probably the worst journey of my life. I was getting more and more anxious knowing they couldn't set off until we got here. Let's hope I never get a repeat of that.'

'Whatever's wrong?'

'Daphne and Gerald Williams own and run the campsite and they're heading off to be with their daughter, Zoe.'

I draw in a huge breath. 'Is she ill?'

'No. She's expecting their first grandchild. It's not due for another week, but she thought she'd gone into labour in the early hours of this morning. Zoe's husband is away, and a neighbour took her to the hospital, which thankfully is only a five-minute drive away from her house. Gerald headed straight there, as Daphne doesn't drive. Besides, one of them had to stay behind in case there were any problems here on site. The pains were coming at five-minute intervals, apparently, but an hour after Zoe arrived at the hospital they stopped. Gerald took her home and stayed with her. They didn't want to leave her on her own for long in case the labour pains start up again.'

'No wonder they both looked so panicked.'

'They'll be staying until her husband gets back, hopefully some time tomorrow morning, but they couldn't leave the campsite until we got here. Gerald has left a list of instructions and if anything crops up that I can't handle, I'll give him a call.'

'Oh my! I did notice that your eyes were glued to the speedo on the dashboard. You should have said something.'

'Why? What's the point of spoiling the ride for both of us?'

Hmm . . . that's one way of looking at it, I suppose.

'Does their daughter live very far away?'

'About half-an-hour's drive.' He throws his arms around me, and I can feel the tension in his body easing already.

'So, we're staying for how long, exactly?'

'As long as they need us. The original plan was that we cover the absence of Gerald's second-in-command. He flies home to Holland for two weeks every summer. Daphne said first babies often arrive late and we were expecting a leisurely handover. This morning's little emergency wasn't a part of the plan. They weren't concerned when I called them the day before yesterday to say we'd be a day late arriving.'

'Oh, right. What exactly will we be doing?'

'Assisting the staff in any way we can to make sure everything continues to run smoothly. I've never covered for their office manager before, but I know how everything works. I usually stay for about two weeks, but last year I stayed for an extra week as Daphne tripped over and sprained her wrist.'

'No wonder you were tense on the drive here. I'm glad I didn't know the situation, as I'd have been biting my fingernails the whole time. I'm sure Daphne and Gerald will feel a lot calmer once they're back with their daughter.'

Luke and I turn to see a camper van about to pull into the entrance, and another one following on behind it.

'Yeah, that's for sure. I felt so bad when I received their

text this morning. Anyway, I'll just move Reba and then we'll head into the office to find out where we're staying.'

It seems that we arrived just in time. I can't wait to find out what working on a campsite entails, I only hope we're not sleeping in a tent.

12

A Different Sort of Celebration

'You're doing *what*?' Beth sounds a little disbelieving, and I don't blame her.

'Helping to build a play den in the middle of a forest, a few miles from Limoges. I haven't got my bearings yet, as we only arrived yesterday afternoon and it's been a bit hectic.'

When I catch her up with the tales of our adventures since the last time we spoke, she starts laughing.

'Only you, Freya. Honestly, from the romantic strains of Puccini in the grounds of a château, to foraging in the forest. Why are you building a den, anyway?'

'They run children's activities here and Tristan, the man in charge of organising the events, wants to build a little mini campfire setting. It's great fun, actually. Anyway, enough about me. What's happening at your end? How's Nancy doing?'

There's a little groan. 'She redesigned our property information form. Apparently, it saves a lot of time, as the layout is now in the same order as the basic details that appear in the property brochures. Incomplete forms have to be flagged and she's happy to liaise with our clients to fill in any gaps.'

'I know it's beginning to wind you up, but anything that saves us time too is a double bonus.'

'Yes, but she's so pedantic about . . . every little thing.'

If Beth has one flaw, it's her admin abilities and she knows it. But it sounds like Nancy is set on making improvements and I see that as a good thing. 'Then take her on a field trip. Get her to see what it's like at a listing appointment and how little time we often end up having.'

'What a brilliant idea! Other than that, Ethan sings her praises but then in her eyes he's Mr Perfect.'

'Oh, is he?'

'Yes. He's rather like you, a bit OCD. And you're right, he's too good to stagnate here as the office manager. Nancy is more than capable of running things and she's dropped enough hints about enjoying working full-time, albeit for just a couple of months. It's funny, people work all their lives to retire early, then find what they miss is the company of other people. Anyway, Ethan made a few phone calls last week, just acquaintances, and we're about to take on two stunning new properties.'

'That's great news all round.' Should I feel a bit miffed that everything is running smoothly without my presence, or is that daft?

'You sound relaxed, Freya. I bet you have a nice tan already.'

I glance down at my bare arms, which are looking a tad bronzed. 'Yes, I do, but it's certainly not from time spent sunbathing. I've never felt fitter and I'm sleeping like a proverbial log.'

'Really? Is it all that fresh country air, or succumbing to the charms of the man lying next to you in bed?'

'Both.' I give a wicked laugh. 'Anyway, I have to go. There's an outdoor karaoke session on this evening and we've a stage to build, among other things.'

'Go! Have fun and sing your heart out. My granddad says music is good for the soul and it gives us a sense of freedom.'

'It does?'

'It gives your mind *wings*; that's the terminology he uses, anyway. Having said that, he was one of the hippies who attended Woodstock in 1969. Way back then he was twenty-six years old, and my dad jokingly says a lot of Granddad's theories on life were influenced by mushrooms . . . of the magical variety.'

My jaw drops. 'Wow!'

He could be right. Last night I was only under the influence of a couple of glasses of Le Château de la Fontaine's finest Pinot Noir. However, there were several moments when I found myself staring at Luke, thinking that whenever I'm around him it's as if I've stepped out of my life into . . . where exactly, I don't know. Was I getting a glimpse of another path I could travel, one in which Luke was there with me?

The sound of Beth muttering a low 'Hmm' brings me back into the moment. 'Granddad says I take life a bit too seriously sometimes. But then I take after my dad, and I guess he never really had an appreciation for Granddad's relaxed attitude towards life.'

'Maybe we're all a little too intense at times, Beth. I hope we don't end up being the "what if/if only" generation.' Did I really just say that, because it's not the me I've come to know; I don't look back with regret, I keep my focus firmly on the future.

'Sorry to leave you to it again this morning, Freya.' Luke leans in to plant a kiss on my cheek as I'm sitting at the desk in our quaint little gîte. It was formerly one of a collection of four stone outbuildings, and what it lacks in size, it makes up for in charm.

'It's fine. There are plenty of things to do around here and I'm sure Tristan can find something to occupy my time.'

He looks at me, rolling his eyes. 'Today is a big day and he'll need all the help he can get, but don't fall for that flirty chatter of his.'

'He's just being friendly, Luke.'

'Well, don't let him get too friendly. We have a lot of people checking in today ahead of tonight's celebrations and

I'm hoping the majority of them will arrive by lunchtime. Gerald said he'd call me this morning to talk me through this afternoon's prep.'

We're both assuming that as Luke hasn't had any texts, there wasn't an overnight dash to the hospital. 'Will Gerald and Daphne head back here once Zoe's husband is home?'

'That was the plan yesterday, when we spoke briefly before they left. But I'm going to press on with everything on the to-do list they gave me, rather than assume we'll have two extra pairs of hands. Right, text me if you get any problems with you-know-who.'

This time, Luke kneels down to give me a lingering kiss on the lips. When he pulls away, I gaze at him, a playful smile tugging at my lips. 'Don't worry, I'm a big girl and I can handle a charmer.'

I don't know whether to be concerned, or flattered, that Luke is feeling a little anxious about me working with Tristan again. Tristan's official title is camp organiser, which seems to cover just about anything not to do with checking in new arrivals or housekeeping.

As Luke disappears, I finish tying my hair back in a ponytail. Then I quickly tidy the tray with the remains of the continental breakfast basket and the coffee mugs a member of staff from reception delivered to our door earlier on and head off to start my day.

'Ah, Freya!' Tristan breaks out into a beaming smile the moment he spots me walking towards him. 'Did you sleep well?'

'I did, thank you. What's our first task today?'

'We fly the French flag. Well, lots of them! *C'est le quatorze juillet!*' He laughs, his eyes sparkling as he looks at me. I don't think he's flirting at all; he's simply full of energy and enthusiasm. That wonderful French accent adds a tantalising warmth that could be . . . misinterpreted.

'Forgive me, but I know very little about the celebrations. The people rose up and stormed the Bastille and there was a lot of bloodshed, which signalled the start of the French Revolution, if I remember correctly.'

'That's about right. But today we also celebrate the Fête Nationale. Thousands of Parisians line the Champs-Élysées, for a magnificent military parade to honour the French nation's unity. In every city and village, it is the occasion for fireworks and *bals dansants* . . . you say, eh, dancing? Also, local parades and picnics. Here, we celebrate with a barbecue, music, karaoke and fireworks; it is much fun.'

'It sounds wonderful.'

The eye contact is getting a little intense for me, so I let my gaze wander around the courtyard.

'First, we will set up the gazebos for the caterers who will arrive later this afternoon. We have more people coming to help but first we need to move a lot of things from the storeroom. It is a little dusty in there, is that OK with you?'

'Yes, that's fine. I've come dressed to work,' I inform him.

His eyes travel over my well-worn jeans, and navy blue and white striped T-shirt. He grins at me. 'You look *adorable*, Freya.'

I can't help but give a dismissive chuckle. If that's a chat-up line, he's missed the mark by a mile . . . well, I guess I should say *a kilometre*. I'm pretty sure the last time I looked adorable was probably around the age of five, when I dressed as a fairy for a friend's birthday party. I only did it the once. Instead of floating around looking like a delicate little thing, I stomped. And as for the wand with a star on top, well, it ended up being taken away from me the third time I got it caught up in someone's hair.

'At last! What a day it's been.' Luke eases himself into the bubble bath I ran for him when he texted to say he was running late. He lets out a satisfied groan of relief, as the warm water and the fragrant smell of the bath salts start to do their job.

The party kicks off in just over half an hour's time and he's feeling the pressure. I'm sitting cross-legged on the bathroom floor, as this is the first time we've been alone together since early this morning.

'I think everything that could go wrong, has,' he mutters.

'Yes, I heard about the water leak in the shower block. That was unfortunate.'

'Did you hear about the little boy on his bicycle?'

'No. What was that about?'

Luke grimaces. 'A group of children were being chased by two little lads on their bikes. Unfortunately, they collided and one of them fell against the side of someone's caravan. There was quite a ruckus and one of the campers ran over to the office to say things were getting heated. Trying to calm everyone down when there was a language problem, with a lot of angry words and pointed fingers in both German and French, wasn't easy, until they realised the poor lad had probably broken his arm.'

'How awful!'

'Suddenly, a dent and scratch on the paintwork paled into insignificance and things soon quietened down as we manoeuvred the boy into his parents' car. They whisked him off to A & E. They aren't back yet.'

'Poor you, having to deal with that on top of everything else.'

'It has been a little overwhelming, with a full campsite and everyone stretched thinly getting things ready for tonight. Finding a plumber who could come out at short notice was a nightmare. We had to shut the office for forty minutes, as there was only the two of us to get the water mopped up so we could reopen the block.' He closes his eyes, as the tension in his body gradually eases. 'But you and the others did well, getting things set up for this evening. The flags around the barbecue area and the small stage is very festival-like. The only thing I haven't yet sorted out are the fireworks. I'm hoping Tristan has a bit of a clue about that. Oh!' Luke's voice perks up. 'I forgot to mention that Zoe is officially in labour! I got a text about two hours ago, so it's a waiting game now.'

'That's wonderful news! If the baby's born before midnight, every year his or her birthday will be a national holiday. How great is that?'

'Well, it's certainly taken everyone by surprise. Right, as much as I'm enjoying just lying here, there are things I need to check on.'

'Another five minutes won't make any difference. What can I do to help?'

He turns his head, giving me one of his cheeky smiles. 'If you could keep checking in with the caterers, in case they need anything, that would be amazing. Tristan will oversee the music and will compère the karaoke, apparently. I want to go and see the guy whose caravan was damaged and check he's calmed down. It'll be an insurance job. I should ask around in case anyone has heard anything more about the little boy. Then, I guess I'll be reading up on firework safety before I open that huge metal box in the outhouse. To be honest, if they're monster-size and need special staging, I might have to deliver the news that the display is cancelled. Even though it won't make me Mr Popular, I can't risk anything going wrong, can I?'

'No. Safety first, including yours. Hopefully at some point our paths will cross a bit later, but I'm off to check in with the caterers and then see if Tristan has any last-minute panics of his own.'

I kneel, leaning in to place my lips on Luke's. It's hard to tear myself away, but once tonight is over things around here should be a little calmer. Luke really does take his responsibilities very seriously indeed. No wonder people are happy to put their trust in him. I let out a little groan as I stand. How I'd love to slip into that bath with him, even though I'm fresh out of the shower.

'Don't!' He gives me a warning look as I start grinning. 'I was thinking the exact same thing, but we have work to do.'

'I know. And you can count on me, your trusty assistant.'

Luke's hand snakes around my waist as we tilt our heads skywards. There's hardly any light pollution here in the middle of the French countryside and with the backdrop of a star-sprinkled, stark navy-blue sky, the first explosion is met with excited gasps.

He pulls me closer, and I lean my head against his shoulder. When Gerald's car pulled into the car park just before seven o'clock, I can imagine the look of relief on Luke's face. Even better, there was another man with Gerald, and after nearly two hours of quite intense work with their new apprentice helping, the display was ready to go.

'Do Zoe and her husband have a name for their little girl, yet?' I ask.

'Méline Louise Chapelle. Gerald told me with great pride that her first name means "little honey" and is in honour of Noel's paternal grandmother, and the middle name is after Zoe's maternal grandmother. I guess when it comes to naming babies, it's a great way of keeping both families happy.' He gives a little laugh.

'Well, I was named after my mother's favourite author. Given that I love my Christian name, I suppose I was lucky that my dad happened to like it, too.'

The sound of a massive explosion overhead, as a giant mushroom ball of small, brilliant white lights fall to earth in an enormous shower, makes me jump and Luke's grip tightens.

'I looked it up online and Freya derives from the Scandinavian form Freyja, it means noble lady.' That's news to me. 'There was also a mythical Freya,' he continues. 'She was the goddess of fertility, love and beauty. Sometimes a name is a perfect fit.'

I tut him as I make eye contact. 'We're missing the display, Luke. It's awesome! Look at the colours.' Two sharp bangs go off in unison and I tilt my head again. 'They've created a rainbow!' I declare, and when I turn to look at him, I realise he's still watching me. 'This might be the only Bastille Day firework display I ever see, who knows?'

'But you could come here again with me, next year.'

I stare at him, frowning. I thought I'd made it very clear this was a one-off. 'While you've probably witnessed this at least half a dozen times, for me it's a spectacle I don't want to miss. Besides, next summer I'll be way too busy flitting from office to office, to take a long break,' I jest.

He withdraws his hand as I turn my eyes upwards once more, joining in with the general *oohs* and *ahhs* from the crowd around me. I'm not really aware that he's stepped away until he nudges my arm and I see that he's holding out a glass to me.

'Courtesy of Gerald. He just popped a bottle of champagne to toast the arrival of the baby. They'll be home in the morning and Daphne and Noel are now back at the house getting everything ready for Zoe and baby Méline's return.'

Luke looks so happy for his friends. I hardly know them, but the birth of a baby is always a reason to celebrate. I raise my glass.

'Here's to a future filled with good health, much love and unbridled happiness.'

We chink. 'You forgot to mention wealth,' I point out.

He scoffs, his smile broadening. 'If you have good health, love and happiness, you don't need wealth. Money can't buy any of those things, even though most people think it can.'

I nod my head but, in truth, our opinions differ slightly. I've seen what lack of money can do and how badly it affects people who are living month by month. An old school friend ended up couch surfing with friends when she lost her job and her savings ran out. Alienated from her parents, she lived with me a for a while until she got back on her feet. Every little hiccup along the way can become a potential game-changer and it's a horrible way to live. Luke is worldly in some ways, but he still has a lot to learn.

Now it's my turn. 'Can I make a toast, too?'

'Naturally!'

'Here's to understanding the difference between *wanting* and *needing*, and to knowing when to count the blessings that life bestows upon us all.'

Luke's smile fades, to be replaced by a frown. 'It's all about where each of us chooses to draw the line, isn't it?'

Suddenly, I don't think we're talking about toasting the baby's arrival, but I have no idea why he's straying off topic. 'I should imagine that making a commitment to someone else changes everything. I only have to look at my best friend Beth. Yes, she's happy, but her life is one of compromises. I'm not sure I'm ready for that. I might never be ready.'

'But what if someone could take all your worries away, so that you could live your life truly free? That would be a blessing too, wouldn't it?'

Now it's my turn to scoff. 'Take a good look around you, at people you know. There are no guarantees in life, Luke. No one is ever truly free because there are so many things that can go wrong.'

Luke comes closer, a little smile twitching at the corners of his mouth. 'Maybe the exception proves the rule.'

I burst out laughing. 'What the heck does that mean?' I think maybe he's drunk a little too much, as he isn't making any sense.

A huge boom overhead makes us both look up and, as a finale, it's spectacular. The star bursts are timed seconds apart and as one plume of coloured lights starts to fade, another replaces it at least a dozen times in quick succession. It's strangely thrilling.

'See, that just goes to prove my point.' Luke points towards the sky, as we're both transfixed. 'Just like fireworks, relationships don't fit one mould. Some are meant to burn brightly and fade away in mere seconds, others last longer.'

'Just not long enough in some cases,' I reply drolly, as he looks at me in earnest. 'And what about forever?'

'Maybe some people need to go through an experience that is so overwhelming it's life-changing before they discover who they are and what they want. Only then can they be confident that they're making the right decision.'

I stare back at Luke feeling puzzled but I'm too tired to play this game tonight. 'Time will tell then, won't it?'

'I hope so.'

13

A Well-Deserved Break

The last two weeks have flown by. Every day has been different and today is only the second time Luke and I have spent the entire shift working together.

Luke hesitates for a second before placing the key in the lock of one of the massive sheds. 'I'm glad you were up for this task today. It should be fun. If I pass you the tools, place them in the wheelbarrow, then we'll be all set to go.'

Well, I certainly wasn't too keen to venture too far inside, as I'm wary about snakes. Apparently, you find them in the least expected places. Like above a door frame, or coiled up on a shelf, unless Tristan has been pulling my leg, but I think I'd rather not know for sure.

I wait while Luke forages around, muttering to himself. Last night we had a very enjoyable barbecue supper with Gerald and Daphne, to mark her return to the site. Gerald was only away for seven days in total, but she stayed a little longer. It was my first opportunity to chat one-to-one with Daphne. The guys left the two of us to sit and enjoy a glass of wine, while they carried everything back to the staff kitchen, ready to fetch dessert and coffee.

'I hope your next stop is an enjoyable one,' Daphne remarked.

I'd shrugged my shoulders. 'I'm not entirely sure where

it is that we're going. Luke mentioned something about us having a few days to do as we please.'

She'd seemed a little surprised but nodded her head. 'That's the nature of summer work here in France. Luke has a lot of contacts and it's just a case of getting the timing right. Besides, it shouldn't be all work, although your stint here has been quite full-on given the circumstances.' Her eyes widened and we both gave an acknowledging chuckle.

'Ah, but how lovely that your granddaughter is finally here,' I'd replied, warmly. 'I will admit that it requires a lot of stamina, running a place like this. I take my hat off to you both.'

'People don't realise how hard we work, but we shut down in the winter and that's when we recharge our batteries. It's glorious in each of the seasons and for a couple of months it's all ours.'

'I imagine it's wonderful at Christmas.'

'Yes, it is. You know, Gerald and I always look forward to Luke's visit. It would have been nice to have spent more evenings together around the campfire, as we usually do. This time last year we had no idea at all a granddaughter was looming on the horizon. Life is full of surprises and blessings, too.'

She'd smiled at that thought.

'We're very grateful to you both, Freya, as we wanted to be there for Zoe and Noel. We're always so busy here during the summer that it's hard to take time off. To be together for a few days as a family to celebrate the arrival of baby Méline was truly wonderful. I stayed on to help with the catering. Noel has a large family, and my brother and his wife flew over from the UK for three days, too. It's been like one constant party.' She'd grinned, happily.

'Ah, that's lovely to hear. A new arrival is a blessing and a cause for celebration.'

It was then that Daphne turned to look at me, but I noticed that first, she'd glanced around to check whether the guys were in sight. 'We were delighted the day Luke pulled into the car park and we saw you sitting next to him. For a while, we weren't sure if his plans for this year were going ahead. When he finally firmed up the arrangements, he didn't mention who he was bringing with him. We had no idea he'd met someone.'

It was an awkward moment. 'We've . . . um . . . only known each other for a little while. Luke talked me into taking a couple of months off work,' I explained. 'I'm so glad he did, as it's been amazing. I'm doing things and meeting people I wouldn't have done as a tourist.'

'Then maybe we'll see you next year, too, assuming Luke's summer trips continue.'

I never got to reply, as our company returned at that point.

'Freya, Freya!' Luke calls out, interrupting my thoughts. He beckons me inside the dreaded shed.

'Here you go.' He hands me a long-handled rake and a pair of shears.

After a little back and forth, he takes the full wheelbarrow and I follow behind pulling a little four-wheeled cart containing a large cool box.

We head into the forest, where we're hoping to clear some of the shrubbery in preparation for what will eventually become a crazy golf feature. Thankfully, the area is bordered by tall trees, so we won't be working in the full sunshine as the temperature rises.

It's not that easy trundling anything over areas of uneven ground, but eventually we get to our destination.

'The wonderful thing about all of the places we've visited so far, is the amount of land at their disposal,' I reflect, as I do a three-hundred-and-sixty-degree turn.

The dappled shade is broken by shafts of sunlight that stream through like torchlight. There's a real sense of peace and tranquillity. Even the sounds from the campsite are few and far between, mainly the odd ringing of metal on metal. I bet that's Gerald hammering straight a post after a caravan clipped the corner getting through the gate.

Luke is already sorting the tools into piles.

'This handsaw is pretty sharp, so mind yourself. You'll need these gloves.'

I start chuckling. 'Yes, sir. And I did as you said, I borrowed this old shirt from Daphne so both my arms, and my legs, are covered.'

'Hey, as the supervisor today I'm all about health and safety.'

'The supervisor, eh? Right, where do we start, boss?'

'Gerald has pegged out some areas for us to tackle. It's hunt the wooden stake.'

We wander around and it isn't long before we're hacking away at some wildly overgrown shrubbery. 'We aren't carting this lot back to the site, are we?'

'No. But there are a couple of spindly trees in our way, and I'll use the chainsaw to chop them up for firewood to be taken back to camp. We'll move most of the debris into an open space and, when it dries out a bit, Gerald will have a bonfire.'

'Thank goodness for that!' I was imagining endless trips and that would be exhausting as the day goes on.

It is hot work but extremely satisfying. The shrubs have become woody and are way past their best anyway. It's the perfect spot for something that kids and adults alike will enjoy, and the shadiness is a relief from the vast areas of open pastureland.

We work in silence for a long while, focusing on the task in hand and enjoying the relaxing ambience. After being surrounded by people all the time, it's a welcome change. After a while, my mind starts ticking over.

I stop what I'm doing to look at Luke. 'Are you deliberately keeping me in suspense about where we're going next?'

'No. Of course not. But there have been developments

and I'm awaiting confirmation to firm up the next leg of the journey.'

'Hmm.' I give a low grumble. 'You're seriously telling me that when you fire up Reba's engine tomorrow you have no idea where we're going?'

'We've been offered a week-long break in a beautiful spot. I was going to talk to you about it tonight.'

'We have?'

'Erin, Max, Daphne and Gerald have put their heads together and called in a favour with a friend. A big favour.' No wonder Daphne was a little surprised when I said I wasn't sure what our next stop is going to be. I hope she wasn't disappointed, thinking that perhaps Luke and I aren't appreciative of the offer.

I look at him and frown. 'They all know each other?'

'They're ex-pats. There's an online group who keep in touch. That's how this summer trip came about. Erin and Daphne are old friends of my mum's.'

Now it's beginning to make sense. 'Thank goodness, I was beginning to wonder what the rules and regulations are for casual work like we've been doing.'

'We're simply helping out old friends of my family's. We're not working our way around France earning a wage, are we? We're staying with people I know, and have known, for a long time. Any IT jobs I do are slightly different. I'm paid for those and, naturally, they go through the books, although I do a lot of freebies for friends.' He grins at me.

Why am I not at all surprised; the more I get to know him, the more I realise Luke's world isn't focused on money and things.

'But what about this *free* break? Isn't that a . . . what do they call it, a *gift in kind*?'

'No. They all swap favours from time to time. Max did a ring around and it's a little present from them all; no money will change hands. It's probably a last-minute cancellation freeing up a room, but he did say it was something rather special. It's going to be a bit of a drive in the wrong direction though, as it means we'll be doubling back on ourselves if we take up the offer. The penultimate stop is a farm only an hour's drive from here. The alternative is that we do a little exploring of our own.'

I straighten, easing back my shoulders and he can see I'm tiring already.

'Come on, let's take a break. I'll grab a couple of bottles of water.'

As I yank off the thick gloves, I raise my arm to mop my brow. 'That would be most welcome.'

It's time to saunter over to a cluster of trees and I ease myself down onto the forest floor, leaning my back up against a stout tree trunk. Luke reappears to join me.

'This is bliss,' I groan, as I down a third of the bottle in one go. 'I really needed that.'

'Me, too. Anyway, where were we? Oh, yes. Le Château des Sources. I've never been there before, it's near a place called Creissels. It's in the Aveyron department, which is in the Occitane region, so we're heading further south; it's about a four-hour drive, I believe.'

'And it doesn't upset your plans?'

'No. We're not due at the farm until next weekend and after that our last stop is going to take us through until the end of our stay.'

My ears perk up. 'Let me get this straight. It's Saturday the twenty-seventh of July . . . we drive south for our little break, then head back this way to stay at a farm for . . .' I glance at Luke for his input.

'Three, maybe four days. I haven't yet had an arrival date for our final destination as it involves meeting up with someone at a temporary stop.'

'After the farm . . . we're talking about our last three weeks in France. Is it another château?'

Luke bursts out laughing. 'No, but I want to keep that as

a surprise. You'll love it, but it's not grand. Well, it is in its own unique way. Trust me.'

'Goodness, Luke. Every single step of this journey has been about putting my trust in you.' And that's something that under normal circumstances I'm loath to do given that I'm a control freak, and I'm not ashamed to admit it.

'We've enjoyed ourselves, though, haven't we? And helped a few old friends along the way. So . . . are we heading south, into the unknown?'

'I guess we are.'

As we drive away from the campsite the following day, I reflect that Luke's friends have become mine, too. It's a network of people working hard for what they believe in. They're all building a future and following their dream as they do so. It's not easy, but that's par for the course. It is an eye-opener, though. I had no idea there was a deeper connection between this far-flung group of people. Each one promotes the others, and Luke – it seems – has a strong bond with them all.

As we rack up the miles, I'm content to listen to what Luke calls his 'on the road again' collection of songs and I allow my mind to wander.

When we stop for a comfort break and to refuel, I wander off to give Beth a call.

'Hey, stranger!' The sound of her voice puts a smile on my face. 'I was wondering when I'd hear from you next.'

'I don't want to disturb your leisurely Sunday morning, so it's just a quick catch-up. We're on the move again, heading further south. It's another little detour but this time it's to take a week off to relax.'

'It's about time. After all, it's a working *holiday*.'

'Yes, thankfully, as after a day clearing shrubs in the middle of a forest yesterday, I've got several blisters on my palms that are actually quite painful.'

'It makes a change from blistered heels from all the walking you do when you're here. You said *another* detour. It all sounds a little haphazard, but then you knew what you were getting yourself into.'

'Hmm,' I agree, because I wasn't under any illusions. 'Luke comes across as someone who decides everything last minute but I'm beginning to see him in a very different light.'

'The surfer dude persona has morphed into the experienced traveller, has it?' she muses.

'As surprising as it sounds, the answer to that is *no*. It's more that Luke doesn't like to let anyone down and he's willing to change his plans to fit in with someone else's agenda. At first, I thought it was because he doesn't like to feel constrained by anything, but that's not it at all. He's mentioned the word "flexible" several times and that's exactly what he is.'

'Your attitude is changing big time,' Beth declares, sounding surprised. 'Please don't get the travel bug and say you're extending your trip. I miss our daily chats.'

'But everything is good your end, isn't it?' I check.

'Yes. We've been really busy, but it's not the same without you in the office. And some of your clients have been asking after you.'

'I'm sure Ethan is charming them.'

'Your Mr Coffee Shop Guy stopped me on Friday morning to ask where you were. His jaw dropped when I said you were touring France in a VW van. I didn't mention Luke, of course.'

I roll my eyes. 'A bit of friendly banter when our paths cross at The Coffee Shack, close to work, doesn't make him *my* Coffee Shop Guy. I don't even know his name. You should have. Mentioned Luke, I mean. He wouldn't have asked after me again!'

'No . . . when you get back you never know what might happen. Absence makes the heart grow fonder and he looked very disappointed when I said you weren't back until the beginning of September.'

'Beth! He's not my type. He's way too serious.'

'Ooh . . . too serious is bad now, is it? Luke's growing on you, isn't he?'

'He's a nice guy and we're having a good time, that's all. Now, I must go as he's probably waiting for me at the coffee machine. I just wanted to check in.'

'Aww . . . it's nice to know you're missing me.' She giggles.

'I feel like I've been away forever and there are moments when I get a little homesick. I bet the garden at my cottage is bursting with colour. Still, I left it in good hands. My neighbour, Roger, will be in there every single day, watering. Right, we'll speak soon. Enjoy the rest of your day!'

Luke is standing by the van chatting to someone, a takeaway coffee in each hand. I hurry over to him as he bids a fellow traveller a safe journey.

'Sorry, I gave Beth a quick call,' I explain. 'I'm guessing that man is a VW enthusiast?' The van does attract a lot of attention wherever we go.

'He said I was driving around in his dream vehicle,' Luke replies, sounding pensive. There's a fleeting look in his eyes that causes him to furrow his brow.

'I bet a lot of people would love to swap places and drive around in Reba for a day, let alone two months,' I acknowledge.

Luke nods his head as he hands me a coffee, and we get ourselves settled in for the next leg of the journey. But his mood is suddenly very sombre, and it takes a while to wear off. Why on earth would that comment unsettle him? It's not like he's stolen Reba, he's borrowed her for a while. No doubt someone owed him a huge favour and being in the IT business, I bet he has a few of those to call in.

We drive through several small villages and we're feeling hungry now. Most of the little shops we see are closed and everything has that lazy, Sunday feel. Eventually, we approach a crossroads and I point to a folded chalkboard perched on one corner.

'There's a café!' I point, and Luke immediately slows down.

'It looks a bit . . . shabby.'

I shrug my shoulders, nonchalantly. 'The paintwork, yes, but what glorious hanging baskets. Anyone who looks after their plants cares about the small things. I'm up for it, if you are. I'm starving.'

'Judging by the size of the rough bit of ground next to it, I'd say this is the equivalent of a transport café back home. It'll be rustic inside.'

'That's the fun of being on the road.'

I'm sure his intention was to drive in and then straight back out, but he merely shrugs his shoulders as we park up.

It's an old building on the corner of a four-ways crossroads. Today's a scorcher, and as we stand here, the cars and lorries driving by throw up dust from the road. Yes, the wooden windows have been painted and repainted many times over, and are peeling a little in places, but the panes of glass sparkle.

Luke walks over to the A-framed chalkboard sitting on the pavement and reels off the *menu du jour*.

'I got chef's terrine, some sort of beef with green beans and then crème brûlée, is that right?'

'Spot on. What do you think?'

'OK, let's do this.'

We push open the front door and enter a narrow passageway. It feels like we're walking into someone's home, and I wonder if there's another entrance we haven't spotted. There's another half-glass panelled door, and when we open it, we're surprised to see a room full of tables of various sizes and shapes, and most of them are full. The buzz of conversation stops for a few seconds when we enter, before it returns to normal.

Luke leans in to whisper in my ear. 'Obviously this is where the locals come to eat, so the food will be just fine.'

An older woman dressed all in black comes bustling towards us. She talks fast and her accent is thick. There's some back-and-forth conversation with Luke and she beckons us over to a table for two, on the far side of the room.

It's a restaurant with a difference; there are family pictures hanging up on the walls and a large display cabinet with a whole array of different pieces of china. Probably family treasures collected over many years. It's like being invited into someone's house and anyone is welcome.

The woman gives us a warm smile as she indicates for us to take a seat. She says something about wine and Luke nods his head, rewarding her with one of his best smiles. Then she hurries away.

'The wine is included in the price,' he informs me. 'She asked if we wanted to see the wine list, but I thought she might be offended if I refused the house wine.'

We both gaze around, and everyone has the same carafe on their tables, no one has bottled wine. The woman returns with a large pitcher of water and a generously sized carafe. From behind her a younger man steps forward, placing an empty plate down in front of each of us.

'*Merci*,' I mutter. He says something very fast that I don't catch. I watch as they both walk back through the swing doors into the kitchen and spot an old woman standing in front of a huge range cooker stirring a pot. She waves her other hand in the air, directing someone I can't see to do something.

'What did he say?' I ask Luke, as he starts to pour the wine.

'Only that the entrée is on the way. They're just waiting for the bread to come out of the oven. I'm going to water my wine down, as I'm driving.'

All around us the background chatter is rather nice, it

feels homely. We're the only non-French-speaking people here by the sound of it and yet, aside from the stares when we first entered, I'm really comfortable.

Luke raises his glass, and we chink. 'Happy Sunday, and *bon appétit*!'

'I hope so.' I gingerly take a sip. 'Hmm . . . not bad. A robust and fruity red wine. I'd be happy if I'd paid a tenner for a bottle of this in my local supermarket.'

Luke's eyes light up as he looks over my shoulder. 'Uh-oh . . . you wait until you see what's coming.'

The young man is back and he's carrying a large wooden platter at shoulder height. He approaches the table and lowers it so it's within reach. He indicates for Luke to serve himself and they exchange a little conversation. I have never seen such a large block of pâté before. It's obviously been made in a deep dish, and it stands about six inches high. About a quarter of it is gone and Luke picks up a large palette knife to cut off a slice. He eases it onto his plate, then hands it over to me and I pass him mine.

Our waiter seems pleased as I stare down at it. 'I'm not sure I can eat all this.'

Luke thanks our waiter and then grins across the table at me. 'Oh, I'm sure you'll manage. It looks and smells amazing. It's wild boar, with cognac. The bread and home-made onion chutney are on the way.'

I take another sip of wine. 'I'm so glad we stopped here. I love the ambience. It's the equivalent of going out for a Sunday roast to my favourite pub. Surrounded by a crowd of regulars, good food and a decent wine, what more could you ask for?'

Luke reaches out across the table to interlace his fingers with mine, just as the woman comes back with a dish of chutney and a wooden board with a roughly cut baguette.

She smiles down at us, apologising for the interruption as she makes space for it on the table and then leaves us to it. Now that's what I call service. What was it Erin said to

Luke . . . something about good waiting staff make it look easy. And they know when to disappear.

We eat, laugh and enjoy what may well turn out to be the most memorable lunch of the entire trip.

Luke

14

Living in the Moment

Only with Freya could lunch at a rough-and-ready roadside café turn into a romantic meal for two.

As we lingered over dessert and coffee, several of our fellow diners wanted to chat, asking where we were from and where we were going. My French is good but there are times I struggle a bit, as often people talk faster than my brain can process the words. But natives also like to demonstrate that they can speak a little English, and one man assumed English people also understand German, which I don't. Freya came to the rescue there, telling me that at school she switched languages after the first year. I did wonder why her French was rather limited. She went on to say that she did a foreign exchange trip with a student who lived in Cologne. It was her first time abroad.

What a fun day it's been so far, and as we near our destination I'm getting rather excited at the thought of staying somewhere I haven't been before. It's a while since I veered off the beaten track, as they say. Every summer for the last seven years has been more or less the same routine. It's always flexible, as when you're helping friends out there are often last minute changes. Like this year, with Zoe expecting a baby; that was a real surprise and added a little pressure.

'You've gone very quiet,' Freya remarks.

'I love driving and the roads over here are easy. I think

we're probably only ten minutes away from our destination. Could you go online and look up the website for Château des Sources? It's near a place called Millau. If it's in the middle of a town, they might not have parking on site. If they do, maybe just put in the name and see what comes up.'

'No problem.'

She sounds happy and carefree. The Freya I first met at the gym was so intense that I thought twice about even approaching her. She was focused on getting in there, doing her thing, and getting out. Like it was some sort of punishment. When, after numerous attempts to get her to chat, she told me what she did for a living, I could understand why she was stressed. It was the way she spoke about it. She didn't just have a job, her job was her reason for being, it made her who she was.

For a while, we were stuck at the exchanging an awkward little smile every time our paths crossed stage and a casual 'Hi, how are you doing today?' But as the weeks went on, it progressed a little into 'How was your weekend?' Her response was usually something to do with gardening and mine was often beach related. However, the first serious question she asked me was, 'What do you do for a living?' It was huge, because it meant she was interested. I simply said I was self-employed.

I remember how her eyes had flickered over my face, curious about what I did, but feeling it was rude to ask. 'I'm in IT,' I'd blurted out, breaking the awkward silence.

'Oh, right. I guess that field lends itself to being a contractor, once you know what you're doing. Who have you worked for in the past?'

It was then that I realised she was a conformist. 'I've never had a permanent salaried job, I worked as a temp for a while. I dropped out of uni during my first year and just wanted to get hands-on and gain some experience. Then I did a bit of coding for someone, and they recommended me to a friend, and my business sort of grew from there.'

I remember the look of shock on her face and, for some reason, I felt I had to explain myself.

'I love surfing, and being a free agent allows me to work as, and when, I please.'

At that point she said she had to go, as she was meeting up with a friend. I feared it was just an excuse to cut our conversation short and I was in danger of blowing what might turn out to be the only chance I'd get to make a real impression. 'The only rules I follow are the ones that keep me out of trouble; I always pay my taxes and my bills on time, but I don't set an alarm clock every morning, and I don't stick to a set timetable. Only the timing of the tides.' But my attempt at injecting a little humour seemed to throw her into a state of confusion, and I knew it was time to shut up. I've never been glib when it comes to chatting someone up and it's fair to say that my nerves were jangling like windchimes that day.

Although it was obvious from the beginning that there was an attraction between us, it was a while until we spoke again, as she seemed to be purposely avoiding me. I did consider returning to Cornwall early. It was just my luck to feel that spark with someone who makes to-do lists and sticks to a rigid routine. I thought that was a waste, so I hung in there and it paid off. The woman I'm with now is radically different to the one who sat next to me when our trip began and it's hard not to fall madly in love with her. I could . . . and I think I am scoring some points, but she deserves a man who has it all sussed. Unfortunately, I'm still figuring it out and making stupid mistakes along the way.

'Luke, this place is unbelievable!' Freya bursts out. 'Seriously, it's quite something and there is parking on site, plenty of it too, as it's set in vast woodlands.' Freya continues scrolling through the website. 'It's a twelfth-century medieval castle that has been turned into a top-class hotel. Have you heard of the Millau Viaduct?'

I shake my head. 'No, can't say I have.'

'Well, apparently it offers a superb view of it, and the foothills of the Tarn Valley and the Larzac Plateau. There's a lounge/library, a billiards room and a gym. And the main restaurant is in a cave beneath the original castle.'

I slow down and take the next turning on the right. Seconds later we spot the sign for the hotel. Around us there's a hamlet of charming stone houses. I ease the van up a rather steep cobbled incline and pull into a generously sized car park nestled between two old stone buildings.

'There's a sign with an arrow saying Reception,' Freya points out.

'Let's leave everything in the van and check it out first.'

As we begin walking, ahead of us is a lawned area and beyond that a huge swathe of trees. When we turn the corner, we get our first glimpse of the front of what is a rather stately castle, with a square stone tower and a parapet. Behind us, what I thought was the side wall of a stone barn, turns out to be an old church; it even has a bell tower with a beautiful spire. In front of us, the main building is rectangular and beyond that there's a newer, more contemporary addition that's set back.

'Wow! I wasn't expecting anything this grand,' I admit.

'The castle has all the character of a medieval building, but it doesn't have an overbearing feeling, does it?' Clearly Freya is entranced, as she draws to a halt to soak up the ambience.

'No. There's a nice feel to the place.'

'I think the fact that it's spread out is why it's so charming. Usually, castles have courtyards surrounded by high walls. I'm sure it was like that once upon a time and this area might have housed the stables.'

I know exactly what she means. I've often wondered with old castles whether it was as much about keeping people contained, as it was about keeping intruders out.

The cobbled area, which runs along the entire length of the series of buildings, abuts rolling lawns now interspersed with a whole variety of specimen trees. There's a collection of white cast iron tables and chairs, with pale coffee-coloured umbrellas shading them from the sunshine. But it's the prolific climbers growing against the castle walls, and the riot of colours in the many flower beds, which creates such a wonderful atmosphere.

Freya reaches out for my hand, leaning her head against my shoulder.

'I could happily sit here all day drinking coffee, reading a book and just relaxing.'

I glance down at her, as she stares up at me, wistfully. 'Then that's just what we'll do. Come on, let's check in.'

'Can you believe this?' Freya is sprawled across the queen-size bed, which faces out onto the gardens.

We're on the first floor so the view is amazing, and we even have a balcony with stone pillars. I grin at Freya as I pop a coffee pod into the machine on a small table in the corner. 'I was expecting it to be a little dark and dingy inside, the contemporary decor is a real surprise.'

Two of the walls are bare stone. The headboard wall is made up of dark-coloured copper tiles, with a hint of a green patina to them. The bedding is white, as is the wall opposite the bed, and I'm guessing we have one of the superior rooms.

'It's handy that the owner, Catherine, Erin and Daphne, all know each other,' I laugh. 'I doubt we'd have stumbled across this place but for their generosity. I was thinking of finding a campsite for our little break.'

Freya sits up, leaning against the headboard. 'Really? You mean sleeping in the van?'

I glance at her, pointedly. 'With facilities on the doorstep, obviously.'

She rubs her hands over the crisp white duvet cover, looking very happy indeed. 'Well, I thought it was going to be hard to beat a manor house and an awesome château but this is something else, so I'm not complaining.'

'Shall we take our coffee out onto the balcony?'

Freya didn't mention the cottage at the campsite. I smile to myself as I carry the mugs out through the French doors. I can't wait until she sees our next accommodation. She did warn me at the start that she's a lady who likes her creature comforts. While it's not as basic as the campsite, it's what I call an alternative lifestyle.

'This is bliss,' she says, as she takes a seat. 'It's also making me a little homesick for my garden.'

'I'm sure your neighbours will take good care of it for you.'

'Who's looking after your place?'

'I have an arrangement with my friend Maggie, and her husband. They live just around the corner.'

She grins at me. 'It's their second home, then.'

'I guess it is. Maggie loves the view and she's an obsessive cleaner. I daren't leave anything out, no clutter at all, as she tells me off. You'd like her.'

'Are you saying I'm fussy?'

Oops. 'Hmm . . . not fussy, but you like a place for everything and everything in its place. To be honest, I'm the same.'

'That's—'

'True,' I reply, cutting her short. 'Go and look at the bathroom if you don't believe me. Everything you put in there is lined up neatly on the countertop. You even straightened the few things I put there, and you can't exactly call me messy.'

Freya bursts out laughing. 'I guess I do like things to be aesthetically pleasing. Does it annoy you?'

'No. It makes me want to take you home with me.'

She shakes her head, still laughing. 'Nice try, but I don't intend spending my life picking up after any man.'

'Not even one who brings you to a place like this?' I reply, feigning an air of disappointment.

'I'll reserve my judgement until the trip is over. For all I know, our next stop might be a tent in a field next to the crop we're going to be picking at this farm place you've briefly mentioned.'

I think it's time to change the subject. 'Did you see the menu next to the coffee machine? It sounds wonderful but after our heavy lunch, I'm thinking we save the restaurant for tomorrow night and eat in the bar. What do you think?'

'I'm so glad you suggested that. It'll be more relaxing, too, for our first evening here. Anyway, what do you think of that view?'

'Breathtaking.'

We sit in silence for a while, gazing off into the distance beyond the gardens and the park. Breathing in the heavily scented air from the lavender bushes below the balcony, we're looking out over the vast Tarn valley. It has that lush, verdant look of an agricultural area, beyond which the foothills of the incredible limestone Larzac Plateau loom up. After a while I pop back inside to fetch a little booklet giving all the information about the château.

'The gorges were formed in the Jurassic period by the sinking of an ocean, imagine that! As for the castle, Henry II built it in the twelfth century as a place to live. Oh . . . even the bar is rather grand by the sounds of it. It's a vaulted stone room formerly known as the Guards' Room. I bet it could tell some tales.

Freya wrinkles her forehead. 'On the website it said the restaurant is in a cave beneath the castle. That's not a euphemism for a former dungeon, is it? Does it say anything about that?'

I scan the pages, shrugging my shoulders. 'Not that I can see. We can ask Catherine this evening. Anyway, I'm here to protect you, even from ghosts.' When I start chuckling, I can see that Freya isn't appreciating my sense of humour.

I glance through the doors and that bed looks cool and inviting. We've an hour or two until dinner, so my mind goes off on a totally different tangent. And who could blame me, because as much as I try, I can't fight my feelings for Freya. It's fast becoming hard not to say what I'd like to say out loud . . . that every single day I fall a little more in love with her, when I didn't even think that was possible.

It's obvious to me that the timing isn't right. It may never be right and that's a scary thought. I'm living my life one day at a time; it's all I can handle right now, but that's not the way to impress a woman like Freya and I know it. I need a master plan for the future, and something tells me that I'll only have one chance to get it right.

When we enter the impressive bar, Catherine is on the phone. The barman is busy serving a French couple and when she puts the receiver down, Catherine hurries over to us.

'How is your room?' she enquires.

'Absolutely amazing,' Freya answers, readily. 'It's the perfect blend of the old and the new. You have some wonderful pieces of furniture here, Catherine.'

'That's down to Yves' family. It's taken them three generations to seek out little treasures to complement what has been an ongoing process of restoration. What can I get you to drink?'

I look straight at Freya. 'Something from a local vineyard?' she suggests.

'Perfect! I suggest a bottle of the Côtes de Millau. It's medium bodied and smooth, with an earthy undertone and notes of blackberry. Are you eating here tonight?'

'Yes,' I confirm. 'But as we had a heavy lunch it'll be a light meal. Can we also book a table for the restaurant in the cave for tomorrow night at seven thirty?'

'Consider that done. You can either eat in here tonight, or on the terrace along the rampart.'

Freya's eyes light up. 'Outside would be lovely.'

'Ah, here he is! Yves, come and meet Freya and Luke!'

A distinguished-looking guy, with flecked grey hair, walks towards us. He shakes my hand firmly, then leans in to kiss Freya on both cheeks.

'Welcome. Is good to meet friends of great friends!'

I can see how entranced Freya is, not least by that warm accent of his. An English guy doesn't stand a chance next to someone as suave as Yves.

'They're eating on the terrace; can you take them up and I'll follow with the drinks and the menus.'

'It will be my pleasure. This way.'

We chat as we walk, and I ask Yves about his family's connection to the castle.

'My great-grandfather sold off his inheritance to move here, after falling in love with the woman he called his angel. She lived here with her parents, but it was not in a good state. Now it is a place to be proud of and Catherine and I are lucky to be able to continue his good work.'

It's hard not to be touched by his words and it's clear to see it means a lot to him.

'Here, you have the best view of all. The Millau Viaduct is at the heart of the Aveyron department,' he informs us, proudly. 'It spans the river Tarn and is taller than the Eiffel Tower!'

The view of the viaduct is unimpeded, and it is a spectacle. It's a very unusual design, but the simplicity and symmetry of it doesn't look at odds with the vast rolling countryside and curves of the huge valley below it. It rests on seven rather slender-looking pillars and the cables above them look like the elegant sails on a yacht.

'How long is it, Yves?'

'Two point four kilometres. It is the final link of the A75 highway, which goes from Paris to Barcelona. It was opened in 2004 and won an award a year later.'

Catherine comes bustling towards us.

'Do you want me to pour?' She checks, but I shake my head.

'No, we're fine, thank you.'

'Here are the menus and someone will pop back shortly to take your order.'

Yves bids us, '*Bon appétit!*'

Catherine turns her attention to us. 'Wine doesn't come any more authentic than this. The labour is all done by hand due to the rough terrain and numerous streams that run through the vineyard. And it doesn't break the bank. Enjoy!'

It's time to peruse the menu, but first a toast.

'Here's to a wonderful break!' I raise my glass and Freya raises hers, giving a chink and then taking a sip.

'Hmm . . . this isn't bad.' I give it a swirl in the glass, breathing in the heady aroma and then taking a second slurp. 'I'm picking up a hint of cherries and cranberries. What about you?'

Freya looks at me as if I'm mad. 'It's smooth and it tastes nice.'

I give her a pointed look.

'I thought you were the expert now? Hmm . . . it's a bit . . . earthy, maybe? Whatever, it's really drinkable.'

We exchange a mirthful glance.

'I didn't know you were a wine buff,' she remarks.

'I'm not a wine snob. But I've had a few glasses in my time. For an affordable wine this isn't bad. What I love is that Catherine and Yves support local winegrowers – that's so important.'

'You're thinking of Frédéric, aren't you? The two of you spent quite a bit of time together.'

'We did. It's a pity he doesn't know Yves, I must mention that to Erin. Frédéric has taken on a huge amount of responsibility and the worrying thing is that Iris has no idea what shape the vineyard's finances are in. I took a look at their website and made a few suggestions, which he's going to look into.'

'Like?'

'Reaching out to local hotels and restaurants. Offering them special discounts to stock the château's wines and starting a monthly blog.'

Freya looks at me quizzically. 'How will that help?'

'People are interested in the process of winemaking and a monthly diary of what goes on at the vineyard is informative. But to make it fun, I suggested they could include tips about which wines go best with what dishes, and maybe even share a few local recipes. But equally as important will be featuring any new sales outlets by way of a quid pro quo to spread the word.'

She nods her head in agreement. 'Ah, like the website here has links to some of their food and wine suppliers, and tourist attractions in the area?'

'Precisely! Now, I don't know about you, but I'm actually beginning to feel a little hungry.'

But Freya is studying my face quite intently. I think I just might have succeeded in impressing her. 'It was common sense to me, but Frédéric was quite excited and couldn't wait to talk to Sabine about it. It turns out she's not new to social media and he thought it was something she'd love to throw herself into.'

'The thing with common sense,' Freya says, giving me a heartfelt smile that sets my pulse racing, 'is that it's often experience based. The fact he hadn't already thought of that means you've opened his eyes to a new opportunity. That's what an entrepreneur does, they see things that other people don't always notice.'

Just when I think my cause is lost, Freya says something that makes me believe she's not writing me off. Today has been a memorable one and it's given me hope.

August

Freya

15

A Reason to Celebrate!

What an enjoyable week it's been just doing as we please. Travelling around in Reba to see the sights has been like a mini trip all on its own. But it's been leisurely, and in between Luke and I have spent plenty of time sitting out on the terrace enjoying the sunshine and being in nature. The gardens are a sheer joy and it's a long time since I can recall seeing so many butterflies, which constantly catch my eye.

I've been content to sit and read, but Luke's been glued to his laptop. He's very intense when he's online and I half wonder whether periods of enforced digital detox over the past few weeks means he's getting withdrawal symptoms.

There are times when I miss the people I work with and I find myself occasionally wondering whether any of my prospective purchasers have found the perfect property. Particularly clients who moved out of their homes into temporary accommodation and are growing weary as the search seems endless. It's like finding a partner, it has to be the right one. If they haven't succeeded, I know it won't be due to a lack of effort on the part of Beth, or Ethan.

Tonight is our last night at Château des Sources. We're dining in the restaurant here again, as the last two evenings we ventured into Creissels to eat. The food was fine, but not quite up to par with the marvellous cuisine here.

I turn the final page of the book I'm reading and place it down on the table. Luke is sitting opposite me, and the movement immediately makes him look up.

'You've finished it?'

'Yes. I'm always a bit sad when a story ends. It often leaves me wanting to know what happened next, even when there's a happy ending.'

'On to the next one, then.'

'I only brought one paperback with me. You said we were travelling light, remember?'

'We are. The van can only hold so much.' He gives me an apologetic smile.

'My tablet has a whole library of eBooks, but it's a holiday thing for me. An indulgence. There's something about turning a page, rather than flicking right.'

We both give a chuckle.

'It feels like I've been flicking right all my life,' he states. 'The last physical book I touched was in school, probably.'

Luke's phone pings, and then pings again. He gives it a cursory glance, rolls his eyes, then places it back down on the table. 'Does this mean you're bored? Do you want to jump in the pool?'

'No. I'm quite happy to sit and watch you.' He gives me a nervous look. 'What are you doing?'

'Nothing much. Just work.'

'Work?' I thought he might be playing a game.

'A friend had a problem that I can fix remotely.'

'It seems to me that most of your clients are friends. Do you have any actual paying customers?' I'm pulling his leg, but his face gets serious.

'Course I do! I'm good at this IT lark. I thought you'd gathered that by now.'

'What do you enjoy most about it?'

'The variety, I suppose. Programming and coding is serious stuff and time-consuming, but it's satisfying. Fixing problems is usually quite basic by comparison.'

'Basic for you, but not for the people with the problems,' I remind him.

'Yes. Most problems can be solved by simply getting on the net and doing a bit of research but some, what I refer to as *users*, are concerned that they'll lose their files or get the dreaded black screen of death. You should read the texts I send out. I bet four out of five of them simply say *do a restart*, or if it's stuck in a loop *switch it off at the wall and fire it up again*.'

'Oh, so when you're texting it's work, not play?' I say that teasingly, but I did wonder as he does get quite a few messages. As if to prove a point, his phone pings again.

'Aren't you going to check that?'

'No. It's not a client.'

'Is that a guilty look I see on your face?'

Luke's eyebrows shoot up. 'If you must know, it's family stuff.'

Now I feel awful for messing with him. 'Sorry, I didn't mean to pry. If you want some privacy, I'll go for a walk,' I offer.

'It's not anything to worry about. It's just . . . it's my birthday so I'll get a few more of these.'

My hands fly up to my face. 'Luke! Many happy returns. Why didn't you tell me?'

'Because you would have made a fuss, like you're doing now. I don't celebrate birthdays. It's not a big deal.'

'That's a sad way of looking at it.'

He shakes his head at me, as if I'm being predictable. 'I always think it's the mothers who should receive the congratulations, for bringing their offspring into the world. That series of pings was my mum thanking me for the flowers I sent her. She always does, but she knows better than to say the dreaded words to me, so she just adds "HBMS".'

HBMS . . . ah, happy birthday my son. Aww, that's so sweet of them both.

'And your dad?'

'He never remembers anyone's birthday except his own.

I usually remind him of Mum's, and their anniversaries. That's probably why she hasn't divorced him yet.' He gives me a wink, so I assume it's a joke.

'I would have bought you a present if I'd known.'

'That's exactly why I didn't tell you.'

'Dinner is on me tonight and we'll crack open a bottle of champagne,' I declare.

'You don't have to do that; we're going halves on the food and drinks, remember? It's no big deal to me.'

'No, I insist. There is one positive thing I can say about it,' I state firmly, unable to stop myself from grinning.

'I know you're going to tell me, even if I don't ask.'

'Today you're only eight years younger than me, until my birthday, of course. It doesn't sound quite as big a gap as nine, does it?'

'Stop teasing!' he retorts, laughing. 'Eight, nine . . . what does it matter?'

'Because I believe they're the most formative years of your life. You hit adulthood and for some people it can take the whole of your twenties to discover who you are and what you want out of life.'

'Ah! You're telling me that at the grand old age of what . . . thirty-four isn't it, that you have it all sussed out now? Did it cross your mind that I might, actually, be an early developer, and I've cracked it already?'

'You can't even keep a straight face as you say that, Luke! I'm being honest here. I think the last four or five years of my life have been a real turning point for me. I set myself a series of goals, like buying the cottage and throwing myself into work. Suddenly I stopped measuring myself up against other people and focused instead on the things that make me happy.'

He looks surprised. 'Why didn't you just do that in the first place?'

I tilt my head back, in serious thinking mode. 'Most of my friends, including Beth, are married. Some have kids and more than one. A lot have drifted away, because we don't have anything in common any longer. When I woke up and realised that I don't need someone else in my life to make me feel complete, it was liberating.'

'That's when you stopped dating and why at first you tried to freeze me out?'

'Ooh . . . that's a little harsh. You were just a tad annoying. I go to the gym because it helps combat stress, not to rekindle my social life. It's also why I don't do dating apps or let my friends arrange dinner dates for me anymore.'

'But I talked my way into your life, anyway, didn't I?'

'You did. Persistence pays off and maybe our paths crossed for a reason. And this little adventure is it.'

Luke looks off into the distance. 'Wouldn't it be wonderful if life could be one permanent road trip?'

'Goodness no; that would be awful. I miss the cottage and my garden, and everyone in my life.'

He narrows his eyes and I find myself holding my breath, wondering what's coming next.

'But you've got me, well, for another four weeks at least. And I'm an addictive distraction, admit it.'

How can I resist that cheeky smile, and it is his birthday, after all. 'You're growing on me, that I can't deny. Can I change my mind about a dip in the pool, or do you want to finish off what you're working on?'

He snaps the lid of his laptop shut. 'I'm all yours, whenever you want me, you only have to say.'

Oh, Luke. My world would stifle you, and your world would drive me mad. But we're already over halfway through our time together and I'm determined to enjoy every single moment we have left. A bit like one's first love, you never really forget it . . . except that mine was when I was only seven years old. When I bumped into him many years later, I was so glad he dumped me for my best friend at the time. It turns out that as grown-ups we have absolutely nothing in common. Maybe that's why I'm a realist when it comes to making someone a permanent part of my life. It has to be a forever thing, or not at all. And how can anyone be sure of that?

As I'm sitting in front of the mirror blow-drying my hair, my phone pings. It's a text from Beth with a photograph of a magnificent bouquet of flowers. Puzzled, I turn off the hairdryer and call her.

'Hey, you. Gorgeous flowers, it's not your anniversary . . . is it?' It's not her birthday as that's next month, I'm hardly likely to forget it.

'No. They're for you, silly! Mr and Mrs Pierson got the keys to their new home this afternoon. They don't know that you won't be back until the end of the month. What do you want me to do?'

'Oh no . . . I have their email address, so I'll drop them a line to say thanks and congratulations. I just won't mention that I'm still on my travels. I'm thrilled for them, though. And how are you?'

'Reeling,' Beth sighs.

My pulse quickens. 'Why? What's wrong?'

'David has decided he wants us to look for another fixer-upper. We've only just finished renovating this house and he wants us to start all over again! Seriously, it's just nice to have the place to ourselves again. All those trades traipsing through; no dust, no dirt . . . it's peaceful.' She sounds miffed.

'Can't you talk him out of it?'

'I'm trying. But given how fussy he is, there's nothing I know of that would catch his eye, so maybe by the time he finds the perfect project, I'll be ready too. Anyway, how about you? Have you moved on again?'

'Tonight's our last night at the castle and it's a special dinner as it's Luke's birthday, but I only found out this afternoon.'

'Your toy boy is growing up,' she laughs, rather uncharitably. 'What's that saying . . . another year older, another year wiser. He's catching up!'

'Beth, it goes two ways. It won't be long before I'm celebrating reaching my mid-thirties. It's a sobering thought, as forty is now clearly on the horizon.'

She guffaws. 'Freya, five years is a long time. Think back to your thirtieth birthday and everything that has happened since then. You've packed in a lot of living and a lot of achievements. You're in a whole new place and I bet way back then you couldn't have guessed where you'd be at now.'

'You mean touring around France in a VW van with a handsome young man, like I'm some sort of cougar taking a break from real life?'

She bursts out laughing. 'I wouldn't have put it quite like that, but the answer is a well-meaning – because it's just what you need – *yes*! Where are you heading next?'

'A farm near the village of Saint-Laurent-de-Céris.'

'What part of France is that?' Beth's interest in our travels makes me wonder whether she's getting the travel bug. It's much more exciting than booking a package holiday.

'The Charente department. The nearest city is Limoges.'

'Ah, right. Gosh, this trip you're on is covering quite a distance.'

'Yes, and we're going back on ourselves . . . well, sort of, but further west.'

Beth giggles. 'I'm guessing Luke will be doing the driving.'

'Yes, although I have been behind the wheel. It's a five-hour-plus drive this time, but we're going to use toll roads for a large part of the journey.'

'It's a pity you don't have time to stop along the way and explore,' she replies, wistfully.

'I know, but we're helping harvest a lot of veggies ready for a special annual market apparently, and Luke promised we'd be there late afternoon tomorrow.'

'Well, wish him a very happy birthday from me and travel safe!'

'Thanks, I'm in good hands. And don't worry about David

and a potential move, we both know it isn't easy finding the right property, so it'll give you time to adjust to the idea.'

'I know . . . these things are sent to try us but he's worth it!'

Now that's a sign of true love.

When I walk into the Guards' Room bar, Luke is sitting at a table nattering away to Catherine. It isn't until I'm a few footsteps away that he spots me out of the corner of his eye. He jumps up out of his seat and stands there, gazing at me with a silly grin on his face.

'At last, but my . . . it was worth the wait.'

Despite the fact that Catherine is standing there watching, he leans in to plant a quick kiss on my mouth.

As he steps back, she gives a little laugh, handing him a napkin from the wicker basket in the crook of her arm to wipe off a trace of my lipstick.

'Oops,' he says, smiling.

'Your table in the restaurant is ready if you want to head down there,' she confirms. 'I can't believe it's your last evening. You will return at some point in the future, won't you?'

Luke immediately responds. 'Whenever we're back in France together we'll make sure it's on our agenda, Catherine.'

Luke's diplomatic answer is so typical of him; why not just say it's unlikely if he feels uncomfortable admitting we're enjoying one fun summer together before we go our separate ways?

Her eyes light up as I join in. 'It's been a wonderful week, truly wonderful. If any friends, or customers of mine, are heading to France I'll be pointing them in your direction.'

Catherine's cheeks start to colour up. 'Aww . . . thank you, Freya. And the two of you have been good for business.' She smiles.

'We have?' Luke questions.

'Whenever anyone sees a couple who are obviously madly in love with each other, it sets the scene. Hearts melt and it often encourages them to rekindle their own spark if it's started to fade a little. Now off you go, have a truly wonderful evening.'

She turns on her heels to finish laying the tables, leaving both Luke and me speechless as we make our way out onto the cobbled terrace at the front.

We walk hand in hand in companionable silence, neither of us knowing quite what to say. The chemistry between us is undeniable but love is about so much more than that. Beth was right, I do have a mental tick list because what happens when that initial spark does begin to fade? If that's all two people have in common, it's never going to last.

We follow a narrow path around to the side of the building and, on turning the corner, the gradient falls away quite sharply. Luke slips his arm in mine.

The cave is hewn into the rocky ground beneath the castle and despite my fears about it having been a dungeon, Yves told us that it was formerly a storage area for wine and food. The temperature inside remains constant all year round. On entering, it's a pleasant relief from the muggy, sticky heat of the evening.

'*Bonsoir!*' Our favourite waiter, Jules, hurries forward to greet us as we enter the small foyer. 'How was your day?'

'Good, thank you. Very relaxing before our long road trip tomorrow.'

He looks at me, pulling a sad face. 'Ah, your last meal with us, but tonight's menu is very special indeed. Come, let me show you to your table.'

Instead of taking us into the main part of the cave, we follow him into a smaller alcove off to one side. It's really a series of cave rooms; overhead the arched ceilings have been lined with bricks, the stone walls are painted white, and the floor is made up of irregularly shaped limestone tiles.

Jules pulls out a chair for me, then disappears and Luke looks at me, puzzled.

'I asked for a quiet table tonight and chef is going to prepare you a special birthday meal!'

He rolls his eyes at me. 'I told you, it's not a big deal for me but . . . thanks, Freya.'

'It's the thought that counts, and as I don't have a present for you, I want you to know how grateful I am to be here to celebrate this day with you.'

On cue, as if he'd been waiting in the wings, Jules reappears with a wine bucket and places it next to the table. He wraps a white linen napkin around the neck of the champagne bottle and eases out the cork with quite a pop. Jules very deftly grabs a fluted glass to capture the first of the bubbles. When I glance across at Luke, the light from the candles lined up on the table flicker over his face, and happiness seems to radiate out from him. For a man who doesn't like celebrating his birthday, he seems rather content to me.

As Jules melts into the background, we raise our glasses to meet in the middle and I give Luke a nod of my head. 'I think you should make the toast tonight.'

'Oh, right . . . um . . . well . . . let me see . . .'

There are moments when he looks so vulnerable, and this is one of them.

'It doesn't have to be anything clever, or prophetic,' I reassure him.

He clears his throat, nervously. 'Then I'll just say that as far as birthdays go, this is the best one ever. Sitting opposite a beautiful woman, in a cave dating back many hundreds of years and sipping champagne, I can honestly say that it doesn't get any better than this!'

As we chink glasses, a momentary stab of pain in my chest makes me realise that his words have gone straight to my heart. I draw in a deep breath, feeling a sudden wave of sadness wash over me. This can't surely be the highlight of his birthdays. What about the celebrations he's had with his family and friends? And then it hits me. For whatever reason, Luke doesn't feel worthy . . . but of what? Love? What happened in his past to make him undermine himself in that way? I wonder.

Two waiters approach us, and I welcome the interruption because I have no words to express how I feel; this is a happy occasion and it's time to live in the moment, which is precisely what Luke is doing.

As a plate is laid in front of me, the waiter talks so fast that I hardly catch anything he says. Fortunately, the other one realises my French isn't that good.

'Tonight, you have seared diver-caught scallops, with a watercress velouté, brown shrimps, anchovy and dill. Enjoy!'

It looks amazing on the plate, the creamy velouté sauce is drizzled over the beautifully pan-fried, seared scallops and the accompaniments add both colour and texture.

'Wow! This almost looks too good to eat,' Luke quips, but he's soon tucking in.

As I put the first forkful into my mouth, my taste buds explode. The scallops are divine, the caramelised buttery brown coating giving it a distinctly nutty flavour. Chef Raymond was so accommodating when I explained that tonight was a special occasion and asked if he was happy to recommend some of his favourite dishes. He simply told me to leave it to him and, oh my, is he giving us a gastronomic treat.

Luke is about to top up our champagne glasses, just as Jules appears to take away our empty plates.

'Ah, *non*!' His hand flies up in the air as he gives Luke an apologetic look. 'Chef has chosen your wine for the next course. I will be back shortly.'

Luke sits there grinning at me. 'I feel like an honoured guest,' he chuckles.

'Tonight, that's precisely what you are!'

He slides his hand across the table, and we intertwine our fingers. Overhead, the inset twinkly lights add to the romantic setting.

Jules returns, presenting the bottle to Luke who reads out the label. 'Corton-Bressandes Grand Cru 2019. I believe that was a good year, please thank Chef on our behalf.'

Jules pours a little wine into the large, bowled glasses and waits for Luke to take a sip, but he indicates for me to do the honours.

'Freya is the wine expert,' he insists, trying hard not to smirk.

Jules turns to look at me and I swirl the wine in the glass as Iris showed me and sniff appreciatively, before taking a sip and letting it coat the inside of my mouth.

'Excellent choice!'

They both smile at me but when Jules is out of sight, I give Luke a knowing look. 'You've never even heard of this wine, have you?'

'No, but it would have been rude not to appear impressed, although I knew you'd do a much better job of tasting it than I would. I'd have downed that taster in one.'

It's good to hear his light-hearted laughter and see how much he's enjoying himself.

When our main course arrives, to my utmost surprise Chef Raymond is a few paces behind the waiters. He watches as they place the dishes in front of us and then steps forward.

'I 'ope this will meet with your approval. It is dried, aged Charolais beef sirloin with Jerusalem artichoke, cep purée, sauce Bordelaise Grand Cru, lemon verbena and gratin dauphinois. Please to enjoy on your special evening!'

'*Merci beaucoup*, Chef.' Luke stands, offering his hand and the two men shake. '*C'est magnifique.*'

'*Bon appétit!*'

What a wonderful evening it's been. As we wander around the grounds hand in hand to walk off the magnificent meal, we're both full. Having resisted the cheese course, we went straight to dessert. Who can resist a tarte tatin? The caramelised apples accompanied by the crème anglaise was utterly amazing.

'You've spoilt future birthdays for me going forward, you

do know that?' Luke half whispers, as he spins me around so that I'm facing him. We're standing beneath the leafy canopy of the trees, which have probably been here for a hundred years or more; there's a gentle breeze going as night falls and his eyes are full of laughter.

'Why?'

'Because I'll always remember tonight, and nothing can beat it. Absolutely nothing.'

His kiss is gentle, then ardent but we have a bit of walking to do before we head back inside to end a romantic evening in the only way lovers can.

Catherine was right in one way; but the dream will, eventually, end as all dreams do because the reality of everyday life back in the UK will turn this into just a memory. Albeit, one to treasure forever. I know that Luke is feeling that, too.

16

Living Off the Land

Today we're heading back to Limoges, so the five-hour-plus journey is like déjà vu, spotting landmarks I'd noticed on the way to Creissels. Being a Sunday, the smaller roads are a little quieter but even the volume of traffic on the toll roads is running smoothly, as Reba eats up the miles.

We listen to music, sing along to a few of Luke's wonderfully nostalgic and eclectic mix, and even play a very competitive, and argumentative, game of I-spy.

We stop at a boulangerie to grab a baguette and some pains au chocolat, then a small supermarket to pick up a Camembert and a punnet of strawberries; our late lunch is a quick roadside affair sitting in the van with the door open. The next stop is a garage to fuel-up and use their facilities.

When Luke fires up the engine he looks at his watch. 'We're about a fifteen-minute drive away from the farm,' he confirms.

'You've been there before, obviously.'

'Yes, numerous times.'

'Numerous?'

'Sometimes I pop over in the spring, or the autumn to visit them, too.'

I'm expecting him to continue, and when he doesn't, I decide to question him. 'Are they nice people?'

'Lovely, very down-to-earth.'

Honestly, just when I think he's about to open up, he snaps shut tighter than a clam. Now I'm beginning to wonder whether that's not intentional, but a result of working on his own for long periods at a time. 'They're particularly close friends, then.'

'Yes. You're not going to give up questioning me, are you? OK, let me see . . . what would you want to know.' He pauses, glancing briefly at me with his eyes narrowed. 'The farmhouse is quite big and what you'd call rustic. There are bare stone walls in most rooms, creaking wooden floors overhead and big old beams everywhere. It sits in three-plus hectares of land.'

'How rustic is . . . rustic?'

Luke gives a dismissive laugh. 'It's rural living, although they don't have a TV out of personal choice; but they do have Wi-Fi and all mod cons. The room we'll be staying in is very comfortable and there's a shower room and facilities next door. It's not exactly basic, if that's what's worrying you.'

'Do I sound concerned?' I reply, indignantly.

'We'll eat well because they live off the land. We're going to help harvest some vegetables and fruits ready for a special annual farmer's market on Tuesday, but I think I already told you that. Oh, and on the actual day, we'll be helping to set up the stall.'

'How long are we staying?'

'Three or four days, probably. I definitely mentioned that. It depends whether there are any larger jobs Warren needs a hand with outside. They have a couple of locals who help out part-time on the farming side and temporary help late August and September. Last year the main task was to finish off building a new greenhouse.'

'It sounds like fun. I might get hands-on with a hammer, then?' I can't suppress a giggle.

'Hmm . . . probably not. Have you ever made jam, or chutney before?'

'No. Why?'

'Vicky is always bottling something or other up to sell, or to see them through the winter months.'

'I can follow instructions and I've always fancied having a go, particularly at making jam, but you need to know what you're doing. And after that?'

'It'll be our final destination for the trip.'

'It's the fourth of August today and if we're only spending a few days at the farm, we'll be spending three whole weeks in the same place. We'll end up heading back home in need of a rest!'

'No, not at all. It won't be physically tiring.' I can see by his expression that he feels relaxed about it. 'For me it's an IT job, which I could possibly have sorted out back in the UK, but for various reasons it's easier for me to do it on site.'

Oh, that's a bit disappointing. 'That's why you said it was going to be a surprise. What will I be doing? Reading and sunbathing?'

'No, you'll be my assistant.'

'I will? You do know that while I use a PC, I have no technical knowledge whatsoever, don't you? I'm what you refer to as a user, which to me sounds a bit derogative.'

He starts laughing, his shoulders beginning to shake. 'I think I've sussed that out, as if you were even remotely interested in the subject, you'd have quizzed me about what exactly I do. It's not meant to be mean, the expression . . . but most people use a PC or a laptop, not so many know how to sort them out when they go wrong.'

'That's OK then.' I'll let him off lightly this time.

'You're constantly on your phone taking photos, so I'm going to put you behind the lens of a proper camera.'

'Really? And that's going to help you . . . how?'

'You'll have to wait and see, but I think it's going to be the perfect ending to a perfect trip. Trust me.' Honestly, if he says that once more . . .

We drive through the small village of Saint-Laurent-de-Céris, and after a couple of miles, Luke slows the van to take a left turn off a dusty, county road. The signpost reads 'La Ferme du Vert Pâturage' and I'm beginning to get excited. I've never stayed at a working farm before, so it's yet another first for me.

We travel for about a mile on a narrow road before driving through an open gateway and onto a curving gravel track. There are a few trees, but it isn't some sort of grand entrance, although it's a pleasant drive up to a series of farm buildings.

'We're here!' Luke announces as he parks between two barns.

I'll be glad to stretch my legs and I am curious as to whether there are animals. I'm not sure how I'd cope around cows and pigs, but as I swing the van door shut all I can hear are birds and ducks.

'It's not a livestock farm, then?' I question.

'No, just ducks, crops and herbs.' Luke reaches out to grab my hand. 'That felt like a long—'

'Luke!' A rather handsome looking man comes striding towards us, throwing his arms around Luke and hugging him like a brother. 'It's good to see you, mate. It's been way too long this time around, but it is what it is. Life, eh?'

Luke stands back to introduce me. 'Freya, this is my good friend, Warren Daniels.'

I extend my hand to shake, but instead he steps forward and gives me a hearty hug. 'Any friend of Luke's is a friend of ours,' he says, with gusto.

'Thank you and it's lovely to be here. What a beautiful place you have.'

Warren raises his eyebrows, his eyes smiling. 'Beautiful but hard work and two extra pairs of hands is really appreciated. Come on, let's head into the kitchen. I'm sure you guys are ready for a nice cold drink. Have you eaten?'

'Yes, but a drink would be heavenly!' I reply, as we walk towards a very pretty, two-storey, stone farmhouse with a lean-to, open-fronted extension to the right-hand side of the property.

It's oozing charm and sits on what is a rather flat landscape. While the front lawn is so large that to me it looks almost like a field, it also feels very private. Some might say isolated. I can't imagine what it's like to live here in winter, as I can't see any sign of neighbours in the vicinity. The two sun loungers, set beneath an enormous apple tree, look like dots on the landscape.

Warren swings open the wooden front door and ushers us into a cosy sitting room. It has two solid oak upright pillars supporting a criss-cross of wooden beams overhead. A log burner sits in a surprisingly modern-looking fireplace with a tiled hearth and the plastered walls are painted white.

We follow him through into a passageway, past a second larger sitting room. I stop for a moment to take a quick peek inside. It has a floor-to-ceiling fireplace that is obviously original, and the room is twice the size of the first room.

'The cloakroom is in there.' Warren points to a door on our right and then we take the second door, stepping into a surprisingly spacious country kitchen.

'Just in time!' The woman, who is probably about my age, rushes over to greet Luke with the same level of enthusiasm as Warren. 'I've just pulled some scones out of the oven. It's Freya, isn't it?'

Goodness, Luke has actually told them about me. 'Yes,' I reply, smiling.

'I'm Vicky. As you've probably already discovered, we're huggers!'

I have no problem with that but it's the sheer delight with which we're being received, that tells me Luke is very close to these two people.

Vicky moves on to give Luke a hug, and they linger for a few moments. She pats him on the shoulder. 'How are you doing?'

'I'm fine. Just fine.'

'Sit down,' she insists. 'Make yourselves at home. Warren,

there's a jug of lemon verbena in the fridge. If you sort the drinks, I'll serve the scones while they're still warm.'

I know we've eaten but who can resist a warm scone?

The two of them bustle around while we settle ourselves down at the huge pine table, which has probably been here for a very long time. Every dent and ding tells a tale of family life both past and present.

'You have such a lovely place,' I remark, eager to make polite conversation.

'It's cool in summer and freezing in winter.' Vicky laughs. 'The land is fertile though and it's been quite an adventure, hasn't it, Warren?'

'You can say that again.' His response sounds a tad jaded.

'Problems?' Luke asks.

'Same old, same old,' Vicky replies.

Warren remains silent as she carries a large platter over to the table. Warren and Luke have at least one thing in common, I muse . . . being oblivious to the fact that people feel awkward when conversations don't flow. It's supposed to be a two-way thing.

Once we're all seated, Vicky passes around some plates and the smell wafting around us is divine. 'Help yourself to cutlery and napkins. These are blueberry scones; in this dish there's strawberry conserve, and this is a lemon jelly. Tuck in.'

Warren is busy filling tumblers from a jug filled with a pale straw-coloured liquid; floating on the top are fresh raspberries and slices of apple.

Luke and I both happily reach for a scone. I cut mine in half and go for the conserve first. It's packed full of fruit and when I take that first bite, it embodies summer. It's not sugary, but naturally sweet from the small berries.

'This,' I state, pointing to my plate, 'is delicious!'

Luke's mouth is too full to speak, but Vicky is grinning from ear to ear.

'She's a good cook,' Warren agrees, as we all look at her.

'But you're the chef, and always will be,' she replies, smiling at him.

'You're a chef?' I ask, rather surprised.

'I was . . . now I'm a farmer.'

Vicky wipes her fingers on a napkin and stares across at her husband. 'Luke will agree with me that it's a waste, Warren. We've built this up from nothing and now someone's interested in buying it from us, this is the chance you've been waiting for.'

Warren mutters a disparaging 'Harrumph.'

'Is this for real?' Luke uncharacteristically blurts out.

'Yes,' Vicky confirms. 'A couple who came to stay with us for a few days while they were looking for a property got very excited when we gave them the tour. They're moving from the UK and want somewhere to set up a business. The moment we mentioned the word "organic" their eyes lit up.'

'It's not an option, Vicky. Setting up a restaurant isn't cheap and there are no guarantees it'll be a success.'

It's obviously a sore point between them and Luke rather diplomatically changes the subject. He's trying to keep the peace and that means he's aware of the issues.

'This drink is very refreshing. What's in it?'

'Water from the well, lemon verbena leaves, and I have one of those carbonator gadgets. The fruit adds a little extra flavour.'

I take a sip and Luke's right; I hate canned drinks and I guess this is the healthy version. 'You could bottle this and sell it!'

Luke has already drained his glass and pours himself another.

'There's so much potential here,' Vicky continues. 'The problem is that everything takes time and money. Just keeping the place ticking over is tough on us both, that's why I'm trying to convince Warren we should consider the offer. This couple are in a position to invest serious money and we'd be cashing out to realise his dream.'

Oh, dear, I walked into that one. Luke very gallantly comes to my rescue.

'Aside from that,' he says, rather gingerly, 'how is this summer's harvest going?'

Both Warren and Vicky start laughing, and the moment of awkwardness has passed. They're a fun couple and even though I know nothing at all about them, it's obvious that they work hard, and that Vicky isn't happy for Warren to give up on his dream.

'Bountiful and there's a lot that needs picking.' Warren's face is expressionless. I would have expected a farmer to have a big smile on his face as he said that, and Warren doesn't.

'I told you that you'd like this room,' Luke says, pointedly, as we lie next to each other on the bed.

I'm smiling and I can't deny that he's right. The second floor of the farmhouse goes up into the eaves, so the ceiling slopes gently on each side of what is a nicely proportioned room. Overhead there's a skylight in each of the sloping parts which let in a huge amount of light. In contrast, the stone walls have a series of tiny box-shaped windows giving glimpses out across the fields, but only if you're lying in bed.

The headboard wall is plastered and painted white; the only features being the three natural stone walls and the gorgeous beams overhead.

'It's simple, rustic living but I'd have been disappointed if it had been modernised and was characterless.'

Admittedly, the shower room next door is small, but it does have a toilet and a sink, and rather bizarrely a washing machine. We have everything we need to be comfortable. It's not exactly living off-grid, but the water comes from a well and they use solar panels; plus, they have a generator.

'Why is Warren so against Vicky's suggestion?' I ask. 'Wasn't it risky coming here in the first place?'

Luke sighs. 'It's complicated.'

'Do you want to enlighten me?'

His eyes are closed and he's pretending to have a nap before dinner.

'I know you're not asleep. Why don't you want to talk about this? I think Vicky was rather hoping you'd be on her side.' That was obvious to me, but clearly not to Luke.

'Does interfering in someone else's life ever have a happy outcome?'

Goodness, that comment takes me by surprise. 'I don't know but Vicky promised me a tour of the site before dinner. What if I unwittingly say the wrong thing? If I can't understand what's going on, how will I avoid doing that? They're a genuinely lovely couple and I'd hate to put my foot in it.'

He rolls over to face me, then eases himself up to lean on his elbow. 'Does the surname ring a bell?'

I look at him blankly, casting my mind back.

'Erin and Max?' I gasp. 'Don't tell me that Warren is their son?'

'Yep.'

I hoist myself up the bed to lean against the headboard. 'Why on earth didn't you warn me?'

'Because I didn't think it was relevant. How was I to know there have been developments since I was last here?'

'You'd better catch me up on what I need to know pretty quickly.' I'm feeling annoyed with him now. He doesn't seem to appreciate what a difficult situation this is and here I am, slap bang in the middle of it, knowing only half the story.

'Sorry. I didn't think it mattered.'

'I'm telling you that it does, so talk to me.'

He groans as he lifts himself up so we're both at eye level.

'Max and Warren had a falling-out three years ago. It was a bad time all round. Erin really misses Vicky. She took a lot of the pressure off her and, even though Max is too stubborn to admit it, the same thing goes for him, too. Not having his son there to back him up is taking a huge toll. This is about nothing more than ego. Warren was fiery, wanting to forge ahead and change the menus; he wanted to experiment. Max is old school in many ways, and they kept butting heads. Warren and Vicky ended up moving out and plunged all their savings into putting a deposit on this place.'

I'm aghast. 'And you didn't think it was important enough to share this with me?'

'I thought Warren and Vicky were happy here. Last summer there wasn't even a hint that they were having second thoughts.'

'Luke, you need to start reading between the lines. It's often what people don't say that is meaningful.'

He looks chastised and rightly so. 'Do they know that Max and Erin are struggling?'

'No, because they haven't talked in a long while. Erin and Max don't even know this is one of my stops.'

I groan out loud and he winces.

'You need to say something, Luke.' He can't stroll through life ignoring the tough bits. It's time to man up.

'I can't.'

'Why?'

'Because neither side will ever trust me again.'

I sit here letting that sink in for a moment. Luke's right. Maybe meddling in other people's affairs is just looking for trouble, but having met them all, it's a sad situation all round.

'I'm not trying to make you feel guilty, and I totally understand where you're coming from—' I give him a sympathetic look '—but this is crazy. People change over the years but if they won't talk to each other, how would any of them know that?'

Luke's frown is deep. 'I can't get involved, Freya, I just can't. What if I ended up making it worse?'

With that, he grabs a towel off the dressing table and disappears into the shower. I let out a deep sigh, my heart feeling heavy. Sometimes being a friend isn't easy and I think this is probably one of those times. In my opinion, it's wrong of Luke to keep Warren in the dark about the fact that his parents are having problems. It's time to man up.

* * *

'Did you make this wine?'

We've left the men to chat in the kitchen so that Vicky can give me the tour. Warren is cooking and happy to do so.

'No,' she replies. 'If we were staying, I'd love to plant some vines. We're a part of a group of local farmers and we all exchange produce but none of them grow grapes unfortunately. Anyway, let me show you the outbuildings and our herb and veggie tunnels.'

It's rather nice to walk, talk and take the occasional sip of wine as we do so.

'This is where we keep the tractor and all the attachments, and the sit-n-ride mower, which is my favourite piece of kit. Warren hates mowing the lawn.'

I can't help laughing. 'It's quite a lawn,' I admit.

'It's one of my favourite jobs, actually. It's a real change from being in the kitchen, weeding and planting or picking herbs, soft fruits and vegetables. Let's walk over to the duck pen.'

My eyes dart around trying to take everything in. The ducks are housed in a huge fenced-off area behind two of the outbuildings to the rear of the farmhouse. It even has a pond with a little island in the middle of it.

'My goodness, they have their own houses.' I have no idea what keeping ducks entails, but these are some very lucky ducks.

'Ducks all have a unique personality.' She smiles at me. 'The problem is that we've grown so attached to them they're more pets than anything else. We're grateful for the eggs, though.'

Ah, farming isn't always easy. 'They are noisy, but when they quack it's like they're talking to us!'

'One of my French neighbours said the mistake I made was in naming them. However, the eggs sell well.'

'They certainly look happy.'

'They were here when we came, and they've grown in

number as I can't bear to sell them. Or worse.' Her look is one of abject horror.

I've eaten duck on many occasions, but I fully understand where Vicky is coming from. Getting up close and personal, they're so darned cute and maybe this will make me think twice before I order it again.

'But you enjoy the lifestyle here in France?'

She nods her head, as she leads me back across the vast lawn, to the fields beyond. 'I do. We're free, but the working day is a long one and there are never enough hours to get everything done. Winters can be difficult. We offer bed and breakfast all year round, but we don't advertise it, it's more word of mouth. If any of our neighbours are full, they give out our telephone number. We have three guest bedrooms, but it's disruptive to our daily routine. That's tough, as we operate on the bare minimum of staff.'

We're approaching several poly tunnels and a huge orchard of fruit trees. 'How do you manage when it comes to harvest time for this lot?'

'There are casual pickers who go from farm to farm; most are students. There are locals, too, more than happy to spend a couple of days out in the sunshine for not a lot, knowing that it helps to keep us going. If we have a bumper crop of anything, we look after our friends.'

It's a lovely way to live, but the reality is harsh, by the sound of it.

The poly tunnels are a surprise and when we step inside it's like a forest of greenery in miniature. 'We supply herbs to a lot of the local restaurants. We've only recently added a second tunnel to double our production and the bonus is that it extends the growing period.'

'There's something so satisfying about growing things. My garden at home is my sanctuary and I am missing it.' I can't help sounding a little wistful.

Vicky smiles at me, congenially. 'What do you do when you're back home?'

Oh, so Luke only mentioned my name and left it at that. Why am I not at all surprised?

'My best friend and I run an estate agency in Sevenoaks and we're hoping to open a second branch in the near future. It's a huge step for us.'

'Ah, and there's always a risk, isn't there? It's like that for us. If we stay, we might only ever eke out a living; if I convince Warren to open a small restaurant somewhere, he's right when he says there are no guarantees. But at least he'd never be able to say, "what if" and that's my biggest fear: looking back and regretting not taking a chance.'

'What did you do before you and Warren met?'

We start the long walk back to the farmhouse. 'I managed a shoe shop. He swept me off my feet and I ended up in France.'

And I know exactly where in France, but I say nothing as it's not my place. She can see I'm amused as that's quite a change.

'Who knew I was going to be good at making conserves and deep-diving into the use of herbs for all sorts of things? The leaves and flowering tops are used in food, drinks and medicines. Did you know that lemon verbena is good for treating a whole range of things, from respiratory conditions to digestive issues, asthma, colds, fever and skin conditions?'

I shake my head in surprise.

'No, neither did I!' she confesses.

It's late for us to eat, gone half past nine by the time we sit down. We're sitting in the lean-to that Warren built onto the far end of the front of the farmhouse. It's very pleasant gazing out over the lawn as the light fades. Fairy lights hang from the rafters above us and several large citronella candles in stout, wrought-iron sconces help deter the insects.

With its tiled roof and open sides, it's like eating in the garden. There's even an outdoor kitchen with a grill, but tonight Warren is serving what he calls his classic rustic menu.

It begins with a salad of mâche, sweet tender lettuce, and baby arugula topped with golden, crispy shallots. On the side is a basket of bubble-topped brioche which Vicky made. Essentially, they're rolls cooked in small tins and the bread bubbles out over the edges, hence the name. That's followed by a rich cassoulet, with Andouille sausage and confit chicken thighs. It literally bursts with flavour.

Luke's plate is empty as he sits back and lets out a satisfied sigh. 'That was truly awesome, Warren.'

He gives a toothy grin, as he and Luke exchange smiles. 'I hope you have some room for dessert. We have your favourite apricot and almond galettes.'

Vicky stands and begins clearing the plates, so I give her a hand.

'While that sounds delicious, I don't think I can eat another thing,' I admit.

'Why don't you guys set up the armchairs under the apple tree?' Vicky suggests. 'I'll make some coffee and we can sit for a bit before serving dessert.'

'Great idea,' Luke endorses, and he follows Warren over to help carry four comfortable-looking folding chairs.

'That meal was wonderful, Vicky, but I'm so full. I kept telling myself one more bite and then suddenly it was all gone.'

She draws in a deep and sorrowful breath, letting it out slowly. 'Warren's a great chef and his talent is wasted here, but he won't listen.'

Luke must make it known that Max is struggling. It's something only a long-time friend can do and I'm gutted that Luke is choosing to ignore my advice.

It's gone eleven by the time we eat dessert, and it doesn't disappoint. When we finally crawl into bed, it's well past midnight and as soon as my head touches the feather-soft pillow, my eyelids droop. I'm not even sure I said goodnight to Luke . . .

Luke

17

Up With the . . . Ducks

When Freya and I make our way down to the kitchen, both Warren and Vicky look up in surprise. It's not even seven o'clock, but they've obviously been up for a while and are sitting having a simple breakfast of coffee, fresh fruit and croissants. The kitchen smells like a bakery and there are two baguettes cooling on a wire rack.

Vicky stands, hurrying over to pour us some coffee from the percolator sitting on the top of the range cooker. 'We were rather hoping you'd have a lie-in after your long drive and a late night.'

I pull out a chair for Freya and then sit next to her, opposite Warren. 'Nature's alarm clock woke us.' I grin.

'Oh . . . you had the dormer window open at the back. I meant to warn you. The ducks wake up early and their pen is only a few metres away. Sorry about that.'

'No, it's fine,' Freya joins in. 'We both slept soundly and we're looking forward to today.'

'It's going to be a hot one, so it's good to start early,' Warren agrees. 'We usually have a long lunch as is the French tradition. No one wants to be working at midday and I often take a nap afterwards.'

'That reminds me, we must sort you out a hat, Freya.'

Freya nods her head, gratefully, at Vicky. 'Thanks. Is it all right if we use the washing machine upstairs?'

'Of course, whenever you want. If you have a really large load, there's another one in the utility room down here.'

I glance at Freya, a smile tweaking at my lips. 'We're travelling light, much to Freya's annoyance.'

'My only gripe,' she responds, 'was that I had to buy a new wardrobe of summer clothes that could be rolled up and didn't crease. But now I'm all set, I'll never carry a travel iron with me again!'

There's a lot of laughter and banter around the table this morning, as early as it is, but last night was a bonding experience. I knew Freya would fit right in. The fact that they're so appreciative that there are two of us again this year, they welcomed her with open arms as I knew they would.

'What's first on the agenda?' I ask.

Vicky glances at me, then at Freya. 'Tomato picking. And there are a lot of them. I thought that Freya and I could tackle that this morning. If we don't sell out at the special Summer Festival Market tomorrow, I'll be turning whatever's left into a sauce to bottle.'

She walks over with two coffee mugs, as Warren tops up the plate in the centre of the table with croissants. Together with the freshly picked strawberries, it's the perfect start to the day. Especially after that huge meal last night.

'We'll feed the ducks first, Luke, then start digging up the carrots and radishes, if that's OK with you?'

'Perfect. No more building works on the go?'

'No,' Warren confirms, not looking happy. 'We've added another poly tunnel since you were last here, so we won't be tackling any more projects until we see how much this year's crops raise.'

'Hopefully—' Vicky holds up crossed fingers '—a handsome bounty.'

I hope so, too. If anyone deserves to reap the rewards of their labour, it's two of my best friends. We were mates back in the UK and this was supposed to be the good life for them; well, joining Warren's parents to help run their business was the original idea. This deviation is down to two stubborn men butting heads.

Warren tasks me with carrying the fruit boxes into the poly tunnel for the girls to make a start. Vicky shows Freya what to do, and as I walk back and forth, it's clear that it's taking her a little while to get the knack.

If you pull too hard on the fruit, you risk pulling the plant away from the stake and there are lots of green tomatoes still to ripen. Vicky has already filled one of the boxes and walks over to get another, while Freya's is only half full. She won't be happy with that, as she's very competitive and sets her own bar very high.

As I walk past Freya, she gives me a smile. 'The more I pick, the headier that slightly earthy, yet sweet aroma gets. It's rare to get tomatoes in the supermarkets back in the UK that have this distinctive smell. It reminds me of my dad's greenhouse, when I was little.'

Vicky walks over, taking some boxes from the stack and placing them at intervals along the row.

'These plants were grown from seed by one of our neighbours. The old tomato varieties are becoming more popular, as they have the taste that a lot of the new varieties just don't have.'

'That's good to hear.' I stop to give Vicky a hand, before I head out.

'This might be a silly question,' Freya says, 'but are we putting all the ripe tomatoes in the box, or keeping misshapen ones separately?'

Vicky gives a little giggle. 'Our customers don't worry about the size, or the shape, just the quality. In fact, if everything is uniform their eyes tend to skip over the produce.'

'Right, that's me done. I'm off to find a spade. See you later, ladies!'

In the background I hear Freya saying, 'I guess I've a lot to learn and the day has only just begun!'

* * *

I enjoy working here, but this year the stay is cut short because I'm doing another mate a huge favour. That's why the last leg of the trip will be a relatively long one, but I will feel sorry to move on. Warren and Vicky have been good to me over the years and seen me through some bad spells.

It's time to drag out one of the wheelbarrows and gather the gardening tools we'll need to start digging up the vegetables. On my way over to the smaller of the two barns, while I do miss heading down to the beach, I realise that this setting has its own appeal, and I could get hooked on it. Manual labour is honest work and satisfying, I've come to discover. I spend so much time at home in my office, that I'd go mad if I couldn't get out and feel the sun, wind and rain on my face. But I could quite happily live here, leading the simple life.

I root around and the barrow is almost full when I hear footsteps. 'You're taking your time!' Warren quips.

'Give me a break. It's been a while since I was last in here and you've moved things around.'

'That was top of my list last winter to get this lot organised. Right, I'll wheel the trolley over and we can load up any debris for the compost heap.'

It's a fair old walk over to the field on the far side of the property. Fortunately, it's bounded by a stone wall, as this was a part of a much larger estate at one time. Maintaining a fence to keep out the smaller animals would be an arduous task, although last year we did some dry-stone walling where a section had collapsed.

'It's all looking good, Warren. Together with the two poly tunnels, it should be a profitable year once everything has been harvested.'

The effort involved in wheeling the barrow makes me a little breathless, but Warren has the harder job as the handmade wooden trolley is heavier. He's solid muscle though, having soon lost a few extra pounds when he switched from virtually living in the kitchen, to being out on the land. Which reminds me that Freya is right, I do need to have a word with him about Max. But I'll save that for later.

'Freya's a bit of a surprise. You're punching above your weight there,' he laughs.

'I know I am. You have no idea how hard it was to get her to take two months off work to join me.'

Warren casts me a sideways glance. 'She's worth the fight though.'

'Yep, but the problem is that she doesn't really take me seriously. I have no idea what will happen between us when we get back. Freya has her life all mapped out and it didn't include getting involved with someone, as she's focusing on her business.'

Warren grunts. 'Hmm. Well, as I've discovered, you can plan all you want but that doesn't mean something won't throw you off course. Vicky was delighted you brought her along; she says you're perfect for each other. Women can sense these things, apparently, but it's obvious even to me that you're the happiest you've been in a while, mate.'

'It's been a tough year, Warren, I can't deny that.'

'Gardening is therapeutic,' he insists. 'Once you've dug up a dozen crates of carrots, your mind will be focused on those aching muscles. That'll stop you pondering about the future, trust me!'

'I can't wait. Anything that . . . stops me thinking these days . . . is . . . a relief,' I reply, my breathing quite shallow now, as we negotiate the five-bar gate.

I take a moment to regain my composure. The field is quite a sight to behold. 'You're going to need a small army to get this lot out of the ground,' I exclaim.

'Next week we have three foreign students arriving for a two-week stay to work on the farm. It means I'll be doing a lot of cooking, as that's a part of the deal.' Warren gives me a wink. 'They're always keen, and by then I'll be ready for a bit of a rest. And I brought some gloves. You'll need to wear them if you don't want to get blisters.'

'Cheers for that. Come on, let's make a dent in this little lot!'

A lukewarm shower before lunch, a simple meal, and two hours lazing on a sun bed beneath a shady tree, sets us all up for an afternoon's toil. It's almost three o'clock and while the sun is still blazing in the sky, there's a bit of a breeze going and it's very welcome.

When Warren asks if I want to connect up the tipping trailer to his beaten-up old tractor and drive it along the lane to the other entrance to the farm, I jump at the chance. While I'm gone, Warren, Vicky and Freya begin stacking boxes and crates ready to be loaded.

Sitting in a loftier position, where I can see over the tops of the hedgerows, makes me marvel at how they've managed to turn this farm around. When they arrived here, three years ago, the fields were pastureland and there was only what I'd call a small holding, enough to feed the family of six, who lived here before. Now it's a real business but scaling up isn't easy and it's costly. There are also hoops they have to jump through, but Warren has help locally; anyone who speaks fluent French fits in more easily than people who don't make the effort.

By the time I get to the far side of the farm, they're all sitting on the ground under an enormous oak tree that marks the gateway. It's rare that I have a chance to get behind the wheel of something this old, but each time I'm here I'm happy to volunteer just because it's fun. If I meet a car coming in the opposite direction they have to back up because this bad boy doesn't manoeuvre that well, but it can certainly pull a heavy load.

'Slacking on the job I see,' I call out, as I jump down from the cab. 'Let's get this lot loaded and then we can all get back to work.'

Freya eases herself up, pushing the wide-brimmed straw hat Vicky insisted she wear firmly down on her head. 'We'd almost given up waiting,' she retorts, good-naturedly.

'There was a bit of a tailback of cars. That'll teach them to take a short cut!'

Warren starts belly-laughing. 'Been there. It's unbelievable how hard some people find it to drive in reverse gear.'

It takes a while to get everything loaded up properly with the heavier crates on the bottom and the lighter, more delicate produce on the top, as it's quite a haul. Before I head back, Vicky suggests that she make her way to the large barn to help me unload.

'It's certainly hot, thirsty work,' Warren grumbles.

'I know. When we return, Luke and I will grab some bottles of water from the fridge. We'll meet you over by the radish patch? After that, we can pick some peas.'

'Will do!'

I watch as they all set off together, chattering away like old friends. It's good to see.

On the slow drive back, I come to the decision that I can't talk to Warren about his dad, unless he raises the subject. Which he clearly isn't going to do and by the time I reach the barn I've psyched myself up to mention it to Vicky. But I'd rather like her to be the one to raise the topic first, so I need an opener to start up that line of conversation.

However, we end up working together in silence and before I know it the job is finished.

'Thanks for giving me a hand, Luke. We'd better grab that water.' Vicky swipes the back of her hand across her forehead, smiling. 'It is hot work, but I can't believe we've filled a whole trailer. Come on, they'll be wondering where we are.'

We up the pace as we walk towards the farmhouse. 'Freya's great company. How did the two of you meet?'

I do my best to hide a little smile. That's a very diplomatic way of asking about our relationship.

'At the gym. We had a couple of dates but she's a busy lady.'

I can see I've piqued Vicky's interest. 'Not too busy to spend the best part of the summer in France with you, though?'

'I guess when you put it like that, I should count my blessings.' That little smile turns into a smirk. 'I think she'll blow me out when we get back to the UK, to be honest with you.'

'Oh, Luke, it would be such a shame if the two of you part ways. You're perf—I mean, you get on so well.'

'We do, but she says this isn't real life.'

Vicky bursts out laughing. 'It isn't?'

'She's a nine-to-five, well . . . nine to however late it takes to get the job done, lady. Freya and her best friend are partners and they're both ambitious people. Me, on the other hand, I'm coasting along.'

'Hardly! Come on, Luke, you're doing yourself an injustice.'

'She doesn't think I'm serious enough. With age comes wisdom and all that stuff.'

I follow Vicky inside and the coolness is a relief.

'Oh. And, just like Warren, you hate sharing the emotional stuff, don't you?' She turns to look at me and I see empathy reflected in her eyes. 'I get it, she's a little older than you and thinks maybe you still haven't got into your stride. But you've been through more in this last couple of years than most people much older than you. It just depends on what life dishes out, and when, doesn't it?'

Vicky turns and I follow her through to the kitchen. 'You need to open up, Luke.' She talks over her shoulder, turning her head slightly to check I'm listening. 'If you don't, you could end up losing her. Freya's a keeper and you know it, I can see that every time you look at her.'

This isn't the way I wanted the conversation to go, but Vicky is expecting a reply. 'I'm working on it. And myself. I'll get there. Anyway . . . talking of awkward stuff.' I pause as Vicky opens the fridge door and hands me two bottles of water. 'There's no easy way to say this but you need to know that Max is struggling. Actually, Erin is too and it's putting a strain on their marriage.'

Vicky closes the fridge door and leans back against it. 'Ugh. And you want me to pass that on?' She grimaces.

'I know he doesn't want it all raked up again, but Max thought he'd finally found the right replacement for Warren and now that isn't happening—' I draw to an abrupt halt.

A look of sadness passes over Vicky's face. 'Leave it with me. I won't say that in so many words, but it's high time he rang his parents just to catch up. It's ridiculous ignoring each other, as if someone has died.' Vicky's jaw drops. 'I . . . sorry. An argument is just an argument, and they'll get over it.' When she starts speaking again, her voice softens. 'You will talk to Freya when you get back to the UK, won't you? Sit her down and explain about your father and the pressure—'

'Yes. I will, I promise. I'm fine now, really.'

'I do hope so, Luke. Forgiveness is a selfless act and sometimes we're all too quick to judge.' She sounds sad.

'If Warren can suck it up and make the call, I'd bet money on it that he won't get a rebuff. Max is exhausted and Erin is worried about him, because he needs his son by his side, but he doesn't know how to say sorry. If you have a serious buyer, now's the time to sell. You've turned this farm into a going concern, one that will make money but it's time to change gear.'

Vicky's eyes dart around, as if fearing Warren will walk in and overhear our conversation. 'What we need is more help on a regular basis, or it will all be for nothing. I'm tired, Luke. So is Warren.'

It's hard to see her so dispirited when they're doing so well. 'You've three new helpers on the way to get you through the next bit, but you know what you have to do.'

She nods her head and walks towards me, nestling the bottles against her body so that she can throw her free arm around me. 'You're an old head on young shoulders, Luke. You always have been. Just let Freya see that side of you, too.'

Freya

18

The Big Summer Market

On our fourth day at the farm, it isn't the ducks that wake us bright and early this morning, but the alarm clock. By six o'clock the farm's Renault van is loaded, and we follow Warren and Vicky to a neighbouring farm just a few miles away. As we pull into the field it looks a bit like a fête, with lots of covered stalls sporting colourful banners.

'Gosh, we're among the last to arrive.'

Luke pulls Reba into a space alongside Warren's van, and as I glance around, the VW is beginning to attract attention even before we're out of the vehicle.

He hurries over to join Warren and Vicky, who already have the back doors open.

'Right.' Vicky immediately begins issuing orders. 'Warren and Luke, can you start assembling the tables, please? Freya, I can't remember where I put the table coverings . . . the last time I saw them they were in a pile on the side in the kitchen.' She holds her hand to her forehead and a look of panic fleetingly flashes over her face.

'In a bag underneath the passenger's seat,' Warren calls over to her.

'Thank you! If we start carrying the trays of soft fruits over first,' she says, gingerly sliding off the first one, 'we'll be set to go once we can get the tables covered. Doesn't it all look wonderful with the heavily laden stalls?'

Two ladies approach as I grab a tray and carry it around to the rear of the stall. They're chatting away, their arms waving in the air as they point and laugh. What I didn't expect was the fast babble of French from Vicky. I hear my name and the ladies both turn to give me a welcoming smile and a wave. Several men are hot on their heels and are admiring Reba, so Warren stops what he's doing to go and greet them, giving Luke an apologetic glance.

'All of this wonderful produce and it's the VW that gets the attention.' I lean into Luke, my voice low. 'I had no idea how fluent they both are. Is this a well-known festival? It feels like a celebration.'

Luke shakes his head. 'It started out as a bit of a cooperative. Just a small group of farmers gathering together to buy, or barter, each other's organic produce. It expanded as the years have gone by, and now they get a really good turnout from the general public.'

'You were here last year for this?'

'Yes. Although I also come over to help with the planting in the spring and then a bit later, for the final big harvest.'

I help Luke by clicking the fasteners on the legs on the fourth table and we turn it over. He hurries over to the van to collect the tablecloths, but then he, too, gets pulled into the conversation. Now he's sliding open the side door to the VW and the chatter increases.

'I'm on my way,' Vicky calls, waving the tablecloths in her hands.

'They'll be a while. She is a beauty and they're all used to Luke pulling up in an old transit van. Mind you, it was useful.' Vicky raises her eyebrows, a broad smile on her face as we each grab an end of one of the plastic cloths and shake it in the air. Like a parachute it hovers over the table and within minutes we're transferring punnets onto the tabletop.

'It's a lovely atmosphere.'

'The French farming community around here is close and if we hadn't had help at the very beginning, we wouldn't be where we are today.' Warren and Luke stride over, their arms full. 'Stack them along the back guys.'

'Do you want me to sort the orders?' Warren checks.

'Please. And, Luke, can you dig out the scales and place them here in the centre of the four tables? Thank you! Warren, please say you brought the cash box.'

He turns to smile at his wife. 'Yep, it's under the driver's seat.'

Most people around us have finished laying out their goods and down at the far end of the field there are two refrigerated lorries and several smaller vans with open sides that are obviously selling dairy produce.

We work in silence as cars are beginning to filter in and park in an area that has been cordoned off.

I follow Vicky's lead. She's very particular in the way in which she displays the wicker baskets. Once she can see that I'm happy to just get on with it, she disappears into the back of the van and returns with metal hooks that clip onto the sides of the baskets to display the prices.

I'm beginning to get a little anxious. 'I'm not sure my French is good enough for me to serve.'

'Don't worry. Watch and learn; you'll soon get the hang of it. Everything is measured in kilos. You simply punch in the price, pop the goods onto the metal tray and it tells you exactly what to charge. We're not expecting you to jump in and do that, but for those who don't bring their own bags, or baskets, you can help wrapping things up. There's a huge roll of paper that Warren will fetch in a minute.'

And relax. I must admit I did a bit of tossing and turning last night worrying that I'd be thrown in at the deep end.

'Warren is sorting the orders as some farmers phone ahead. I love the exchange system, as it means we can stock up on meat and dairy, so he'll be putting baskets full of produce aside for that to be collected too, at the end of the day. But now that it's open to the public, it's a big draw and the extra income is what will fund additional help when it's fruit picking time in the orchard.'

She's already visibly calmer as the table gradually fills with colour. The rich reds of the tomatoes next to curly-topped carrots, heaps of peas that give off a slightly bitter/sweet smell, and a mountain of French beans I'm layering up, makes two days of solid work seem worthwhile.

'Given the size of the poly tunnels, I'm surprised you didn't bring more trays of herbs.'

'A lot of it is sold direct. You will have noticed that we grow them in pots, so local restaurants pick up their orders from the farmhouse once a week and people who use aromatic herbs to produce say, soap or essential oils, buy in bulk. We don't offer a delivery service, although Warren does a few special runs for customers who can't get to the farm. Mostly elderly people living in more isolated areas. He calls it his meals-on-wheels service.'

'*Bonjour!*' Our first customer is already inspecting the produce and she picks up one of the small baskets to begin loading it with punnets of raspberries.

Vicky stops to have a chat, while I finish off filling baskets. When I eventually get to stroll around to the front to survey the tables, it's incredible to see. We picked this little lot, and my back is still aching from all the bending, but I wouldn't have missed being a part of this for the world. Next time I visit a farmer's market back home, I'll be more appreciative of the toil that goes on unseen and the care with which the farmers tend their crops.

I draw in a deep breath. 'I can smell coffee!' I exclaim.

There's a chorus of 'Yes, please' from the others and I grab my bag from the van to do the first of what will probably be several runs today. It's like I've stepped into another world, and I wish we were staying longer. That thought makes me smile to myself; I'm enjoying getting hands-on and being out in nature. Goodness, I haven't had a headache since we set off and as for the racing heart . . . I've never felt better. But my heart is beginning to ache a little. We have one more stop and although it'll take us right the way through until the end of August, I can't even imagine how I'm going to feel when this is over.

'How's it going at the farm? Hard work?' It's good to hear Mum's voice.

'I will admit that I am aching in a couple of places, but it's been an amazing few days.' I tell her all about the fête and practising my French. 'In conversation, I'm picking up more and more; enough, as it turns out, to serve a whole host of non-English-speaking people today. Sadly, my answers in French are usually short and to the point, though.'

She laughs, but I can tell she's happy to hear that I'm enjoying myself.

'Have you heard from Beth?'

'No. Not for a few days. Why?'

'I popped in to say hello when I was in town shopping and she's fuming. David has found a property he wants her to look at, but it's at auction. And guess who's selling it?'

'Oh no . . . it's not one of Quentin's properties, is it?'

'That's partly why she's annoyed about it, but I don't think she's ready to move just yet. When she calls you, don't mention it, let her tell you all about it herself.'

That's going to be quite a call. Their house isn't even on the market, and bidding at auction requires the funding to be in place. That can only mean that David wants to find the money from another source. Beth won't be happy about that, as it raises the element of risk significantly. With our expansion plans for the agency, this is the last thing Beth needed right now.

'How are things with you?'

There's a telling pause. 'Um . . . wonderful, actually.'

Wonderful? 'Why, what's happened?'

Another short pause. 'Nothing in particular. George did a little job for me and last night I took him to the cinema by way of saying thank you. He won't let me pay him for his time and I was feeling awkward about it.'

'Well, now you're no longer in his debt, Mum.' I know that won't sit well with her, but it seems to me he makes it his business to know when she has a problem. 'Everything else is ticking over in the house, is it?'

'Yes,' she replies, confidently. 'It's all good.'

I must make a point of asking her that question more regularly in future. I'd rather arrange for a contractor to go in than give George another reason to come to her rescue. Perhaps that's the answer.

What I find rather disconcerting is that every time I visit Mum and he's there, he immediately makes an excuse to leave. In fact, he can't get out of the house quickly enough and that, to me, is a red flag. George certainly doesn't want to enter into a conversation, probably because it's only natural that I'd want to know a bit more about him if he's spending time with Mum.

'If you do get a problem, you can always call me. I have a phone full of telephone numbers of tradesmen who handle all sorts of things.'

'I know—' Suddenly, I hear a noise in the background. 'I must go.' Mum's voice is muffled, and I think she just put her hand over the mouthpiece. 'I . . . uh . . . have a washer load that's spun and needs popping into the tumble dryer.'

Then I hear the same sound again, like a heavy object coming into contact with a hard surface. 'Have fun, lovely, and let me know once you're at your final destination.'

'I will and take care. Love you, Mum.' As we disconnect, I have the distinct feeling that she has company; I can only hope it's not George poking his nose in again. Dad would expect me to watch out for her.

I make my way out to the garden to rejoin the others, feeling concerned, but try my best to brush it off.

'How's your mum?' Luke asks, as I sit down next to him at the table in the outdoor kitchen cum dining room.

'Fine, according to her.'

Luke raises an eyebrow, but I say nothing.

'Are we all ready for dessert?' Warren checks and receives a chorus of yeses.

He disappears back into the farmhouse, and I turn to Vicky. 'What's the plan for tomorrow?'

Luke sits there, twiddling the stem of his wine glass in one hand as he gazes out over the garden. The light is going and everything has that dusky look to it. It's bliss here, so quiet when the ducks aren't quacking, and restful. However, the isolation must take a lot of getting used to, and it's clear that Vicky and Warren love having company.

'We didn't bring back as much as I'd thought, so it's a case of spending two or three hours at most in the kitchen blanching, freezing and doing a bit of a cook-up.'

Luke turns to look at me. 'Ah, Freya, you'll miss out on making chutney and jam!' He laughs. 'I know you were looking forward to that on our last day at the farm. It looks like we'll be heading off a bit earlier than expected.'

I pull a sad face and Vicky smiles. 'It's been a joy having you both here. You don't have to wait a full year to come back, Freya. In winter there's less to do outside and the farmhouse is cosy with the log burner going.' She sounds wistful, but whether that's because it's her favourite season, or the fact that she's enjoyed our company, it's hard to tell.

Warren appears carrying a large tray, which he places very carefully on the countertop next to the barbecue grill. 'What have I missed? You're all looking down in the mouth.'

'I was telling Luke *and* Freya that they're welcome here any time.' Vicky and Warren exchange a warm smile.

'They're both aware of that,' he replies, giving me a subtle wink. 'Anyway, tonight, I'm making the ultimate crème brûlée, to celebrate our last night together.'

We all sit entranced, as we watch him fire up the culinary cooking torch. A sprinkling of sugar and in minutes he stands back, looking happy with the result.

He adds a pile of fruit to each dish and, with great pride, ferries them across to the table.

My mouth instantly begins to water. The caramelised sugar looks amazing and together with a small pile of fresh raspberries and blueberries, I'm impatient to tuck in.

We wait until Warren is seated. '*Bon appétit!*' he says, raising his wine glass and we all toast. 'Thank you both for three very hard, but hopefully enjoyable, days.'

I can tell from Luke's expression that he would have loved to stay longer; me too. But all good things come to an end and tonight is a celebration.

'Oh . . .' Luke is the first to taste Warren's efforts and the moment the spoon is in his mouth he makes an appreciative sound. 'Coffee! That's a first. It's perfect with the fruit. This could be my favourite dessert of the entire trip.'

Warren's face lights up as he watches me taking my first bite.

'This is a showstopper, Warren,' I endorse. 'Heaven on a plate. That caramel is crisp, the underneath deliciously creamy and the coffee with the fruit is a real delight.'

'It's not exactly a French classic,' he laughs, slightly embarrassed.

'But who wants a classic when they can have the inspired?' Vicky looks at her husband with pride in her eyes. 'This is precisely why you need to spend more time cooking and less time tending the soil.'

It's true but given the situation it will require a lot of hard thinking to sell this place and venture into the unknown. I can only hope they find the perfect solution, because in a way it feels like paradise here, to me. But a fleeting visit is just a snapshot of their day-to-day lives, and I can imagine that, at times, it's hard on them both.

'It looked like you and Vicky had a very productive morning.'

We're on the road again after a bit of a tearful goodbye, Vicky making me promise I'd keep in touch. I was happy about that and delighted that even after only a few days we'd developed a real connection.

'We did. It was fun, and when I get home, I'm going to start making my own tomato sauce for pasta, in future. It was so easy and smelled divine. I said I wouldn't be confident enough to bottle it, as Vicky does, but she said it freezes well and defrosts quickly. Her top tip was to add in a splash of wine and heat it up in a small saucepan.'

Luke gives a chuckle. 'It was really your thing, wasn't it? Getting hands-on gathering the produce and experimenting in the kitchen.'

'Surprisingly, it was. My garden is all flowers and shrubs, but I'm going to change it up a bit next spring. I think I might treat myself to a greenhouse and maybe add a raised bed for herbs and lettuces.'

'Life-changing stuff, then.'

Now he's making fun of me, and I nestle back in my seat, content to look out the window at the trees, fields and pretty little villages flashing by. After a while I stop feeling cross with him and decide it's time to ask a few questions.

'We're obviously heading towards Poitiers, what's after that?'

I glance at his profile and watch as his face breaks out into a smile. 'You really do hate surprises, don't you? It's about a four-and-a-half-hour drive, so we'll probably only have one stop for a comfort break and a coffee. After that amazing lunch Warren cooked for us, I think we'll last until this evening.'

If it weren't for all the manual work, I swear I'd probably have gained half a stone over the last few days, I reflect.

'Anyway,' Luke takes my silence as a hint for him to get to the point. 'After that we hit Tours and then on to Orléans—'

'Yes, but what's the destination?' I'm growing impatient with him now.

'Montereau-Fault-Yonne bridge.'

'Where on earth is that?'

'It's south of Paris.'

231

'Why are we heading for a bridge?'

'Because that's where we're going to park up Reba and begin the final leg of our adventure.'

He's obviously not going to share any more information with me, and I yank the phone out of my pocket to text Beth.

> How are you doing? We're on the move again. To somewhere south of Paris, but it's a surprise.

I turn to stare out the window again. A forest of trees flashes past so quickly that it's just a green blur, until I hear a ping and look down at my phone.

> Good. Well, work is fine but home life at the moment is rather tense. It's a long story. Let me know when you're settled, and we can have a chat. Hasn't Luke sussed out by now that you don't like surprises? ☺

I pull a grimace as my fingertips tap away.

> Aww . . . sorry to hear that. And he does know, but he seems to find it amusing winding me up. ☹ I'll be in touch, hopefully tomorrow. This is what I'm seeing out the window right now – a massive field of them! 🌷

It's a while before she replies with a thumbs up, which means she's busy and I heave a sigh.

'Problems?' Luke glances at me, briefly.

'No. And keep your eyes on the road. I just texted Beth to say I'd give her a call soon to catch up.'

'Oh, right. I meant to ask . . . can you swim?'

'Yes. Why?'

'In the pool at the Château des Sources you didn't venture down to the deep end.'

'Um, because the best view was up at the shallow end,' I reply, stating the obvious.

'Ah, right. I was showing off a bit doing all those laps up and down the pool,' he admits, and I can see that he's grinning to himself.

'Well, I didn't really notice,' I reply, nonchalantly.

So, we're heading for a *bridge* and it's obviously over *water*. A riverside setting, maybe? Now that would be awesome.

19

Cruising Along

It's just gone half past five in the evening when Luke mumbles, 'We're here' and I glance up to see a sign saying Rue Port des Fosses. He slows the van and turns into a large car park surrounded on three sides by a mix of buildings. Some are obviously commercial properties, but not all.

Unusually for Luke, he takes his time choosing a space that's set on a slight angle. I look at him quizzically.

'She's going to be parked up for a while and there's no chance anyone will dent the sides if they open their car doors.'

We're in the far corner, beneath a massive tree. Still, it's a shady spot and if this is our destination, Reba's going to be here for three whole weeks.

'I just need to go and grab a bunch of keys,' he informs me.

I watch as he walks across the car park and disappears into an alleyway between two of the buildings. We're on the edge of a place named Yonne and it has a village feel to it. To my surprise, he's only gone a few minutes and when he returns, he's beaming ear to ear as he opens the passenger door and extends his hand to help me climb out.

'I think you're going to love this but first we need to get some supplies.'

He locks the van, and we walk back along the road we just came for about twenty minutes where there's a convenience store. After filling a small hand basket with fruit, cheeses, bread rolls and two classic tarte aux fraises, we return to the car park.

'Are we taking everything from the van, tonight?' I enquire.

'I think we can manage it all. We're literally no more than a ten-minute walk away.'

As I extract the handle of my cargo hauler, Luke slips on his large backpack, and I take the carrier bag of food as he grabs our two smaller bags.

'Right, let's go!'

We cross the road and after a few yards take a right turn. To my delight, ahead of us is a wide river.

'That,' he informs me, 'is the Seine.'

'Oh, yes. We drove over a bridge on the way in.' I'm impressed. The view is lovely and as we walk a large commercial barge chugs by slowly.

How wonderful to wake up and look out the window to see this each morning. The bridge behind us has three arches which gracefully span the large body of water. On the opposite bank, a row of old stone houses has a marvellous backdrop of tall trees extending way back and the riverside setting is a nice change of scenery.

'This is it.'

Luke draws to a halt, and I follow his gaze.

'A boat?'

He catches his lower lip between his bottom teeth, as he waits for my reaction. 'Yes. She's called *La Belle Vie*. She's a Pénichette 1500FB. The range is modelled on a classic French barge.'

I have no problem with the idea of staying in this barge-style boat, as she's a beauty and must be at least fifty-foot long. There's a row of windows below deck at the front and the back. In the centre is a raised cabin with 360-degree visibility and a door that leads out to a sun deck with two double sofas, a table and two chairs.

'We're staying here for the whole three weeks?'

'No. Tomorrow morning we set off on our travels. She's

got a powerful diesel engine and a comfortable cruising speed of eight knots,' he informs me, as if that makes a difference.

I look at him rather aghast. 'Luke, I've never been on a boat other than a ferry before. Who's going to steer this monster of a thing?'

'Captain Luke at your disposal, ma'am. And don't look so shocked. It's not the first time I've been her skipper, and it won't be the last, as the owners are good friends of mine. We meet up a couple of times a year.'

Everyone is good friends with Luke, but I can't help noticing that none of them are permanently in his life. Back in Cornwall he says he's not very sociable and doesn't invite people back to his house. I'm beginning to think he has something to hide, but what?

'Come on,' he urges me. 'Let's get a move on because I'm ravenous.'

I heave a sigh as he helps me on board. He thinks it's because I'm not too impressed and I don't feel inclined to dismiss that assumption. Luke thinks I'll just go along with his plans even though boats aren't my thing. He's crossed the line; he should have at least run the idea past me and not simply sprung it on me. I don't appreciate being taken for granted. Home is just a plane ride away and if this begins to turn into a bit of a nightmare, I'll be doing just that!

After a good night's sleep, I think I might have overreacted a little yesterday. I don't do what Beth laughingly refers to as 'roughing-it' holidays, but I can't really complain. It's hardly getting back to nature, considering that we have absolutely everything we need albeit in a confined space.

Luke is actually a lot more organised that I originally gave him credit for and this morning he's given me a lot of information to read while he cooks us French toast for breakfast. My induction into the boating world feels a little overwhelming, as I wade through some basic guidance on the rules and protocols of cruising the waterways.

'You're not expecting me to get behind the wheel of this thing, are you?'

He flips the toast and then does a half-turn to glance at me. 'No. But give it a couple of days and I promise you that you'll be eager to at least have a go. I'm fully trained in taking first-time boaters through the handling procedures and the rules of the waterways. It's something I learnt on my first summer jaunt here, and my mate's the expert.'

'Hmm . . . just don't bank on me taking over the wheel at any point,' I warn him.

Last night after a buffet up on the sun deck, Luke sauntered off and reappeared carrying a sturdy box. 'I'm glad to see that our kit arrived safely.'

'Kit?'

'Wet-weather gear and manual inflatable vests.' He proceeded to unpack one of the vests. It looked like a simple harness to me, with padded straps on the front. It turns out there's a plastic pulley and the padding each side was actually the airbags that get deployed. 'You don't need to wear it all the time, but you ought to when up on deck. Certainly, until you get your sea legs.' He'd grinned at me. 'I don't want to lose you overboard. But we need to use them every time we're going through a lock.'

I'd quizzed him about how he knew what size weatherproofs to buy me, curious because most men wouldn't have a clue. He admitted that he'd looked at the size label in the back of some of my clothes.

Luke carries the plates over to the table and I tidy the pile of papers in front of me, then jump up to refill our coffee mugs.

When I sit back down, he's drizzling a honey dipper over his toast, eager to taste the local offering we bought at the little convenience store yesterday evening.

'After breakfast we'll run through a few things I'll be expecting you to do as first mate.'

I almost choke on my coffee. 'First mate? Seriously, even under instruction there's a chance I might mess it up.'

'Oh, you'll soon get the hang of it. You're going to be tying off the ropes when we moor up or go through a lock and unhooking them afterwards. I might get you to top up the water tank. On the way, even some of the smaller pontoons available to tie up overnight, have water and electricity we can link up to.'

While the idea of living on a boat sounds idyllic, I'm beginning to have my reservations. 'On our way where?'

I spoon a few raspberries onto my plate and drizzle some honey over the toast, then start tucking into the golden brown, deliciously eggy brioche.

'A place called Auxerre, which is the capital of the department of Yonne, in the far north of Burgundy. I guess it's about sixty kilometres in total but don't quote me on that. Don't worry, Ben and Hilary Gardiner, who own this boat and run a successful boat hire business, have everything already mapped out for us. There are a lot of locks, which will probably double our journey time. We'll only be travelling about four kilometres a day, though. We have a full tank of fuel, which in theory should get us all the way there.'

I'm fascinated listening to him talking and, thankfully, the sumptuous richness of my breakfast begins to quell the butterflies in my stomach. I'm still adjusting to the gentle movement of the boat whenever something sails past us. Maybe this won't be quite as bad as I feared at first and a confined space could also be construed as cosy.

It's like a mini house floating on the water. In the kitchen, which is referred to as the galley, this table would comfortably seat eight people with its wrap-around banquette. Opposite us there's a free-standing cooker with a full oven and three rings on top. There's a full-size sink, with a double cupboard beneath it and two three-drawer cabinets next to it. The fridge/freezer and pantry is in a recess to my right, which is beneath the upper sun deck. Beyond that we step down into a saloon with more banquette seating and in one corner the office area is equipped with a desk and a computer chair. Each of the four cabins, all doubles, have an en-suite shower compartment, toilet and handbasin. I have no doubt at all that this is luxury boating, it's just taking a while to get my head around the size of it.

'You've gone very quiet.' Luke interrupts my thoughts. 'Was this a bad idea?'

'No.' I sit back, wiping my mouth on a piece of kitchen towel and then I reach out for the mug of coffee. 'On reflection, I'm glad you didn't tell me in advance, as I would have been imagining something dark, cramped and smelly. Whether I'll see this through to the end, depends very much on how it goes. Every time the swell from a passing boat makes the barge move a little, my stomach turns over.'

He starts laughing. 'That's understandable if you've never been on a small barge before.'

'I don't call this small, but I am nervous about cruising, not least because locks are narrow. But, you seem confident it won't be a problem, so what's the plan for today?'

I'm not about to give up just yet.

'We clear everything away then go up on deck and I'll show you how to tie off the ropes. Then we set off and head towards our first lock. The plan is that we travel each morning and I'll be online all afternoon. I have my work cut out as I'll be building Ben and Hilary a second website from scratch and updating some of the photos on their existing website for their boat hire company.'

'And what plans do you have to keep me occupied? You said something about taking photographs.'

He gives me a sheepish grin. 'Let's leave that discussion until we get to our first mooring for the night. I have a few ideas I'd like you to consider.'

'Oh, so you meant it when you said that I won't be sitting around reading and sunning myself?' I quip.

'Anyone would think this was a holiday,' he retorts. 'You have to earn your supper, just like me!'

* * *

It's early evening and I decide to call Beth. Luke is on the phone to Ben, thrashing out some last-minute details with regard to the design of the new website.

When Beth picks up, it's good to hear her bubbly voice. 'Hey, you! I got your text. So, are you really afloat and it wasn't a joke?'

'We are. I'm sitting on the sun deck gazing out onto a narrow canal lined with trees as far as the eye can see.'

'Is it likely this could turn into a new hobby? You seemed a bit disgruntled when you texted me but this evening you sound relaxed.'

'I am because we're moored up and the ropes are firmly tied to two bollards; I know that for a fact as I was the one handling them.'

Beth gives a tinkling little laugh. 'You? That year we took the ferry around the Greek islands you weren't that excited about being on the water.'

I give a little groan. 'It was a bit stomach-churning at times as the water got very choppy, but this is different. It's more sedate. Just the wash from the other boats and Luke knows what he's doing.'

'Hmm . . .' There's a hint of suggestiveness in her tone. 'As it turns out, he's a man of many skills and I can tell you're impressed by it.'

I can't deny it's true, but that's enough about me. 'How are you and David?'

A gentle sigh filters down the line. 'He's doing everything he can to convince me that we should bid on this wreck of a property. He wants me to put our house on the market now; his parents have offered to loan us the money until ours sells.'

'Goodness, he really is serious.'

'If he just wanted to do it up and sell it on again, I'd dig my heels in but, oh, Freya . . . he wants to make it our forever home. He showed me some rough sketches he'd drawn up and it could be stunning.'

'When's the auction?' It's obvious Beth is tempted, even though they've hardly had time to enjoy all the work they did on their current house.

'Next Thursday, the fifteenth. Time is running out to make up our minds. The loan doesn't worry me, that's between David and his dad; he says the money is just sitting in the bank waiting for their retirement and I know our house will sell quickly. The property we're considering was rented out for a long time and then it was empty for a while.'

'That's never a good sign.'

'Basically, the tenants had trashed it and the landlord couldn't afford to bring it back up to meet the regulations. It will mean some re-plastering, a new kitchen, replacing all the bathroom fittings, sorting out the flooring and the gardens on three sides are like a jungle. If it weren't for the fact that it's set on a big corner plot in a nice part of Aylesford and has some mature trees, I wouldn't even consider it. I'm sending you the link to the details now.'

I wait for that familiar ping as Beth continues.

'It's going to cost around eighty-thousand pounds on top of the purchase price to turn it into something special. That includes doing a loft conversion to make it into a five-bed home.'

I flick through the online brochure. It looks what it is, sad and neglected. There's no kerb appeal at all. You can't even see the front door, as a massive shrub is obscuring it and most of the path, too. 'It's in a nice cul-de-sac,' I reply.

'Yes, although Ditton is a bit further afield than I'd like,' she concedes. 'It would be a twenty-five minute drive to work. We don't intend to sell it on, but I'm hoping it will be a good investment. What do you think?'

It's fifteen miles from Sevenoaks and I'm already doing an online search of house prices in the area.

'Done to a good standard you should get in excess of

five-hundred-and-seventy thousand, looking at what's been sold recently.'

'If we get it at auction for say, four-hundred thousand and with fees end up spending another hundred thousand on top, that's not a bad profit.'

'You're clearly coming around to the idea, so what's holding you back?'

She clears her throat. 'He's suggesting that we move in with his parents, rather than renting somewhere, while the work is carried out. It could take six to eight months, but the saving would be, he says, worth it.'

Oh dear; it's not that Beth doesn't get on with them, but I can understand her reluctance when she should be enjoying the beautiful new home they've created together. 'Having a tight deadline in which to make the decision is a lot of pressure to handle.'

'Tell me about it. Still, change happens, often when we least expect it. I certainly didn't see this coming, but he's given me twenty-four hours to make up my mind. He wants to have a second tour of the property and he's going to take a structural engineer with him this time.'

Reading between the lines, I think the decision has already been made but Beth is struggling to catch up. She'll get there, because it sounds like the potential is huge.

'If you want to talk at any time at all, just give me a ring. How're things going at work?'

'Good. The team has really bonded; we had a work's night out. I felt that given the recent upheaval and changes, a leisurely meal out together was in order.'

'Aww . . . I wish I'd been there!'

She chuckles. 'Don't pretend you're missing us; you have way too many distractions there to waste time thinking about work. Anyway, I must go. David wants to go over his draft plans again tonight.'

'Well, good luck and I know you'll make the right decision for you both.'

'Thanks, Freya. Life isn't the same without you here and I'm crossing the days off on the calendar. Have fun and we'll speak soon.'

As the line disconnects, I wonder whether Beth simply needed to hear someone else confirm that taking a calculated risk is sometimes warranted, without using those exact words. I can imagine that her own parents would be concerned, particularly about her and David potentially owning two houses for a period of time. But with big risk, comes big rewards. A forever home is special, and I know that only too well; it took me twelve years of renting to be able to afford to buy the cottage and now it's my sanctuary. When I shut the door, I'm shutting out the world.

As the light begins to fade, the trees become mere silhouettes but, on the horizon, it's like an artist's impression of a glowing, soft pink sunset. I take a quick photo and send it to Beth with a smiley face. Then I give up waiting for Luke and open the bottle of wine sitting in the cooler on the table in front of me. There's a cold pasta dish waiting in the fridge, so I jump online to do a little research on boat hire websites.

Twenty minutes later, Luke calls out. 'Sorry,' he apologises as he climbs the three rather deep steps up to the sun deck. 'That went on a bit longer than expected but we haven't had a chance to speak since I left the UK.'

He looks tired, but content.

'This is quite a big job, isn't it?' I pour him a glass of wine and he takes a sip, sitting back in his chair and letting out a sigh of satisfaction.

'Now I have a clearer idea of what he wants, it's not difficult. However, it is a fair bit of work.'

'I should imagine it's like drafting an article; anyone can throw some words together quite quickly, but a professional takes time to polish and perfect it.'

'Correct. You end up poring over every single word.'

'You've written some articles?'

'I used to blog about quick fixes for IT problems. You'd be amazed how many hits it attracted but I don't get time for that anymore. The website still attracts new business, though. People who are so desperate they turn to the internet, and when they've tried everything, they reach out. A lot of things can be fixed with some over-the-phone guidance; if it's a company, sometimes I can sort it remotely, taking over their PC, which is cheaper than a visit. Wow . . . look at that sky, it almost looks unreal, like the artist went overboard on the pink and red streaks.'

He's ready to relax, so I leave him to enjoy his drink while I do a couple of trips to and from the galley to lay out our late supper. Luke deserves a little spoiling. I'd have rejected the suggestion of a holiday aboard a boat without even giving it a second thought. It's certainly something I'll probably never do again but I'm so glad I didn't miss out on it. Sometimes taking a risk reaps surprising rewards.

20

I Do Love a Challenge

This morning I feel a lot more confident casting off for an early start. I was pleased that my first attempt, yesterday, at tying a figure-eight hitch around the metal-horned cleats located fore and aft on deck, held. The terminology confused me at first, but I'm getting used to it. It's simply a foolproof way of ensuring the rope doesn't come untied when you wind it around a stout metal fixing with a protruding bar at each end.

The fact that you can steer from up on deck and also from inside the cabin is handy in wet weather but today it's sunny and Luke is up top. After washing up the breakfast things, I'm about to join him.

I saunter over to give him a hug and a quick kiss on the cheek, happy to stand and chat.

'We have two locks to negotiate this morning. Even the automatic ones close between noon and one o'clock, so we need to press on. The next overnight stop will be within easy cycling distance of a Sunday farmer's market, as we're running low on supplies.'

'I did notice we had an alternative form of transport. It's been a while since I last rode a bike, but it's like driving a car – you never forget.' Or, at least, I hope it is.

Boating people are very friendly and whenever someone passes, they usually wave, and we acknowledge them back.

'Are all the canals like this?' I ask.

'It's considered to be one of the quieter routes. The Canal du Nivernais links the river Loire with the river Seine,' Luke explains. 'This is what they call a canalised river, that's why it's wide in places and narrow – as you'd expect a canal to be – in others. There isn't as much commercial traffic because of that, and this stretch also has the most locks of all of the three main routes in central France. That sort of puts people off. Not all of the locks are straight sided, some are sloping with a pontoon in the centre to raise or lower the boat.'

'Does that matter?'

He smiles at me knowingly. 'It will to you, when it comes to tying off the ropes. Imagine the boat being lowered six feet, if there's no one topside to throw the ropes to you, how do you hook, and unhook them, if the sloping sides mean it's too far to reach with the telescopic pole?'

I grimace.

'Don't worry, there's *un éclusier* – a lock keeper – who will assist us. That's why locks close for an hour at noon, because it's their lunchtime. Sometimes there are little stalls next to the lock keeper's house and you can buy local produce, or they might have a shop and sell things they make. When I was here two years ago, I bought a carved wooden owl for my mum, at one of the stops. She loved it, as she has a collection of owls, mainly china. Anyway, it's good to see you wearing your life jacket.' He turns to grin at me, cheekily.

Before I can respond, and without any warning, he sounds the horn, making me jump. 'We're just approaching a blind bend so that's something you need to remember.'

'Right. Well, I'll make a mental note of it in case I ever get behind the wheel.'

'And you can only travel at six kilometres an hour on canals, which is roughly three point three knots; it's eight kilometres an hour on river sections.'

'You do know that this is all going straight over my head, don't you?' I complain. 'I'll stick to handling the ropes, cooking and cleaning. After all, you're the captain.' I lean in, resting my head against his shoulder.

'This is peaceful, isn't it?' he murmurs. 'But this afternoon it's back to work.'

'For me, too?'

'You bet!'

Luke has turned the table in the galley into his temporary office, as he says the light is better. It's such a beautiful afternoon that he suggested I try out one of the bicycles, take his camera and just snap away at leisure. He gave me a dizzying explanation on how to use it, to take both photos and video footage. Whether I'll remember what all the buttons do when it comes to using it, is another matter. When I asked what he was expecting, he said he needed photos for both websites. Ben is providing some specific shots, but my task is to give people thinking of hiring a boat a feel for the delights of canal cruising.

Having been given my instructions, I begin my journey along the towpath, albeit with a wobble, or two, until I get into the swing of it. When I find a spot where I think I can grab some great shots, I prop the bike up against a tree and unpack the camera case from the rack attached to the seat. I'm sitting on the grass trying to figure it out, when a woman approaches, walking a dog on a lead.

When he spots me sitting on the grass alongside the towpath, he instinctively wants to check out what I'm doing, and she struggles to hold him back. It isn't long before he's within arm's reach and, looking extremely apologetic, she stops to let me smooth him before he literally pulls her over. '*Pardon*,' she says, awkwardly, but her accent is unmistakably British.

'It's fine, he's just curious.'

'Ah, a fellow Brit! Bartie is a typical cocker spaniel,

he's so nosey. Don't let us disturb you though.'

But as hard as she tries to entice Bartie away, his curiosity doesn't wane. 'It's not a problem. I'm supposed to be taking photos, but it's stuck in video mo—ah, at last!' I peer through the viewfinder and Bartie's head almost fills the screen, so I snap away but the button is stuck. 'Do you mind? I need to practise, as it's not my camera, and I have no idea what I'm doing.'

'Oh, go ahead. He loves attention and it's not like I can stop him. He has a will all of his own, but he's got such a sweet nature. Do you mind if I join you? I'm trying to tire him out. It's our first holiday renting a boat and while we had a short training session, it's still a little stressful at times. I think Bartie senses that and he takes ages to settle down for his naps.'

I check the setting but there's a light at the bottom of the screen and I'm not sure why it's on. Maybe it's the auto focus setting.

'No, please do and I totally understand. It's my first trip, too.'

'Commiserations,' she laughs. 'My other half said it would be a relaxing holiday before he starts his new job but it's not quite as easy as it looks. Still, by the time we've finished this trip I'm sure we'll feel like real pros. Our first lock sent us both into a bit of a panic. The lock keeper was shouting instructions at us, but our French isn't that good. Luckily, a passer-by stopped and helped us out in his broken English. We got through it and each one gets a little easier.'

I'm still trying to take photos, but something isn't right, so I end up putting it down on the grass between us. Bartie is now lying about two feet away, making the most of the shade.

We chat for a while until Bartie decides he's had enough and starts yanking on his lead. 'Oh well, so much for resting my legs. I'm Patricia, by the way. Maybe we'll bump into each other at one of our stops. We're on a mooring about a ten-minute walk that way.' She points to our left.

'I'm Freya, it's nice to meet you, Patricia. We're way back there. That's the beauty of a bicycle and it's so pleasant on the towpath. What's your boat called?'

'*Centaurus*. It's white with a stripey blue awning over the aft deck.'

'Ours is white with a green stripe on the side; she's called *La Belle Vie*. I'll keep an eye out for you.'

Bartie is impatient to get off and we part ways with a brief wave. I decide to give up on the camera and pack it away. On my way back to the boat I stop a few times, using the camera on my phone. It's quick and easy, and if I've messed up using the camera, at least I'll have something to show for my first excursion.

Catching sight of a wonderful vista off to the side, I stop once again. It's a clearing in the midst of a cluster of trees and streaks of dappled sunlight filter through between the canopy of leaves overhead. It almost looks as if there's a ball of light in the centre of the open space. I'm not sure Luke will think it's worthy, but it's rather magical. As I'm about to climb back on the bike my phone pings, and it's a text from Vicky.

Just checking to see how it's going and let you in on some news. Warren called his dad, and they had their first chat in a long, long time. Fingers crossed it'll be the first of many! ☺

I smile to myself as my fingers get busy.

Oh, Vicky, that's awesome. Luke will be delighted to hear that. It's all good here. We're having a boating experience. I'm learning fast! ☺

Warren said he'd give Luke a call soon. If it weren't for your visit, he wouldn't have reached out to them. I'm so glad he has, because family is important. Take care and I'll email you those recipes I promised in the next day or two. x

'I don't like the look of those clouds. I think we're going to get some rain before the night is out.' Luke scans the darkening sky.

'I'm sure the plants and the grass will be glad of it,' I reply, pushing my plate away from me. 'That was lovely, but it's my job to cook. You've had an intense afternoon.'

He does look tired but relaxed, as he cradles a wine glass in his hand. 'It was a productive session. Sorry I was a bit preoccupied when you got back.'

I give him a warm smile. 'It's understandable. I know how hard it is to switch off when you're in the flow.'

On my return I'd decided to head straight for the shower to give him a little breathing space. The cycling was hot work and rather than let my hair dry naturally, I wanted to blow-dry it. When I finished, he was in the galley cooking and ready for company.

Luke adjusts the angle of his chair, easing his legs out in front of him. 'I'm used to spending a lot of time on my own and sometimes it shows, I'm afraid. Anyway, how was your afternoon?'

'It was—'

His phone starts ringing and I indicate for him to take the call, while I clear the table and fetch our dessert.

'Mate, it's good to hear from you. How's it going?'

As I descend the steps carrying the tray, I have a feeling it's not Ben checking in to see how's he's doing. I take my time, doing a bit of tidying up but, if anything, Luke is even more regimented than me at putting things away. On a boat, oops barge, it's even more important. It's wide, probably four metres across and I'm guessing the hull is almost flat, as it seems to sit on the water, rather than in it. I guess that helps on the river sections as I have no idea how deep the channels are.

We really do need to go shopping and the best I can do is yoghurt with the last of the soft fruits we bought at the convenience store in Yonne. By the time I arrive back on the sun deck Luke is sitting there, looking content.

'That was Warren, you'll never guess what? He called Max.'

Not wishing to spoil his revelation, I do a double take. 'That's brilliant news.'

Luke shakes his head, smirking to himself. 'Warren decided to act as if nothing was wrong between them. He talked about what he and Vicky have been doing at the farm; he said the words just flowed out of him. When he stopped, he held his breath for a few seconds, not even sure that Max would respond. But he did. He simply said that his dad sounded relieved, and they went on to talk about Erin's plans for the future and the fact that Max has misgivings about it.'

I place the tray down on the table and Luke lifts the dessert bowls off the tray, as I sit next to him. 'It's quite something that they can talk openly.'

'Max is a wonderful man, but he's stubborn – much like Warren. Neither was ever going to kick off the conversation with an apology, were they?'

'I guess not. Sometimes you simply have to draw a line under the past and move on.'

'It's a great start and you were right; my conscience wouldn't allow me to bring up the topic. I took the coward's way out.' The corners of his eyes crinkle up as he smiles at me.

'You did?'

'I talked to Vicky. Guys talk about lots of things, but seldom about emotional stuff. Warren would have changed the subject the minute I raised it, and I didn't want him to feel uncomfortable. I don't know what Vicky said to him, but it did the trick.'

'Sometimes it's a case of simply sowing the seed. A word here, or there, at the right time is often all that's needed.'

'You sound like an expert,' Luke chuckles.

'With age comes wisdom!'

'Not again . . . with experience comes wisdom. Who have you been . . . let's call it *nurturing*, lately?'

I pause for thought, marvelling at the clarity with which Luke can often appraise things. 'I guess it's Beth, at the moment. I think I mentioned to you about the property David has seen at auction; well, it's getting serious as the date draws near. It would be a huge undertaking and risky, as are all new ventures. But they could end up with their dream home.'

'I thought it was just another renovation for them to sell on?'

'That was the initial impression I got, too. But Beth actually said it could be their forever home. That's when I knew she wasn't asking for advice, she just wanted to gauge my reaction. I wished her luck and said that I knew she'd make the right decision.'

Our eyes meet. 'That's what good friends do. They don't judge and they don't force their own opinions on other people.'

'David is an astute businessman and Beth is in the property business. It's a great combination. They made a resounding success of their first project, so they're not going into it blind. Now if she'd said he wanted to sell up and spend life cruising the French canals, I would have sown a few seeds of caution.'

Luke bursts out laughing, his eyes glinting in the moonlight that is streaming through those ever-darkening clouds. We're going to get some thunder, I'm sure of it.

'Come on, let's eat up and get inside before it starts raining,' he suggests, and I agree.

* * *

The pitter-patter of raindrops on the deck above and on the windows means sleep is almost impossible but it's strangely comforting being tucked up in bed. I admit to Luke that I think I messed up with the camera and ask him to run through the instructions with me once more. I hand it to him and he snuggles closer while he figures out what I was doing wrong.

Suddenly, I can hear my own voice.

'Who's this?' Luke asks, as Bartie's head fills the screen.

'Oh, it was in video mode!' I laugh, as we listen to Patricia introducing herself.

'Nice dog,' Luke interjects.

We spend the next five minutes listening and watching. I kept moving the camera around as I fiddled with it, taking shots of my lap, my feet, the sky and a lot of footage of Bartie.

'Well, that was fun,' he comments when it finishes. 'We'll have to keep a look out for *Centaurus*, as I'd like to meet Bartie in the flesh. I had a black cocker spaniel when I was a kid; his name was Marley.'

'Ah, how sweet. You don't have any animals now?'

'No, sadly. They're good company but I travel too much.'

Luke very patiently runs through the various buttons again.

'Sorry I messed up, but I did take quite a few photos on my phone. Here, trawl through these and let me know if that's the sort of thing you're hoping to get.'

'Actually, if it weren't for the more random shots in the video – like your lap – it's a bit like a podcast. If you can get to grips with it, how do you fancy doing short clips narrating it as you go? Maybe even talking about your experiences as a newbie to boating?'

I wasn't expecting that. 'I'll give it a go but check out these photos.' Handing Luke my phone, I glance over his shoulder at the first one. 'Oh, that was the last one I took so you'll need to flick left, not right. There are probably at least thirty of them.'

Give him his due, he studies each one and I feel quite pleased, although a few of them are what I'd call arty. Like the golden ball of light in the middle of the clearing between the trees. Suddenly, he's staring at a photo of himself, and I grab the phone out of his hands.

'That's it!'

'You took a photo of me sleeping?' It's obvious he's highly amused by that.

For some reason I feel flustered. 'You were snoring.' He wasn't, he was lying in this bed and looking cute. It sounds daft but I wanted it as a . . . memento for when I'm looking back nostalgically on our time together.

Last night I just lay there wide awake, wondering what I've got myself into. When he returns to Cornwall will we text and call each other until enough time passes for the contact to tail off? Or will he turn up on my doorstep every few months when he's passing through?

I can't bear the thought of Luke adding me to the long list of friends he collects, so that he can flit in and out of my life when he's at a loose end. I'm not in the market for an occasional lover who comes and goes at will, disrupting my routine and my life, no matter how much fun I'm having.

He's hardly going to give up the somewhat nomadic life he leads for me. And I have no intention of wandering from place to place until he's ready to put down some roots. It's all, or nothing, and my head is telling me to prepare myself for the inevitable. But how do you stop caring for someone when they've touched your heart? The answer to that is probably bit by bit, I suppose.

'Anyway, what about the shots of the countryside?'

'They're great. You've managed to capture some real gems that will give potential new customers an idea of how different everything looks when you're on the water. Ben is going to be delighted. But I loved the video, and it wasn't just Bartie's presence. Say if you don't feel comfortable filming the scenery and talking about your experiences, it's a lot to ask.'

'I'll give it a go.'

'Just short clips Ben and Hilary can post on the blog. People do a lot of research for their holidays, especially anyone considering renting a boat for the first time. It would really help if they can find everything in one place.'

I'm fine with that. 'Do they own many boats?'

'Three other Pénichettes similar to this one, and a few smaller boats, but they're about to start a second business offering gourmet canal cruises. Now the boat they've bought for that is something rather special.'

'Gosh, it's quite a change of direction.'

'Not really, Ben used to be a chef, but Hilary soon tired of the late nights and long hours.'

'And running two businesses isn't as bad?' I query.

'It will be, but they're together most of the time and that makes all the difference. But a chef can never completely step away from the kitchen. When you have a passion for something, it's hard to let it go. Just look at Warren.'

'It's nice that Hilary understands.'

'Yeah, it is. This is a bit of an indulgence for him, but he'll start off by offering a few select dates in the most popular months. If it takes off, I'm sure he'll scale it up and get help, but will still keep his hand in every now and again.'

It's time to lie down and, being a little cooler, it's rather nice to need a thin cover over us. We can even lie in each other's arms quite comfortably tonight.

Luke lets out a deep breath.

'What's that for?'

'This was a good idea of mine, wasn't it?'

I grin to myself. 'Yes, it was. And even though I hate surprises, I love this one.'

Oh, Luke . . . that inner voice pipes up, *how can I say the word love without thinking of you?*

In a perfect world where there is nothing to tie us down, or hold us back, this would be that vision. If only life were that simple. For a holiday, this is wonderful, but it's not a lifestyle I'd choose forever. I think that's where the two of us differ. I am, gradually, seeing a side of him I had no idea existed, and I could envisage him living permanently on a boat. Luke and his canine companion, who would sleep half of the day, keeping him company while he worked. Then they'd go on long walks together, enjoying the fresh air.

When it comes to choosing a partner to spend the rest of your life with, that's when things get complicated. It would be impossible living with someone who holds the emotional stuff in. Sharing is caring . . . in more ways than one. It not only lessens any sense of burden but it's about having someone you trust enough to share your deepest, innermost thoughts with. And being happy to do so without fear of being judged.

Either Luke isn't ready, or I'm not the right one for him. It would be foolish of me to kid myself that I could change him. That's how so many relationships fall apart, isn't it? It could take him a long time to learn how to open up and feel comfortable doing that.

The act of wanting to change someone doesn't sit well with me. It means I'm comparing our lives and judging him, as if the path I'm on is somehow better. It might be safer, more practical even, but the things that I regard as important aren't necessarily important to Luke. We're like two people standing either side of a deep valley, both thinking the view we're seeing is perfection and wanting the other person to join us. It's a daunting trek and what if I make the journey only to discover it's a mirage? Luke's head is in the clouds whereas my feet are firmly planted on the ground. That sobering thought makes my heart ache.

21

Le Marché

Negotiating the boat into one of the finger berths, extending out from a sizeable floating pontoon, isn't easy even for Luke. He uses something called a bow thruster in short bursts to manoeuvre *La Belle Vie* into place before I tie her up fore and aft.

'Great job, captain!' I salute him as I stand on the wooden pontoon. The boat fits nicely in between the two fingers and we're one of over a dozen crafts already moored up.

'We're staying here for two nights,' Luke informs me, when I jump back on board to help get the bicycles. 'Once we've stocked up on provisions, I thought I'd go online for a short stint and then maybe this evening we have ourselves a romantic dinner for two, something a bit special. What do you think?'

'It sounds good to me. It can't be all work, can it?' Steering the boat seems to be a real pleasure for Luke and most of the time it's relaxing, but negotiating locks is time-consuming and a bit fraught. Well, it is for me, and I notice that he watches me like a hawk when I'm up on deck.

As we cycle along, I'm curious as Luke seems to know exactly where he's going. 'Have you been to this market before?'

'Oh, yes. Twice before on this route. Ben and Hilary often invite me to join them on one of their little breaks. It's good to catch up and I usually do a bit of work for them online while I'm here. Sometimes, though, it's at the start, or the end, of the peak season, if they have a boat that isn't booked up and it's not always on this canal.'

'Lucky man, you have some fun friends.'

'Well, a lot of them started out as clients. Usually, it's because they had a problem with their IT kit, or their website, and someone they know recommended me. I like to be fair, and I have no problem at all working for bed and board. It's just up ahead; turn into that gravelled drive and it's to the rear of the stone building.'

It's obviously a yard used by a working farm, as to one side there are several tractors and some attachments lined up in front of a low stone wall. There are a lot of cars here and, in the field beyond is a large collection of stalls. We lock our bikes and grab the cool bags from the panniers.

As we walk hand in hand, today everything feels fresh after last night's showers, but the sky is a an almost opaque blue, subtle as opposed to the vivid blues we've had day after day. It's like everything has cooled down a little and it's a relief.

'*Fromage* first!' Luke states. He pulls me in the direction of a white van, the side of which is open, shading the produce in the long display counter. It's filled with so many cheeses, it's hard to know which to choose.

When we step forward, Luke and I take it in turns to point as he chatters away to the man behind the counter. We decide to split up and I go to buy some vegetables and fruit, while Luke heads off to buy fish and meat.

With a wicker basket already filled with carrots, French beans, lettuces, tomatoes and some baby potatoes, I'm just about to grab a few bunches of herbs when I hear my name being called.

'Freya, Freya!'

Patricia comes rushing towards me, followed by a man with an empty shopping bag in one hand and Bartie's lead in the other.

We hug like old friends. 'I did wonder if we'd bump into each other! We saw your boat moored up, but no one was around. This is my husband, Ant.'

'Hi, Ant, it's nice to meet you. And hello, Bartie!' I stoop to ruffle his fur and his tail wags.

'Are you staying here overnight?'

'Yes. Two nights, actually.'

'Ah,' she replies. 'We're off in the morning. Another boater told us about this market and what a find!'

Out of the corner of my eye, I catch Luke hurrying over, eager to meet Bartie.

'This is . . . Luke. Luke, meet Patricia and Ant.'

They shake hands, then Luke places his cool bag down on the grass and kneels to fuss over Bartie, who is delighted. 'Now aren't you a handsome one, Bartie.'

I swear that dog couldn't wag his tail any more if he tried. It's whipping back and forth so fast, it's like a blur.

'He's a beauty and a beast.' Patricia smiles, watching them both as Bartie hunkers down for more. 'He's so full of energy it's hard to keep him on the boat. I spend as much time walking him on the towpath as I can to tire him out.'

We can't stand chatting for long as we have goods that will spoil, but we end up inviting them over to join us for dinner this evening. Patricia kindly offers to bring something along, but Luke insists he'll do the cooking.

When we part company and hurry back to the bicycles, I turn to look at Luke. 'That's kind of you to invite them. I know you had a special dinner for two in mind.'

'We've plenty of time for quite a few romantic meals together before this trip is over. I thought you'd enjoy a little company in case you were tiring of me.'

As we carefully distribute our goods between the panniers either side of each bicycle, I stop to shake my head at him. 'You're much too fun for me to tire of you.'

'Oh, so I'm entertaining, am I? That's not quite the reaction I was hoping for.'

'Come on, we need to get this back to the boat. It's bad form to fish for a compliment.'

With that I set off, smiling to myself quite happily as Luke hurries to catch up with me. The sun is out, the rain has pepped up some of the wilting flowers and leaves, it's not too hot and life feels good. Another memory to cherish and more still to come.

'Hey, Mum. How are things with you?'

'Freya, it's really good to hear your voice! I'm fine but I can't lie, you've been on my mind a lot the last couple of days. I nearly dropped my phone when I read your text message saying you were on a canal boat.'

'I know,' I acknowledge, rather meekly. 'I'm sitting on a bank next to the towpath as we speak, just watching the world go by and unable to believe how quickly I've adjusted.'

'But you do have all the facilities . . . don't you?'

Aww, bless her. She knows I'm not the caravanning and camping sort.

'We have four en suites,' I laugh. 'Admittedly, each one is more of a little cubicle with a shower, loo and handbasin packed in it, but the water's hot and everything is immaculate. With just the two of us onboard, it's roomy.'

She heaves a sigh of relief. 'Four?'

'Yes, one for each double bedroom, as it caters for eight people. It's a luxury barge. We have a fully kitted-out galley and diner, and a separate saloon with a computer desk.'

'I wish you'd mentioned that,' she grumbles. 'I've been imagining you on some cramped little boat trying to pretend you're having a good time.'

'I am having a good time, really. And learning a lot.'

'Like what exactly?'

'How to negotiate a lock and how to tie a knot so that the boat doesn't float away while we're sleeping,' I muse, trying to imagine the look on her face.

'And how's Luke?'

'Aside from being an excellent captain, he's doing an IT project for the owners, so he's been working quite hard.' I go on to explain that I'm the designated photographer, which makes her laugh.

'You sound happy, which is the main thing. You wear a life jacket, don't you?'

'Stop worrying. It's a huge boat and it has a guard rail around all the walkways. We even have a sun deck, where we sit and relax. Tonight, we're having a dinner party onboard with another British couple we've met on our travels.'

There's some interference on the line and then I realise that once again Mum has company, and her head is turned away from the phone while she whispers to someone.

'Have I caught you at a bad time?' I ask.

'No. Not at all.' I hear another muffled sound before she begins speaking again. 'Did Beth call you?'

She's changing the subject on purpose in case I ask who's there with her. I know the answer, it's George.

'No, I rang her. The auction is this coming Thursday.'

'Do you think they'll go for it?'

'She was still thinking it through; obviously it was a bit of a shock at first. I can't wait to find out what happens.'

'I don't know . . . all these changes going on, just when it looked like you were all settled. As if the two of you don't have your hands full running the business.'

'Mum, if Beth and David do get that house, they can handle it. And as for me, another few weeks and I'll be back home, then everything will return to normal.'

In the background I can hear someone hammering now, which sends Mum into a bit of a tizzy. 'I must go and investigate that noise. Take care, darling, and don't forget to wear that life jacket! Love you.'

Beth is family to both me and Mum. We've known each other since we were toddlers, and as I didn't have any siblings, she's like a sister. I think Mum worries as much about her as she does about me.

I stand, determined to get to grips with the camera. Now, I'd better not zoom in on people, or the names of boats, so I wait for a while until there's nothing in sight. Then I walk and talk, pointing out the beautiful surroundings and even succeed in filming a family of ducks. They paddle along effortlessly, sending little ripples across the surface of the canal.

Further on, an old stone building lies abandoned just a stone's throw off the path. It's half covered in a climber with vibrant pink flowers and surrounded by knee-high weeds.

When I pan around, I focus on the bicycle leant up against the tree and talk about the joys of cycling on the towpath. Most of the people on the boats and barges that go by wave, and when I see two following each other, I stop filming to wave back. It's time to go a little further and take a few photos before I head home to help Luke in the galley. *Home*, how easily that word popped into my head.

As I cycle, I start humming to myself. The sun on my skin feels glorious. When I glance in the rear-view mirror I look, and feel, tanned and revitalised. A new version of me, more relaxed, no doubt due to what has turned out to be a bit of a digital detox for me, too. Who wants to spend time online when there's so much to see and they're in good company?

My big fear in coming away with Luke was that we'd end up getting on each other's nerves. Me with my need to plan everything and him with his seemingly relaxed attitude. How the tables have turned. He's the one with the schedule and the plan, I'm the one taking it day by day. Who would have thought that would happen?

After a delicious meal, Patricia can see that Bartie is in need of a walk and she grabs his lead, but Luke immediately jumps to his feet.

'I'll take him,' he offers.

'Are you sure?'

'I'd love to. We'll be fine, won't we, Bartie?'

Bartie spent most of the meal sitting at Luke's feet, and I think everyone can see that they've already become firm friends.

As they set off, I start clearing the table and Patricia gives me a hand. Ant is busy going through the gallery of photos on his iPad, after hearing about Luke's project. They spend their afternoons venturing a little further afield than me. When I asked if he had any photos of small villages within easy walking – or cycling – distance of the canal, he simply said, 'Of course. I snap away all the time, much to Patricia's annoyance as it slows us down. I'm sure I can find a few that might be of use to you.'

As Patricia follows me into the galley, she gives me a warm smile. 'You've just made his day,' she declares. 'Not that he's one of those people who bore their friends with holiday snaps but, as an amateur photographer, he likes to capture the essence of where we've been. Which is just as well, as I'm not the sort to stand there posing for him.'

I give her a knowing smile. 'Me neither. And I don't do selfies.'

'We only have another week before we drop the boat off. Then it's back to work for us both. Ant is getting a bit twitchy about the new job, but he'll be fine.'

Patricia manages a clothing shop in Ipswich; Ant is a buyer for a large retail chain and has recently been poached by a competitor.

'Would you take a boating holiday again?'

'Yes, we would. I wasn't sure how we'd find it being closeted together all the time,' she admits. 'We're like chalk and cheese. Ant spends a lot of time at the gym, but I prefer yoga and tai chi. The gym bores me rigid. I like reading and he likes long walks so he can take a few photos.'

'Luke and I met at the gym.'

Patricia's eyes light up. 'I notice you don't wear a ring. Is this a fairly new relationship, because the two of you seem very close?'

How do I explain the unexplainable? 'We're not actually a couple, we're just good friends. I was badly in need of a break from work and Luke's working holiday meant he needed a companion, although he had to talk me into it. He usually travels with one of his best mates.'

'Oh, I see; you're two people unexpectedly thrown together for a summer adventure in France, how romantic,' she remarks, trying not to look a little surprised.

I find myself frowning, as I stare out the window at two people walking along the towpath hand in hand. 'I think that sums it up perfectly.'

'And when you get back?'

The chances of crossing paths with Patricia and Ant again is pretty slim. I turn to look at her. 'That's a question I keep asking myself.'

She's buffing the wine glass in her hands with a tea towel, and she pauses for a moment. 'When I first crossed paths with Ant, I was fresh out of a two-year relationship and had decided I needed some time alone. You know, to discover what I really wanted out of life and to understand why it took a friend to enlighten me that my man had been cheating on me. Ant was different, and I knew that from the moment he started chatting to me. It still took a lot of courage for me to give him my phone number. My head was saying "it's too soon" but, like you, I got talked into it. He wasn't pushy, just persistent in an endearing way. A year later we were married. You never know what the future holds, do you?'

'No, that's true.' Never, ever did I think that after giving in and letting Luke take me for a drink, we'd end up here, alone together on a boat in France.

When we wave Patricia, Ant and Bartie off the next day, they insist on exchanging details in the hope of meeting up at some point when we're back in the UK. To my amazement, Luke is keen. Admittedly, they're a genuinely lovely couple and Bartie is also a little darling, but they see us as a couple, which we aren't.

Sometimes I wonder if he's given any thought at all to what happens when we return home and go our separate ways; I can't blame him, as I was the one who said this was a trip with no strings attached.

'Oh, what I'd give to have a dog like Bartie,' Luke comments, as he grabs my hand and we watch them sailing away.

'Maybe you'll be in a position to get a canine friend one day very soon.'

Luke's grasp tightens a little as we stroll back to *La Belle Vie*. 'I hope so, Freya. Come on, let's grab a coffee and look at your footage and photos from yesterday. I'd like to select a few stills to add to the home page. I'll download the ones that Ant emailed over, too. It'll make his day if we can use a couple and credit him as the photographer.'

'The start of a new career?' I jest, raising my eyebrows.

'Everyone has to start somewhere. If you follow your passion then a job isn't really work, is it? It's more of a vocation.'

'Honestly, Luke. Sometimes I think I should be noting down some of those little throwaway lines of yours. *Life according to Luke.*'

'Now you're poking fun at me, but what I said is true. And there's more to me than meets the eye, you know.'

Hmm . . . I can't argue with him there.

'Right, I'll watch your video first while you download the photos and share the folder with me. Then I'm going to be really boring and spend all morning working, if that's all right with you.'

'It's fine. I'll take a cycle ride and film another video.'

He stops to spin me around, placing his hands around my waist. 'You're the least demanding person I think I've ever met.'

'Oh, I can be demanding when I want to.'

There's laughter in his eyes.

'This afternoon I'm all yours and this evening we will have that romantic dinner for two under the stars, I promise.' His lips on mine are warm and inviting but there's work to do.

The problem I have is that Luke is so . . . enticing. He makes life feel easy; there's no drama, no expectations, just living in the moment. There is a sense of joy in that simplicity, but maybe it's amplified by the ambience of being in a country setting. There are no crowds of people, no constant background hubbub going on.

Just nature, the water and the two of us.

22

The Final Week

It's Monday, the twenty-sixth of August and on Friday morning we'll be mooring up the boat for the last time. The last two and a half weeks have flown.

Breakfast today is a rather subdued affair as it begins to sink in that we're on countdown. It's like the bubble has burst and we're both feeling a little deflated. Luke keeps glancing at me nervously in between tucking into a plate of scrambled eggs. Even his choice of dish this morning is a reminder of home.

'Any further updates from Beth?' he asks, tentatively.

I put my elbows on the table, holding a mug between my hands and peer at him over the top of it. 'Fingers crossed; it looks like they might get an offer on their house tomorrow. It's an agonising wait as today is August bank holiday back in the UK. One couple did a second viewing yesterday afternoon. They were there for over an hour, as David and Beth offered them coffee, which bodes well. People often like to talk directly to the owners when it comes to asking questions about the property.'

'Even though Beth is an estate agent,' Luke chuckles, as he loads his fork.

'It wouldn't be professional for Beth to do the viewings herself, so Ethan did one on Thursday and two on Friday. There are two couples who expressed a serious interest, but to book a second viewing so close to the first – and on a Sunday when they know the homeowner is likely to be there – is a good sign indeed.'

Luke pushes the plate away, lazing back in his seat. 'Are you worried what's going on in her life will affect things when you get back to the office?'

He thinks that's why I'm subdued, but it isn't that. I can't put into words why I feel so lacklustre today, as all holidays come to an end. 'No. Our friendship comes before business and if it means we delay our plans to expand for a year, it's no big deal. These things don't happen overnight, anyway.'

We lapse into silence, and he suggests we take our coffees up onto the sun deck.

'I love early mornings,' he muses, as I follow him up the steps.

'What's the plan for today?'

We were supposed to be spending two nights at our previous stop, where we refuelled and used the facilities to pump out the wastewater and fill the clean water tank. On Saturday, when Luke suggested we move on after only one night instead of two in the berth, it was the first time he'd deviated from Ben's schedule.

Given his generally relaxed attitude, it surprised me. It was only then it dawned on me that, deep down inside, he's a bit of a secret worrier. He wanted to get us a few kilometres closer to our final destination near Auxerre. We're not going quite as far as the boat harbour itself, but a quieter mooring a couple of kilometres away. One of Ben and Hilary's staff will be meeting us there and, in case of any last-minute problems, he doesn't want to risk being late.

'Freya, you haven't been listening to a word I've said, have you?'

Guilty as charged. 'Sorry, my mind keeps wandering. You have my full attention now, I promise.'

He grins at me; oh, how I'll miss that cheeky look and the glint in his eyes that accompanies it.

'Our next two mapped stops are just floating pontoons with no need to book and no facilities, so if we sail on this morning and cover a few more kilometres, we'll be closer to our final mooring on Thursday, ahead of the handover the following day.'

'It's going to be a long haul back to the UK.'

'If it all goes to plan, Claude will have Reba there waiting for us. I've never met him personally, but Ben assured me that he'd take her steady and was excited to be driving a VW van. We'll be on the road by ten o'clock, hopefully. With a forty-five-minute stop either side of the tunnel, it'll take us about eight hours.'

'So, our last morning's cruise will be a short one.'

'It'll be a gentle start before we head for your place. As for today, we should push off soon and find somewhere to berth before noon.'

I know he's nearing the end with his project but he's not there yet and time is fast running out.

'What's on your agenda for me, this afternoon?' I laugh, determined to shake off my reverie. I don't want to spoil what time we have left; that wouldn't be fair on Luke. We set off on this trip with a no-strings-attached mentality. There was no way of knowing it would stir up a whirlwind of emotions within me. Although I've laughed it off whenever he's hinted that it could grow into something bigger between us, he seems to accept that it'll soon be over. I should be relieved . . . shouldn't I?

'I'm keen to get the pages fully populated ahead of the new website going live and the revamp on the old one being revealed. To do that, it would help if you could work alongside me. It's time to change out some of the photos I used as placeholders, as there's such a vast library now and you've caught some superb shots. Then we need to go through your video diary.'

'My what?' I exclaim.

'Think about it. Little clips, each in a new setting and you talking about your experiences. All the new things you've learnt about sailing a barge.'

'About being a lackey, you mean.'

'No. Being the captain's mate is an important role and you have been behind the wheel a few times.'

That makes us both laugh. 'With you no more than two paces away,' I declare.

'It's the little squeal you let out every time we pass a boat, which makes me a tad nervous.'

'That's not fair. It's just the bigger boats around us that really disturb the water and I feel *La Belle Vie* being pushed off course. Sometimes the bank isn't that far away and there's no room for error, is there?'

'I'm teasing you and I shouldn't. You've done absolutely brilliantly, Freya. Boating may not be your thing, but you'll give anything a go and I admire that. Besides, I really couldn't have completed this project without your help. You're pretty darned good behind the lens, too. It would have been too much work for one and the quality of the photos wouldn't have been half as good.'

He leans in, throwing an arm around my shoulder and pulling me close to him on the sofa, as we gaze out over the canal. Times likes these are the ones I'll remember forever. The stillness all around, the sense of being alone together in the French countryside and knowing that for some reason this was meant to be.

When it's all over, will this turn out to be *the* highlight by which I measure every experience I have in the future? How do you know for sure whether a single moment in time is that what if/if only moment, or simply one that wasn't meant to last a lifetime anyway? *Stop with the thinking, Freya*, that inner voice warns me. You dared to dream and look where it's got you.

* * *

'Aww . . . Bartie!' We're watching that first accidental video I made, and Luke pulls a sad face.

'It's not the lovely Patricia and Ant you're missing, it's your canine friend, isn't it?' I ask, accusingly.

He shakes his head at me. 'Kindred souls . . . what can I say?'

Luke can sort out his feelings for a dog, but not for me. The truth is that he's just not ready to settle down. I can't help but raise an eyebrow at him as we press on, watching video after video. Each one is probably no more than six minutes long, but he's right, it is like a video diary.

'You know, they're all good. If you're happy, I'll share the whole folder with Ben and Hilary. They'll credit you, of course.'

It's a lovely way to repay our hosts for this amazing experience aboard *La Belle Vie*. 'That's fine by me.'

'And who knows? You might even become an internet sensation. You could then set up your own website and post an *At Home with Freya* series.'

Now he's belly-laughing.

'Doing what?'

'Taking clients on viewings? Or maybe, since Vicky sent you a lot of her recipes, an at home in the kitchen series?' He muses.

I know he's being tongue in cheek, but I'm warming to the idea. 'It would certainly help fill all those dark evenings when winter arrives. I've spent enough time around some great chefs to learn a thing or two and I could recount little snippets of my travels and add photos, of course.'

Luke's eyes widen. 'Well, there you go! Now, on to the photos. Being honest—' he gives me an awkward look '—there are only three of Ant's I think we can use. The rest have people's faces in the background so we can't use them, and a couple just aren't up to your standard.'

'Really?' Is he pandering to my ego? One glance tells me that Luke is simply being pragmatic. 'The hard work is going to be in not duplicating the scenery you've caught in your video clips. I do love some of the ones where you focus on the boat and, of course, the expertly filmed one of you demonstrating how to tie a cleat hitch, then coiling the ropes so they aren't a trip hazard.'

'Because you took it!'

His eyes light up. 'Naturally. I'm going to email Ben and Hilary a link to the video folder to see what their reaction is, then I'll load a few of the photos we're already agreed on. If you're happy to wade through the rest and save copies of the ones that make your final cut into a separate folder, I can take it from there.'

He leans in to kiss my cheek and even though I know his thoughts are elsewhere, we both have tasks to attend to. I can't even imagine how much it costs to rent this boat for a week, let alone three and I can't lose sight of the fact that to Luke, they're important clients.

'That was . . . an interesting evening,' I chuckle, as Luke pulls me into his arms. Lying here in bed, it's still raining outside but inside it's cosy and comforting.

'What . . . the getting soaked to the skin, or the dark trek back through the menacing forest?'

I have to think about that for a moment. 'When that couple stopped to talk to us and suggested a quaint little restaurant close by, we should have realised that, as joggers, close is a case of perception.'

'But it was a real gem of a place. And they were so obliging. Did you notice we were the only ones with not one, but two candles on our table?' Luke turns to grin at me.

'I did. And it was a real find; it had that intimate feel. The other diners were so friendly, and the hosts were jolly.'

'It's not often you get free wine *and* a complimentary aperitif.'

'I know . . . and I can't believe it was the first time I've tried pastis. When it arrived, a seemingly small drop in a tumbler and I watched you add water from the jug, I wasn't too impressed to begin with. It looked like cloudy lemonade but the taste . . . well, aniseed is very pleasant to drink, and the water didn't make it feel like alcohol, at all.'

Luke smiles. 'I didn't like to tell you, but the correct ratio for the water is one to five, and you flooded yours a little. But it needs that, as it's so strong. Don't quote me on this, but I think it's something like forty-per-cent proof.'

I gasp. 'Thank goodness you stopped me from trying it neat! What does it consist of?'

Luke puckers his lips as he thinks. 'Well, aside from alcohol, I believe there's star anise, peppercorns, cardamom, nutmeg, cloves . . . what else? Cinnamon and liquorice, if I remember correctly. It's one of Ben's favourite drinks but he'll often have one before, and one after, a meal as he isn't into wine.'

'It's a shame I won't get to meet him and his wife in person.'

'I know, and they feel the same way, but they're busy putting together the menus for the Gourmet River Cruises and are set to do their first trial run at the weekend. If we were staying longer, we'd have been invited, as it's not paying guests just friends and acquaintances.'

'Ah, what a shame.' Luke's body starts shaking and I know he's laughing. 'What?'

'Us, walking back in the dark with only the light from our phones and seeing shapes behind every tree.'

Before long I'm laughing, too. It was spooky. 'Tripping over the rotting branch from that fallen tree was rather unfortunate. How's your leg?'

'Sore!' he complains.

'I'm sorry I laughed. I thought you were safely over it when I moved my phone.'

'It was how hard you laughed that got me. I mean, you were doubled over!' But he knows it was just one of those reactions you can't control.

'It was the way you fell. Your arms flew up into the air!'

'Yes, and what did you do? You certainly didn't hurry over to check I was still alive.'

I touch his cheek, as he stares at me.

'You were groaning but I knew the moment you stopped that you'd want to know exactly where your phone had fallen.'

He presses his lips together for a second or two. 'You're right. There's no way we could have found it, foraging around in the dark. So, thank you.'

We lie here for a while listening to the gentle raindrops pitter-pattering on the windows. It was a lovely meal and a wonderful evening. It's certainly one of the memories from this trip that will always come to mind. The walk through the forest was scary. Luke was trying to pretend he wasn't as spooked as me, and after the pastis, and two glasses of wine, I'd have laughed even if I were the one who tripped over the fallen branch.

'You've no regrets about coming on this trip with me, have you?' His voice is low, his arms tightening around me.

'No. Not at all. I've met some interesting people; I've done some things I never, ever, dreamt I'd do and spending time with you has been wonderful, Luke.'

He falls silent for a while and just when I think he's asleep, he suddenly turns his head to face me once more.

'We could escape together, you know.'

I give a chuckle. 'Escape what?'

'It's more a case of expanding our horizons.' His tone is serious and his look intense as I study his face, but I don't know what exactly he's expecting me to say to that, so I say nothing.

'Has this break changed anything for you?'

Oh gosh, now he's asking me to evaluate our time together and I can't do that. My head and my heart are fighting each other, and deep down I know that my head usually wins.

'I've learnt a few things about myself, if that's what you mean.' I'm skirting the issue and the light I see reflected in his eyes dims a little.

'Have you?'

This is painful and an ache begins to fill my chest. I do my best to reply in an upbeat manner. 'I can steer a boat if I put my mind to it. And I chop vegetables consistently enough to please a chef. Oh . . . and harvesting fruit and vegetables is hard work, but so rewarding when you know the person who planted them.'

'Is that all?'

I let out a gentle, but well-meaning sigh. 'It's been two months, Luke. Every single day has been filled with fun, laughter, new experiences and challenges. It's been amazing, totally amazing.'

Even in the darkness, I can see that he's not wearing the customary smile he has when I'm talking to him.

'I'm glad it didn't disappoint.'

I'm mortified when I can't stifle the yawn that suddenly erupts and Luke reaches out to push a few strands of hair away from my face, scooping them behind my ear. 'It's been a perfect summer,' I mumble, tiredness beginning to overwhelm me.

Was it what I was expecting? No. Did I learn anything new about myself? Yes. I discovered that the tussle between heart and head is an impossible battle ground. The answer to happiness, I believe, lies somewhere in the middle. But it takes two people to understand that, in order to move a relationship forward.

Luke's voice floats around me but I struggle to distinguish the words as sleep tries to claim me. The words 'need' and 'you' seem to float in the air, as I'm being spirited away into a dream about forests and shadows. Then I hear 'hopeless' or was it *hopeful*? The darkness around me is closing in fast and I'm powerless to stop it. The adventure is almost over and yet a part of me wants it to go on forever. Sadly, my head is telling me to let go – or is it my subconscious easing me into sleep mode? I wish I knew which . . .

December

23

Lost . . . and Found

'Freya, it's Luke.'

The sound of his voice makes my entire body quiver and I almost drop the phone. 'I . . . I can't talk right now.'

'Bad timing. I understand. How are you?'

It is a struggle to hold back a sarcastic laugh. It's been three months since our return and there's been no contact between us at all. His parting words were that he'd be in touch; he didn't say when, but I didn't think it would take this long. Sadly, it's an easy way out when it's hard to know what to say, isn't it? I just feel stupid that I didn't suss that out at the time.

'Fine. And you?' The coldness in my voice as I say the words chills even my heart. Where once there was this inner excitement, as the weeks have passed I had no option other than to accept the truth. It was over. I forced myself to let that silly bubble of hope deflate.

'Life's been crazy. Look, I know you're at work, so I won't keep you. Can I call around to your place tonight?'

He's back then. A part of me begins to crumble. The hardest part has been hiding my sense of disappointment and also rejection, from the people I love. They'd be gutted to know that I'm hurting and just as I was getting stronger, this happens. I should say no but I want . . . no, I need to understand what happened.

I know I made it clear to Luke at the very start that it was just a summer adventure, but I changed on that journey and I really thought that he had, too. I understood that it was difficult for us both settling back into our everyday lives. But as the days rolled on and there was no word from him, I knew I had to accept that while he has feelings for me he's not ready to make a commitment.

In hindsight, I guess it was mean of me to keep testing him, because that's what I was doing every step of the way. I wanted . . . no . . . needed him to open up his heart to me. If I were *the one* for him, he would have done that, wouldn't he? And now I've become one of his long list of friends. But we were so much more than simply good *friends*.

'I'll be home by seven. I have a viewing at six fifteen.'

'Great. See you then.' I can tell from his voice that he's smiling. He sounds upbeat and happy. I guess in Luke's world, three months without so much as a text to say he's still alive and kicking is normal. I was right all along. Thinking we could make a life together is like trying to mix oil and water.

As I press end call, Beth gets up from her desk and saunters over to me. 'Fancy a coffee?'

I look up and give her a fleeting smile. 'Yes. That would be great, thanks.'

'Good. Grab your coat.' She turns to Nancy. 'We're just popping out for half an hour.'

I'm a little thrown, as I assumed she was heading into the kitchen. Obviously, Beth has something on her mind.

It's freezing today. It's only the second of December, and they're already taking bets on a white Christmas. All bundled up, Beth and I walk the two-hundred-or-so yards to The Coffee Shack.

'I'll get these, you find a table,' she insists.

It's busy here today. They're running a special offer and who can resist a warming Santa Special hot chocolate, with a free gingerbread Christmas tree. I hurry over to the far corner where a man is just slipping a laptop into his bag.

'Are you going?'

'Yes. I just need to clear this away.'

'Oh, I'll take the mug and the plate back, while you finish packing up.'

He gives me a warm smile. 'Thanks. This is fast becoming my second home,' he laughs. 'I'll make sure no one else grabs the table.'

Beth is at the counter being served now and I pop the dishes onto one of the trays in the rack and hurry back.

'There you go. It's all yours. I've seen you here before. Do you work nearby?'

He's winding a knitted scarf around his neck as he stands.

'Yes. The estate agent's, a bit further along the rank.'

'Ah, I know the one. I've recently purchased one of the flats in Dewsberry Road.'

'Oh, nice. Great location.'

'Yes. Close to everything. I'm here every day. I like the noise and the bustle . . . and the coffee. Working from home can feel a tad solitary at times. Maybe our paths will cross again.'

Beth approaches carrying a tray and he strides off.

'What is it with you and stray men. He was chatting you up. It's a good job Mr Coffee Shop Man isn't here today.' She smirks as she checks him out.

'No, he wasn't. Just a local guy who works from home. If you spend enough time on your own, you'll chat to anyone, I should imagine.'

'Well, you put a big smile on his face, that's for sure.'

She settles herself down and I survey the goodies. 'What's this all about?' I ask, as I grab the coffee mugs and place them in front of us.

'The gingerbread Christmas trees were on the house, and I know you love shortbread biscuits. You look in need of pepping up this morning.'

Oh no. This is going to be about me.

'Do I?' She's right and I grab a biscuit, demolishing a third of it in one go.

'See. I know you. It's not what you say, it's what you've not been saying that concerns me. And whoever it was you were talking to on the phone just now, well . . . the colour drained from your face. What's going on, Freya?'

I can't help but sigh. 'Life. That's what's going on. Everything passes in time.'

Beth tips a small packet of sugar into her drink and begins stirring as she gives me one of her intense looks. 'Since you've been back it's like a part of your mind is elsewhere. You said you had a great time, but you were glad to be back. It hasn't given you itchy feet, has it? You know, the yearn to travel.'

That remark makes me splutter and some crumbs go down the wrong way, sending me into a fit of coughing. Beth freezes as I compose myself. 'No! Of course not.'

'Thank goodness. I've been imaging Luke turning up on your doorstep and the two of you driving off into the sunset. I have no idea what I'd do if you suddenly announced that you were walking away from our partnership. I can't afford to buy you out, not until the new house is ready for us to move into.' She looks miserable. 'And that sounds mean of me, when you were good enough to agree to putting our expansion plans on hold until—'

'Listen, the timing wasn't right anyway, and we both know that. I've been on catch-up and we're coming up to the quieter season, anyway.'

'Yes, but you did it for me because we're friends and you understand that there's only so much utter chaos I can cope with at any one time.'

I unwittingly give a little snort. 'You mean, the delights of living with your in-laws.'

Beth rolls her eyes. 'Sorry, but it's not easy. I thought I was doing a better job of hiding it. It can't go quickly enough for me. And we're running behind schedule, but who's counting?' She laughs and I join in.

'You'll get through it and judging by the architects'

impressions, it's going to be one amazing house when it's all done.'

She gives me a poignant look. 'It will, but this interim situation I got myself in is my problem, not yours.'

'Beth! I would never leave you in the lurch. Besides, I haven't heard from Luke since we returned. Well, until this morning.'

'I did notice that you started mentioning his name less and less as the days passed.'

'The truth is that the trip messed with my head a little. It made me think about the long-term future. I might start dating again.'

Beth sucks in a deep breath. 'With Mr Coffee Shop Guy or this new admirer of yours?'

'No! I don't mean now, this second. I have some loose ends to tidy up with Luke, first.'

Beth leans in, her eyes searching my face for clues. 'Like what? Oh no . . . don't tell me you fell for those gorgeous eyes, with that slightly lost look?'

'Lost?'

'You know exactly what I mean. You can only rescue someone if they want to be rescued.'

We sit, sipping our coffees in silence for a few minutes. Hot coffee and sweet, buttery biscuits soon perk me up.

'He's coming to my place this evening so we can say a proper goodbye. That day he dropped me back home we were both struggling to find the right words. It was such a wonderful, inspiring and happy trip. Two months is a long time and to go from that to knowing we might never see each other again, well, what can you say?'

Beth peers at me over the top of her mug. 'You have a speech all planned out?'

'No. I just want to thank him, really. Before we left, I was so intense about everything, and I was stressed. You know me, everything has to be planned out ahead of time and I'm like a bloodhound following a trail. But I had the time of my life. The transition back to normal life has been tough because I now have a new normal.' I can't help smiling as I think back fondly of some of the many highlights of our trip.

'I like the new normal for you,' Beth says, softly. 'I was just a bit worried it's taken you a few months to adjust.'

'Old habits die hard, but I didn't want to fall back into the same old routine. I'm glad Luke rang because it's like drawing a line under the past. Well, that's how I feel, anyway.'

'So, it's all good, then?'

'It is, Beth. What I realise is that I don't want to live the rest of my life alone. Oh, I love my cottage and the garden is my pride and joy. But it's no substitute for having someone by my side.'

'You should definitely come in here tomorrow for a coffee, about this time. On your own, naturally.'

That sparks another coughing fit as I was just draining my mug. 'Beth, stop it. I'm not ready, but I will be. Hopefully, quite soon.'

When the doorbell rings, my hands begin to sweat. I'm not sure I can do this, but I have no choice. I need to get through it and start living as the new me.

'Luke, come in. I hope that's rain, not sleet.'

I stand back and he steps forward, kissing each cheek and then going for the third as if we're back in France.

'It's sleet, I'm afraid, but it won't come to anything.'

He has a carrier bag in his hand, which he places on the floor before slipping off his wet coat and hanging it on one of the hooks in the hallway. Then he slips off his shoes. There's a hole in his left sock and I stare down at it.

'Sorry, I dressed in a rush this morning. It's been totally crazy, and I'm exhausted.'

And yet he's buzzing, I can see it reflected in his eyes.

'You mentioned that. Come on through to the kitchen and I'll make us a drink. Tea, coffee, wine?'

'Black coffee would be amazing, thanks.'

He leaves the carrier bag on the floor beneath his coat.

Luke pulls out one of the tall stools at the breakfast bar on the other side of the kitchen and we lapse into silence as I boil the kettle. This is awkward. It would have been easier if I'd suggested he call, rather than come round in person.

'How did the viewing go?' He's feeling awkward, too.

'Great. They're going to call me in the morning, and I'll be very surprised if it isn't with an offer.'

'Wonderful. You haven't lost your touch, then?'

Is that supposed to be funny or is he struggling for things to say? It feels like we're old friends meeting up after many years apart, having gone off in different directions and finding we have nothing in common anymore. At least that makes it easier.

I carry the mugs over to join him. 'I never got a chance to say how much I enjoyed being driven around in Reba.'

When he dropped me home that last night it was late and it was raining heavily. I assumed he'd stay, but he said his friends were expecting him and he was heading home early the next day. My sense of disappointment took a while to shake off; but I kept telling myself that he'd get in touch. Now I'm digging deep to maintain my composure as this is precisely what I thought he might do: think we can pick back up whenever it's convenient to him. And that's not going to happen.

'It was an amazing experience,' I continue. 'As holidays go, it was probably one of the best I've ever had. I got to see and do things off the beaten track, so to speak. It was . . . great, Luke.' But it was just a holiday.

Without any warning, he reaches out to grab my hand and it catches me unawares. I can't look him in the eye.

'It changed everything for me, Freya. I've put my house on the market.'

My jaw literally drops, and I immediately tilt my head to look at him. 'You have? I thought you loved the view out over the water.'

'I do and I will miss it. My parents . . . well, my mum didn't take the news well when I said I'm moving to France.'

So, that's what this summer was about. 'I'm pleased for you. It's a huge step to take but I genuinely believe you'll be happy there.' And I mean it. I just wish he'd been honest with me from the start. But then I was the one who laid down the ground rules. No strings attached and that's exactly what I got.

'I want you to come and spend the weekend with me at the house before I accept an offer on it.'

'You think the price isn't right?'

'No.' He gives me a strange look. 'Because it will explain a lot of things that I couldn't share with you. One last trip in Reba, eh? I'll take you down to the beach where I surf, and we'll eat handmade Cornish pasties from the best bakery in the whole of Cornwall.'

'I can't just drop everything, Luke. It's a kind offer, but Christmas is looming, and I've got . . . a lot of things to do.'

'Hmm . . . now you're making excuses. My estate agent tells me this is the quiet time of the year for both viewings and taking on new properties.'

I can't argue with that.

'I bet you've worked every Saturday since you've been back.'

He's right, but keeping busy while my heart mends is important. I don't want to break it all over again.

'Please, Freya. Four days – the weekend after next – that's all I'm asking for and it'll be fun.'

Fun for him, maybe, but I fell for that once before and look how it ended. Talk about mixed messages!

'Sorry. I know you mean well, but—'

'Oh, I have something for you!' He jumps up off his stool and heads back out into the hallway, leaving me feeling confused and bewildered.

'Here you go. It's quite heavy.' Luke hands me the carrier bag. 'Don't open it now but I guarantee it will put a smile on your face after I leave. I feel a bit like Santa, as I just popped in to see my friends. Anyway, I have to get back and it's a long drive in the dark.'

'You drove all the way from Cornwall to Kent just to drop off some presents?'

'Yes.'

I look at him askance. 'You're mad.'

'I know. Normally, I'd post them but it's really good to see you and I wanted to deliver this in person. Anyway . . .' He picks up his coffee mug and downs half of it in one go, even though it must be a little hot still. 'I need to get back on the road.' With that he walks over to the tap, adds a little cold water and drains the remainder.

I think about Reba and wonder what he's driving now. It's hard to suppress a smile, as I imagine an old pickup truck with a tailgate. Something in which he could safely transport his surfboard without damaging it.

'Don't give me your answer now, just think about it. Text me tomorrow, OK? Right, I'm off.'

Less than a minute later, I'm left standing in my hallway wondering what on earth that was all about. And then I walk back into the kitchen and open the carrier bag. It's quite a heavy box, beautifully wrapped in plain silver-coloured paper. I rip it off to see that it's a vintage bottle of champagne from Le Château de la Fontaine. It's in a fancy wooden display case. The front is embossed with a bunch of silver grapes and the vineyard's distinctive logo.

I find myself frowning until the penny drops. Luke is serious about moving to France. He didn't buy this while we were there, which means he's been back since. So, after visiting Max and Erin, he took an hour's detour to see Iris just to bring me back a souvenir that would make me smile. And it has. That's Luke all right, expect the unexpected and a part of me hopes he'll never change; it takes courage to stay true to yourself. Especially when it means putting everything on the line. I hope he finds what he's looking for and can finally put down some roots.

The next morning Beth can't wait to join me in the kitchen at work to quiz me about last night. When I tell her what happened and how confused it left me, she goes very quiet for a moment or two.

'Freya, maybe he's hoping you'll talk him out of selling his house.'

That's probably the last thing I was expecting her to say.

'In which case, why put it on the market if he needs a second opinion to tell him he's doing the right thing?'

She gives her head a little shake. 'Don't you think it's a little odd, coming back and suddenly deciding to move to France?'

'Hmm, I guess it is, but maybe that was his plan all along. He was making sure that's where he wanted to be, and I was just along for the ride.'

Her frown tells me that was a little blunt. 'Maybe he returned from your little jaunt as unsettled as you are.'

I raise my eyebrows. 'I'm not unsettled. I've just started seeing things from a slightly different perspective, that's all. You and David have been trying to get me to go on a blind date with some of his eligible friends for months. I thought you'd be pleased I've finally decided to let down my guard a little and am considering it.'

She snorts. 'You let down your guard and some, pretty quickly with Luke.'

I'm flabbergasted. 'I can't believe you said that. I wasn't letting down my guard, I was having a harmless summer fling. I made it very plain from the start.' And ended up getting hurt.

'Because he's young and he doesn't know what he wants to do with his life yet, I know. You said all that before. But maybe he needs someone who has come to know him a little better, to save him from making a big mistake.'

Does Beth think that I should set my feelings aside and rush to his aid? Surely there are other people in his life he can turn to. 'You think I owe him something?'

'I think you want to do the right thing, but you're scared.'

Now I'm feeling cross. 'I'm not scared. It's over between us, because the truth is that it was just a fun interlude. I think he's running away to France because he's doing what he always does, not facing up to his problems. They were all there waiting for him on his return, and this is a classic case of avoidance.'

'Then be the person, the friend, who helps him break the pattern. And then you can get on with your life with a clear conscience. Four days you said, the weekend after next. There are plenty of people to cover, we're not exceptionally busy.'

Inwardly, I groan. 'If I manage to find Mrs Rowe the property of her dreams in the next week, then I'll head off to Cornwall, a week on Friday. Seriously, she's at the end of her tether, with no home in sight yet and the lease on her rental property ending mid-January, time is running out. She's put her trust in me and I'm not going to let her down.'

'That's a tall order, but if anyone can do it, it's you. But I'm here and I wouldn't leave her hanging. I say that because I don't think you're capable of walking away from Luke knowing that he's about to make a huge mistake. On some level the two of you bonded and there's no denying it, Freya.'

If only I didn't have a conscience, that inner voice pipes up. Then I grimace. A conscience is all that separates good from bad. My dad used to say that if you can't do something good, at least do no harm. It's been a long time since that phrase has popped into my head, but maybe it's come to the forefront of my mind for a reason.

'I'd better start phoning around and chasing some of the valuations I've done going back a while.' Who knows, I just might make the right call, at the right time, and find Mrs Rowe exactly what she's looking for.

'Freya! Listen to me. You get too caught up in people's situations. Sometimes clients are their own worst enemies, we both know that. Mrs Rowe has this vision in her head of the perfect house to turn into her new family home. Maybe it doesn't exist, but if it does, it'll probably be way over her budget. That happens when people are downsizing, particularly after a divorce. The right property for her, and her daughters, will come up at the right time. You head to Cornwall, and I promise I'll look after them for you.'

Beth means well but if I don't succeed, then that could be a sign telling me sometimes you can't tie up all the loose ends. But Beth has, unwittingly, put me on a bit of a guilt trip. I can't leave Luke in the lurch, either.

24

Doing the Right Thing

Luke was ecstatic when I called him to say that I'll be travelling down to Cornwall by train. At first, he insisted that he drive up to collect me, but I immediately rejected his offer. Next week is going to be a long one, with a spate of evening viewings I told Beth I'd cover. I simply said that I was looking forward to the journey as I'll need to unwind.

When I arrive at Mum's house early evening, I drop into the conversation that I'm off to Cornwall for four days at the end of next week.

'In the rain?' She laughs, shaking her head at me. 'It's a lot nicer in summer.'

'I know, but Luke is making some life-changing decisions, and he needs a listening ear.'

'I thought that was . . . um . . . done and dusted.'

'It is. This is just looking out for a friend.'

Mum's eyes search mine. 'You didn't part on bad terms, did you? Because I did wonder—'

On my return, all everyone wanted to do was chat about my holiday. Given that I had no idea what was happening with Luke, I simply put on a brave face. I talked about the wonderful things I'd seen and experienced but tried my best not to mention his name any more than necessary.

'Not really, but it was hard to say goodbye, you know,

find something fitting to say other than "*au revoir* and have a nice life",' to which she chuckles.

'You two got very close, Freya, so it's important you end it on a high note. You don't want to spoil all those wonderful memories.'

Mum is being careful what she says, but it's what she's not saying that tells me she knows I got my heart broken.

'That's why I'm heading down to see him. He says he's selling his house and moving to France.'

'Ah. That's the beauty of being footloose and fancy free, as your grandma would have said. You can do whatever you want, whenever you want.' Mum gives me a pointed look. 'The problem is there are times we all need someone to be there to save us from ourselves.'

I don't think Mum is talking about me, but I sit quietly facing her and settle myself back against the sofa cushions.

'This is hard, Freya. I know you and George don't see eye to eye, but while you were away . . . well, we started having our evening meals together. We took it in turns to cook and it was nice, as we'd chatter away over a glass of wine and then a coffee, afterwards.'

'I warned you that letting him pop in to fix this and that would give him the wrong impression. Seriously, you have more than enough friends to keep you company and it's worrying that every time he does a little job for you, you feel you owe him.'

Mum looks down at her hands. 'The thing is, Freya, I enjoy George's company. In fact, his visits brighten my day. So, we've recently started it up again.'

I draw in a sharp breath and find myself holding it for way longer than I should. When I exhale, it's followed by an embarrassing gasp.

'I knew you'd be upset. Please listen because it's taken a lot of courage to broach this subject. George makes me laugh and he has a good heart. It would be nice if the three of us could have a meal together sometime, so you can get to appreciate what I see in him.'

They're seeing each other? Is Mum being serious? But the look on her face tells me she is. 'Oh. Right. Maybe after I get back from my long weekend away,' I bluster, unwilling to make a firm commitment. I ease myself up off the sofa. 'Anyway, it's just a flying visit. I'm having my next-door neighbours in on Saturday night for a meal to thank them for looking after the garden in the summer. I've been so busy I haven't had time to get around to organising it and I was wondering if you wanted to come. Unless you have other plans?'

'No, that's . . . um . . . fine, darling.'

'Great. Does seven thirty work for you?'

'Yes. Perfect.'

She sounds a little disappointed, but there is no way I'm going to invite George. The last time our paths crossed he was under Mum's kitchen sink tightening up her cold tap. He couldn't get out of the house quickly enough, once he knew I'd arrived. Why would he act that way, unless he has something to hide?

On the drive home, I can't help but worry about what Mum is getting herself into. She hardly knows the man and it's not like her to blindly trust just anyone. She's not naive, but what really upsets me is that George is clearly a charmer. I'm not even sure whether Mum would realise if he were manipulating her.

Argh! This is turning into a nightmare. Why couldn't a nice family have moved in next door to her? I'm going to have to keep a close eye on how this develops. Still, one thing Mum is very savvy about is money. After twenty years as a finance officer managing a small admin team, she'd never fall for a quick-return investment, or any of that nonsense. Gosh, listen to me. The child is becoming the parent! Do I spend more time worrying about Mum now, than she spends worrying about me? I wonder. I just don't want to see her get hurt in the way that I have. It snuck up on me when I least expected it and now I'm paying the price. Besides, George is no replacement for Dad.

Since my return from France, I spend a lot more time in the kitchen. One of my recent successes, if I say so myself, is coq au vin, one of the recipes that Vicky sent me. Anything that cooks in one casserole dish is perfect for me. If I get the timing of the roast potatoes wrong or forget to put them in – which I have done – I can simply put the grill on low to keep it hot and turn up the oven.

In the background my neighbour, Roger, is opening a bottle of wine. His wife, Ursula, is talking to Mum.

'Oh, Kathy, how wonderful to live next door to a man with some DIY skills. Our overhead light in the sitting room stopped working and it took the best part of three weeks to get an electrician to finally turn up.'

'I did offer to get the stepladder in and take a look at it,' Roger points out.

'And risk you getting an electric shock? I remember when you decided to loosen the wall sockets when you did some painting.'

'Hmm. That was different. One of the wires worked loose and when I eased it off that's what blew the fuse. It could have happened to anyone.' He sounds miffed.

I half turn and catch Ursula giving Mum a look of exasperation. I, too, am feeling a tad exasperated at the mention of George, as Mum continues.

'It's very handy, I will admit.'

'A bit of company for you, too,' Ursula adds.

As I start carrying the hot dishes over to the dining table, Roger very kindly moves the wine glasses away from the trivet in the centre. 'There you go, Freya. Goodness, that smells good.'

'Well, this meal is way overdue, Roger. I can't tell you

what a relief it was knowing that you were looking after the garden for me while I was away. July and August are the hottest months, and I would have been heartbroken to come back to find my garden bone dry and dying off.'

'See, Ursula, there are some things I do well. Each to their own, as they say.'

'Oh, I know how lucky I am, honey. But plumbing and electrics are entirely different skill sets. We won't talk about the time you decided to replace a washer on one of the taps, will we?'

Roger bursts out laughing. 'Now that was a bit of a mistake. In my defence I didn't have the right tools.'

The banter between them is rather endearing.

'Exactly! Do you and George have anything in common, other than the fact that you're both on your own, Kathy?'

I walk back to the table, putting the serving spoons down with a bit of a clatter but no one takes the hint to start helping themselves. 'Roger, please tuck in.'

He grins back at me and grabs one of the spoons.

'A few things, as we've discovered. Neighbours are so important, Ursula, aren't they? Having someone you can call upon close at hand is a blessing.'

I reach for my wine glass and take a hefty sip as Roger turns his attention to the dish of roast potatoes.

'Oh, very much so,' Ursula agrees.

'We spend a couple of evenings together each week playing board games. George is very good at chess.'

'It's nice to have something fun to keep you occupied in the winter. Maybe the four of us could get together for a games evening. What do you think?' Ursula proposes and Roger nods his head in agreement.

'You could join us, too, Freya,' Roger adds.

Mum starts laughing. 'I'm afraid my daughter doesn't approve of my friendship with George.'

My mouth goes dry as all eyes turn in my direction. I lift my plate and start spooning some of the casserole onto it, acting nonchalant. 'I just think it's prudent to take your time to get to know someone, that's all.'

Mum turns to look at me, her expression rather sober. 'George has lived next to me for sixteen months now, Freya. I think the time for prudence is over, don't you?'

Well, that puts me firmly in my place. 'I think an evening of board games would be fun, Roger.' And that's what a dutiful daughter does to please her mother.

I guess she's right. It's time to give George the benefit of the doubt, but he'd better not put a foot wrong. No one is going to mess with my mum's affections. Dad would have expected me to look out for her and that's precisely what I'm doing.

The weekend seemed to flash by and it's Monday morning before I know it. Today I'm taking Mrs Rowe to view two properties. She's had the details for both of them for a while but had ruled them out. However, as time goes on, she's finally realising that she won't get everything on her tick list and is ready to accept that it's going to be a compromise. Oh, how many times have I been here before? But there is a third option I'd like to show her. It isn't even on the market yet and I do need to clear it with Beth first.

I walk over to her desk, and she looks up. 'Can we grab a quick coffee?'

She gives me a knowing look. 'You want to check on Mr Coffee Shop Guy? Aren't you better off popping in on your own for a takeaway, in case he is there? He might invite you to join him.'

I roll my eyes at her. 'I meant out the back.'

'Oh. It was just a thought,' she laughs as she follows on behind me.

I switch on the kettle and grab two mugs.

'How did the dinner party go?'

'Awful.'

'Really?' She pulls a long face. 'What went wrong?'

'The four of us and George are going to be having an evening of entertainment. Playing board games at Roger and Ursula's house.'

Beth laughs. 'Oh dear. You know, Freya, you have to stop being so overly protective of your mum. She's astute enough to know if a man is trying to worm his way into her affections for the wrong reasons.'

'Then why does he avoid me?'

'Maybe because you aren't prepared to give him a chance and he can sense that. Your mum obviously likes him.' Her voice is full of empathy.

I let out a gentle sigh. 'It's just—' I take a deep breath. 'No one can replace Dad.'

'Oh, Freya. You need to back off and let them work it out for themselves. If it doesn't come to anything, that's just the way things go. I know you don't want to see your mum get hurt, but if that means never taking a risk then she isn't living her life to the fullest, is she? Your dad wouldn't want her to be lonely, would he?'

It took a lot of courage for Beth to voice those words. 'Point taken,' I reply, noting the empathy in her tone. 'I've already agreed to this games night, albeit grudgingly.'

'By then, you might have a guy of your own to take along. Seriously, you could do worse than a date with Mr Coffee Shop or, dare I mention it, the new man who recently started working at David's office.'

I stir the coffee and pass her a mug. 'Enough of that. I need to talk to you about Mrs Rowe. I'm taking her and her daughters to look at two properties she'd already ruled out, without viewing. You know what it's like, when people start looking they expect a photo to make them instantly say "that's the one!" and they discard details for the most bizarre reasons. It's about the bricks and mortar, not the furniture, and the internal decoration is easy to change.

'However, you remember when I did that phone around? Well, one of the couples are almost ready to put their property on the market but they want to freshen up some of the paintwork inside first. The thing is, I think it's perfect for Mrs Rowe and her two daughters. It'll be another two weeks until they finish the work, so they aren't quite ready to sign a contract.'

Beth frowns. 'And you want to talk them into letting Mrs Rowe and her daughters have a look around today?'

I nod my head. 'I know it's not our policy to do that. But Mrs Rowe is desperate, and I'd hate for her to settle. She's still reeling from her divorce and with two teenage daughters, it's all about reinventing herself and making a new home for them. There's a good chance this property won't end up going on the market until after Christmas. The owners obviously want it to look perfect, but it's fine as it is, a bit of fresh paint won't make any difference. You know what it's like. Some people don't even make their beds before a viewing, but this couple are the sort that will give it a good clean every time just so everything sparkles.'

Beth and I take a seat on the sofa.

'I understand where you're coming from, Freya. It's just a bit of a risk. If Mrs Rowe doesn't fall in love with it, it might put this client off signing with us.'

'I know. That's why I haven't said anything to either of the two parties yet. If you think it's the wrong thing to do, then that's fine by me.'

'Oh, it's hard when you care, isn't it? Maybe this is one of those exceptions to the rule.'

'I'm glad you agree. I'll ring the sellers and make it happen!'

And that's precisely why I love working with Beth. Her heart is in the right place, and it isn't always about the money.

* * *

'Thank you so much for arranging these viewings at short notice, Freya. I think I can speak for myself and both of my daughters, when I say that the first property is lovely, but I can't see us living there. However, this one . . .' She looks back at the house across the street, that we've just viewed. Then she glances at each of her daughters in turn. 'The garden is smaller than we're used to. And we'd have to get builders in to make a few changes inside. What do you think, girls?'

The eldest, who is probably about seventeen years old, speaks up. 'The garden will do, Mum. The inside is fine, plus we can have two sitting rooms, in addition to your home office. That's a bonus, isn't it?'

Mrs Rowe's other daughter saunters up to her mum, putting an arm around her. 'It means we won't be driving you mad when we play our music or are on the PC gaming.'

Mrs Rowe glances at her, with pride reflected in her eyes. I can see that they all want the search to be over, but Mrs Rowe just can't quite bring herself to say *yes*. Having downsized from a really impressive five-bedroomed country house, this is an adjustment.

'There is one other property I could show you, but it's not on the market yet.' They all turn to look at me. 'We don't usually let our clients view anything until the owners have signed a contract because there's no guarantee they won't have second thoughts about selling or signing with us.'

Mrs Rowe makes direct eye contact with me. 'But you've talked them into letting us have a look around anyway?'

'I have.'

'Why?'

'Because when I went to see them a couple of weeks ago to value it, I instantly thought of you. I think it ticks off pretty much everything on your wish list. It's in immaculate condition, but the people who own it didn't want to show their home until they've refreshed some of the paintwork.'

'We can't put forward an offer on it, even if we like it?' Mrs Rowe looks confused.

'No. You can do that, but what I'm saying is that they might prefer not to accept any offers at all until it's on the open market.'

'Is this about price? Is it possible they'll get more than one offer and it'll end up in a bidding war? My budget is fixed, I'm afraid, and I just can't afford to stretch it.'

This is precisely why we don't do viewings on a property before we've formally taken it on; things aren't clear cut. 'No. For some people it's about working through the process of moving on. Preparing their house for sale is just that, for them. But when I explained that you've been looking for quite a while and you have a deadline to vacate your rental property, they agreed to a pre-marketing viewing.'

I can see that this resonates with her but maybe for all the wrong reasons. 'The people who bought our old house fell in love with it straightaway.' To my horror, she looks tearful and both of her daughters rally around her. 'I'm fine, darlings. It's all going to be just fine. I hadn't realised how hard it would be having everything in storage and feeling . . . misplaced. The rental property has never felt anything even remotely like home, has it?'

They both nod in silent agreement and I look on, trying not to show how harrowing this is to witness. 'Then I think it's the right thing to show you all this house. Even if they take a month to consider an offer, if it's the one, it'll be worth doing whatever you need to do to wait for it. But I will warn you that there is a risk. Sometimes people change their minds at the last minute. It's rare, admittedly, but it does happen.'

All I can do is explain the pros and cons; the decision lies with Mrs Rowe. People can be unpredictable at times and that applies to me, too. That thought makes me groan to myself as I think of Luke. Some lessons are meant to be learnt the hard way. I thought I was sparing Luke getting hurt but, as it turned out, I was the one who veered off course.

25

A Friend in Need

A heavy frost overnight has turned everything I see from the train window into a glistening winter wonderland. Even the bare trees look beautiful, encased in their delicate white coating. The scene looks crisp and wintery, unlike when the snow comes, which quickly gets trampled and then ends up looking a mess.

What a week it's been. Mrs Rowe burst into tears when I put forward her offer on what she said was her dream house and it was accepted. It was quite a moment in the office, as it's easy to forget that it's the future of people's lives we're involved in. After a strong cup of tea, she left on a high. As for the sellers, there's a house they've had their eye on for a while and hopefully we can get it all tied up in record time. Happiness is infectious and while there's a lot of frustration in this business, there's also a great deal of satisfaction.

But after a monumental high comes the low. It's time to prepare myself for the emotional upheaval ahead. That inner voice speaks up. *Three months, Luke . . . that's a long time to wait to say our final goodbyes. It's like writing the last page of a book, it's not over until you write 'The End'.* And I'm about to do just that.

When my phone kicks into life, I assume it's Luke checking I'm on the train but to my surprise it's Mum.

'Hi, Freya. You certainly chose a cold snap to venture down to Cornwall. I hope you packed lots of layers.'

That's Mum, always worrying. Ha! Just like me.

'I did. Um . . . how's George?'

There's a slight pause. 'He's fine. Actually, my gas boiler wasn't working, and he managed to solve the problem.'

'He did?'

'Yes. The overflow pipe was iced up. He used an old coat hanger to dislodge a rather long icicle and behold, the system fired up!'

I can hear the happiness in her voice.

'Don't mention that to Ursula,' I laugh. 'George might end up getting panic calls from her!'

Mum chuckles. 'He wouldn't mind. George is a kind man; he likes to feel useful. He says doing little jobs keeps him active, and being active keeps him young.'

And I'm beginning to see that I never gave the poor man a chance. 'Well, thank him from me, as I couldn't bear the thought of you sitting there shivering, wrapped in blankets.'

She bursts out laughing. 'I'd have lit the fire in the sitting room and used the sofa as a bed until I could get a plumber in. You don't have to worry about me, I'm doing just fine.'

'But it's nice to know you've got someone close by looking out for you.' The tone of my voice softens.

'Yes. I think so, too. Now, text me when you get there and then switch off your phone. Sort out Luke and make sure when you come back that your head is in the right place, then I'll be happy.'

'Will do. Love you!'

'Love you too, Freya. Just follow your gut instincts and you'll be fine.'

As we disconnect, I find myself staring down at the phone. What does that mean? Luke's his own man; all I can do is point out the pitfalls of his decision but at the end of the day it's down to him. Rather like my clients, sometimes a risk pays off, but that isn't always the case.

* * *

After a hug that is embarrassingly long, with passengers having to dodge around us, Luke and I trudge across the car park. He insists on wheeling my suitcase, leaving me with just my handbag.

Even though there's a little awkwardness between us, I'm glad I came. I care too much about him to walk away when it's obvious he's at a crossroads in his life. I like to think I know enough about him to listen and maybe point out any pitfalls in his plan.

When I spot Reba parked up, I'm shocked. 'You have her again?'

He turns to look at me, puzzled. 'She's my only form of transport.'

'But I thought you'd borrowed her from a friend. She'd just come out of the garage after a refit.'

'You did? I don't know what I said to make you think that. And, yes, it was her first time out on the road after two long months of using a rental car.'

I cast my mind back; on reflection, he's right. I assumed he'd called in a favour. Talk about not judging a book by its cover. This is probably his most prized possession and now I feel badly that I didn't make more of a fuss about it.

He undoes the lock and stows my case away in the back, oblivious to my puzzlement. VWs aren't cheap and neither is a complete refit with a new engine.

'Come on. It's freezing. I should have brought you down here for a visit before we headed off on our big adventure.'

'That's exactly what my mum said. I mean that Cornwall is glorious in the summer.'

'Although, in winter there's a lot less traffic. I wanted to share the view with you, and I did promise, didn't I?'

'You did.'

Luke walks me around to the side of the van and opens the door for me. He comes close, planting a kiss on my cheek and I hesitate, wondering if he's going to do the French thing but as I start to turn my head, he steps back. It's an awkward moment and we smile at each other, nervously.

'Come on. The one thing I can say about my house is that the heating is brilliant and it's close to the station.'

He said house, not home. Maybe France is where he's supposed to be, he has a lot of friends there. Perhaps he won't miss his daily trips to the beach and riding the waves as much as I thought.

Luke shuts the door, and I watch as he walks around to the driver's side. It feels like forever since I was last in this seat and yet, on the other hand, that cosy familiarity is there – instantly. It's a little unsettling, and I take a silent, but deep breath, as he pulls on his seat belt.

'Oh, before I forget, thank you for that wonderful bottle of champagne. And it did put a smile on my face.'

'Good. I knew it would and it was a perfect year for the grapes, apparently. Could you taste the difference?'

'Oh, I haven't popped the cork yet. I think a vintage champagne is worthy of an extra-special occasion, don't you?'

'You're right. Is there anything specific you had in mind?'

It's hard to suppress a giggle. 'My mother's friendship with George seems to be developing into a thing.'

'A thing?' Luke queries, and as I check out his profile, I can see he's frowning.

'They're getting on really well. I've been trying to ignore the signs but now it's so blatantly obvious they've moved on beyond having dinner together most evenings.'

'But you don't like George, do you?'

'No. Well, only because I feel I'm betraying Dad.' Gosh, did I really just admit that?

'It's only natural you should feel that way, Freya, but life goes on and your mother has a lot of good years ahead of her.'

'I know.'

Luke begins slowing down but my eyes are firmly fixed on the view to our left. The road is literally on the banks of an estuary, the other side of which are rolling fields. 'Wow!' I exclaim. 'That's a breathtaking view. Imagine waking up to that every day.'

'I do. This is the house.'

The engine idles as we wait for a car to pass and then Luke pulls onto a paved driveway in front of a spacious double garage. In estate agents' terms my head is going into overdrive, as if I'm writing up the blurb. It's a luxury detached contemporary-style home, set over three floors, on the outskirts of Newquay with far-reaching views over the water and the countryside.

'Don't tell me . . . it's not quite what you were expecting.' Luke is studying my face, his look almost apologetic. 'It's just a grand beach hut really.'

I don't quite know what to say. I mean we're talking a million plus, here. Maybe a million and a half.

'And you're selling it?' On a house like this you don't put up a sign in the driveway, it's about reaching out to find the right purchaser. Then I find myself wondering whether he's house-sitting for a friend, having already sold his own property.

'Yes. Unless you think I'm being rash. Well, are we going to just sit here, or shall we take your things inside?'

Even though there's a numbingly cold wind blowing in across the estuary, I find myself standing on the drive just trying to take it in. The architect has done a clever job, as while it's overtly contemporary it doesn't stand out like a sore thumb. It has that coastal-living look, with pale grey cladding interspersed with large windows, and two sets of French doors to maximise on the views. The ground floor has been extended to create a huge terrace with a glass panelled balustrade. On the top floor there's an inset balcony, providing a cosy, all-weather nook off what I assume is the master bedroom.

'After you,' I say, snapping myself out of my reverie. 'I can't wait for the tour.' Or to get to the bottom of what's really going on. I'm not easily impressed, although having said that, this place is mind-blowing. Whoever owns this house is a very lucky person indeed.

Luke deposits my case at the bottom of a wide flight of stairs which, from my vantage point, has at least three turns in them, if not four.

'That's the trouble with a three-storey house, the stairs are a killer. I expect you're hungry. I nipped out to my favourite bakery, and I'll pop a couple of pasties in the oven. Shall we have a glass of wine while we're waiting for them to heat up?'

'That,' I state, firmly, 'would be very welcome indeed.' I thought I was prepared for this, but I'm not. My pulse is racing and I'm beginning to think that it was big mistake coming here.

'My parents think I'm crazy selling up to move to France, but this was only ever an investment for me.'

He's serious and I don't know quite what to say.

'I mean, it turned out great. The architect did a wonderful job, and my cleaner loves me. I live and work in the same room, as I have a pull-out bed in the study. She said if I ever get married and have kids, she'd insist I double her wages with all these sleek, shiny surfaces.'

I think I need to sit down, and I must look a little wobbly on my feet, because suddenly Luke walks back to me, taking my hand firmly in his. He pulls out a tall stool tucked beneath the oversized island and manoeuvres me onto it. His cleaner is right, everything is super shiny, from the white and grey veined granite countertops to the off-white floor tiles. I watch as he walks over to the fridge to grab a bottle of rosé wine.

All I can think of, is why wasn't Luke straight with me from the start? I feel I don't know him at all. Not only is this house not his style, it's like something out of a magazine. And it's out of character for the man I've come to know.

He carries over two glasses, pours out a little wine and returns to turn on one of the two ovens.

'Do you want anything with this?' he checks.

'No. It's fine as it comes.' While his back is turned as he searches for a baking tray, I lift the glass to my mouth and take a quick gulp. He spins around and catches me. 'Sorry, I couldn't wait.'

Luke gives me a guilty look and abandons the tray to walk over to join me. 'You want some answers, but it's tough because it rakes up things that I still find hard to get my head around. If it weren't for you, I couldn't have handled this summer. Not travelling on my own, if I'm being honest.' He holds up his glass. 'Having you there by my side, got me through it.'

We chink glasses, and as our eyes meet, I can see how emotional he's feeling. 'Look, you don't have to explain anything to me, Luke. It was a fun summer, one I'll always remember with great fondness.'

'Great fondness,' he repeats, frowning as he stares back at me.

'We don't owe each other anything. That was the agreement, Luke.'

'But I want you to know that I didn't lie to you; I just didn't tell you the full story.' He hoists himself up onto the seat. 'Every year since I was eighteen, my brother Ollie and I did the tour. He was a sous-chef who started small and was trying to make a name for himself. Max and Erin were hoping that after last summer he'd join them full time. I tagged along doing work here and there. Max let me work in the kitchen doing some of the easy prep, but when Ollie worked in some of the other restaurants on our travels, I'd work at places like the campsite you and I stayed at.'

I'm not sure if he's pausing to collect his thoughts, or waiting to hear my reaction, but I sit here quietly sipping my wine.

'You see, he didn't think he was good enough to make

it. There was always something new to learn and it drove him crazy. This was going to be *the* year when he made a commitment to join Max to replace Warren, and in doing so show my father he was worthy.'

I watch as Luke swallows hard before continuing. He turns his head towards the window for a few moments, staring out at the unbelievable view over the estuary and beyond. He can't bear for me to see the pain in his eyes.

'It's all my fault you see, and it's all so messed up.' He stops short, his expression dour. 'I dropped out of university in the first year because I was bored. I was making enough on the side sorting out people's computer problems and working as a temp for an agency, to rent a flat and get out from under my father's feet. Ollie was the successful one and I was glad for him, as he had real talent.'

He pauses and I can see how tough this is, so I quietly sit here trying not to watch his every move.

'I started setting up websites, that sort of thing. Then I got into developing apps. My name got around, and things took off. I made a lot of money in a very short time, and all the while Ollie was diligently honing his craft. You see, I was the dropout, the failure. Because of all this—' Luke holds his hands up, as if what we're seeing around us is a burden '—my brother saw it differently. I let my father talk me into buying a house; I guess he thought I might fritter what he referred to as my little *windfall* away. Ollie had a brilliant future ahead of him but I just struck lucky. Then, just before Christmas last year, we were due to meet up in town. I tried his phone, but he wasn't answering, so I went to see what was happening. He shared a house with a mate who worked at the same restaurant.'

Luke grinds to a halt and gulps half of the wine in his glass down in one go.

'Ollie had taken an overdose. And just like that he was gone. My father warned him that he was putting too much pressure on himself. At the time I hated him for saying that, as my brother took it to mean that Dad didn't think he had what it took to step up to the next level and become a sous-chef at Le Manoir du Bois. But maybe he saw what the rest of us couldn't; that it was Ollie who didn't believe in himself. And the fact I blamed my father when I didn't spot that, will always eat away at me. I failed my brother when he needed me the most because I was too busy getting the house fixed up, just to prove to my father I knew what I was doing.'

Poor Luke. If every single person who knows him has avoided raising the subject for fear of causing him distress, they might not even be aware that he blames himself for what happened. Left alone to deal with the pain and his regrets, he might even see it as the punishment he deserves; how awful is that?

I slip off the seat and throw my arms around Luke's shoulders. It's the first time since my father's funeral that I've seen a man shed tears, but my instincts are telling me that's exactly what Luke needs. There's only so long you can cheat your emotions and it does more harm than good to keep them bottled up.

'How was the shower?'

I look up as Luke saunters back into the kitchen, looking relaxed and with his hair still damp.

'Good. I feel refreshed. And guilty. It wasn't a part of my plan to go to pieces on you. I'm not really sure if any of what I said made sense. Ollie would have eventually made quite a name for himself; of that I have no doubt at all. He had a real talent and a fierce passion. I should have spent more time with him, rather than working.'

'Luke, your brother wouldn't want you – or anyone else – to feel guilty for what happened, as tragic as it was. He lost his way and that's the thing with life, it's no one's fault, not even theirs. Some people put too much pressure on themselves, and it doesn't take much of an imagination to understand that it can lead them into a very dark place indeed. Occasionally, they can't find a way out and it's heartbreaking to witness, but you can only save someone who wants to be saved.'

I pass him a mug of coffee. 'The thing is, Freya, money means nothing, nothing at all. It's all about doing something you love, creating something. Ollie was a creator; I wish you could have tasted some of his dishes. That's why Max and Erin were so dispirited; we all thought this was the summer Ollie would don his white chef's hat at Le Manoir du Bois.'

At least he's calmer now and in the twilight of the early evening, the soft lights around us at least make the house feel a little cosier.

'You and your family have been through a horrible experience, and you can only take it one day at a time. Losing someone close to you under any circumstances, is life-changing and grief is a long and lonely journey.'

I know that from personal experience, but when it's a young man with his whole life ahead of him, it must be truly devastating.

'Reba belonged to Ollie. He was going to take her to France. Mum and I couldn't sell her off and that's why I had her refitted for the trip in his honour.'

'Oh, Luke, that's a lovely thing to do to remember him by.'

He looks at me and sighs. 'I should have read the signs better. When I asked him about her name, he said it stood for Re-born-again. He was trying to tell me something, something he couldn't put into words. Maybe he knew, even way back then, that he'd never make the trip.'

'It's time to let go of the bad stuff that you can't change, Luke. You didn't do anything wrong. When you think of your brother you need to focus on the good times, the laughter and the fun you had on your travels. You've got to live your best life, because that's what he'd want for you.'

'Yeah.' Luke leans back against the countertop. 'I've told myself that but there are times I feel . . . I wonder if I'd just—'

I reach out to touch his arm, giving it a gentle squeeze.

'Stop. That's the sort of negativity that drags a person down, and if it gets out of control, you'll lose your way, too.'

He draws in a deep breath, and I watch as his chest expands, and he pushes back his shoulders.

'It's taken me a while to sort myself out since our trip. I realised that even though you sensed a part of me was broken, it didn't stop us growing close. When I got back home I knew something had to change. I had to take a long hard look at myself and you're the one who inspired me to do that. I need you in my life, Freya.'

I open my mouth to speak, but no words come out. My own emotions have been on a roller-coaster ride since the moment I saw Luke at the station. We've shared tears, I've felt the rawness of his loss, and the haunting depth of the turmoil inside of him. And now I can see that I judged him unfairly.

I was wrong to think Luke was casually breezing his way through life as if it were a form of rebellion, or a way of avoiding responsibility. In reality, he was going through the grieving process, stumbling around in the dark as he tried to find a way through it. The man I see standing before me now is a man who has a plan to rebuild the pieces of what, for one so young, has been a life-shattering experience.

On our trip together, my head was telling me something wasn't quite right. If only Luke had opened up to me back then, but he wasn't ready to tackle his demons.

Now I'm the one who is struggling to understand what I really want out of life. I used to be so sure of myself and now it's as if the ground has shifted beneath my feet. I'm falling, but where will I land?

26

Daring to Dream

As the evening goes on, the hurt I felt deep down inside for what I saw as Luke choosing to distance himself, has evaporated. It's been replaced by a scary sense of excitement, tinged with disbelief that any of this can be happening.

Neither of us really touched our food, we just pushed it around the plate as we talked. This time it was a happier conversation, reflecting on our time in France together and then filling each other in on what we've done over the last three months.

We retire to the huge sitting room to relax. With patio doors leading out onto the raised terrace, it's a shame it's too chilly to sit out there to enjoy our nightcap.

'Your gut instincts about Ethan proved correct, then?' Luke smiles at me, as if he never doubted that for a moment.

'Yes. He's doing really well. Now that Beth is getting used to Nancy's dry sense of humour—' I chuckle to myself '—Ethan can focus on sales and generating new leads. He's in his element.'

The flickering candles on the coffee table in front of us make Luke's eyes sparkle. I can't believe the change in him. It's like a weight has been lifted from his shoulders. All he needed was someone to tell him that his brother's death wasn't his fault. It's a shame his parents didn't understand that.

'You sound very relaxed about work. France was good for you.' He flexes his eyebrows, giving me one of his mischievous grins. 'Was it enough to tempt you to return . . . with me?'

'Oh, Luke,' I sigh, softly. 'If only it were that easy. I have a business partner to consider. Another year and we're looking to get that second branch set up.'

His grin begins to fade. 'That's still your dream?'

'That's the plan, Luke. Dreams and plans are two different things.'

'Are they? I love you, Freya. I know that probably hasn't been apparent because I've been so screwed up emotionally. A part of me is scared that now I'm seeing things more clearly, it's too late to change the perception you have of me.'

'Oh, Luke . . . you've touched my heart, and I can't deny that. And, after what you've told me today, maybe moving to France isn't a rash decision for you. It could be a new start and that might be exactly what you need.'

'But.' He furrows his brow.

'Yes, there is a *but*. I can't leave Beth in the lurch. Then there's my mum. If George turns out to be genuine, then her life is about to change. Love isn't something you can switch off and I know that she'll always love my dad, so it's not going to be an easy thing for her letting someone else in. She's always been there for me, now it's my turn to be there for her as she resets her life.'

The silence between us is heavy. 'Ten years ago, I was carefree, and I would eagerly have let my heart rule my head, but now I realise that life isn't just about me and what I want. I have responsibilities. It's easy to take risks when the only person it affects is you.' And that's where Luke's life is at.

'Just do me a favour.' His gaze is intense, as he stares back at me. 'One last adventure, because I value your opinion and your judgement. If I get this next step wrong, I'm sunk, and you know me better than anyone, Freya.'

My heart sinks in my chest. 'Why do I feel that this is going to be something really crazy?' I mutter, speaking to myself more than to him.

'Let me show you my new life. Check it out for yourself and then tell me, honestly, if you think it's way too ambitious. It's not too late to backtrack, or maybe tackle it in a slightly different way. A way that might not involve me moving to France at all. Would that make a difference?'

My head is whirling and I don't know how to answer him.

'Freya, I'm so glad you rang. It's a little late and I was getting worried because your text was very short.'

'I know, Mum, and I'm sorry. I'll explain when I get home but there's been a bit of a change to the itinerary. Luke and I are heading off to France. I'll be back on Monday, as planned, but it will be quite late.'

'France?' As I expected, Mum sounds rather shocked. 'On a whim?'

'I know it sounds crazy and my initial reaction was that I couldn't possibly go, as what about my passport? Then I realised that it was still in the zip pocket of my handbag and it just seemed like a sign. How could I possibly say no, after that?'

Mum chuckles. 'That's so unlike you, so maybe it is!'

'Luke's just figuring out the easiest, and quickest way, to get us there. I don't know whether we'll be flying, going by ferry, or driving, at the moment. He needs advice about whether he's making the right decision, and I can't help him unless I know what he's getting himself into.'

'And that someone has to be *you*? Why not his parents, or another friend? This won't unsettle you again, will it?'

I can understand her concern. This is going the extra

mile, but when you really care about someone you can't abandon them in their time of need.

'It's complicated, Mum. He's been through a lot and now I'm aware of that, I can't possibly let him down.'

'In that case, just travel safely and please text me when you get there. And when you're back in the UK. I won't go to bed on Monday night until I've heard from you.'

'Mum, everything is going to be fine.'

'Freya.' Luke walks into the room waving some pieces of paper in his hands.

'Sorry, Mum, I've got to go. Take care and I love you!'

Luke pulls a long face. 'I bet I'm not her favourite person dragging you all the way to France and back.'

'Mum's fine with it. So, how do we get there?'

'A flight is out of the question, unless we want to fly at different times and one of us waits around at the airport. Then there's still the hassle of the hire car. I've checked all the ferries and the various ports. Looking at the available sailings, the time to get to the port, the crossing itself and then the road trip the other side to our destination, it's swings and roundabouts. And that's without adding in waiting time.'

He looks at me and I know exactly what he's thinking.

'The Channel Tunnel is easier, because if we miss our booking, the next train isn't far behind.' We're going to retrace our steps. 'So . . . how long will it take?'

'Worst case, thirteen hours door to door.'

I gasp. 'That's a marathon of a drive, Luke. We're going to have to take it in turns driving.' I'm trying to plot it out in my head.

'If we set off very early tomorrow and drive all day, we'll get there early evening. Then we'll have all day Sunday for me to show you what the big plan is, and you can point out the drawbacks. Then we'll set off on Monday morning and I'll have you home by bedtime, I promise.'

I shake my head at him. 'You do know this is ridiculous, don't you?'

'Yes, but as I said, I really value your opinion. I'm sinking everything I have into this new opportunity and if there are pitfalls I haven't picked up on, I'd rather know that now.'

'Then let's do it. We'll share the driving and make it happen.'

One last adventure together. If I know he's going to be happy, then I can let him go.

'We're about a twenty-minute drive from our destination, according to Luke, Mum.'

'Thank goodness the bulk of the journey is behind you. I bet you're exhausted.'

'We've both had little catnaps, as we've driven in three-hour stints. We've stopped to refuel, so I thought I'd set your mind at rest.'

'I hope you can satisfy yourself that he's doing the right thing. You find it very hard to let people go, Freya, always did and always will. But if it's the right thing to do for you both, then accept that everything happens for a reason. It would be a sad world indeed if we can't help each other in times of need. Maybe that's why your paths crossed.'

'His brother died shortly before last Christmas, Mum. He's still reeling from it.'

I hear her sigh. 'Oh, Freya. It must be so hard to lose a sibling. It's sad losing anyone, but when it's a young life it's a tragedy.'

'It is but I think he's finally ready to put himself back together. Anyway, stop worrying about me, I'm fine. I've already had two croissants and I'm looking forward to eating a few more on our way back.'

Mum laughs. 'You'll sleep well tonight.'

'We both will. When we were awake, we sang our hearts out, as Luke downloaded some classic Christmas songs. It was like the car journeys we had with Dad when I was a child, lots of laughter and fun.'

'Ah, that's good to hear. It's a long way to go when you only have tomorrow to check everything out.'

'Yes, but if it reassures him, then it's worth it. I probably won't even need to say a thing. I think when he gets there he'll instinctively know if it's right, or not. Anyway, he's on his way back. I'll be in touch when I can. Love you!'

I put my phone away as Luke opens the car door.

'Is it much further?' I ask and he gives a little laugh.

'That's your equivalent of "are we there, yet?" and the answer is that I'm surprised you don't recognise this road.'

'It's a dark winter's evening, everything looks different in the daylight,' I throw back at him.

When the engine kicks into life and he pulls away, I peer out the window trying to spot any landmarks I might recognise. We passed the turn-off for Saint-Quentin about forty minutes ago, so it's clear we're not going to stay overnight with Erin and Max.

Then I spot a familiar triangle of trees where the road forks. 'We're going to the vineyard?'

'We are. Iris has a room all prepared for us. I mean . . . she assumed—'

'It's fine. The destination is a bit of a surprise, that's all. It'll be lovely to catch up.' Last night we slept together in the same bed, but it was different. Luke just needed comforting and I was happy to be there for him.

Emotionally, we were both exhausted, of course, and sleep came in fits and starts. It's nice to be needed, though, and last night Luke needed me.

'We'll get to meet the new baby.'

'Oh . . . I forgot about that! What did Frédéric and Sabine have – was it a boy, or a girl?' I feel guilty now for not giving Iris a call to enquire, as I knew the baby was due in early November.

'A boy. He'll be what . . . five weeks old now.'

As we negotiate the uneven lane leading up to Le Château de la Fontaine, the memories of the wonderful night we spent there come flooding back. It was truly magical and something that will live on in my dreams forever.

The crunch of tyres on the gravel sounds the alert and the front door swings open wide. A shape appears backlit as the light floods out onto the terrace. The person waves and strides forward. Frédéric descends the stone steps two at a time, rushing over to greet us.

He kisses both of my cheeks, his welcome full of enthusiasm. Then he turns to give Luke a hug and a fist pump. 'At last! You have an hour and a half before dinner. Everyone is excited to greet you, but I said you would be dusty and tired. Come, let me show you to your room.'

It's weird retracing my steps, as it's something I never expected to do again. Even when I'm in the shower, I feel like pinching myself to check that I'm not dreaming. When Luke unexpectedly joins me, suddenly everything begins to feel very real indeed.

Iris's eyes light up when Luke and I walk into the grand dining room.

'My dears! We thought you'd appreciate eating a little later. How was the drive, aside from being long and tedious?'

Iris steps forward and we hug. She looks a little emotional. 'Sabine and baby Géron are away and won't be back until tomorrow. He's visiting his other grandparents,' she explains as she turns to hug Luke. 'They've only been gone two days but I'm missing them terribly.'

'And I'm catching up on some much-needed sleep,' Frédéric comments, to which Iris shakes her head and tuts.

'He has a good set of lungs on him, does our little boy. Anyway, take a seat and relax. Frédéric, I'll leave it to you to pour the wine while I check where we're at in the kitchen. I think Cook is ready for the trolley to be brought through.'

I love this room with its tall ceilings, wonderfully restored cornice and wood-panelled walls. As you would expect, the top half of the room is wallpapered, and they chose a print very in keeping with the style. The silver-grey background is decorated with large white mop-head roses interspersed with an occasional soft-blue flower. It has that regal look to it.

The fact that, with just the four of us here tonight, we're clustered around one end of the oversized table, makes me smile. How often, I wonder, does Iris seat twenty-plus people around this table? But when she does, I bet it really brings the place to life.

'Here we are!' Iris returns carrying a tray, and behind her a young woman wheels in a posh version of what my mum would call a heated hostess trolley.

Luke jumps up to take the tray from Iris, who turns to the young woman, giving her a nod and a smile, as she manoeuvres the trolley back against the wall. '*Merci, Eloise.*'

'*Bonne soirée*, Madame.'

'*A vous aussi.*'

Luke acts as waiter, placing the starters in front of us and pulling out a chair for Iris to take a seat.

'This is so exciting,' she says, glancing at each of us in turn. 'I can't wait to hear all about Frédéric's and Luke's plans to guarantee the future of the vineyard for generations to come. I appreciate that the last couple of months have been very intense for them. I'm assuming you're as eager as I am to hear the details, Freya?'

Luke's face pales.

'Yes. But I'm sure this evening will enlighten us.' I glance at Luke and he looks anxious, but Frédéric is clearly excited.

'Let's begin eating and the pair of you can take it in turns to give us an overview. But first—' Iris raises her wine glass in the air '—we should toast our new partnership.

Welcome to the vineyard, Luke. You are now officially a part of our family.'

Trying not to look as shocked as I feel isn't easy. I just hope my smile looks natural and not forced, as I try to hide my sense of confusion. If it's a done deal, then why on earth did Luke bring me here? His decision has already been made.

The sound of Beth's voice is immediately comforting. 'Hey, Freya. How's the impromptu trip going? I couldn't believe it when I read your text.'

I'm staring out of the bedroom window, feeling tearful, as I try to gather my thoughts together. 'I've just used you as an excuse to take a much-needed breather.'

'Oh no! I'm sorry to hear that. Do you think Luke is about to make the biggest mistake of his life?'

Where do I begin to explain how confused I'm feeling right now?

'Look, take a deep breath,' she continues, 'and when you're ready, start at the beginning.'

Twenty minutes later and I can tell from the stunned silence that Beth's as confused as I'm feeling.

'Let's see if I have this right. Luke says he wants you in his life but he's planning a move to France. Now you're there together, are you saying that he's having second thoughts and he's hoping you'll give him the courage to admit it's not right for him . . . or for you?'

'I don't know. I'm getting so many mixed messages and it's because his head is all over the place. He's swamped with emotions he can barely handle. But he can't mess Iris and Frédéric around like this. When Iris made that toast his face froze. Is it me he wants, or is he using me to get him out of a hole he's dug for himself?'

She breathes in suddenly, catching her breath. 'What's your gut instinct telling you?'

'That it isn't over between us, but if he can't sort himself out it won't work. He's made a firm commitment to be a part of the vineyard. If he pulls out now, what's to say he won't change his mind about wanting me in his life when we're back in the UK?'

Beth gives a gentle sigh. 'He's not the only one whose emotions are in turmoil. Be honest with yourself, Freya. You took a big risk spending the summer in his company and I think everyone who knows you wondered what was really going on. You don't take risks and you don't let anyone distract you. But Luke did.'

There's no point trying to deny it because it's true. 'But he's a mess, Beth. I can't be a crutch. I need to be with a man who has a vision, who knows exactly what he wants out of life and we both have to want the same thing.'

'What if he isn't getting cold feet about the move but he's worried you're not onboard with the idea and he got it wrong?'

My head is beginning to ache; I'm feeling weary and conflicted. 'What should I do?'

'Let it all play out. If it's you he wants, then together you'll make it work. Whether that's in France, or in the UK. Don't return home with any regrets because you didn't hear him out. He's not the best communicator in the world, is he? And, given what you've told me about his past, he's still grieving over the loss of his brother and finding someone he wants to spend his life with has thrown him.'

Knowing Luke, he sees even that as either some sort of betrayal because he doesn't deserve happiness, or worse – that he'll only mess it up, anyway.

'Thanks for being a listening ear and trying to help me make some sense of this, Beth. It means a lot.'

'Just promise me you won't be too quick to judge. See what tomorrow brings.'

'I will. Sleep well, and I'm really grateful for the advice. I was about to jump online and find a hire car, so I could head for home in the morning.'

'Now that would be a huge mistake. Whichever way it goes, this is the defining moment.'

'I know and it's scary.'

Luke

27

The Chance to Create a New Reality

What I'd hoped would be a pleasant catch-up over a delightful evening meal, took an immediate turn when Iris proposed a toast to the new partnership. For the second time in two days, I'd unwittingly succeeded in unsettling Freya to a point where she was struggling to understand what was going on.

Iris's announcement came out of the blue, and it made me stifle a groan. I was touched by her words, but when I glanced over at Freya there was a fleeting look of disappointment on her face. She masked it well, instantly plastering on a smile, while wondering why on earth I'd dragged her all the way to France.

Frédéric immediately launched into a broad outline of the master plan. Erecting a bespoke building to house a new bottling plant alongside the old one would ensure continuity. I went on to explain that once everything was up and running, the old plant would be dissembled, and the building converted into warehousing. I'll also be taking over responsibility for the running of the website and marketing, which is something I'm excited to get started on.

'It's ambitious,' Iris pointed out, 'but without this investment I know our long-term future here is in doubt. Together, the two of you will make a great team.'

There was a distinct buzz in the air but as soon as we'd finished dessert, Freya excused herself saying she'd had a text from her business partner, Beth, a little earlier that she had to deal with. Iris had no idea that our partnership was news to her, or that she was reeling over it, and she simply gave Freya a big smile and suggested we delay coffee until she returned.

Being polite, Freya simply said, 'Of course,' before hurrying away.

I'm such a fool; I've made a right mess of this. I just can't seem to find the right words when I'm around Freya. There's so much going on inside my head, so many things I want to tell her, but it's all a jumble. No wonder she's confused.

'Sorry, that took a little longer than I expect—' Freya enters the room looking slightly flushed and surprised to see me sitting here all alone. 'Oh! Iris and Frédéric weren't offended by my delay, were they?'

'No. Sabine texted, and they've gone off to the sitting room to make a video call. Are you all right? I'm so sorry I didn't forewarn you. I had no idea Iris was going to make a big deal of it. I was going to run through it with you tomorrow when we weren't so tired. I thought it might be a bit too much to take in, all at once.'

'It was just a shock to hear it was all going ahead and her words were so heartfelt. You asked me to come with you because you said that you weren't sure you were doing the right thing, Luke. But you've already made the commitment.' Her eyes search mine, looking for the truth.

'Look, it's not quite what it seems. Having made an investment in the infrastructure, as I told you, I don't have to move to France. Frédéric is the plant and production manager, and he's the expert. I'm taking over sales and marketing, which can be done from anywhere. With conference calls and the odd trip back every now and again, it would still work. Business is one thing, my life . . . *our* life together, is another.'

She makes no attempt to come and sit down and stands

there looking ill at ease. Whether that's because Iris and Frédéric could walk in at any moment, or because she's angry with me, I can't tell.

'How was Beth?'

'Fine, it was just work stuff.'

My heart sinks in my chest. Beth is her confidante and the first person she goes to for advice. The silence between us is tense.

'Look, why don't we grab our coats and wander out onto the terrace so we can talk frankly?' I suggest.

'I think that would be a good idea.' She's doing everything she can to avoid eye contact and I wonder whether I've left it too late – have I already lost her?

We saunter back upstairs, grab our thick coats and scarves, and it isn't until we're at the edge of the terrace staring out over the floodlit lawns, that she finally turns to look directly at me.

'I sat there wondering why, when you'd found the courage to tell me about your brother, you stopped there. Why couldn't you be honest and tell me everything? It's obvious you want to make the move. Why pull me into it at this late stage?'

'Argh.' I look away for a split second, wondering where to start. 'I'm just not used to expressing my emotions. I meant it when I said that I love you. I wanted to prove to you that I can make sound decisions about the future. You need a plan, and I get that, so I made one.'

'But when it comes to a relationship, it's usual for two people to sit down and plan their future together, Luke.'

'And we can! I freely admit that I'd love to live here and get hands-on tending the grapes and learning from Frédéric, but if it means losing you, then that option is out the window. I'd still have to sell the house to free up some equity, but I don't even have to stay in Cornwall.' She's still not getting it, and I frantically search around for a way of lightening this moment. 'I know a good estate agent who's based in

Sevenoaks. I hear it's a great place to live.' The uplift in my voice instantly catches her attention.

'You'd do that for me?'

'I'd do anything to have you by my side for the rest of my life, Freya. Anything at all.'

We stand together gazing out into the floodlit darkness until the cold makes her shiver. I wish I could rewind the last couple of days and start all over again. The very first thing I should have said to Freya when I saw her was 'I love you and I did from day one.'

The following morning, as soon as breakfast is over, I'm keen to take Freya for a walk. As we're about to step outside, Frédéric strides into the hallway carrying a suitcase in each hand. Sabine follows in his footsteps, carrying the baby in her arms. He turns to kick the door shut behind them.

'They're home!' he calls out, as we go to greet the new arrivals.

Sabine's eyes light up. 'Freya, Luke! Oh, it is so good to see you both!'

Kisses and hugs are forgotten, as Freya and I peer down at the baby.

'Meet Géron David Beauchêne,' she says, proudly. 'He has the Christian names of both of his great-grandfathers.'

'He's totally adorable,' Freya gushes. 'And so tiny, still. How old is he now?'

'Five-and-a-half weeks.' The look on Sabine's face is one of pure joy. 'He might look small, but already he is getting to be an armful. Are you off for a walk around the grounds?'

'Yes. I thought I'd show Freya the outbuildings.'

Sabine gives me a knowing smile. 'Enjoy! We'll catch up later. This little one needs to see his *grand-maman* for a cuddle, or I will be in trouble.'

'Well, I hope I can steal one too, a bit later. It's lovely to see you and meet baby Géron, Sabine.' Freya's smile is sunny and warm.

As we step out into the crisp morning air, she's still smiling to herself. 'They all look so happy, don't they?'

A part of me is wondering whether Freya is in the mood to talk about the future. Last night she was as frosty as the thin white covering coating everything we see around us. But, to my utmost surprise, she doesn't need any prompting.

'That's why Iris is so excited about the plans you and Frédéric have made. She knows he would have struggled, just like his father, to do it all on his own. This is the right thing for you to do, Luke. Of that I have no doubt.'

I wait, thinking she's going to continue, but instead she starts walking across the terrace towards the steps on the far side. I follow her, my heart beating so fiercely in my chest I begin to sweat. I'd say something if I could find the right words, but – as usual – I'm scared I'll say the wrong thing. Did Freya agree to this trip because she feels sorry for me and not, as I'd hoped, because she was waiting for me to prove myself to her?

We walk in silence, everything still except for a handful of birds flitting in and out of the shrubs searching for food, attracted by the bright red berries. Then on past the bottling plant and across a wide courtyard.

If I don't say something, and quickly, then it really is all over. I need her in my life and now I've finally got my act together I'm not about to accept defeat. I know she loves me, even if she won't admit it to herself because she's scared I'll let her down.

'Two of these three buildings are used as storage for the wine and the other one is used by the gardeners.'

Freya turns to stare at me puzzled, questioning why I'm even bothering to give her the tour. There's a distant look in her eyes as they sweep over my face. Then it's like she gives herself a mental shake.

'They're pretty buildings but they need some work. Are these a part of the plan, too?'

It's true they need some re-pointing, but the roofs are

sound. It's mostly cosmetic but my plans are way bigger than that.

'This is the reason I brought you here.' I draw to a halt.

'This . . . what?'

'This courtyard and these buildings.'

She frowns and then sighs. Her patience is wearing thin and while the last thing I want is to annoy her, I need Freya to figure it out for herself. She has to want this too.

Then I can see that it's finally beginning to sink in. I'm content to stay where I am, as she wanders around to get a better look.

'I have the keys in my pocket if you'd like to take a peek inside,' I offer.

'All right.' She's not going to make this easy for me and I guess I deserve that after last night and the way I've mishandled things.

'This is the first of the two main storage barns. They're both filled with racks that extend way back. All of this will be rehoused once the new bottling plant is up and running. It won't be visible from here and because the old stone plant building backs onto the courtyard, the high wall makes it very private.'

When I swing open the magnificent double oak doors, Freya catches her breath. 'It's enormous,' she remarks, stepping inside. I turn on the lights and then close the barn doors behind us.

'Impressive, isn't it?'

She turns to look at me rather intently. 'It's a blank canvas inside, right up to the rafters.'

'It is, *but* – you knew there'd be one, didn't you?' I laugh.

At last, that sparkle is back in her eyes. 'Yes. Come on then, tell me what you're thinking.'

'The partnership aside, these three buildings could be turned into a wonderful home. Buying this plot of land and the buildings on it from the Beauchêne family, would involve investing every penny I have. It might even mean selling

Reba. But it would be the start of a brand-new life. It's not just about investing in a business I know has a great future, it's a place where *we* could make a life together – you and me, Freya. *If* that's what you want.'

The stout walls keep the temperature in here almost constant, like a huge cave. But trying to imagine it as one's home requires a massive leap of faith and I'm hoping that she's brave enough to make it.

I wouldn't have brought Freya all the way here if I had any doubts at all about her being able to envisage the dream, it's whether she's willing to put her trust in me. I knew that words alone wouldn't influence her, she had to see it and feel it for herself.

'A life in rural France, in a vineyard setting. You'd have plenty to keep you busy, but what would I do?' Her laugh isn't dismissive, it's curious as if she's slowly trying to piece it together in her mind.

'Whatever you want. The vineyard isn't far from town, although clearly there are an endless number of jobs that need doing here. As the business grows, it's only going to get busier. And Frédéric would love to do wine tours and wine tastings on site, again. That side of the business was shut down several years ago. Naturally—' I look at her in earnest '—there are other options.'

'Like?'

'I know there are no guarantees in life, or even in love. But it's not too much of a stretch of the imagination to think about settling down at some point and having a family, is it?'

'Is that a proposal?' she questions, her eyes shining. 'It's usual for a guy to get down on one knee!'

I stride towards Freya, wrapping my arms around her. 'If you're willing to take a risk on me, then yes, of course it is. Because I know I'm ready and I wouldn't consider moving here – as perfect as I think this place is – unless you're prepared to come with me.'

She leans her head against my shoulder, giving a deep

sigh. 'Oh, Luke. You're . . . impossible at times. You make huge decisions sound simple.'

'I know I'm asking you to give up so much. And your mum and Beth aren't exactly going to thank me for whisking you away to France. But once they see how happy I'm going to make you, they'll soon forgive me. And who wouldn't want to come and visit us, here at the vineyard. They're only a car ride away. It's an easy journey from Kent.'

That makes her smile. I know I'm grinning like a mad fool, but I can't help myself. When I'm with Freya everything seems different. Life is full of light and hope, instead of darkness and shadows.

'Can you imagine us here together?'

I watch as she walks around the huge, rectangular courtyard. With high stone walls on two sides and the row of buildings taking up the third, I can't tell what she's thinking.

'At the moment it looks a bit like a farmyard,' she remarks, chewing on her lip. 'We could fill the courtyard with islands of potted plants and have a few bistro tables and chairs dotted in between. It could be amazing.'

She tilts her head to look at me.

'Our little piece of heaven on earth, you mean?' I grin back at her.

I catch her hand in mine and lead her towards the two smaller detached buildings that sit alongside the storage barn.

'The one at the far end is a lot bigger and it could be turned into a wonderful three-bed gîte, perfect for when family come to stay. However, I was thinking that it would be fun to join the barn to the middle building with a glass corridor.' I turn to look at Freya and suddenly I know I have nothing at all to worry about.

She imagined spending her life with a man who wears a suit to work; instead she'll take a risk on me because it's what the heart wants that truly matters.

'I love that idea,' she enthuses. 'A touch of the contemporary will make all that beautiful old stonework look even more amazing.'

I knew this place would inspire Freya once she could see beyond what it is now. 'You wait until I talk you through my plans for the storage barn. Five bedrooms, all en suite, a wall of glass doors that concertina back at the touch of a switch—' Now I'm starting to ramble and she puts a finger to my lips.

'Together we'll make it all work and turn it into a beautiful home.'

Our lips touch and her breath is warm on my face. 'I knew I was in trouble the moment you picked me up at the station,' she admits. 'And I'd never let you sell Reba, no matter what.' Freya sighs, happily. 'What I realise now, is that people learn from each other and you've inspired me to think outside the box.'

'And you'll keep my feet on the ground. Striving to be the best version of me is all I need to focus on now, isn't it?'

She gives a gentle laugh. 'You simply need to believe in yourself, Luke, that's all. Wisdom is the result of life experiences, because you were right all along – age is . . . just a number. I love you, Luke. I tried so hard to deny my feelings, because it just seemed too easy.'

'When something's right,' I reply, softly, 'that's how you know . . . because everything comes together naturally.'

We walk and talk, and even though her head must still be spinning, we begin to make plans for the future. There are a lot of things to sort out but her main concern is not leaving Beth in the lurch. We discuss the possibility of Freya becoming a silent partner maybe, and Beth simply taking on another sales negotiator. Or even opening a branch in France. Her eyes lit up at that suggestion, as she said lots of people are looking for a bolthole this side of the Channel. Freya said they'd be the first estate agency in Sevenoaks displaying French properties.

Just the fact that she's already considering the options, tells me I was right. If we'd tried to make a life together back in the UK, it wouldn't have been a fresh start. And Beth, and Freya's mum, will simply want what's best for her, knowing that they'll always be a big part of our lives here.

We seal our future with a loving kiss and suddenly the things we both thought stood in our way, are no longer stumbling blocks. When something is right, there's absolutely no denying it, no matter how crazy it might appear to be on the surface of it. All it requires is a little teamwork to find the perfect solution.

One summer in France was simply the beginning. A seemingly impossible dream is about to become a reality and, suddenly, an exciting future beckons. The adventure has only just begun . . .

Acknowledgements

Special thanks go to editorial director Cara Chimirri, for taking the story to the next level. It's a joy working with you!

A virtual hug to the amazing editorial team on this project and sincere thanks to the awesome cover designer.

I also want to acknowledge the network of people behind the scenes who beaver away to promote and generally spread the word about my newest release.

Not forgetting the other incredible driving forces behind the Embla team – *because our lives are built on stories, and each book does matter*! It's a thrill to be a part of it.

Grateful thanks also go to my wonderful agent, Sara Keane, for her sterling advice, support and all those long phone calls putting the world to rights. It's been an amazing journey since the day we first met, and your friendship means so much to me.

To my wonderful husband, Lawrence – always there for me and the other half of team Lucy – you truly are my rock!

A special mention to Félix for his guidance to ensure the French words and terms used are as accurate as possible. Oh, how I wish I were a gifted linguist . . .

This story was inspired by my very own French adventure with my husband. It was a summer we'll never forget.

There are so many family members and long-term friends who understand that my passion to write is all-consuming. They forgive me for the long silences and when we next catch up, it's as if I haven't been absent at all.

Publishing a new book means that there is an even longer list of people to thank for publicising it. The amazing kindness of my lovely author friends, readers and reviewers is truly humbling. You continue to delight, amaze and astound me with your generosity and support.

Without your kindness in spreading the word about my latest release and your wonderful reviews to entice people to click and download, I wouldn't be able to indulge myself in my guilty pleasure – writing.

Wishing everyone peace, love and happiness.

Lucy x

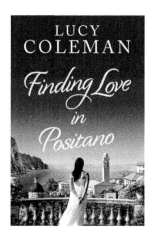

One summer in Italy might just change everything . . .

Marci James loves her job so much she's not had a holiday
in 5 years. But after receiving a mysterious letter from her
godfather, Richard, Marci must pack up for a summer on the
Italian Coast. Tasked with sorting through Richard's antiques
shop, Marci is determined to find the right balance of work
and pleasure.

But when Marci arrives it's apparent that the task is far more
daunting than she imagined, and it isn't long before Nico, her
gorgeous local guide, offers to step up and lend a hand. As
the two enjoy the Positano summer, and all that the Amalfi
Coast has to offer, Marci finally lets herself relax and the
sparks between the pair soon begin to fly.

But Richard hasn't just left his possessions behind, he left a
secret, one that Marci unwittingly stumbles across. Will it
break her heart after the happiest summer of her entire life?

**Perfect for fans of Karen Swan, Rosanna Ley and
Sarah Morgan.**

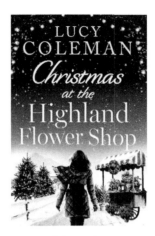

Four months. One impossible task. It's time to save Christmas at The Highland Flower Shop...

Bella Reed has worked at The Highland Flower Shop ever since she left college and now her Aunt Jane has handed the keys and the lease over to her. With the business under her reign, Bella is ready to hit the ground running – until she's dealt a massive blow. **They're being evicted.**

When dashing businessman **Maverick McIntyre** turns up in Fort William, Bella discovers the reason they're being kicked out. He has no intention of honouring a ridiculous deal his father made many years ago.

As Maverick and Bella lock horns, they both begin to see different sides to one another and before long the two strike up the most unexpected of friendships. Bella knows she has to keep business separate, but when her head and her heart are saying two different things, life starts to get complicated.

No matter her feelings, Bella isn't about to let anyone down and the entire town's counting on her to save Christmas.

A sparkling Christmas romance from bestselling author Lucy Coleman to curl up with in front of the fire this holiday season!

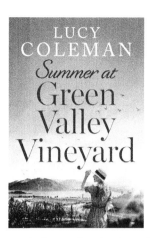

A beautiful vineyard. A new beginning. A summer that will change their lives forever...

Linzi arrived at Green Valley Vineyard nine years ago, in need of a fresh start. In the lush emerald countryside and ripening grapes, she finally has a place to call home.

But Linzi's world is rocked when the owner announces he is retiring, and his grandson is taking over.

When **Elliot Montgomery** first sets foot at Green Valley, Linzi's worst fears are realised. He's stepped straight out of the boardroom in shiny shoes and a tailored suit. How will a numbers man like him ever understand the magic of what they do here?

Elliot has his own demons, carrying the grief of his father's death. Despite their differences, he has come to the vineyard for a new beginning, much like Linzi once did.

As the summer unfolds, Elliot and Linzi find themselves in an uneasy alliance while old secrets threaten to be revealed.

Could more be about to bloom here among the twisting vines than they ever thought possible?

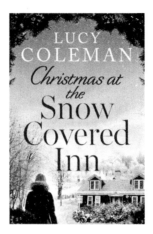

Ria's Christmas wish list: A secluded inn, beautiful decorations, lots of snow and a man who could change her life forever . . .

After a messy breakup, interior designer **Ria Porter** has been dedicated to her job. Now one of the best in the business, she's been hired to work on a beautiful inn nestled in the snow-covered mountains of New Hampshire. A career-making opportunity she couldn't refuse, Ria's determined to make it her finest work yet.

Successful businessman **Hayden Reynolds** has carved his own path in life. But this December he is flying back home on a mission to save his grandfather's beloved inn.

Between interfering family members and a tight deadline, Ria's got her hands full. The last thing she needs is Hayden distracting her with his good looks and kind heart. But as they work together to bring the inn back to life, Ria finds her resolve thawing and it harder to keep things professional.

With Christmas Eve approaching, Ria has a decision to make. She can keep her focus on her work or she can allow herself to dream, letting this beautiful place open up a future she never thought possible . . .

About the Author

Lucy Coleman always knew that one day she would write, but first life took her on a wonderful journey of self discovery for which she is very grateful.

Family life and two very diverse careers later she now spends most days glued to a keyboard, which she refers to as her personal quality time.

'It's only when you know who you are that you truly understand what makes you happy! Writing about love, life, and relationships – set in wonderful locations – makes me leap out of bed every morning!'

About Embla Books

Embla Books is a digital-first publisher of standout commercial adult fiction. Passionate about storytelling, the team at Embla publish books that will make you 'laugh, love, look over your shoulder and lose sleep'. Launched by Bonnier Books UK in 2021, the imprint is named after the first woman from the creation myth in Norse mythology, who was carved by the gods from a tree trunk found on the seashore – an image of the kind of creative work and crafting that writers do, and a symbol of how stories shape our lives.

Find out about some of our other books and stay in touch:

X, Facebook, Instagram: @emblabooks
Newsletter: https://bit.ly/emblanewsletter